DEEP IN THE HEARTWOOD, WHERE MAGIC GROWS—

there are many quests fulfilled, adventures begun and ended, spells cast by and upon those who dwell in or wander into the forest's depths. Now today's finest word weavers lead you into enchantment's green realms with such spellbinding stories as:

"Out of the Woods"—Was he a madman, or a poor soul who'd finally escaped the enchantment that for centuries held him captive in the woods?

"Fiat Silva"—Though he was only a boy, his ability to believe with all his heart and soul might be the only magic that could bring new life to the trees. . . .

"Weeds"—It began as just another college field trip but what found them in the forest would transform their lives forever. . . .

"My Soul into the Boughs"—She'd come to care for her dying grandmother—only to discover that she'd been chosen for an even greater responsibility. . . .

More Spellbinding Anthologies Brought to You by DAW:

WEIRD TALES FROM SHAKESPEARE *Edited by Katharine Kerr and Martin H. Greenberg.* Welcome to the alternate Shakespeare, in which today's top fantasists provide such unique entertainments as: a computer-peopled "King Lear," a vampiric Romeo, an unforgettable Midsummer's Night encounter with Puck, an arachnid Queen Lyr, and a fairy queen determined to find true love—or at least a truly magical moment of passion.

ANCIENT ENCHANTRESSES *Edited by Kathleen M. Massie-Ferch, Martin H. Greenberg, and Richard Gilliam.* Melanie Rawn, Jennifer Roberson, Andre Norton, Harry Turtledove, Tanith Lee, William F. Wu, and their fellow weavers of spellbinding legends bring you such memorable tales as: a poignant recounting of unrequitable love, a new interpretation of an "evil" Arthurian sorceress, and the working of a sorcery more powerful than death.

WITCH FANTASTIC *Edited by Mike Resnick and Martin H. Greenberg.* Thirty-two tales of curses cast or lifted, enemies defeated or reformed. Let such masterful magic makers as Jane Yolen, Judith Tarr, Katharine Kerr, and David Gerrold lead you to the secret glens, the inner sanctums, the small-town eateries, isolated farms, and city parks where the true practitioners of magic play their own private games of power to transform our world.

ENCHANTED FORESTS

**Edited by Katharine Kerr
and Martin H. Greenberg**

DAW BOOKS, INC.

DONALD A. WOLLHEIM, FOUNDER

375 Hudson Street, New York, NY 10014

ELIZABETH R. WOLLHEIM
SHEILA E. GILBERT
PUBLISHERS

First Printing, December 1995
1 2 3 4 5 6 7 8 9

DAW TRADEMARK REGISTERED
U.S. PAT. OFF. AND FOREIGN COUNTRIES
—MARCA REGISTRADA
HECHO EN U.S.A.

PRINTED IN THE U.S.A.

ACKNOWLEDGMENTS

Introduction © 1995 by Katharine Kerr.

The Forest's Not for Burning © 1995 by Katherine Lawrence.

"I'll Give You Three Wishes. . . ." © 1995 by Kevin Andrew Murphy.

The Triple Death © 1995 by Ken St. Andre.

Out of the Woods © 1995 by Lawrence Watt Evans.

Viridescence © 1995 by Connie Hirsch.

Fiat Silva © 1995 by Jack Oakley.

Weeds © 1995 by Julia and Brook West.

Benbow © 1995 by Nancy Etchemendy.

The Prism of Memory © 1995 by Jo Clayton.

The Force that through the Green Fuse © 1995 by Mark Kreighbaum.

My Soul into the Boughs © 1995 by Teresa Edgerton.

These Shoes Strangers Have Died of © 1995 by Bruce Holland Rogers.

The Clearing © 1995 by Lois Tilton.

How the Ant Made a Bargain © 1995 by Karawynn Long.

In Fear of Little Nell © 1995 by Gregory Feeley.

Wood Song © 1995 by Kate Daniel.

Virginia Woods © 1995 by Janni Lee Simner.

Ties of Love © 1995 by Lawrence Schimel.

The Heart of the Forest © 1995 by Dave Smeds.

Holy Ground © 1995 by Thomas S. Roche.

Ghostwood © 1995 by Michelle Sagara.

The Monsters of Mill Creek Park © 1995 by Susan Shwartz.

The Memory of Peace © 1995 by Kate Elliott.

Everything Has a Place © 1995 by Barbara A. Denz.

Trees Perpetual of Sleep © 1995 by Nina Kiriki Hoffman.

Both this book and I owe a thousand thanks to Jo Clayton. Last year, when I was drowning in personal disasters, Jo stepped in and lent a hand with finishing up the anthology. Without all her help, this project never would have been finished on time. Thanks, Jo. I appreciate it more than words can say.

CONTENTS

CONTENTS

INTRODUCTION

by Katharine Kerr

The forest was our first alien world. Our species evolved weak except for our shaped stones, defenseless except for our foul smell. We needed an open view, where we could see the leopard stalking the grass, the hyena pack spreading out to surround. As we moved out of the Rift to migrate through and then beyond the water meadows and grasslands of the area that's now the Sahara desert, forests began to loom dark at the edge of our view, always alien, always dangerous, but always, since humans are who we are, inviting us in with questions about what we might find there.

The history of Europe is the history of the death of forests. Hunters might stalk through them, shamans and priests might retreat into them, shepherds and horse nomads might shun them, but the farmers, Europe's real settlers, slashed and burned their way through, even though it took them thousands of years to kill all the wild places. In China, in India, the primeval forest also fell before stone ax and fire. In America the history reads the same, though the axes flashed with steel. Our once vast forests of the Eastern states, at least, have dwindled into parks among the plowed fields.

Yet somewhere deep in our collective psyche, the enchanted forest still stands, fearsome and inviting all at the same time. In forests lurk monsters but treasures as well, evil witches but wise hermits, tests to fail, tests to win, roads that lead to places where magic lives and things are made new. For this book, I asked twenty-five different authors to take a fresh look at these forests of the mind. Although some themes have emerged from the collection, I've been fascinated by the wide variety of the stories I received. I hope you enjoy them as much as I did.

WOODWORK

*Humor and ingenuity are part
of the job requirements*

The Forest's Not for Burning

by Katherine Lawrence

The 1994 Pima Canyon fire in Arizona's Catalina Mountains inspired this story by Katherine Lawrence. She spends much of her time exploring the boundaries of the Enchanted Forest as an animation scriptwriter for such series as CONAN THE ADVENTURER.

Have you any idea what it's like to live at the edge of the Enchanted Forest, and be the Woodcutter's eldest daughter? You know, the one out supporting the family after our parents died?

You guessed it. I was at the local market when the Duke arrived and found my younger sister hauling water from the well. I hear they have two children now.

My youngest sister was pulling up carrots when the Prince arrived. I was out trying to find a new stand of trees to harvest. At least I got an invitation to the ball they threw last month.

Oh, I've met my share of royalty, but they never quite did anything for me. I mean, they were handsome, but obsessed, every one of them. They had to have the most beautiful woman, the most magical sword, the strongest spell, whatever. Not one of them was seeking a competent partner with whom to share their life.

So when those high-efficiency ceramic stoves came into use, and the need for stacks and stacks of wood declined, I figured I needed a new career. Woodcutting wasn't cutting it anymore, if you'll pardon the pun.

In the Enchanted Forest and surrounding area, we have all the witches, wizards, sorcerers, kings, princes, dragons, princesses in peril and whatnot that anyone could want. More than enough, for my tastes. So obviously those careers were out.

What we didn't have was a plain, old (both of which descriptions were applied to me, then all of 25 years old) private investigator. So I did my research and found a school for that sort of thing, not too far around The Corner in the Real World.

What do I mean by around The Corner? It's difficult to explain, but you know how sometimes you see something wonderful out the corner of your eye? When you look full-on, it's gone, but you know it was there? Well, many of those living on the edge of the Enchanted Forest can walk around that corner and end up in the Real World. I'm one of them.

It took a year of studying combined with part-time jobs, too many roommates, and too few visits back home, but I finally got my Investigator's License and certificate of graduation. Okay, the license was only good in the Real World, but the King wouldn't know that. She wasn't allowed to leave the Enchanted Forest, and as a result was a bit naive about these things.

When I finally returned to the Enchanted Forest, I didn't have a home. The cottage I'd grown up in, and planned to continue living in, was gone. It and quite a bit of the Enchanted Forest itself.

The fire was all anyone could talk about. The King of the Enchanted Forest had set all her wizards on the case, but no one had been able to figure out the cause. It was magical, but it wasn't a spell. They were baffled.

Eager to show off my newly-learned skills, I went to the King and offered my services. Once she finished laughing at my business card, "Kit Marlowe, Private Investigator," she accepted. After all, if no one else could solve it, what did she have to lose?

Five gold a day plus expenses, I told her. She gasped, but the Treasury was good for it.

So I had my first case. Solve this one, and my career was made. Fail, and I'd at least have the money to find a new home.

I'd attended a lecture on arson investigations, so I knew where to start: First establish that an act of arson was committed.

I talked to the nearby Villagers, and got my youngest sister's daughter, the Princess, to talk to the animals. No one saw the fire start, but they all had the same answer for where it started— between my old cottage, and the edge of the Enchanted Forest. A place with no trees, just grass. There were a few stumps, but that was it. It definitely looked like arson.

Next step: Search for an incendiary device or inflammables.

I searched the area, and there was one stump more burned than the others. Only a hole in the ground, really; it had completely disintegrated. The damage appeared to have radiated outward from this spot.

I took the ashes of what remained of that one stump around The Corner to my favorite instructor at the School, who had connections to the County Forensics Lab. They owed him a favor, and were happy to have him collect on something this easy.

It was even easier than I'd anticipated. There was no sign of any of the usual inflammables. All they could detect was that it had incinerated. Well, at least that ruled out the obvious Real World possibilities.

I returned home and handed a bit more of the ash to the Court Sorcerer. He could tell me there was magic of some sort on the ash, but of a level so low, he couldn't figure out what it was. He also assured me a normal *or* magical fire shouldn't have been able to enter the Enchanted Forest. He'd reinforced the spell himself!

He thought a bit more and wondered if perhaps the fact that it started within the old boundary had something to do with that.

I thanked him, then took my expense report-to-date to the Treasury. I was now ten gold richer, and no closer to a solution.

What did that leave? I began to make lists. My new cottage quickly became filled with scribbled lists, logic flowcharts, and transcripts of interviews.

The overflowing stacks of paper reminded me of the records my father used to keep, from his days as Head Woodcutter. He was, if you'll pardon the expression, anal retentive. Yes, that's a term I learned from the lectures on Psychology of the Criminal Mind.

Father was incapable of cutting down a tree without noting its original location, where the wood was processed, and what it was turned into. He kept the records at the Palace, not at home, so they should be intact.

In the ninth musty storeroom the Palace Majordomo opened, we found the records. Being even more anal than my father, he refused to let me remove the records, but did condescend to letting me bring a lantern and a chair into the room.

My father had inherited a map of the original Enchanted Forest that numbered every tree and showed it in its original location. The map had been passed down in the family since the Enchanted Forest was discovered, so it had everything. Each tree had been carefully numbered and coded with the year it was found, since there were occasionally new trees, and the year it was cut down.

It took days, but I copied the section of the map that covered the meadow behind the old cottage.

Then I took the map and walked the burned meadow. I had to put in for several replacement pairs of boots before I was through, but I finally found which tree was the one that had disintegrated.

Next day it was back to the Palace, and the records. After several hours, I found the file for that particular tree.

I flipped through the pages and found not only confirmation of the date the tree was first noticed and the date the tree was cut, but what I really needed—what the cut tree was used for. The tree had been sold to Sorcerers Publishing, along with a couple of other trees.

Next morning, I headed to the publishing company. The Sorcerer-in-charge handed me off to his Apprentice, who threatened to turn me into a toad if I didn't go away. I informed him of the identity of my client. He went to check the files.

He came back with the dustiest book I'd ever seen, and plopped it on the desk. Naturally, or more likely magically, all the dust blew in my direction.

I decided to ignore him, for now, and opened the book. For some reason best known to Sorcerers, each magic spellbook has to be made from one and only one tree. So each book requires a separate tree. No wonder there were so few spellbooks!

Anyway, this particular tree, assuming the numbering was accurate, was turned into a spellbook for the Wizard Mendip. I looked up and caught the Apprentice making some rather spectacular passes in the air, in my direction.

One nice thing about those wizard robes—there are lots of places to grab. Once I bounced his head on the floor a couple of times, emptying his pockets of not just various spell components but some of my gold pieces, he agreed to look up an address for Wizard Mendip.

Unfortunately, Wizard Mendip had disappeared fifteen years ago. No body was ever found, so his record had a question mark next to it. That was a great help.

I didn't know whether the tree and book had anything to do with the fire, but it was the only lead I had, and now it hit a dead end. I was not a happy Investigator.

I looked up, and slowly smiled at the Apprentice. He backed away, his face pale. He backed up so quickly, he fell through the doorway behind him, and down the stairs. I figured it was a good time to find my own way out.

I went back to my quickly rebuilt cottage and stared at the assorted lists. I refused to fail on my very first case. There had to be another way to come up with the data I needed. But what?

No brilliant ideas had occurred during the night. They rarely do, despite "common wisdom." I needed help, and there was only one person I trusted on this sort of case.

Thomas was not just my favorite teacher at Investigators' School, but he was also a private investigator himself. I took my notes and went around The Corner to visit him.

I explained the situation, and he reminded me of the very first lesson he'd tried to beat into our heads in class: never make assumptions. Everyone assumes wizards stay in the Enchanted Forest. What if he'd come around The Corner and was living in the Real World?

So with Thomas' help, we checked the databases. These are the lists of everyone in the Real World. It's amazing how much one can learn about them. That's what made it so difficult for me; until Thomas "adjusted" things, I wasn't on the lists.

Anyway, there he was—Magnus Mendip, right in the same city, too. Like me, he must have stayed just around The Corner, so he could get home if he wanted to. But if that's the case, why didn't he?

I took the bus and found the Wizard's house. It looked like every other house on the street, except for the boy on a skateboard gliding down the front walk. I asked the lad if Mr. Mendip was home, and the kid punched me and took off.

I'd taken the required self-defense classes, but I hadn't expected to be punched by a twelve-year-old. I ended up on my rear end, on the grass.

A woman, whom I at first took to be the boy's mother, rushed out of the house and helped me to my feet. She apologized profusely as she helped me brush myself off. Apparently Kevan was going through "a stage" and was very difficult to deal with.

I kept my thoughts to myself, and asked if she was Mrs. Mendip.

She tittered, a sound I'd only heard a mouse make before, and one hand covered her mouth. Around the hand she informed me she was Mrs. Hodgson, the baby-sitter, and Mrs. Mendip was at work. Mrs. Mendip was expected to be home shortly, however.

Well, at least I knew I had the right household. I asked for Mr. Mendip, and was told that he had died in a car accident less than

a year ago. A drunk driver, you know. I expressed the proper
sympathy while thinking there went my lead.

Mrs. Hodgson asked me in, and naturally, I accepted.

By the time tea was served, Mrs. Mendip arrived home. On
the off chance that she might know something, I asked if she
knew of any rare books her husband had owned.

Turns out he had several. I explained that I'd been sent to find
one book in particular, as it was worth quite a bit both sentimen-
tally and in a monetary sense. She told me the special books
were kept in his study, and offered to show them to me.

The study was immediate confirmation that he was the wizard
I was searching for, in case there'd been any doubt. It wasn't a
matter of dead animals, or that sort of thing, just the general atmosphere. When you live as close to the Enchanted Forest as I
do, you develop a sensitivity to magic.

The books were in a cabinet behind his desk, and to Mrs.
Mendip's surprise, the lock had been jimmied. The doors opened
at a touch, showing an empty shelf.

Mrs. Mendip was horrified, and ready to call the police to report a burglary when the skateboarder, Kevan, walked in. Mrs.
Mendip told him to get washed for dinner, but he ignored her. He
headed straight for me.

He demanded to know what I was doing there, what I wanted
with his father, and in the same breath cursed me more ways
than most of the witches know, for daring to enter his father's
study.

I carefully stayed out of reach as I explained that I was searching for a particular book that his father owned.

With great pride and belligerence, Kevan informed me that if
it was one of the books his dad kept in that cabinet, then he'd
burned them all.

My brain started making connections immediately, so I almost
missed what he added—that the magic spells in them didn't
work anyway.

Now, you and I know that only wizards can read magic spells
in a Wizard's book. I looked at the boy more closely, the back
of my brain solving the arson case.

His mother looked at him sadly and told him to stop lying.
There was no such thing as magic. And those books were empty
anyway. The pages were all blank. She'd had to look when the
lawyers came in to check everything after he'd died.

The boy glared at his mother, calling her a stupid cow. For just a moment, I thought I saw her pink dress turn black and white. Kevan was untrained, but pretty powerful.

I asked his mother if I could have a private chat with Kevan, and she reluctantly agreed. Fortunately I at least look harmless.

Kevan refused to sit down when I suggested it. He stood in front of me, arms crossed defensively.

I asked him how badly he wanted the magic to be real.

He turned away from me, but I could read the combined pain and longing in the hunch of his shoulders and the way his arms wrapped further around, to hug himself.

I told him about the Enchanted Forest, his father being missing for fifteen years, which told me, at any rate, that he must have had very good reasons, quite likely his family, for not returning home in all that time.

A small voice muttered that this was his dad's home, which at least meant Kevan was listening to me.

I then offered, if he would consider leaving home, the chance to become a wizard like his father. I admitted it would be difficult, and he'd have to lie to his mother about where the "boarding school" was, but he could come home anytime for vacations, if he wanted.

He turned around and the fierceness of his glare as he searched my face for falsehood made the gold I'd earned seem an insignificant reward. This was the real reason I had become an investigator. Hope is the most difficult, and the most rewarding thing anyone can search for.

It took some time, and he wasn't able to come with me immediately, but I started his mother thinking about the idea of sending him off to a special school. And I promised Kevan I'd be back, with someone who'd worked with his father.

When I turned The Corner back home, after telling Thomas what happened, my eyes were more than a bit teary. I adore happy beginnings.

I still had to report to the King, but that was the easiest part of the day.

It took some time for me to explain, but the Court Wizard understood immediately, and was abashed at not having realized it sooner. One of the founding principles of magic is that a piece of a thing is the same as the whole thing. It's called sympathetic magic. What a wizard does to a single stone, affects all the stones in the castle, if the spell is properly cast.

So when an extremely talented, though untrained, young wizard burns a book made from a tree on the edge of the Enchanted

Forest, the remains of that tree incinerated. The fire simply spread from there. Sympathetic magic.

Arson by accident.

The King happily paid me the remainder of what I was owed, and I had my first reference. Not bad, for the Woodcutter's eldest daughter. Beats marrying a prince any day.

It's not so bad having one for a brother-in-law, however, or a Duke. The Duke heard of my success, and sent me a message that he needs to see me, at my soonest convenience. Wonder what he wants?

"I'll Give You Three Wishes...."

by Kevin Andrew Murphy

Kevin Andrew Murphy's last exploration into the realm of faerie was in The King Is Dead, *wherein he had Elvis stolen by the elves. He also has stories in* I, Vampire, Weird Tales from Shakespeare *and several other anthologies.*

"Good morrow, young man, and pleasant journeys," said a voice from the roadside. "What brings you so far, this sunny morn, and why so dour a face? It doesn't suit you by half, and the look in your eyes suits you even less. So take off that tired and world-weary look and tell me how you came to be wearing it."

Conrad looked to the roadside, and there, between the dandelions and the boundary stone, sat a witch.

Conrad knew she was a witch. The rats' nest hair was one sign, artfully arranged with just the right number of dead leaves and twigs, as if the old woman had once been a young maid who put flowers in her hair, then had forgotten to ever take them out.

Then there were the clothes: layers of skirts and shawls patched over and over again, stained with berry juice and with mice peeking out of the pockets—making him wonder if the woman's hair actually had been *done* by rats, instead of just looking that way. If a couple popped their noses out then and there, he wouldn't have been surprised.

The dead giveaway, however, was the dialogue. No peasant woman spoke like that. Being a peasant himself, Conrad had been around enough to know. Peasant women just said, "Mornin', boy. What's the problem?" then spat on the ground for punctuation.

He tried to remember his grandmother's tales and recall the proper form of address for a witch: "Prithee, good dame . . ."

The witch looked at him expectantly.

"Grandame . . ." he tried.

The witch continued to look at him, smiling.

Conrad kicked a rock off into the grass at the side of the road. "Listen, lady, why don't you just turn me into a toad and get it over with, okay? I'm in no mood for this."

The witch smiled. "My, the world has shat upon you, young sir. Shat upon you most mightily. Tell me, child, what has transpired, and how for did you come to this sorry pass of circumstance."

Conrad looked at her and sighed. "You obviously don't listen to the Royal Proclamations, grandma. I'm a woodcutter. This," he said, taking the ax from his belt and flourishing it, "is a woodcutter's ax. Except the King decided that everyone who cuts wood in the Royal Woods needs a woodcutter's permit. Except the permit costs more than I make in a year. So the only choice I have is to starve, or to poach wood from the Royal Woods. And if I get caught poaching—and that's an easy thing to do, since it's easy for the King's bailiffs to find a woodcutter who's selling wood without a permit—then I get arrested and have to work off my sentence doing guess what? Chopping wood in the Royal Woods. And once I'm paroled, I'll have no trade, and a criminal record, so I'll have no choice but to get arrested again so I won't starve." Conrad spat on the ground. "The King's slick as a slug in a grease pit."

The witch leered. "Slicker, in fact. That plot is worthy of the Prince of Darkness himself."

Conrad shrugged. "I guess so. Doesn't matter. The only place I can cut wood legally is Wild Wood over there." Conrad pointed to the forest just across the meadow. "Except everyone knows it's haunted, and filled with fairies and goblins." He paused, looking at her. She was obviously enjoying this. "And witches. And everyone told me the wood nymphs would turn me into a tree if I dared to cut their woods, but I'd rather be a tree than chop wood for the King. And there it is."

The witch chuckled and snorted. "Oh my," she said. "Oh dear. I haven't heard anything so funny in quite a long time. You! A tree!" She laughed until tears ran down her face, mice from her skirts, rats from her hair, and what Conrad had taken for a tatty black stole was revealed to be an even tattier black cat. "A tree! You! Turned into a tree! By the wood nymphs!" The witch laughed and pounded the ground, giggling like a village girl who'd just seen a naked man for the first time.

Conrad exchanged glances with the mice and rats and the cat and the pair of toads who had crawled out of her shoes. They all looked embarrassed. The cat began washing one ear, pretending not to notice her mistress' conniption fit.

Conrad decided to take the cat's attitude, because now that he was actually looking at a toad, being one didn't seem quite so preferable to just being an unemployed woodcutter.

The witch at last recovered, wiping the tears from her eyes and collecting her retinue back into her skirts. "Oh my, young sir. I haven't had so fine a laugh since my youth, and for that I will reward you." She looked at him again, leering. "You don't get the jest, do you?"

Conrad shrugged. "No."

"The wood nymphs," the witch explained, "only take the handsomest young men. And you—That nose! Those teeth!" The witch burst into renewed peals of laughter.

Conrad considered his ax and the helpless witch on the ground, but the cat looked at him and her expression was clear: *Don't even think it, buster.*

Conrad shrugged again. The witch reminded him even more of the village girls, who had been the first to laugh at his nose and his teeth. "So what would the wood nymphs do with me?"

"Oh, they'd probably just drop a branch on your head and have done with it. But you've made me laugh, young sir, so I'll help you." She rubbed her hands with glee. "Oh yes, I think this may be quite profitable for both of us."

Hector the mockingbird knew it meant trouble when the woodcutter came to the forest. "Woodcutter. Woodcutter. Always trouble. Always trouble. Sharp ax. Sharp mind. Cut, cut, trouble, trouble, trouble."

Prissy the squirrel threw an acorn at his head: "Loud mockingbird! Too loud! Bad Hector! Bad-bad-bad!"

"Woodcutter! Woodcutter! Trouble, trouble, trouble!" Hector whistled, laughing, and did a back flip to dodge another acorn. "Woodcutter! Woodcutter! Chop-chop! No trees! No nuts! No squirrels!"

Prissy paused, cocking her head and another acorn. "No nuts?" She dropped the acorn in shock. "No nuts!" She ran off, sounding the alarm: "No nuts! No nuts! No nuts!"

Hector did another back flip, proud of himself, then winged

off through the forest, singing his song: "Woodcutter! Woodcutter! Trouble-trouble-trouble!"

Conrad stayed close to the witch. The birds and animals seemed upset, and one squirrel sat on a high branch and scolded him, throwing acorns at his head.

The cat put her head up and hissed. The squirrel dropped her nuts and took off down the branch, chattering wildly.

"That's right, Mehitabel. You tell that nasty squirrel." The witch stroked the cat's tail. "Destroy the forest? Of course not. Just select portions. Parts that have crossed us."

The witch led the way straight to the door of her cottage, through a garden filled with belladonna, henbane, monk's hood, skullcap and a bush heavy with the luscious purple berries of deadly nightshade—and a paranoid-looking black goat tethered in the middle, carefully cropping the few nonpoisonous plants in between. A broomstick hung over the threshold for those still slow on the uptake.

"Welcome to my humble dwelling, young woodcutter," the witch opened a door decorated with a freshly painted pentacle and a skull that evidently belonged to some former goat who had no doubt finally nibbled the wrong bit of greenery, "but before you enter, give me your name."

Conrad knew it wasn't the wisest thing to give one's name to a witch, but then again, she could probably turn him into a crab apple without it, so it didn't really matter. And with the starving goat behind him, the last thing he wanted to be was a crab apple. "Conrad, uh, good dame."

The witch cackled and ushered him inside. "Call me Dame Margot. That name should do as well as any."

"Yes, Dame Margot."

The hut was low-ceilinged and grimy, and Conrad had to hunch over almost as much as the witch to keep from knocking his head on the bundles of moldering herbs and various and assorted spiders. There were tables and mixing bowls, mortars and pestles, shelves of pickled whatsises better left unidentified, and off to one side, a lectern carved with bats and cats and rats and all the other fuzzy little animals favored by Forces of Darkness.

Atop this, in a place of honor, lay the witch's books of forbidden lore. Or at least that's what Conrad assumed they were. Being illiterate, he couldn't read the titles, but given the setting and the leering pride with which the witch gestured to them, he suspected they were something aside from chivalric romances.

She then pointed to a stool by the hearth. Conrad sat down without question. Beside him, the obligatory cauldron simmered, brownish gruel swirling in the depths.

Dame Margot stumped about her hut happily, humming some little tune: " 'Today I'll bake, tomorrow I'll brew, the next day the Young King's child I'll stew . . .' No, that's not it. 'Be he dead or be he alive, I'll . . .' No, not that either. Oh, I don't know why I bother with these silly dwarven songs. The only point to them is to have something to do with your lips in between mouthfuls of beer." She came back with two mugs and set them down to warm by the fire. "Dwarven ale. The best kind."

She cackled in delight, then got a long spoon and a wooden bowl and dished up a mess of the stuff in the cauldron. "Here, young woodcutter. Eat well and hearty, so that we might better discuss business."

Conrad took out his horn spoon and tasted the stew. It was better than he'd expected, but not much, with little bits of unidentifiable meat which may have once belonged to the undiscriminating goat. But the ale was much better, and he could understand why the dwarves got their lyrics mixed up.

The witch sat down on the stool opposite him, Mehitabel jumping down and stretching out before the hearth. "Now, tell me what you know of wood nymphs, young woodcutter." She produced a crust of bread and broke it up for the mice and rats, who began to nibble it and look at him expectantly.

Conrad paused. "Wood nymphs. Um, they live in trees. They're really beautiful. They turn men into trees sometimes . . . but only the handsome ones. The men, that is, not the trees. And sometimes they can give you wishes . . . except they never turn out right."

"Aha!" said the witch, stamping her feet in delight and frightening the toads from her shoes. "There you have it! There's the rub and there's the problem and there's the trouble with wood nymphs. They have magic, true enough, but it's natural magic, and cursed to boot, at least if you have the wood nymph's ill will. Can't wish for castles and crowns and kingdoms with a wood nymph's wishes. Just small, simple, natural things or natural magic. Not that you'd want to anyway, since people who get their wishes from bullying wood nymphs end up with sausages stuck to their noses. Or was that noses stuck to their sausages? No matter, I've heard both, and I've heard much worse than either. Oh yes, much worse." The witch cackled a bit more and rubbed her hands. "Why, I could tell you a few tales ... but never mind. Listen to me, young Conrad, and heed well my lore and learning. The only folk who've ever had happy dealings with wood nymphs are the ones who've gained their love, and most of them ended up as trees, so it's a tricky business. And if you're handsome, they'll take you as a tree, to keep you with them. But if an ugly man could gain a wood nymph's good will, why, then ..."

Dame Margot rubbed her hands and cackled. "You're a merchant, aren't you, young Conrad? There's more to being a woodcutter than just chopping wood, isn't there? There's selling it, too, and it's in the selling that there's the profit. And you get happy customers when you sell them something they want." Dame Margot leaned close, and the cat and rats and mice and toads all leaned in to listen, too. "Now let me tell you my plan. ..."

Lindy the Linden was absolutely terrified. The woodcutter had been walking all over the forest, singing fiendish woodcutting songs, and now he had come and sat beneath her tree for the third time that day.

And he was sharpening his ax.

She was an old linden, but a small one, and she hadn't any limbs large enough to drop on his head, and the thought of even losing one of her limbs ...

She quaked like an aspen. To lose a limb, then have beetles crawl under her bark.... Oh, terrible, terrible! But to be cut down altogether ...

She did her hair up as prettily as she could with her springtime flowers and arranged her gown of bark as nicely as possible, then slipped out the back of her tree and came round to where the woodcutter sat, polishing his terrible ax. He was young, but as ugly and horrible as any of the forest dwarves, and brawny besides.

She wrung her hands as she had been told was wise and tried to look as plaintive and miserable as she could. "Oh please, good Woodcutter," she said. "Please do not cut down my tree! If you promise not to cut down my tree, I'll give you three wishes!"

The woodcutter looked up from his horrible ax and smiled. "Hello, good wood nymph. Is this your tree here?" He reached back and patted the trunk of her precious linden, and Lindy felt his hand running up and down her leg.

"Yes, good Woodcutter! Please, do not cut down my tree or I will perish! I will give you three wishes if you promise not to harm me!"

The woodcutter smiled more and stroked the root that corresponded to her foot. "Never fear, good wood nymph. I was not planning to cut your tree. You may keep your wishes, and your life. Indeed, your tree is far too young and pretty to cut; it would be a crime to rob the forest of its beauty." He patted the root again and Lindy felt him stroke her foot. "I only sat here because I find yours the most fine and beautiful young tree in the forest, and I wished to have a pleasant place to sit while I tried to decide which of the old and ugly trees to cut down for firewood."

Lindy paused. "You do not wish to cut down my tree, good Woodcutter?"

"Of course not, beautiful nymph. To all things there is a season, and it would be a crime to cut short the life of anything so young and beautiful." He ran the whetstone across the ax blade and looked at the other trees nearby. "It is just so hard to choose which of the old and ugly trees to take. To decide which the forest would be better off without. I take my responsibilities as a woodcutter seriously and would only cut down a tree that had outlived her usefulness." He looked at Lindy and smiled, buckteeth protruding. "I don't suppose you'd know of a tree that fits that description?"

Lindy held a finger to her lips, amazed at her good fortune, then pointed right across the way, to where Becka the Beech lived. "That one. Right there. That bitch has been blocking my sunlight my entire life, and her roots take most of the water, too!"

The woodcutter polished his ax, looking at the beech tree. "Are you certain? As I said, I take my responsibilities as a woodcutter seriously, and I would not want to take any tree that did not absolutely have to go."

"Oh, she has to go all right," Lindy said. "That bitch thinks she's the Queen of the Forest, when all she is is a sun-hog and a breeding ground for bark beetles and woodpeckers. The forest would be a lot better off without her."

The woodcutter sharpened his ax, looking at Becka the Beech bitch. "Are you certain? It is an old tree, certainly, but I am not certain that should be the one I cut down. . . ."

Lindy paused, thinking of how much easier her life would be without Becka blocking all her sunlight and taking all her water. "I'll give you three wishes. . . ."

"Three wishes?" said the woodcutter. "Well, if you feel that strongly about it, I suppose she has to go. . . ."

Witch Margot kicked up her heels and danced with the cat. " 'Oh, today I plot, tomorrow I scheme/The next I realize my dream! And that will be good and better than good/With wood nymphs stacked as kindling wood!' "

"Meow!" shrieked Mehitabel. "Meow!"

"That's right, Mehitabel. All those nasty wood nymphs who've crossed us will be gone, and we'll be rich in the bargain!" The mice and rats played the fiddle, and the toads played the mandolin, and teaching them that had been more of trick than she liked to think about. But it was worth it for moments like this.

" 'Oh, today we dance, tomorrow we drink/Get piss blind drunk till we can't think! For each revenge we get a wish! Get what we want . . .' " Witch Margot paused, trying to think of a good rhyme.

"Meow! Meow!" cried Mehitabel, dancing the Mazurka.

"Yes!" said Witch Margot. " 'And cream and fish!' We'll have it all, Mehitabel!"

Margot hitched up her skirts and danced round the kitchen once more. Blessed be the day she'd bought those books from the magic peddler! Who ever would have thought they'd hold such lore and knowledge, or explain the way of the world so well and clearly? "Wonderful!" she exclaimed, dancing over to the lectern and giving a reverent pat to the *Deutsche Volksmärchen* and the *Collected Works of Hans Christian Andersen*. "Lovely, lovely, lovely books! And you, the most precious of all my darlings!" she cried, picking up and kissing the *Folktale Motif Index*. "Oh, I wish I had all the books in your bibliography!"

Witch Margot paused, but no library suddenly appeared.

She shrugged and laughed. "Ah well, Mehitabel. We'll get them soon enough. 'Oh, today we dance/Tomorrow we bake/ Have lots of beer—' "

"Meow!" shrieked Mehitabel.

" '—and fish," Margot translated and nodded in agreement, "and cake!' Blessed be the peddler and the day he sold me my books!"

She cackled with glee, dancing around holding her prized *Folktale Motif Index* over her head, altogether too caught up in her good fortune to notice the mockingbird and squirrel peeking through the tear in the thatch.

* * *

Conrad stood up, polishing his ax. Three wishes, in advance . . . He smiled, remembering what the witch had told him to wish for. "For my first wish, I wish to live a long, healthy life."

"It is done," said the wood nymph, clinging to her linden tree like a harlot on a lamppost.

Conrad suddenly felt very, very healthy and the wart on his thumb dropped off onto the ground.

For the second wish, the witch said he could wish for anything, except to be handsome: "I also wish to be strong. Incredibly strong. Even stronger than Ernhardt the Blacksmith."

Conrad felt all his muscles swell up and the laces on his jerkin stretched tight and then popped. He looked down at his bulging arms and chest, though this was rather hard, since his clothes were now much too small and he didn't seem to have a neck anymore, at least not one that was smaller than his head. But he certainly felt strong.

"It is done," said the wood nymph. "What's your third wish, good Woodcutter?"

Conrad finished admiring himself and figuring out how to move without his thighs rubbing together, then looked back at the wood nymph. "Oh, that. Yes. I wish that the old lady who gave me such good advice would get the third wish. To use however she wants." After all, Conrad thought, that was the deal, and he knew enough of his grandmother's stories to know that you always played straight with witches. Unless you wanted to be a toad, and being a toad—even an incredibly strong, healthy, long-lived one—was not something that Conrad wanted to be.

"It is done," said the wood nymph. "Are you going to go cut down Becka's tree now? I'd really like to have some more sunlight."

Conrad tipped his hat, getting used to the way his new muscles were rubbing on each other. "Of course, good wood nymph. I'm a man of my word, and we're agreed—the beech tree has to go."

He walked across to where the tall beech stood and looked up. A branch dropped down, landing beside him, and he smiled. The linden tree had been as good as her word; the branches were missing him. Well, time to be true to his. He inspected the trunk of the beech for the right spot to cut, and another branch landed beside him.

The linden was right. The beech tree was a bitch.

Conrad spat on his hands and readied his ax, but before he

could swing, the beech's nymph stepped out of the trunk. She was tall and grand, looking like some ancient queen, with a crown in her hair and a mantle of squirrel skins. "Woodcutter," she intoned, "spare my tree and I will reward you with three wishes!"

Conrad smiled. Dame Margot had also been right. The wood nymphs were just giving them away.

"Sorry," he said. "I think I'll just cut down the tree."

"What is—" she began, then did a double take. "What? Doth mine ears deceive me? Didst thou just refuse my three wishes?"

Conrad nodded. "That's right. Lot of good board feet of lumber in this baby." He patted the trunk and the wood nymph looked shocked and grabbed her bottom. "Anyway, a dwarf told me if I cut down this tree, I'll find a golden goose inside."

"What? The dwarf lies! I have not a goose inside my trunk."

"Well, honey, you sure act like you've got something stuck up your ass. Let's see what it is, huh?"

"But—Three wishes! I'll give you three wishes!"

Conrad shrugged his massive shoulders. "Eh, I've already had three wishes. I think I'll go for a goose instead." He swung the ax, and the wood nymph grabbed her ass and screamed.

Conrad swung again and again, pleased at how fast the woodcutting was going with his new muscles. At last the screaming wood nymph disappeared, and the trunk gave way. "Timber!" Conrad called and the beech tree listed over, crashing slowly to the ground and flattening a certain small linden tree.

Conrad polished his ax. Just like Dame Margot had said. All the witnesses taken care of, and three wishes in the bargain.

Becka the Beech tree had been right, too. There hadn't been a golden goose stuck up her ass. However, there was an old tinderbox lying on the edge of the stump, just the way the witch had said, and when he looked down the hollow into the cave below, Conrad saw the three dogs Dame Margot had also mentioned, the ones with the eyes the size of teacups, millstones and the Round Tower at Copenhagen, wherever that was.

Conrad took the tinderbox and looked down at the three dogs. "Hey there! Dogs! Remember, I've got the box now, so don't go telling anyone what happened!"

The dogs blinked, panted, and wagged their tails, and Conrad tried to find room for the tinderbox under his arm, which was rather hard, as there was a good deal of muscle in the way that hadn't been there before.

Oh well, he could certainly get used to that. He set off back to

Dame Margot's and wondered what, aside from walking bowleg-ged, he could do to keep his thighs from rubbing together.

Hector the mockingbird and Prissy the squirrel hastily con-ferred in the upper branches of one of the oaks. "Trees no listen!" Prissy squeaked. "Just squirrel! Just bird! Trees no lis-ten! Stupid trees! Stupid-stupid-stupid!"

Hector nodded in agreement. "Woodcutter trouble! Witch trou-ble! Double-trouble! Double-trouble!"

"Who listen, Hector?" asked Prissy. "Who care? Just bird! Just squirrel!"

Hector thought a moment. "King Stag?"

Prissy twitched her tail. "Why care?"

She had a point. "Fairy Boar?"

"Boar old!" said Prissy. "Boar crazy! Boar eat bad truffles!"

Hector cocked his head. "Goblins?"

Prissy twitched her tail, refusing even to comment.

Hector thought a bit more. "Know the thing!" he cried. "Find Dwarf King!"

Prissy paused and cocked her head. "Why Dwarf King help?"

"Profit! Profit! Money-money-money! Dwarf King, triple-trouble, money-money-money!"

"Dwarf King. Triple-trouble." Prissy twitched her tail. "Hector smart."

Hector did a back flip. "Money-money-money."

Conrad sat with Dame Margot, divvying up the week's haul. "Let's see, that's twenty-seven wishes, nine for you, eighteen for me, plus you've got the tinderbox, the golden goose, and this, whatever it's worth." He flipped the small bone he'd found in the crook of an ash tree onto the table. It didn't look like anything important, but it had been shut in a silver chest, so it must be worth something.

Dame Margot picked up the bone and laughed, her voice sounding much nicer since she'd wished herself young and was again the maiden with flowers in her hair that he'd guessed she'd originally been. "Oh, this," said the witch maiden. "It's a wiz-ard's finger bone. Some of the silly old buggers hide their lives in them, then give them to something else to guard. Usually dragons or wood nymphs. If we snap it, the wizard will die."

Conrad shrugged his massive shoulders, finally getting used to the heft of them. "So what do we do with it?"

Margot looked at it. "Oh, we could probably sell it back to the wizard it belongs to, but that's more trouble than it's worth. I know what we do with it." She whistled. "Here, Teacup! Here, boy! We have a treat for you!"

The dog with eyes as big as teacups bounded forward and sat down, wagging his tail. "Woof!"

Margot laughed and flipped him the bone, which he caught and crunched happily. Somewhere, Conrad supposed, a wizard was having a heart attack.

The golden goose honked and Margot gave it a biscuit broken up in a bowl of water. It dabbled happily, though it looked rather strange with the tea cozy firmly attached to its tail. "Golden goose feathers are sticky things," Margot had said. "Once you get stuck by their enchantment, the only thing that can loose them is a laughing princess, and we haven't the time to get one of *those* just now."

Conrad went back to counting the coins from the three chests the dogs had brought. The coppers weren't very valuable, but the gold and silver were worth a king's ransom.

A knock came at the door. Margot rolled her eyes. "If it's any lost children, tell them to go away. I've moved. Children are nothing but trouble."

Conrad nodded, going to the door of the now spacious and pretty cottage. A terrible waste of a wish, in his opinion, but then Margot was free to do with her wishes what she wanted.

He opened the door, and while the height was right for a pesky child, the long white beard and the golden crown were certainly not. It was a dwarf, and unless Conrad missed his guess, it was their King. On his left shoulder sat a squirrel, and on his right, a mockingbird.

"Who is it?" Margot asked from the table.

Conrad paused. "Um, I think it's the King of the Dwarves."

"The Rubezahl?" Margot asked. "Oh, by all means, invite him in. He can help us count the gold."

The Dwarf King's eyes twinkled at the word and he walked in past Conrad. "Hmph, I was wondering when you were going to get around to that." He surveyed the cottage as Conrad shut the door, then looked directly at the chests of gold and the goose. "My, what a nice haul. I was given to understand that you were dealing with wood nymph wishes. I didn't realize that they could do gold now."

Margot smiled. "We had a bit of other good fortune."

The three dogs growled at the Dwarf King, and Margot looked

at them fiercely. "Millstone! Tower! Teacup! Hush! This is the Rubezahl. . . ."

The Rubezahl took in the three dogs and then looked to the table. "You found the tinderbox? My, this *has* been a fortunate week for you. However," he said, sitting down on one of the old stools, "my associates," he gestured to the squirrel and the mockingbird, "have informed me of the scam you're running. Very good. Very clever. I must commend you both."

Conrad considered wishing the dwarf, squirrel, and mockingbird dead right then and there, but he saw the look that Margot was giving the Rubezahl and realized that that wasn't really an option.

The Dwarf King smiled, showing a mouthful of golden teeth. "Now I have a dozen dwarves, with axes, ready, willing, and able to run the same scam. However, the wood nymphs would finally catch on, and that would quickly dry up the market." The Rubezahl steepled his fingers, jewels shining on each knuckle. "It would be far more profitable, in the long run, to continue this as a solo operation." He rubbed his hands together and the rings clicked. "May I ask what split you're operating by?"

Conrad exchanged glances with Margot, and she nodded. "Um, I get two out of every three wishes, but Margot gets first pick of the extras. The tinderbox and the goose and the wizard's finger bone."

The Rubezahl raised his eyebrows. "Finger bone?"

Margot grinned weakly. "I fed it to Teacup."

"Good sense," said the Dwarf King. "Wouldn't want to have to cut a wizard in on the action, too, and they're no end of trouble, at least the undying ones. Almost as bad as children."

Margot nodded. "True."

"Now," said the Dwarf King, "what I'm offering is a three-way split on the wishes, and an even pick of the extras. I'm also offering my expert services as appraiser, as well as the use of my dwarves to insure the secrecy of this operation and guard it against the addition of any fourth parties or unnecessary competition. My associates," he gestured to the mockingbird and the squirrel, "would also like some additional considerations, in exchange for their discretion in this matter."

He conferred for a moment with the squirrel and mockingbird, who chattered and whistled, bobbing their heads up and down.

"Yes," the Rubezahl said. "Yes, of course."

He gestured to the mockingbird. "Hector here would like the

ability to speak the language of all men and beasts. Would that be possible?"

Margot struck three sparks from the tinderbox. "Tower! Go fetch a dragon's heart! There's got to be one somewhere that doesn't need his, and there's a nice treat for you when you bring it back!"

"WOOF!" boomed Tower, blinking his enormous eyes, and bounded off through the ballroom. On second thought, Conrad considered, perhaps the expansions to the cottage hadn't been such a foolish wish after all. They had to have somewhere to keep the dogs.

Margot turned back to the Rubezahl. "And . . . ?"

The Dwarf King stroked the squirrel's tail and conferred again, then looked back and smiled. "Yes. Prissy here would like an endless supply of nuts, and protection for the Great Oak in the center of the Wild Wood."

Margot shrugged. "No trouble with the oak. Everybody knows there's a wizard locked in the trunk, and as you said, wizards are almost as much trouble as children. That wood nymph can keep him and her tree. But as for the nuts . . ."

She looked to Conrad and he shrugged. "I don't know. I've never heard of an endless supply of nuts, unless we're talking about the royal family." He paused. "Maybe the King's granary?"

"Possible," said Margot. "We could always use a wish for it. We have enough. Though it seems an awful waste. . . ."

The squirrel chattered, evidently having a difference of opinion.

The Rubezahl waved one hand regally, dismissing the objection, and showed his golden teeth. "I wouldn't be so eager to use a wish just yet if I were you. You're aware that a wood nymph's wishes are cursed, aren't you?"

Witchmaid Margot smiled. "Of course—but only if you have the wood nymph's ill will. We've been very careful to have Conrad sweet-talk those sawdust brains, then drop another tree on them while they're still happy. No troubles."

The Dwarf King steepled his fingers. "Yet—to the best of your knowledge. Which brings us to an unpleasant bit of business, which, as your new partner in this endeavor, I'm now free to share with you." He paused and looked at the two of them. "Are you aware that the only certain way to kill a willow tree is to burn it out at the roots?"

Conrad and Margot exchanged glances, and Margot raised her eyebrows. "A willow tree? You went after a willow?"

Conrad shrugged and the chair creaked beneath him. "Wareen the Willow. A real bitch. She wanted to pay me only one wish a hit, but I took 'em all anyway and dropped all three oaks on top of her. I've heard of willows walking, but there's no way she walked away from that."

The Dwarf King grimaced. "Well, she may not have *walked*, but Hector spotted a very irate stump *crawling* through the underbrush. Which, I'm happy to report, is now just so much willow-wood charcoal." The Rubezahl toyed with his ruby signet. "Be that as it may, that still means that Wareen the Willow had ample time to curse her wishes, unless you used them *very* promptly."

The Dwarf King smiled. "I trust, at least, that you did proper accounting, and know which wish is which?"

Conrad felt a sinking feeling and looked to Margot. "Did you . . . ?"

She threw up her hands. "What do you expect? I'm a witch, not a bookkeeper."

"Ahem," said the Rubezahl. "I believe I offered my services just in time. We'll have to do a very strict accounting to discern where in the order the cursed wishes lie—assuming, of course, those are the only ones—then we will need to devise some way to disarm them so as to get to the good wishes behind them."

"How do we know they go in order?" Conrad asked.

"Because—" the Rubezahl began, then looked to Margot. "Do wishes go in order?"

"They do with leprechauns. As for wood nymphs, well, I'd expect . . ." She stood up, looking distracted. "Let me go check my *Motif Index*."

The Rubezahl smiled. "From the magic peddler?"

"Of course." She sighed. "I'd better put on the kettle. This is going to be a long night."

"I take mine black," said the Rubezahl and pulled his stool closer to the table. The squirrel and the mockingbird hopped off his shoulders to take places on the edge of one of the bookshelves, and he got out a large ledger, his crown disappearing to be replaced by a green eyeshade and spectacles.

He sharpened a crow quill and dipped it in an inkwell that appeared just as suddenly. "So, boy, who was your last client, and what was the last wish you made?"

Conrad leaned heavily on the table and it creaked beneath his weight. "Well, the last one was Elena the Elm, this morning."

"Time?"

Conrad tried to scratch his head, but that was still hard with all the muscles in the way. "About an hour after sunrise?"

The Rubezahl scribbled in his ledger, and the golden goose honked and eyed the cup of tea Margot set before him. "No, Gee-Gee. Here, have a crumpet." She crumbled some into the goose's bowl, then gave the rest to the squirrel and the mockingbird and her pet rats and mice.

The Rubezahl picked up his tea and smiled. "Thank you, Margot." A moment later, a golden mug with a fine head of foam appeared in Conrad's hand, and the Rubezahl clicked his cup against it. "Here's to a long and lucrative business association, boy."

"Conrad," Conrad said.

"Conrad. Good. Let's be informal. You can call me Rube. To a long and lucrative business association—and to better book-keeping."

"Uh, sure, Rube." Conrad took a sip and smiled. Good strong dwarven ale, most likely from the Dwarf King's private reserve. "To good business and better bookkeeping." He took another draught.

The goose looked up from her scone and honked several times.

The Rubezahl put his pen down. "Indeed?"

The goose honked several more times.

Conrad set his beer down. "Does the goose want a piece of the action, too?"

The Rubezahl inclined his head. "After a fashion. She thinks we should cool it with the wood nymph scam and go for the laughing princess."

Margot flipped through her book. "According to the *Motif Index*, if we go with the goose, we stand to gain an entire kingdom—something we can't get with the wood nymph wishes."

"Sounds like a plan."

The dog with the eyes as big as the Round Tower at Copenhagen (and Conrad still didn't know where that was) bounded in and dropped a large heap of steaming meat on the floor next to them. "*COOKIE!*" bellowed Tower in place of his usual "*WOOF!*"

The mockingbird fluttered down to land on the heap of meat and took a few pecks from it. "Dragon's heart! Really smart!

Take a part! Then we start!" the mockingbird sang, doing a flip and landing on the table.

"So that's a dragon's heart?" Conrad asked.

"With a good bit of the dragon still attached, but yes," said the Rubezahl.

"Well, the mockingbird's got the right idea." Conrad stood up and got hold of the bloody thing. It came off the floor with a soft squelch. "Let me go carve this up. Once we can all talk with each other, we can decide which scam we're going to go with."

"COOKIE!" boomed Tower.

"And," the Rubezahl added dryly, "we should probably go over exactly what everyone expects to get from this relationship. I believe I'll start drawing up the contracts."

"COOKIE!" Tower boomed again, louder this time.

"Get one of the dog biscuits while you're at it, Conrad," Margot said. "Actually, get the jar. This is going to be a long night."

"Got it right!" chimed the mockingbird.

Yes, thought Conrad, it was certainly going to be a long night.

A witch, a dwarf, a squirrel, a mockingbird, two mice, two toads, two rats, a cat, three dogs, and a goose with sticky gold feathers. And the goat out in the garden, depending on whether Margot planned on cutting him in as well. What a crew.

"I wish—" Conrad said ... and paused.

No, he wasn't going to wish anything. Things were complicated enough as it was.

The Triple Death

by Ken St. Andre

*Ken St. Andre is an award-winning fantasy game designer
and one of the pioneers in developing these games. His
Tunnels and Trolls (™) was the second such game in the
United States. He works as a librarian for the city of
Phoenix, occasionally writes fiction, and gets by with a lit-
tle help from his friends.*

"Light the torches!" called Sir Kay as the red light of sunset
faded from the windows. Serving boys hastened to obey, and as
the wood crackled into flame, a flickering light brightened the
huge hall. An angry mutter of conversation filled the dining
room of Camelot. At the head of the table sat Arthur and Guinevere, dressed in their best robes of gold-embroidered wool.
Along the sides of the table sat the foremost knights of the realm
and their ladies, while at the trestles that stretched in aisles
through the large chamber thronged the other members of Pen-
dragon's court, including many lesser knights, squires, church-
men, tradesmen, and their companions. A Welsh bard plucked a
ripple of music from his handheld harp, though it seemed to have
no effect on the impatient crowd. The words "eat" and "when do
we eat" cut through the babble repeatedly. The torchlight picked
out red-gold highlights in Sir Gawaine's mane of unbound hair,
and made the green silk scarf that encircled his throat appear almost black. Just after he thumped his pewter drinking cup down
on the sturdy wooden table his stomach rumbled so loudly that
all conversations around him stopped, and the harper twitched
and broke the smallest string of his instrument.

The Queen leaned over to whisper in Arthur's ear. "Let the feast begin, Sire!" Her stage whisper carried to every corner of the room. "The marvel you desire has been with us all day, for is that not the sound of the Questing Beast in yon knight's stomach? That should be marvel enough for any Christian monarch!"

More than twenty knights and ladies echoed her plea as soon as the general laughter died down. Gawaine hid his blush by refilling his mug from a large chalice of mead, gulping the poorly fermented honey liquor. "At least Arthur didn't laugh," Agrivaine whispered to Gawaine, showing a rare moment of sympathy.

Though a smile curled the corners of the King's mouth, he did not look ready to summon the food. At that moment Gawaine's belly growled again, not quite so loudly, and many other stomachs rumbled in sympathy.

Gawaine set aside his mead cup, and rose to his feet. In a ringing voice he cried out, "Uncle, send for the food, and I shall tell you and this assembly of a right marvelous adventure that happened to me before I became a knight!"

"So be it!" said Arthur with a tired smile. He signaled to his hulking butler.

Cheers and the clanking of cups raised in impromptu toasts to the king, Sir Gawaine, and the food itself filled the great hall with noise. A line of scarlet-clad scullions bearing wooden platters heaped with steaming cuts of venison, boar, and mutton paraded into the room. Two brawny cooks pushed a small cart carrying a cauldron of bubbling turtle soup toward the center of the hall, and small page boys offered polished wooden bowls and spoons to all who wanted them. After placing at least one meat platter on each table and trestle, the servers returned to the kitchens, only to reappear in a few minutes carrying trays covered with hot, roasted chickens and ducks. Some of them brought basins filled with bunches of purple grapes and ripe red apples which they placed on every table.

Sweet grape juice trickled down Gawaine's cleanshaven chin as he reached out with his dagger and nabbed a whole roast chicken from the center of the table, just instants before Dinadan's blade thwocked into the empty wood. "My apologies, Din! I did not mean to rob you." Gawaine extended the prize toward the smaller man, but Dinadan waved it off and took another slightly smaller bird instead. "To the victor . . ." Dinadan laughed. Gawaine pulled the hen back to his plate, sawed off a drumstick, and took a huge bite.

Agrivaine dipped a chunk of hot bread into a puddle of dark pork gravy, and lifted it like a scepter. "Better than the Christmas cod feast back in Orkney, eh, brother?" He gloated for a moment before biting into the sopping loaf.

"Christmas at home," mused Gawaine. He stopped chewing and his eyes clouded with memory. "Remember the time that Merlin feasted with us. Thanks, brother, I think I know what tale can pay for this supper."

An hour later, the feasting slowed. Men groaned happily and loosened their belts while ladies wiped their lips and discreetly adjusted their girdles. Sir Dinadan rose on his bandy legs, wiped the grease from his bushy mustache with his sleeve, lifted his cup high, and called out a toast, "Drink we now to Sir Gawaine, the courteous knight, for he has once again saved this court!"

"Keep now your promise, Nephew, and justify this feast with your tale," commanded the king.

Gawaine arose. In two steps he passed the bard and deftly plucked the harp away from him. The minstrel started to protest, but an exaggerated wink from the knight calmed him without a word. Gawaine staggered up to the high dais (hours of imbibing made it slightly difficult to keep his balance) and hammered on the strings until the hall fell silent. "Hearken, my lords and ladies! I shall tell you of my first meeting with Merlin, the great enchanter, and a marvelous adventure that came of it."

"I was just a lad of twelve summers when Merlin the Prophet visited our court. He brought with him a break in the snowstorm that had blown for all the twelve days of Christmas, and for that, my father decided to honor him with a three-day feast.

"Merlin proved to be a popular guest. Commoners and nobles crowded round him, offering small gifts and asking his blessing or advice. The ladies of our court vied with each other to comb his beard, or bring him morsels from the table. As the day turned to evening, my father's face darkened with jealousy.

"In his wrath, my father decided to test this famed magician. He called me forth and presented me to the Wise Man, saying, 'This is Gawaine, my first-born son. Tell me now how he shall die, if the future is known to you.'

" 'Lot, this is unseemly,' said Merlin. 'No man should know the manner nor the time of his dying.'

"My father stood up and glared at his guest. 'I am King! My word is Law! My whim is command! Tell me of Gawaine's death!' And he glowered, gray eyebrows and shaggy mane of hair putting all who saw him in mind of an ancient storm god.

" 'Very well,' Merlin agreed. 'I am your guest, and I should obey my host, but little joy will you gain from this knowledge.'

" 'Just tell me! Tell us all!' commanded my father.

"Merlin called me to stand before him and placed his hands atop my head and over my heart. Those hands were warm and strong with the best-kept fingernails that I had ever seen, all of a length, unbroken, uncracked, and not caked with dirt beneath the nail. I felt a tingle that made my neck hairs rise on end, and then the wizard—he was not an old man at that time—winked at me with one eye, before turning to face my father and mother at the head of the board.

" 'This boy shall die by falling,' he intoned in a sepulchral voice that filled the hall.

"Disappointment and dismay twisted my father's harsh features. We kings of Orkney are warriors, and doubtless my sire expected to hear that I would die in battle.

"My mother leaned and whispered something in his ear, and his countenance brightened. 'Twice more shall I ask this question, but for now let the feasting and merriment proceed.' I escaped happily to the table in the corner where my brothers and I took our meals, hoping that Agrivaine, or some other child would be the king's subject on the morrow, but on the next evening, when Lot dirtied my face and dressed me in the rags of a peasant boy, there was nothing I could do but pretend to a churlishness I did not feel.

"Merlin seemed to look right through the grime on my face. Neither my slouch nor my ragged garments fooled him. Putting his hand on my head, and staring my father straight in the eye, he announced, 'This boy shall die by hanging!'

" 'Is that so?' asked King Lot, and a gleam of satisfaction came into his eyes. 'Well, I will watch his fate carefully, and he won't go by hanging if I have anything to say about it!'

"Once more my father planned to ask his question, and the final disguise shamed me. For the third occasion I had to play the part of a girl—truly a galling experience for a twelve-year-old boy who thinks he will be a warrior some day. I had a blonde wig, a scratchy dress, a necklace made of wooden beads from my mother's store of jewelry. They cut my fingernails and toenails and painted them red. They stained my lips purple with berry juice, and they padded my hips to make them seem wider. It took all afternoon to dress and prepare me. My mother made me practice walking with a swaying motion. I also had to keep my eyes discreetly downcast. The ladies really tried to make a proper damsel of me, but I fear that I disappointed them." Gawaine paused in his tale to take a drink while laughter rocked the hall.

"Gawaine!" When Guinevere could speak without laughing aloud, she went on, "You amaze me! Perhaps you would accept an honored place among my ladies."

"Nay, lady!" The words came out vehemently, and the queen tinkled with laughter again. "Let me remain as I am, your true knight and defender." The queen nodded her assent.

Gawaine bowed slightly and resumed his story. "After three days of feasting, Merlin seemed to have filled up. To my childish eye, he looked strong and restless. He didn't even wait for the question when my father led me forth with some story on his lips of my being his niece from farther north."

" 'You are quite a trickster, Lot,' he declared, 'but you don't fool me. This boy who is trying to act like a girl to make you happy will die by drowning!'

" 'Ah haw! I may not be a great trickster, but you are not so clever yourself, magician! This young maid is in reality my son Gawaine, and indeed it has been him each night when I asked the question, but you predicted three different deaths for him. You are a fraud, Merlin, and a charlatan who cannot remember his own predictions from one night to the next!'

"Merlin rose to confront my father, and the two men now stood chin to chin and eye to eye like two dogs about to attack each other. 'You set a fine table, Lot, and I thank you for the meat and drink, but your hospitality leaves much to be desired by way of courtesy. Indeed, I knew it was young Gawaine each time you asked your question, but I spoke the truth—he shall indeed die by falling and by hanging and by drowning!'

" 'Never!' howled my father. 'My son Gawaine shall grow to be a great warrior like his father—'

" 'Greater,' Merlin said in a voice so low that only I heard him.

" '—the greatest in the land—'

" 'Perhaps,'' whispered the wizard. He took my hand and gazed deeply into my eyes. 'Fear nothing and you shall be a hero, Gawaine.' His words seemed to be aimed for my ears alone, and no one else took any heed of them. '—and when he dies, it shall be a sword that brings him down!'

" 'That, too,' muttered the wizard.

" 'Fake! Fraud! Your prophecies are all lies and trickery. To-morrow you must leave my dun and never return on penalty of death!' declared my father sternly.

" 'Why wait?' Merlin said. 'I will take my leave now, but you Gawaine shall see me again when you least expect it!' He then cried a word of power, and the hearthfires began to smoke so much that the whole hall soon filled with mists and vapors. We all ran out into the snow to escape choking to death, but Merlin never came out. Nor was he inside when the hall cleared. He vanished, simply disappeared, which really puzzled my royal sire. He felt that somehow he had been made to look like a fool, and he always hated the wizard for showing him up.

"In fact, Sire," Gawaine addressed King Arthur directly at this point, "my father took the field against you when you were newly crowned more because that you were Merlin's protegé, than from any desire to be High King himself." Arthur, who had been smiling and laughing as heartily as anyone, grew sad. "Would that Merlin still graced this company!" he exclaimed. "I could use his wise council in these troubled times."

"Nay, my heart," answered the Queen, "you are better off without the old devilspawn. Surely the priests of Holy Church would not support you so staunchly if you trafficked with a black magician like Merlin."

"Truly, Nephew, that was a strange feasting that you described, yet I think it does not yet justify our meal this evening," said Arthur.

"Wait, Sire, it gets better," Gawaine assured him. "The true adventure and marvel is yet to be told. I need but a moment to slake my thirst with another flagon of mead before I move on to part two of this tale." A serving knave quickly refilled Gawaine's cup and he downed it in one long gurgle. Setting down the empty vessel, and speaking with a bit of a slur, Gawaine picked up the thread of his story.

"In the years that followed, I forgot about Merlin's strange prophecy. I grew from a gangly youth to a young warrior nearly as large and strong as I am now.

"On Midsummer Day of my seventeenth year, I rode out hunting with only a pair of dogs and a single servant to accompany me. I rode beneath ancient oaks covered with mistletoe, and among thickets of furze and blackberries, up hill and down, searching for game. Armed with sword and boarspear, I thought myself a match for any beast I might encounter.

"Deep in the forest, I met an old hermit, and stopped to speak with him for a moment.

" 'Turn back, young sir,' he croaked at me. 'Death haunts this forest today.' His eyes sparkled strangely as he warned me, and I fancied that I knew him, though I had never seen him before."

"A ragged old hermit," muttered Arthur. "Yes, he liked that disguise."

"As I rode into the shade of a king among oak trees, a cold breeze from nowhere riffled my hair and cloak, and for a moment it seemed that day was night—everything around me faded to stark black and white images, and I nearly fell off my steed with sudden dizziness. Then, as quickly as the strangeness had come upon me, it vanished, and I recovered myself to find the dogs leaping and barking at something in the bushes in front of me.

"A sort of grunting came from the impenetrable foliage. I thought my hounds had found a wild boar. To bring back such game while hunting alone—my servant had fallen so far behind that I no longer knew his whereabouts—would be a great honor. I lowered the spear and charged blindly at the source of the grunting noises, though I could not see anything but leaping dogs and thrashing greenery.

"My spear penetrated the foliage and struck something—something not much softer than rock or wood. So great was the resistance that the spear shaft bent like a bow and snapped with a deafening crack.

"Then, a hairy thing, an Ogre, a Monster, surged out of the bushes and attacked my dogs. It was certainly not a wild boar or pig of any kind, and it did not seem to be a bear.

"Ten feet tall, manlike in shape, it had long arms that dangled down past its knees. The face, wrinkled and snouted, had four great tusks that projected out of its maw like four bony daggers. The creature had a large flat nose, scarcely more than two snorting holes. Small red eyes glittered beneath a beetling brow. In one hand it carried a heavy stick which it flailed about. I could see talons a good two or three inches in length on both hands. It bellowed in pain and anger, and as I watched in horror, it tore my spearhead out of its flank. It was the most appalling Thing that I had ever seen.

"I reached for my sword, pulling it out, not because I thought I could fight the monster with it, but just for the comfort of having it in my hand. At that moment, the club hit one of my dogs. The sickening crunch of smashed bones and one high-pitched yipe of pain filled my ears, and the dead animal flew more than fifty feet through the air before crashing to earth.

"The other dog, quite sensibly, tucked its tail under, and ran away.

"My horse reared away from the monster, nearly unseating me, but I tightened my grip with my knees and kept in the saddle. I started to swing at the creature with my sword, but a sideways lurch of my mount left me striking at empty air and clutching desperately at the mane to keep from falling.

"Then the world spun around me. The horse's forelegs came down with a thump that rattled my teeth, and it bolted madly through the forest. I could no more control it than an infant could control its father. All I could do was lean low along its neck while branches and leaves beat at me, and try to hang on."

Gawaine paused from his storytelling and looked at his audience. They leaned toward him eagerly. Guinevere breathed in short gasps and so did many in the crowd. Several knights held their daggers in a swordsman's grip, and glared around fiercely.

"Go on, Nephew!" cried Arthur. "This is no time to stop for a drink of mead!"

"Tell on! Do not stop!" yelled Dinadan. Many voices echoed his requests. Gawaine smiled and bowed and continued his tale.

"It takes a long time to tell all this, and it seemed like a long time while it was happening, but you realize that everything occurred in the space of a few seconds.

"I hadn't ridden very far when a heavy tree bough swept me from my saddle and dropped me in a furze bush. Hundreds of thorny needles jabbed through my clothing and drew points of blood. Half dazed, I pulled myself from the prickly shrub.

"A hideous bellow from the Beast cleared my head. I struggled to my feet and I saw the creature loping toward me on two bowed legs and one arm whose knuckles met the ground with every stride. It held its club poised to strike, and I barely managed to parry it to the side with my sword, which was miraculously still in my right hand.

"Then followed one of the greatest fights of my life. At first I could only parry, sidestep, duck and dodge. It drove me back and back. Once a glancing blow from its free hand numbed my left shoulder and hurled me ten feet to bounce off a lichen-covered boulder.

"There was never a chance to break and run, and in the madness of the moment, I never considered it. My ears rang like church bells; my vision blurred into a red haze; my knees wobbled and shook; yet still I rolled and dodged, and occasionally struck out at it with my sword. Once I connected with its club arm—my blow severed its thumb and scraped along the bone, leaving a bloody wound and disarming it at the same time.

"Still it kept flailing and striking at me. Still I dodged backward, backward, ever backward. Sometimes I hit trees and slid to the side. Sometimes I tripped over roots and fell. Whenever I could, I struck at the thing with my sword, and I began to hit it on every third or fourth blow. It was more like chopping wood than hitting a fleshly thing. Its coarse hairs seemed like steel wires, often turning my blow before it could penetrate—its rock-like flesh opened in only minor cuts whenever a sword blow landed.

"I slipped around the last tree, staggering, barely able to stay on my feet, sword dragging the earth in front of me. Dimly I realized that I was in a high place as the cold wind tore at my wounds. With a bestial growl, the creature rushed me. This time I could not dodge, and iron-hard claws sank into my shoulder and thigh. The thing grabbed me, lifted me off my feet, and pulled me toward its slavering mouth.

"When it lifted me, I summoned the last remnant of strength and will in my being, and brought my brand up in a disemboweling thrust that took the creature squarely in the groin. It was like striking wood, but I pushed harder, pushed till the blood burst from my nose and my ears, pushed until I felt the blade break through all resistance and totally gut this Thing. Its growl of triumph turned into a high-pitched squeal of mortal agony, and instead of biting out my throat, it suddenly went into a spasm, and threw me into the air away from it.

"I sailed up into the sky like a hurled pebble. I knew that I had given it a mortal wound, and despite all my pain, I laughed with exultation as I hurtled through the air—right over the cliff!

"And then I fell. Head downward, I hurtled into eternity. Far below I could see trees and rocks and water, and I knew that I could never survive this fall. The hairy thing had killed me after all—killed me by falling.

"It seemed that time slowed to a crawl, and my whole life flashed before my eyes. I remembered my birth—mostly sensations, going from warmth and comfort, through squeezing, and gasping into a world of bright and dark and pain and cold. Then I remembered the feel of hot sand on bare feet, and the coolness of ocean waves splashing onto my legs as I ran down the beach with other children. I remembered bouncing on my father's knee, and his gigantic laughter as he spun me madly through the sky, and I remembered how he told me stories of the battles he had fought, and what it meant to be a warrior. I remembered my first dagger, and my first animal kill—a chicken that was too slow to escape my thrown rocks, a chicken with a broken leg that my father insisted I must finish killing because a warrior finishes what he begins. I remembered a thousand things, and I relived each event in all its sensations, and finally I remembered Merlin's feast of five years earlier, and how he had prophecied that I would die from falling.

"And, I think I laughed, because Merlin had been wrong after all. It wasn't falling that killed a person, but stopping at the end of that fall. It seemed to me that Life itself was a fall, and Death comes when we run out of space to fall through and hit the ground.

"I had closed my eyes while the memories ran by, but I opened them again and saw I was about to hit the treetops. I barely had time to wrap my arms around my head before I crashed through the upper branches of a great hawthorn tree.

"Then something stopped me abruptly. My booted left foot caught in a fork in a branch and it held and stopped my fall. A pain greater than any I had ever known shot down my leg into my spine, past my heart and shoulders, and exploded through the top of my head. Blackness smothered all my senses and I became nothing but a line of pain existing in a void.

"The chill of water on my face awakened me. I knew that I was hanging upside down in a tree by one foot, like a carcass hung up and left to drain. So this was the death by hanging, but again Merlin seemed to be wrong, because I hurt too much to be dead.

"It occurred to me then that Life was like death by hanging. We are all suspended between beginnings and endings, and much of our life is spent just hanging in one place, waiting for something to happen.

"Then the water forced itself up my nose and into my mouth. I realized that the tree had caught me just before I fell into a stream. I had been holding my breath (or not breathing), but now the insistent water forced its way inside, and my lungs began to fill. Distantly I felt my body shudder and cough, but I had no strength left to pull out of the stream. My consciousness began to eddy away at the edges just like the water flowing past me and through me.

"My last thought was that Life is like drowning, because . . . but all thought and sensation fled before I could finish that idea."

Gawaine returned to his place at the table, handing the harp back to its owner as he passed, then sat down and sighed like a whickering horse. "Well, Sire, Lords and Ladies, that is my tale. I hope it is good enough to earn the feast we have all just finished."

"Whew!" gasped Arthur, releasing his pent-in breath explosively, not realizing until then that he had forgotten to breathe during the end of Gawaine's tale.

"But, Gawaine, that can't be the end," cried Guinevere. "What happened next?"

"I died, of course," said Gawaine with a sheepish grin. "I died by falling, hanging, and drowning, just as Merlin had said I would."

Everyone in the great hall of Camelot sat in stunned silence for a moment; then Sir Dinadan began to chuckle, a chuckle that grew stronger and stronger until it was a full-throated belly laugh. Sir Lancelot picked it up, and then Sir Tristram and then Arthur himself, and a wave of laughter swept through the great hall until finally everyone whooped and gasped with hysterical glee.

After a good two minutes the laughter died down to mere giggles and chuckles. "A great story, Nephew," said Arthur. "You have outdone yourself this time. Yes, indeed, you have justified our feast!" Arthur beckoned to the musician. "Come, bard, give us a tune."

"Wait!" cried Guinevere. "That can't be right! You don't look dead! You don't feel dead! How could you have died? How could you?"

Everyone looked at Gawaine. "I didn't stay dead," he explained, grinning hugely, "but that's another story, one I think I'll save for next Easter in case we have another such wait for our feast."

Out of the Woods

by Lawrence Watt Evans

Lawrence Watt Evans is the author of some two dozen novels and four score short stories in the fields of fantasy, science fiction, and horror. His best-known work is The Misenchanted Sword, *and his latest is* In the Empire of Shadow, *the second volume of the Three Worlds trilogy. He lives in the Maryland suburbs of Washington with his wife, two kids, two cats, and a parakeet named Robin.*

Jenny slammed on the brakes and prayed the car would stop in time. The man who had stumbled onto the road in front of her showed no sign of moving out of the way, he was just *standing* there.

The tires squealed, and the car slewed sideways and came to a stop—and the man wasn't there. Jenny kept her hands locked on the steering wheel as she turned her head and stared out the passenger-side window.

She saw only empty road, huge dark trees, and drifting wisps of mist.

Had she imagined it? These English roads were narrow and winding and made her nervous, and the thick surrounding woods were spooky, but she hadn't thought she was far enough gone to be hallucinating.

Getting out of London for at least a few days of her month in Britain had seemed like a good idea, but right now she wasn't at all sure it hadn't been a major mistake.

The rental car had stalled, and Jenny decided against trying to start it right away. Instead, she turned off the ignition and got out, pocketing the key. She looked around. There was forest on either side, with the empty road curving out of sight in either direction.

And then a muddy shape rose up out of the roadside ditch, not a dozen feet away. She almost screamed, but at the last moment managed to turn it into a gasp. It was the man, the man she had almost run down—he must have flung himself into the ditch at the last instant.

"Are you all right?" she called once she'd caught her breath.

"Aye," he said.

Jenny grimaced. Only in rural Britain would anyone who spoke English say "aye" instead of "yeah."

"I'm sorry I didn't see you sooner," she said. "Do you need a lift somewhere?" The rental car company wouldn't like it if she got their upholstery all muddy, but she was paying enough that they could afford to clean it, and she *had* almost run the fellow down—a lift seemed like the least she could do.

"How do you say, lady?" the man replied—or at least, that was her best guess at his words. It might almost have been "lad" instead of "lady," but she gave him the benefit of the doubt.

His accent was one she'd never heard before—British, certainly, but an unfamiliar variant; she couldn't even be sure it was English. For all she knew, it was Welsh, or Scottish, or even Australian or South African.

And apparently her American accent was giving him a little trouble, too.

"Do you want a ride?" she said, speaking slowly and loudly and, she hoped, clearly.

The man eyed the rental car, then looked Jenny over. "Aye," he said at last. "And my thanks to you, lady."

This time it was definitely "lady."

"Get in, then," she said. She climbed in on the driver's side—the right, that is, a fact she still wasn't entirely used to.

The man approached the passenger side hesitantly and stood, looking down at the door. Impatiently, Jenny leaned over and opened it for him. He made an odd little noise that she took for a sign of relief, then carefully climbed into the car and settled on the seat.

Jenny looked at him, puzzled; she hadn't really noticed when she first saw him in the road, or standing in the ditch covered with mud, but he was dressed oddly—his pants were more like baggy tights, with crude garters just above the knees, and he wore a sort of tunic instead of a shirt. His hair was unfashionably long, but he was clean-shaven—or rather, he had no beard; he was a few days past clean-shaven.

The overall effect was vaguely medieval.

"Are you an actor?" she asked. "Is there some local festival or something?"

"Nay," he said, "I'm no player, but an honest workman."

She started the engine, and he started at the sound.

"Where are you headed?" she asked.

"Eh?"

"Where should I drop you?"

He simply looked baffled, and she gave up. She would just drop him at the first pub she came to and let the locals deal with him. She put the car in gear.

He grabbed at his seat—he hadn't put on his seatbelt, she saw.

She drove slowly and carefully. The fog still lingered, and night was falling, and one scare on these roads was quite enough.

Besides, she wanted to be able to stop quickly and jump out if the man started to act even weirder. Now that she was over her initial concern about sending him into the ditch, she was having second thoughts about giving him a ride at all. Back home in the States she wouldn't have picked up a stranger, so why should she here? Sure, England had less violent crime, but there were still nuts here and there.

Maybe if she talked to him, he'd reassure her—or maybe she'd *know* he was a dangerous loonie.

"So what were you doing in the woods?" she asked.

He hesitated, then said, "Feasting with Queen Mab."

Jenny had trouble at first understanding what he said, but the words did eventually register.

He *was* a loonie, she realized, though not necessarily a dangerous one. She wished she hadn't offered him a ride.

"Oh?" she said.

"Aye. I'd followed a fairy light, and found myself at the Queen's table, whereupon I was bid join the feast, which I did with a will. I passed many a long year there in pleasant company, and but today did I at last depart."

"Oh," Jenny said.

For a moment they drove on in silence; then Jenny asked, just to break that silence, "You said *years?*"

"Aye, I'd say so," the man said. "Surely, years it must have been, for the world to have changed as it has—your garb, your speech, and this carriage are all strange to me."

Jenny blinked, trying to decide whether this was as completely nonsensical as it sounded. "Just when did you follow the fairy into the forest?" she asked, and immediately wished she hadn't—it sounded so stupid.

" 'Twas May Eve, in the Year of Our Lord fifteen hundred and ninety-five."

For a moment Jenny didn't respond.

"That was four hundred years ago," she said eventually.

"*Four* hundred, you say?" The man's eyes widened in wonder. "Zounds, so long as that?"

"Yeah," Jenny said.

They were nearing a village—not much of one, but she thought it would do to get rid of her passenger. She slowed still further and began looking for a sign that would indicate a pub or inn.

"You doubt me," the man said. "Perchance you think me mad. No wonder on it, I'd think the same were I you."

That was the most reassuring thing he'd said yet; she threw him a quick glance.

"What's your name?" she asked.

"William Tinker."

"I'm Jenny Gifford. Look, is there anywhere in particular I can drop you? Anyone who'd know what to do with you? Do you have any money or anything?"

"I've no coin, nay. As for one who'd know to aid me—a priest, perhaps, who knows the ways of fairies?"

"I don't think modern priests know much about fairies," Jenny said, though she admitted to herself that British priests might well know more than the American ones she'd met.

William Tinker hesitated, then ventured, very cautiously, "A witch, perhaps? I'm a good Christian, and would not consort with such, but . . ."

"A witch." Jenny grimaced. A psychiatrist would probably be better.

But then she spotted the pub on the corner and pulled over to the curb.

"Here," she said. "Go in there and ask if they know of a witch. Tell them you've been visiting fairies in the wood for four hundred years."

That was perhaps a bit cruel. They'd mock him, most likely. But then they'd probably send him to the National Health, and get him taken care of.

Tinker looked at the signboard, then pushed at the car door; it didn't open, and he looked helplessly for a handle or latch.

Jenny leaned over and opened the door for him.

He got out carefully, then bobbed to her in something that was almost, but not quite, a bow. "My thanks to you, good lady."

She felt guilty about dumping the poor loonie like this, and she was momentarily tempted to park the car and go into the pub with him, to make sure things didn't get rough—but it wasn't her problem, and she wasn't a native here.

He'd be all right. This was a peaceful English village, not a bar in Detroit or L.A.—or even London.

And it just wasn't her problem.

She took her foot off the brake and pulled away.

Three days later, in her hotel room in Bayswater, she had the TV news on as background while she wrote a letter to her parents back in Cleveland. Something startled her, made her look up, though it took a second to realize what she had heard.

William Tinker, that was it—someone on the TV had said the name William Tinker.

And there he was, the same man she had picked up on that lonely road, with a woman on either side—an overweight matron on his left, a thinner, younger woman on his right, both in long dresses and wearing necklaces.

Tinker himself was dressed in modern clothing now—a simple shirt and slacks—but it was unmistakably the same man. His hair was still long, but looked considerably cleaner now.

". . . naturally, so-called modern scientists are dismissing his story without even bothering to investigate," the older woman was saying, "but *some* of us recognize the possibility of wonders."

The camera cut to a blond host in a tweed jacket. "Then you believe that Mr. Tinker really *has* spent the last four hundred years at a faerie feast?"

Back to the woman.

"No, not literally—but we believe *something* extraordinary has happened in that forest. It may be that Mr. Tinker was affected by forces in the wood that reverted him to a past life, and that he was really only in there for hours and simply swapped identities, or it may be that he really did enter in 1595 and was somehow transported to our own time—my compatriots and I favor this latter explanation, since it would account for his clothing, and the fact that no one fitting his description has been reported missing."

"And you consider this more likely than an attempt at fraud, or a simple delusion?"

"Oh, very much so," the woman said. "What would be the *point* of such a fraud? And we have medical reports that will attest that Mr. Tinker appears quite sane, other than his belief that he spent four centuries in that forest. Furthermore, his teeth show no sign of modern dentistry, and the doctors say he's never been immunized against *anything,* or received any of the other lasting benefits of the National Health. He doesn't appear to have ever seen a doctor before. We've asked linguists from Balliol College at Oxford to tell us whether his speech is authentically Elizabethan, and so far, while we haven't heard their final opinion, none have found any specific inaccuracies."

"And have any historians questioned Mr. Tinker?"

"Not yet," the woman conceded. "After all, he only emerged from the wood three days ago."

"So you believe that in fact, Mr. Tinker *is* from the sixteenth century?"

"Yes, I do."

"Mr. Tinker, do you have anything to add to that?"

Jenny stared as Tinker said, in that strange accent of his, "I do truly believe that I am William Tinker, born in the Year of Our Lord fifteen hundred and sixty-seven, and that I came upon Queen Mab's table in the forest on the last day of April in fifteen hundred and ninety-five—but if you say I am mad, I'll not debate. I think I am not, and yet to pass four centuries with the Good Folk and not age a day is surely a great wonder; were it proven me that 'twas all a dream, that would be no greater marvel. In truth, I wonder whether all I see about me, this world of a twentieth century, is not but a dream."

"Mr. Tinker, you seem to be in remarkably good health for a man more than four hundred years old," the host said, with just a slight sardonic edge to his voice.

"Aye," Tinker said. " 'Tis the magic of the wood, beyond question."

Jenny sat and watched as Tinker and his two companions— presumably the village witches from that town where she'd abandoned him—held their own against the host's growing sarcasm.

The younger witch hardly said anything, but the older argued at length for the existence of powers beyond modern understanding—not fairies, but spirits or powers that gave rise to tales of fairies, or if even that seemed too mystical, she was willing to consider them as energy fields created by the living things of the earth.

Was it so utterly impossible that someone could become caught in such an energy field?

"And these fields," the host asked, "preserved our Mr. Tinker for some four centuries? Would this sort of thing be responsible for the legends of the Fountain of Youth, then?"

"It very well might," the elder witch declared.

Meanwhile, Tinker himself seemed to be growing ever more uncomfortable, caught in the middle of this debate, and when at last the host announced that time had run out, poor Tinker was visibly relieved.

Jenny turned off the set and sat on the hotel bed, staring at the blank screen for several minutes.

Maybe, she thought, he *wasn't* a loonie.

After that she began to watch the news regularly. She saw the reports from the experts, proclaiming Tinker to be either genuine or the best fake ever—neither linguist nor historian nor physician could find anything to contradict his claimed origin.

The real bombshell was when his clothes were carbon-dated and proclaimed authentic late-sixteenth-century.

It was after that that reports of would-be explorers getting out of hand at the forest began. Curiosity seekers had gone poking about there ever since Tinker's first television appearance, but now entire mobs were sweeping through the woods, searching for "Queen Mab's table." The authorities were dismayed, to say the least.

It was a relief to Jenny when the forest was closed to the public; she hated the thought of all those people trampling through the underbrush, scattering candy wrappers and beer cans on the moss.

She watched the televised reports with a sort of dreadful fascination. Picketers were protesting the government's decision to restrict access. There was talk of secret conspiracies to keep the "fountain of youth" energy for the government elite.

And there were a few reports coming in, not very reliable ones, of people disappearing into the forest and not coming back out—presumably, they'd found the fairies.

She spent hours on end in her hotel, watching—she knew it was stupid, a waste of her remaining vacation time, that she should be out enjoying London—but she couldn't tear herself away.

She was staring unhappily at yet another interview when someone knocked on the door of her room.

Startled, she opened the door.

There were three men standing there. One of them held a microphone, another a video camera.

The third, somewhat disguised by a woolen cap and sunglasses, was William Tinker.

"Ms. Gifford?" the man with the microphone asked.

"Yes," she said, puzzled. "What's going on?"

"We understand that it was you who first found Bill Tinker after he emerged from the enchanted forest," the man with the microphone said. Jenny recognized him now; he was a newsman, but she couldn't think of his name.

She glanced at Tinker, who looked apologetic.

"I wished to speak with you," he said, "and I knew not how you might be found. I agreed that I would give your name, that you might be interviewed, if I might accompany them and speak to you in private."

His accent wasn't quite so distinctive any more—he was beginning to adjust to his new surroundings, she supposed.

"I don't *want* to be interviewed," she said. "I'm not part of this."

"Then you weren't the one who found him?" the newscaster asked.

"Oh, sure I was," she admitted. "I almost ran him down, so I gave him a lift into town, that's all."

"And did he tell you he was four hundred years old?"

She glanced at Tinker uncomfortably. "He said he'd been in the forest since 1595," she said.

"And did you believe him?"

"No. I thought he was nuts. But he seemed harmless."

"But didn't you tell him, when you dropped him at the Plow, to ask where he could find a witch?"

"I said something like that," Jenny admitted, embarrassed. "I didn't think he'd want to see a doctor. Listen, I haven't agreed to an interview, and I'm not going to—not until I've talked to Mr. Tinker in private."

It took some further argument, but eventually Jenny was able to close the door of her hotel room with Tinker and herself on the inside, the newscaster and cameraman outside.

"Now, why did you want to find me?" she demanded.

"Softly, pray," Tinker said, holding up a hand. "Your pardon, I pray you, Mistress Gifford.

She glowered at him.

"Prithee, lady, I come to you most humbly to ask a service—

will you even hear me, or have I angered you by bringing with me these relentless hounds with their cameras?"

He pronounced "camera" in very nearly the modern fashion, she noticed—it was presumably a new word for him.

"What kind of a service?" she asked quietly.

"Lady, I beg you," he said, "though I be an Englishman born and bred, and loyal to my Queen, whiche'er Elizabeth it may be—can you take me with you to America? I must escape my own land!"

She stared at him.

"Why?" she asked.

"Need you ask?" he said, gesturing at the closed door. "In mine own land I shall have no peace, 'tis plain."

"Can't you just hide somewhere?"

"Where? This land is so changed I know naught of it."

"You know that forest," she said, a trifle bitterly. "Can't you go back there, to Queen Mab's table, if you can't take the modern world?"

His hands flew up in an odd gesture, then he hushed her and glanced at the door again.

"They'd have that of me," he said. "They'd have me lead them thither, with their cameras and mikers and all."

"Well, why not?" Jenny demanded.

He stared at her, chewing his lower lip, and she stared angrily back.

"You'd have the truth?" he asked.

"Of course!"

"All the truth, then?"

She blinked. "Yes," she said, a bit less certainly.

"In truth, then—there is no Queen Mab in the forest, no Little Folk."

"What *is* there, then? What about the people disappearing in there? Is this all a hoax?" Jenny tried not to let her fury show—he *was* a fake!

"Nay, nay! I am all I say, trapped four centuries in the wood, and I swear it in God's name. But 'twas no fairies that held me, but a demon, a spirit sprung from the wood itself."

"Go on," she said.

" 'Tis plain enough. I was held there 'gainst my will," he said. "I'd followed a fairy light, as I thought it, though now I know 'twas but a lure, and then was I caught and held by the spirit within the wood."

"Why?" she demanded. "What did it want you for?" A thought struck her. "And is it still there?"

"Oh, 'tis yet there, verily. And it hungers, I doubt me not."

"Hungers?" she almost screamed. "What about all those people going in there looking for your fairy queen?"

"I fear that some of them will ne'er emerge," he said, shamefaced. "Oh, 'tis sinful of me, and a disgrace I do not bear easily—but if you only knew. . . ."

"So tell me."

He sighed. "I was not alone when it lured me in," he said. "Else I'd not have been such a fool as to follow. I was with a dozen of my townsmen, gathering wood for a May Day blaze, when we saw the light before us. Kit saw it erst, and called out, and old Stephen warned him to let it go, but Kit laughed. 'What have we to fear, then,' he asked, 'when we are twelve stout Englishmen?' And in our folly we gave chase, into the forest depths—and there our paths turned back upon us so that we traveled ever in circles, trapped therein. And a voice spoke to us that bade us calm ourselves, calm and rest, and at last we did—we lay ourselves down and in our exhaustion we slept.

"And when we awoke, our Christopher was naught but bones.

"We shouted, we fought among ourselves, we attempted flight, but it did no good. We saw the sunlight wane, then reappear, over and over, for time had become strange to us.

"And at last we slept again, and when we awoke old Stephen was as Christopher, nothing but bone.

"And so it went, and we perished, each in our turn, until only I survived, and I knew what my fate was to be when next I slept, and in my despair I fell down upon my knees and cried out to whatever had trapped us, whatever had spoken that first day, and I begged for my life, I bargained, I offered whatever I could if only it would free me, spare my life and let me go."

"And it did?" Jenny asked.

Tinker nodded. "Aye," he said, "but erst it spoke to me again, and told me that it would trade my life for seven others—if I swore, by God and the Virgin, to bring it seven other lives, then I could go free. May God forgive me, lady, I did so swear—and but moments later I was on the high road, where you found me."

"And you sent it seven people?"

"I know not how many I sent it!" he wailed.

Jenny stared at him.

"Look you, lady," he said, "I bethought me that if I spoke of Queen Mab in the village, and said fairy treasure was to be had in the wood, then a few hardy souls would venture forth, and I'd be quit, and at little cost to my conscience, for they'd take the risk upon themselves, would they not? And I'd put that village behind me and ne'er set foot there again, and 'twould be an end on it." He gestured helplessly. "How was I to know of television, or motorcars, or tour buses? To send *hundreds* thither, at risk of their lives, was ne'er my intent, and now all England is cursed of me—my face blazoned on paper at every corner, and on the telly glass in every home! Take me to America, I beg you. Let me put this behind me!"

She stared at his pleading eyes for a moment.

"We have television in America, too," she said at last. "You'd be news there, too."

His expression collapsed into despair.

"And you have to do something to stop them," she said, struck with sudden horrific realization. "All those people going into that forest . . . I bet they're still sneaking in, even though it's officially closed. My God, *I* was tempted to take a look!"

"What can I do?" He spread his hands hopelessly. "A tale once spun has a life of its own."

"That's true," she said thoughtfully.

"And if I speak the truth now, they'll stretch my neck ere morn, for betraying all those fools to their doom."

England wasn't known for lynchings, but this was a special case. "That might be true, too," she said. She considered carefully.

She wondered, for a moment, why she didn't just throw Tinker to the wolves. After all, he *had* betrayed all those innocents. By his own admission, he had meant to send seven strangers to their deaths—but then, he had seen his own companions killed horribly one by one and known he was next. . . .

He'd done wrong, but he knew it, he wanted to make what amends he could. What good would it do to destroy him?

But they couldn't let more people feed the thing in the forest—whatever it was. Jenny didn't believe in demons or fairies, but there must be *something* in there.

And then she saw the way out. If one lie had lured people in, maybe another could turn them back.

"Listen," she said, "you're going to go on TV again—on television—and tell everyone that Queen Mab's angry about all these intrusions on her privacy. Remind everyone that fairies are dangerous. That's something we tend to forget nowadays. Remind them that fairies steal human souls. *That* should discourage most people—and anyone who goes in anyway, it's *his* problem."

"Aye," Tinker agreed reluctantly, after a moment's thought. "That should serve, I warrant. But am I to spend my *life* in television?"

"Oh, no," Jenny said confidently. "Don't worry. You're just a fad. It'll all be over in a few weeks, and you can settle down somewhere—I bet there are colleges that would hire you for their history departments. You must know the sixteenth century better than anyone else alive."

"Aye, perhaps," he said. "You'll accompany me, then, to the television?"

She hesitated, but then said, "Sure." She gestured. "Go ahead and open the door, and we'll tell your camera crew the news."

Jenny insisted they do their interview right there. The first few questions were harmless, asking about how she happened to pick Tinker up.

But then the newscaster asked, "Do *you* believe there are fairies in the wood?"

She glanced at Tinker, there beside her.

"Oh, yes," she said, "and in fact, I believe I've heard their voices."

Startled, the newsman asked, "Oh?"

"When I picked Bill up on that road. Maybe *he* didn't hear them, but I did—they were saying they wanted to be left alone, that he'd abused their hospitality long enough and that any other humans who bothered them would regret it."

She glanced at Tinker, who smiled gratefully at her.

"Indeed, I heard something," he said. "I'd not caught the words, though. . . ."

And together, they blithely made up a whole network of lies.

The broadcast went well—and for the rest of her stay in England, Jenny Gifford found herself something of a celebrity. She spent a good bit of time in Tinker's company, helping him adjust to modern life—an adjustment he made with amazing speed.

And she was only slightly jealous when he bedded that young witch, rather than herself—but really, she told herself, he was a bit old for her, wasn't he?

She giggled at the thought.

By the time she returned to the States, Tinker's moment of

fame was already passing, and her own with it. Within a week of her arrival home, the whole thing seemed like a dream.

But for the rest of her life, she still shuddered whenever she passed thick woods.

SPEAKING WOODS

The view from the branches

Viridescence

by Connie Hirsch

Connie Hirsch got the idea for "Viridescence" when she visited Muir Woods and discovered the extraordinary way in which the Sequoias altered their environment to promote their own well-being. When not writing, Connie makes databases sit up and do tricks, reads a lot, plots expeditions to interesting places, and frets about not writing.

> "Colorless green thoughts sleep furiously."
> —Noam Chomsky

We must have had a beginning; our seed must have sprouted in the manner of unremarkable seed, our shoots yearning up towards the bright, our rootlets drinking moisture, burrowing deeper in the good soil of our slopes and rills, growing in the manner of the Green.

Yet, when did we become aware of our apartness? That while we were of the Green, we were yet apart from it, too awake in the bright day, dreaming too strongly in the dark night. Most of all, knowing that we were different, remembering that we remembered. In some forgotten age of time, we knew that we were ourselves.

Our knowledge made us wonder, and speculate upon our own nature, proposing theory after theory. Perhaps our ancestor seed fell from the sky, carried by some great wind from a distant land so far the Green only whispers dreams of it. Perhaps the lightning struck our ancestral soil with some magical cousin of the hated Fire. Perhaps the fungus that feeds our roots went through a shift of its nature, linking plant body and root body and wood body together as never before. Perhaps all of these, or perhaps none: the result the same. We live, remember, dream together here on our slopes, beneath the sun and the rains.

Once we would have added, "as we always have." Yet that is not true. Changes have come to us, changes we fought or welcomed, changes we have even initiated. It is this lesson we pass to those who will come after us, as the individual members of our self germinate, mature and die in their stages. For it is the remembering that we pass on.

When still the Green whispered of the great glaciers retreating, we were young, and unpracticed in our togetherness. We were still new, learning to use the senses we had been born with: the feel of the sun's heat upon our green body, the patterns of light and dark as sunbright filtered onto our ground, the feel of limb and branch and root, separating out body from member body, yet conscious of the whole. We grew in our capacity to feel, to coordinate, to sense.

But what we sensed did not please us. For the first time, we noticed the depredations of the fleshbeasts that infested us, that were not of the Green. Before, when green body was destroyed or root body disturbed or wood come crashing to the ground, we had no more apprehension of its wrongness than when the Sun disappeared into the darkness of night every day.

Now we knew differently, that these happenstances were not random acts or laws of nature. And perhaps for the first time, at least in our long remembering, we felt emotion. We learned hatred.

Oh, how we resented those robbers, meditated long on their evil, inventing new concepts as we thought on them and their depredations. And in our long resentment, we came to understand that we could no longer be passive with these interlopers, not as we were passive beneath the sun that gave us life, and the sky that gave us the rain. We must take action against the fleshbeasts, a campaign to save our very being.

For long seasons we trained ourselves, forcing our Mind to evolve and strengthen. An infestation of Tinybiters, winging from branch to branch, consuming leaf and tender bark? We learned to poison our sap, to make our green body taste unpleasant. Did we feel too many Gnawers clambering over our branches, eating our fruit before it could germinate? We learned to weaken connective tissue in our wood body, to drop branches, limbs, that the Gnawers clung to. We learned to set springy traps with our roots, to suddenly ensnare the fleshy ones and drag them under, entomb them where they could feed our fungus.

We were fierce warriors against the beasts; they did not pass our boundaries without punishment. Our space became filled with peace, filled with healthy growing, till we could support no new members throughout our boundaries. Vines grew on our trunks, airplants sprouted from our branches, and we ruled supreme in our demesne, but for one thing.

Yes, for all our learning, our many accomplishments, we could not protect ourselves from the Fire. Decades would pass in growth and peaceful dreaming, and then a dry season would come. We could conserve our sap down in our roots, increase the wax that coated our leaves, spread our upper branches wide to protect our lower, younger selves from a sun turned savage. But the dryness, bad enough of itself, could bring the Fire.

Always, we could feel it coming, as the Green cried out around us, as the heat leaped from valley to mountain, from grass to leaves to bark, the wind pulling at our leaves, sucking the very air toward the Fire's hunger, the sun turning cold, gone out as it did in the night.

Then would come the pain, as the fire consumed our wood bodies, scorched our plant bodies, worse than any Tinybiter or Gnawer, so fast, so sudden! The strategies we used against fleshbeasts were useless: the Fire did not crave our sap or our seeds, and we could not pull it under the ground to smother it. Our only hope was to conserve our sap and essence in the roots that would not burn.

Time and again, in the long seasons, we were burned down to those roots. We despaired for the continued existence of our self, but our roots lived, and sent up new shoots, or our half-burned trunks recovered. We grew back each time, adopting new lives into ourselves, until our strength was full—and full of wrath.

We were angered by the unfairness. The Green about us did not seem to suffer nearly so much as we from the Fire, for all they were dumb and silent, and infested with fleshly life.

Eventually our anger gave way to observation. While the fleshbeasts thieved the Green, they gave back in several ways; clearing away deadwood, spreading seed. On a tentative basis we allowed back in a few Tinybiters and Gnawers, watching, weighing their swift activities. We studied them, took their fleshly bodies apart, meditated on their structure.

Then we turned our Thoughts on them. It seemed impossible,

and yet we had patience on our side, and time. First we had to learn to Listen, so very subtle and strange, like and not like the communication among our selves. We had to divine the minds of the fleshbeasts, to look through their eyes and hear through their ears, senses so foreign, beyond all comprehension—almost. We had not known senses beyond those we possessed before: the warmth on our leaves, our roots extending through the soil, the moisture that the sky sent to us, that we drank through our roots.

But we persevered. We learned from the shadows of their beastly senses, ruminated on the cells of their fleshly essences, and finally experimented. Could we affect the tiny individual minds, so insignificant in their aloneness before ourselves, as we were in turn small before the Green?

The fleshbeasts could never be a part of us, but we found we could affect them. We could bend their small minds, influence them to leave healthy limbs alone, to cause the Flitters and the Peckers to find the Tinybiters more efficiently, make the Gnawers spread our seed far afield to the bare patches, gnaw at deadwood until it fell free.

Seasons passed as we experimented, generations upon generations of the swift-living fleshbeasts, generations of our individual members even. As the years passed, so passed our deepest resentment; we had adapted to life besides the fleshly ones. They had become more than interlopers, servants that we depended upon. Peace had come again.

We prospered under the sun again. We kept our land reasonably free of the buildup of dead leaves and deadwood that the Fire loved too much, moved our branches just enough to permit a healthy undercanopy to slow the spread of fire with wet sap and slow burning leaves.

Yet we wondered at how we were changed. It gave us pleasure now to look upon the beauty of ourselves, to hear the wind in our boughs through the senses of our pets. We grew trunks of prodigious size, standing tall, symmetrical, lush, and proud. We were content within our demesne. We could not expand beyond certain boundaries, no more than a Gnawer can grow longer from nose to bushy tailtip: it is the size it is, and no more. We covered our acres, and were content.

New beasts passed from time to time through our domain, and we paid them scant attention so long as they left us alone. The ones we called Two Legs may have come several times before we noticed, thinking perhaps they were deformed Honeyeaters or large flightless Flitters. Our subject eyes chittered at them from high in the branches, our ears twitched in the burrows among our roots, but aside from reflecting on what ungainly beasts they were, we paid no more attention.

Then one day, the Two Legs attacked one of our wood bodies, peeling off the bark with strange claws held in their paws.

Our pain was not so bad, perhaps, only one trunk injured among our many wood bodies, but our shock was profound. Swiftly, we sacrificed branches to drop on the interlopers, sprang the roots to grasp their feet and pull them into the embrace of our understructures. Our leaves trembled for days at the outrage.

"Two Legs" was not sufficient a name. We dubbed them Death-to-Green, as evil as the Fire, and we vowed that their kind would not be suffered to come again.

Alas for us, more followed in their wake, two or three a year. We eliminated them when they came, for here was a danger near equal to the Fire—indeed, we were shocked to find the Death-to-Green actually carried Fire on occasion. Here was a stranger thing than we had ever dreamt.

We were ruthless in eliminating the Death-to-Green who dared our ground, until they came less frequently. Yet, they had not gone far; merely settled nearby valleys, for we could still sense them dimly through the Green.

Equilibrium had been reached and we rested content, sure we had triumphed once again. But as so many other times, this was only a phase: worse was yet to come.

Changes were occurring in the Green, great changes: wood giving way to field, and Death-to-Green behind it. Suddenly, in short tens of decades, they were everywhere, clearing wood bodies to plant lesser Green in strange orderly rows. It seemed that their nature had changed, perhaps a different species infested the land. The sort we had once hated now seemed benign.

Month by month, year by year they drew closer. We thought they would come right up to our hills, but they only settled the valley land, cutting down the wood bodies, flattening out sections, laying down rock dirt that monster rockbeasts moved far too swiftly upon. The Green cried out in agony, and we could not help but hear.

Occasionally, an individual Death-to-Green would pass our boundaries, and though we sent our Tinybiters, our Gnawers, our Flitters to distract it, we could not turn it back. Then we would eliminate it, swiftly and silently. Yet the day came when we eliminated two young ones, and our slopes were suddenly infested with Death, more than we could count.

We were in confusion; too much activity, too swiftly. We held back from retaliating, paralyzed by the thought: what if the Fire they carried should get loose in our glades? We could not defend ourselves against so many: not just these interlopers but the tens of tens of tens of tens that covered the land. But what could we do?

Their minds were strange; so swift and curiously shaped that we had never been tempted to Listen as with our familiar fleshpets. We had not liked the feel, so fleshly and strong. But now we embarked on a program of strengthening ourselves, learning what we could from the bodies of our trespassers.

It was only a matter of time, before a Two Legs came again. This time we withdrew our fleshly allies and sought to insert our Thoughts into the fleshbeast mind.

Stronger than the mind of any Gnawer, the Two Legs resisted us, as spirited as when we resist the Fire, thrashing through our underbrush, making strange noises with its mouth. We could now sense its panic and paranoia: something was watching it, following it, trying to control it. We doubled our efforts, waking up parts of ourselves that had slept for years, determined to succeed.

At last the Two Legs threw itself flat upon the ground, babbling noises at us, its thoughts abject. It was not so simple as our fleshpets, perhaps in its horribly singular way even as intelligent as we . . . but we could use it just the same. It must work to protect us, must bring others of its kind here to be initiated into our service.

A season beneath the sun passes quickly for us, dreaming in the warmth, listening to the Green, managing our acres in peace and prosperity, while the lives of Two Legs speed so quickly.

In time that Two Legs came back, bringing others. We found we did not have to use quite the strength of the first time: the ability of Two Legs to communicate with one another served to prepare them for indoctrination. From time to time we caught glimpses through their minds—puny, solitary things—of worse fates that could have come to us: "subdivisions," "strip mining," "landfills"—all filled with hideous Death-to-Green that we had never contemplated, bad as the Fire.

We permitted them to build paths through us, to facilitate their visits, and keep their clumsy clumping feet away from the tender young groves, subtly guiding the hands of their workers. We found amusement when the crews wondered at the absence of Tinybiters and other annoyances. We wanted to speed their work, after all.

More of our new servants came to visit, bringing their leaders and lawmakers, their minds filled with questions of ownership, as if we could be owned. They put up a fence around us, to keep out wanderers, and gates with signs beside them.

At last we could see in the minds of visitors that our future was assured; we were now a park. Mirth was our response, and thoughtfulness. For now we were safe, yes, but the Two Leg species lives and breeds so quickly. We could continue to manipulate them, the way we bred and trained our fleshpets, to work for our well-being.

Influencing the minds of the Two Legs will be work, yes, but in time, we shall spread the Green back to its size out of history. We shall have our servants take cuttings, culture the fungus in our soil, plant new daughter selves in foreign soil to grow to awareness as once we grew. Our slow, patient years beneath the sun are long and strengthening, and the Two Legs are transitory after all. It shall be enough.

Fiat Silva

by Jack Oakley

*According to Jack Oakley, he grew up thinking he was a
tree, which he says may account for his wooden prose.
When he's not writing pulp fiction, Jack lumbers around
San Francisco in a fir coat.*

Maybe I'll see a bear, thought Adam. He left the path around the
lake and made his way through manzanita and oak toward a
stand of tall trees, stopping once to take a picture of a ground
squirrel with his birthday camera. The campground sounds
faded, the underbrush thinned, and soon he was on a silent carpet
of duff in a spacious grove of sugar pines. Even the sounds of
small scurrying animals ceased in the soft, still immensity.

The clear whistle of a bird pierced the hush. Adam looked up
and searched the vault far overhead. A flicker caught his eye and
he stepped backward for a better look, stumbled on a log, and
pitched over with a painful jolt to his head. He lay on his back,
gazing in a blue aura at the treetops, each faraway needle limned
transparently against the azure shimmer.

The bird called again. "Come here. Come here." He felt for
the camera, staggered to his feet and followed dizzily. A talking
bird? Maybe it'll take me to a talking bear. "Come here." Its call
was the only sound in the nave of a vast cathedral. He trod silently by a tree he recognized from a campfire talk as a sequoia.
Farther on was another and even taller trees. The bird alit in the soaring
cient grove of even taller trees. The bird alit in the soaring
branches of a huge sequoia in the center of a circle of giants.
"Come here," it repeated clearly.

"I'm here," he replied. "What do you want?" He sat and leaned against the base of the tree. "My head hurts."

The bark caressed his back with a profound slow sigh. "Our heart hurts." Adam's belly vibrated and his head stopped throbbing, though the blue light grew more intense.

"What? Who are you?"

"We are the forest, young manikin."

"Are you this tree?"

A calm wave of amusement resonated in his belly. "We are this tree, and we are this grove, and we are this forest. We are this last stand of the sylvan soul which has spread eternal over Gaia since your Paleozoic era, yet shrinks in the blink of mankind."

"I don't understand."

"We have lived through continental shifts, waves of ice, and the heat of star rock collisions. We would live on until the sun's last flame flares, but for your race's frantic spread over Mother's face."

"I know. We're cutting down the rainforests and polluting the streams. I'm sorry."

"We are sorry too, upstart discombobulated sprout without memory of your past. We have waited these million years for clear communication with your kind, but few of you have understood the bird's call and fewer still have spoken."

"Well, who'd talk to a tree?"

Amusement resonated again. "You are."

Adam felt peaceful. "You talked to me first."

"Our way is to wait. All races are born in our garden, some leave, all return. Only the dinosaurs forgot their origin and went too far, too far alone and died. We were sad. Your race is the second who has gone so far, and we fear you won't return before you've destroyed us all."

"I save half of my allowance and donate it to the Nature Conservancy to buy forests."

Now amusement tinged with compassion flooded him. "Yes, you want to help, and in every age there have been people of partial understanding, for good or evil, but no man or woman has fully sensed your participation in us the world's life. Johnny Appleseed was a good man who spread the word, but his ken was limited to one small aspect which benefits your race. Francis in Assisi was dear to us though he preferred a peripheral circle of angels, the quick warm-blooded creatures. Paul Bunyan well intuited our ways but brashly used his knowledge for destruction. Siddhartha Gautama received enlightenment beneath the pipal

tree but misunderstood our message, turning it from the universal
to his human nature within."

"What message?"

"Our roots tap the chthonic creaking movement of the conti-
nents, the mantle, the dumb and blind slow mineral core; our
leaves receive the sun's speech, and through her the stars' song;
our trunks translate the celestial to the subterranean; and through
our atmosphere swim the blooded creatures."

A vision of the slow wheeling progression of galaxies dark and
light, and simultaneously the scent of pine and hot summer afternoon chaparral, and moist spring eucalyptus, and crisp dry fall.

"Our way is to wait, though there is risk. When a species
leaves, it seeks to develop itself alone without consideration for
the farspread web of life, and damage is done, but the rips can
be repaired since the movement takes millennia, and in the fullness of time the race returns for reintegration. But we are astonished and dismayed at the speed with which mankind has
reached the brink of self-destruction. You are something new.
The universe has moved slowly until now, billions of slow
coalescing years, interstellar dust into the rotation of galaxies,
the stately evolution of life. Even the dinosaurs drifted sedately
to their death. There was no danger. But now your demise threat-
ens us all, and your death will come through our destruction, our
link will be broken, and we will all die."

"I want to help, but I'm just a little boy. When I grow up, I
want to be a forest ranger and help save the trees."

"There is no longer time. Soon our extent will be too small
and our soul will fade like the sounds in this grove. The world
has changed, and slow must incorporate the quick before the
quick destroys the slow. We have waited a million years alongside you, but if we continue apart, we will vanish because of
you. We cannot stay ourself and survive. And if we vanish, you,
too, will vanish without our air, our rain, our shade and wind,
our animals and our shelter. None of us can live alone."

"That's what I tell my sister, but she laughs at me."

"There is no longer time to talk and convince. We must both
change."

"I'll do it."

"Beware. The transformation we propose is profound. We are
the oldest race and slow to change, but everything must change.
We must accept the new quickness in the world, and your quick
intelligence must blunt its cutting individuality as you lose yourself in ancient communion."

Into his back emanated a blurred vision of darkness lifting, a hazy sight of early dawn.

"Okay, I'll do it." Proud and scared and responsible.

"You will no longer be yourself."

"I tell my classmates I would die if it would save the earth."

"You will not die, but you won't be yourself."

"Okay."

"Then take this, and be fruitful and multiply." A whisper in the air above whistled and with a crackle a cone bounced at his feet. "The seeds in this cone contain the germ of a new forest. Your breath will fertilize them. Shake out the seeds, breathe upon them, and cast them. As the new forest grows, the particularity of your essence and ours will diminish, will combine, and a new creation will begin."

A sensation of love and urging passed through Adam. A sense of excitement gathered in the airy grove, as if the tall trees leaned forward. He turned the cone in his hands, shook it, and two small brown spheres rolled out. He held them in his palm and breathed softly on them.

Dizziness, a flowing outward from himself; the trunk behind him sighed and its force diminished minutely.

At first he saw nothing but a concentration of green light; then two tender shoots like spring green stalks of grass, which grew an inch, two inches, a foot, thickened and grew thicker like his finger, browned, passed eye level, sprouted branches and green needles.

"So fast!"

"Your quickness intensified by our breadth."

Two trees shot up, one sequoia and one sugar pine. "Two kinds from one cone?"

"The seeds will develop best suited to the conditions where they fall."

"Life!" cried the trees with the wonder of youth in a tone intimately his own, as if he were in the trees, as if he had painted a picture of himself and stepped back to look, yet more than the mute reflection in a voiceless mirror—these trees were part of himself yet not himself, an extension, a bond, a family tie, a union.

"Yes," he breathed. "Yes," sighed the grove. "Yes, ess, ess," twittered the bird.

Adam arose and took a picture of the trees. I wonder if the blue glow will show up. He left the grove in a dream, walked past the silent sugar pines, and found his way through the chaparral. This is a good place for a tree, he thought. He shook the cone until he had a handful of seeds, blew upon them, and scattered them with a sweep of his arm.

Again a dizzy green haze clouded his vision and he weakened as his forces flowed outward. He sat down to rest and watched a dozen spears rise and writhe into the twisted torsos of a young manzanita grove. "Life!" they sang and his stomach sang counterpoint. It was several moments before he came to himself. Good-bye, trees. Good-bye Adam. He found the lake and returned to the campsite.

"I don't want to go home," he said. "This was our best vacation ever."

"It was, wasn't it?" said his father.

"But school starts the day after tomorrow," said Evelyn. "I've had enough of this, anyway. I can't wait to see my friends again."

"I'm going to stay here forever."

"I wish we could," said his father. "But we have our lives to live, you know."

"Part of me will always live here."

"Yes," said his mother. "Part of all of us will."

"Can Evelyn and I walk around the lake one last time?"

"I don't want to."

"Come with me, Evie. I'll show you some neat trees you haven't seen before."

"I've seen enough trees."

"If you come, I'll take your picture."

"Big deal."

"Why don't you go with Adam?" said their mother.

"Oh, okay. C'mon squirt. Why are you bringing that stupid pine cone?"

"It's magic."

"Oh, sure."

When they reached the spot where Adam had left the trail, he said, "This way, Evie, the trees are over here."

"It's getting too dark. I don't want to go there."

"I planted them this afternoon."

"Why do you say such stupid things?"

"Please just come."

"Oh, okay."

As they approached the grove he felt like he was returning home. He was bringing his sister to his tree siblings. "Aren't they nice trees?"

"They're just trees."

"Can't you hear them talk? Feel them? Just sit quiet for a minute."

"Oh, okay." After a minute she said, "You're right, Adam. There's something very friendly here, and it's funny, but it feels like you somehow."

"Yes, that's what I wanted to show you. Now we can go back. I'll tell you why," and he told her about his afternoon.

"Oh sure, Adam. Someday you've got to grow up."

The next morning they rolled up the sleeping bags, folded the tents, and tidied the campsite. "Everybody in the van," said their father. "Let's go."

"Adam, leave that pine cone here."

"It's a souvenir, Mom. Can't I bring it, Dad?"

"You know we're not supposed to take anything from a national park."

"I do know, but this is special."

"It's his magic pine cone, Dad," Evelyn said sarcastically.

"Glen, why don't you let him take it?"

"All right. I hope it doesn't just end up gathering dust under your dresser."

"It won't, I promise."

Adam and Evelyn sat in back facing the rear as they drove down the mountainside. "I'll miss the forest."

"Me, too, but I'm not sorry to be going home."

"Part of me is here."

"Oh, Adam, you're so sappy."

"Really, Evie. The trees are talking to me."

"Okay. Prove it. Show me how that pine cone of yours works."

"I will, but wait till we stop somewhere."

"You're just procrastinating because you made it up and you don't want me to find out."

"Wait till we get somewhere there aren't any trees. Down in the valley."

The day warmed up as the sun rose higher and they descended into farmland. "Is this good enough?" Evelyn asked.

"Yeah. Now we have to get Mom and Dad to stop."

"I'm hot," said Evelyn loudly.

"I'm thirsty," said Adam.

"Okay," said their mother. "We'll stop at the next town for sodas." They left the freeway and pulled into a shopping center's broad asphalt parking lot. Their father opened the back door. "Come in and pick out your drinks."

"I'll stay here," said Adam. "Just get me an orange soda."

"Me, too," said Evelyn.

"You sure you want to sit out here in the hot sun?"

"That's okay."

"Me, too."

As their parents walked toward the store, they heard their mother say, "I can't understand these kids. They want to stop, but then they don't want to get out."

Adam laughed.

"Show me," commanded Evelyn.

"Okay. Watch." He tapped the cone and gathered the seeds. "Now you breathe your spirit into them."

"Come off it."

"Watch." He breathed over his palm and felt faint again, as a small part of himself flowed out. "It feels funny." He closed his eyes and concentrated on establishing a new balance with the warm life vibrating in his hand. "Okay." He tossed them out the door.

Evelyn watched the brown spheres bounce and with a sudden small green flash adhere to the asphalt. "Mmph!" said Adam. Her eyes widened as six green stems shot upward and the pavement rippled in all directions. The spreading roots tilted the van forward and supple green trunks broadened and browned. In a few minutes they sat in the peaceful shade of small stand of live oak.

"Cool," she agreed. "Can I do it?"

"There isn't enough room for more."

"How do you know?"

"I just do. We have to go somewhere else now. You can do it when we get back on the freeway."

Their mother and father returned with a grocery bag. "Where did these trees come from?"

"What trees?" asked Evelyn.

"There weren't any trees here when we parked."

"Oh, Daddy, you never pay attention."

"There weren't, were there, Marie?"

"I didn't notice."

"I swear, when I opened the door, I was standing in the blazing sun."

"Are you okay, Glen? Do you want me to drive?"

"No, I'm fine." He closed the back door. "Still," he muttered, "it's weird." They bumped out of the parking lot to the freeway.

Good-bye trees. Good-bye Adam.

"Okay, my turn now, please, Adam."

"I don't know . . . Are you sure? It does something to you."

"Yes, yes, please, please."

"How can we do it now? We're on the freeway."

"We can open the window. Please, Adam."

Without turning her head their mother called back, "Adam, just let her do it, whatever it is."

"Okay, open the window. Here." He gave her the cone and she shook a few seeds into her hand. "Now breathe."

"I feel dizzy."

"I know. Do you feel yourself moving into the seeds?"

"It's like they're part of me now. Here you go, seeds." She dropped them one by one out the window. "Ooh, it almost hurts."

"They're sprouting."

The van sped rapidly along but they could see a green haze appear far behind. Soon there were no cars following. "I think we blocked the road."

They laughed happily. "Cool!"

"Let's do it again!"

By the time they reached the city at dusk, they were vegetating in a peaceful stupor, a vast part of themselves strewn along a finger of forest for hundreds of miles through the valley to the park. They leaned against each other drained. Their parents opened the door and helped them out.

"Leave that pine cone in the garage, Adam."

"No, it's a souvenir of our best vacation ever."

"Yes, Mom, it's our magic pine cone."

"You, too, Evelyn? Okay, bring it in."

Their father supported them up the steps to the house while their mother unloaded the van. "These kids are as heavy as logs."

"Time to get up," called their mother. "First day of school!" The words came from far away, dimly penetrated the dream of an immense continental forest. Rising from slumber was like uprooting a small tree. Adam and Evelyn pulled themselves out of bed and went to the kitchen for breakfast. The morning newspaper reported the bizarre growth of a mixed deciduous and evergreen forest centered on the southbound lane of Interstate 5. Trees were spreading east and west despite attempts by road crews with chainsaws and bulldozers to clear the highway.

"That's terrible!" said Adam.

"That's strange," said their father. "I didn't see any trees."

"It must have happened just after we passed by."

Adam and Evelyn smiled at each other.

"You kids are going to be late. You'd better make like trees and leave."

They laughed and got their backpacks. Adam put the cone in his and they went out the door. During show and tell, when everyone was telling what they had done during the summer, he took it out and said, "We went camping and I got this magic cone. It grows trees."

His classmates snickered, and the teacher said, "Yes, Adam, it is magical the way new life sprouts from a seed."

"No, it isn't like that. You breathe on the seeds and part of you goes into them and trees grow up right away."

Mrs. Hargrave looked concerned and everyone else laughed out loud. He regarded them steadily with the clear gaze of a spreading forest. "Watch," he said, and shook the cone, breathed on the seed in his hand, and feeling faint, stood, walked to the terrarium on a table in the corner, and dropped it in. He sat woodenly on the floor and saw the green flash and a tingle of motion as a tiny stem twisted into a bonsai cedar that barely peeped above the glass walls.

The classroom was silent. Then his friend Jess said, "Wow," and they all crowded around the terrarium. "May I look at that cone?" asked Mrs. Hargrave with her hand out.

Adam backed away. "No, I'd rather not."

"Let me look at it," said Jess.

"No, no," said Adam. The others pressed close, demanding, and he opened the door to the playground and stepped outside. His classmates followed.

"Wait!" said Mrs. Hargrave. "Come back here!" Some of them hesitated. "Give me that cone, Adam."

"I'm sorry," he said. A crowd stood in the doorway watching as he shook out a handful of seeds and breathed softly, breathed his soul out surrounded by the wavering outlines of the school building and dimming outlines of his friends, inhaled a dream of green life, a wordless song of sylvan speciation, and stumbled and slipped to the ground scattering the seeds.

He became aware again. Evelyn had her arms wrapped around his trunk. She was sobbing and her sorrow distressed him. "Don't cry, Evie," he said and bent his branches to enfold her.

"I was looking out the window and I saw the trees growing up and I knew what you'd done, so I got up to see better and Mrs.

Hascall said to sit down, but I saw you lying on the ground so
I said my brother's hurt and I ran downstairs and you were here
and your skin was getting hard and you wouldn't move and I
held onto you and you changed, and you changed, and now
you're growing here in the yard . . ."

"Evie," he sighed, and emanated a gentle wave of love which
filled her arms and body and flowed through her feet to complete
the circuit underground at his roots. "Evie, you must join us. Everyone must join us. Come into the new garden. We need your
help, we're still too few—they're cutting us down on Highway 5,
you know."

"Yes," she said, "I see," she said, as she saw what he had seen
in the grove and now showed her, the completion of the dimly
sensed vision of integrated intelligence and interwoven life, individual death and the sparkling green continuum of existence. A
crow alit in his branches and laughed with raucous delight. "But
what about Mom and Dad? We can't leave them alone. They'd
pine for us."

"Tell them to come and join us, or else they'll be left behind."

Evelyn heard the murmur of an excited crowd of children
milling around the trees. The principal stepped forward with
Mrs. Hargrave. "What's going on, Evelyn? Where's Adam?"

"He's this tree."

Mr. Thierry frowned. "Evelyn, Mrs. Hargrave says he disrupted
the class and ran out here. We're afraid something's wrong."

Evelyn smiled nervously. "I don't think it's wrong, Mr.
Thierry, but I don't think Adam's coming back. Can you call my
parents and ask them to come right away?"

"There's the pine cone," said Mrs. Hargrave.

Evelyn snatched it up. "Please, Mr. Thierry."

"See if you can get the children back in their classrooms," he
said to Mrs. Hargrave. "I'll call their parents."

"Come with us," said Mrs. Hargrave.

"I'll wait here," said Evelyn.

Mr. Thierry threw up his hands. "Promise not to go anywhere." As they left, she heard him say, "The first day of
school's always tough, but this takes the cake. What are we going to do about these trees? Okay, everybody, back to class."

A peaceful half hour passed in the shade. Sparrows skipped
cheerfully through the leaves and chattered at the crow. A squirrel skittered in from somewhere and shyly extended a delicate
paw, scampered up Evelyn's arm into Adam's crown and chit-

tered busily from branch to branch. She leaned back and listened to a song of sparkling streams.

"This is all very good, Adam, but I'm not sure one cone is enough to change the whole world."

"That is why, O sister mine, we need the others. Tell them, you who still have their attention, what to do. As these groves quickly grow and fructify, each cone contains the same celestial seeds. Bring the children here and let me speak to them."

At recess a swarm of curious children came. The teachers stood in a group by the building and wondered about the new laurel grove, and commented about the students' strange behavior. The children enthusiastically surrounded Evelyn with questions as she called for calm, eventually settled into a generally attentive huddle, encircled a tree, even the skeptical ones, arms on each other's shoulders, stood silently as if listening intently, then lined up to receive something Evelyn shook from a pine cone, dispersed to the edges of the playground, touched hands to mouths and flung them away. The teachers watched in disbelief as the playground flashed, was covered by a hazy verdant stubble which rose and rapidly veiled the adjacent freeway with a tender growth of laurels as the children skipped laughing and shouting under its canopy.

"I think we'd better start calling all the parents," said Mr. Thierry. "Ring the bell for classes. Let's keep the kids inside. And let's call, let's call ... I don't know. I'll call the Park Department." Some of the teachers went inside. The others suggested holding class in the grove; everyone was too overwrought to sit still, and it was a nice day. They gathered their classes and asked what was going on.

"It's Evie! No, it's Adam!" "Where is Adam, anyway?" "He turned into a tree!" "Come on ...." "Yes, he did, I saw it." "That's what Evie says." "I felt it, too, I felt like I was a tree." "Me, too! Me, too!"

Their father arrived. "What's going on?"

"Evelyn's sitting out there in that grove and she won't leave a tree she says is Adam."

Glen was astonished. "Where did those trees come from?"

"I don't know," said Mr. Thierry. "Strange things are happening."

"Where is she?" Glen threaded his way through the trees. Evelyn ran and threw herself into his arms.

"Oh, Daddy! I'm so glad you're here! Is Momma here, too?"

"Not yet, but she's coming. Where's Adam?"

Evelyn drew him and placed his hand on Adam's bark. Through his palm, up his arm, into his heart came the loving word, "Dad."

"Adam!" He touched the tree with his other hand, and his mind filled with a bright starlit vision of immensity and a small green globe spinning in serene joy. "Adam, what is this?"

"We're helping to save the world, Dad, and now it's Evie's turn to join us, but we want you and Mom to come, too. Will you?"

"What does this mean?"

"There is no meaning, Father, only life's dance, and in this place we are the new race of earth being born. If we survive, life will continue here; if not, it will not, and that would be sad, but races like individuals die and creation will continue elsewhere. . . . But life loves living and to live we must evolve, and we must change quickly here. Please come with us."

"Adam . . . what is this vision? How do you know this?"

"We are the primeval forest, Father, we are Adam and we are the birds, we are the life that lives, the love that loves, the past uncounted, the present extended, the future foreknown."

"Yes . . . I feel Adam, and I feel the rest of you. . . . But why now, why here?"

"The eternal is always here."

Marie arrived. "What is all this? Hello, Evie, darling. When did they plant these trees? Where's Adam?"

They showed her. "Oh," she said. "Hello, dear." She embraced him and listened. "Yes, of course we'll come. You're our children. We love you."

"Oh, Momma," Evelyn said with joyous relief.

"Show us how."

"Like this." She shook out a seed. "Breathe on it. Plant it." She sighed and sank down.

"Evie!" cried Glen. They knelt and took her in their arms. A smile played peacefully on her face, her eyes closed, the cone dropped. She grew heavy, they laid her carefully on the ground and caressed her thickening skin; she gently kissed her father's hand. "Her bark is worse than her bite," he said softly.

"What naughty children; they've gone and left us."

"Well, children always do, you know."

"And now we follow," she smiled, and shook the cone, and handed it to him.

Weeds

by Julia and Brook West

Brook and Julia West are a husband and wife team who write fantasy and science fiction. Julia is an anthropologist and botanist and Brook is a physical geographer who spent several years in Japan. Julia was 1994 Grand Prize winner and Brook has been a finalist in the Writers of the Future contest, and they have sold several short stories to magazines and anthologies.

Crisp mountain air, splash and gurgle of water dropping over a ten-foot waterfall, wind through the trembling leaves of an aspen forest; Angie Lindstrom wished she could capture the smells and feeling on videotape, as well as the silver-green flash of leaves. Odd that there were no bird calls or scolding chipmunks, though.

She turned off the minicam—she needed to help her botany students set up camp. Well, it was Dr. Stoker's class, but they *were* her students—she was the Teacher's Assistant.

A hand fell on her shoulder, and she turned, twisting out of Dr. Stoker's grip. "I'm glad you're getting the camp going, Angie," he said. "Where did you leave the cans of herbicide?"

Angie was relieved to see her husband, Kelton, come up behind the professor. "I put them over in that jumble of boulders," Kelton said. "What do you need that stuff for, anyway?"

Dr. Stoker turned to face Kelton. "Call it a personal crusade. I feel that eradicating introduced weeds—like dyer's woad and thistle—is important. This valley may look like an unspoiled Eden, but odds are we'll find noxious weeds up here too, crowding out the native plants."

Angie made a face behind Dr. Stoker's back as he went to inspect his precious cans.

"Wish you'd TA for a different prof," whispered Kelton.

"Kel, you know he's on my graduate committee. I had to."

"Well, he'd better keep his hands off you. . . ."

"Hey, Anj, got a hammer?" called George, a gangling redhead, and one of the better students.

"Sure." She dug it out of her pack for him. "Everybody doing all right? Need any help?"

"What's this?" asked Laurie, whose long blonde braids hung down into a jumble of tent nylon.

"Just leave that for now; it's the rain fly, and you won't need it unless it rains," said Helen, a tall black girl with her hair in cornrows. "I'll give you a hand; I've used this kind of tent."

Angie moved on down the line of tents set higgledy-piggledy in the open spaces beneath the aspens. "Um, Cory. Pull those branches out from under your tent—you don't want to sleep on them."

"Oh, yeah. Sorry, my dad always put up our tent."

Angie chuckled and went to help Kelton set up. Wildflowers were just starting to bloom at this elevation—a tall spike of bog orchid, tangles of blue clematis in the trees, and freckled monkeyflower blooms. The sparse grass was dotted with spring beauty blossoms.

"Shouldn't be hard for anyone to identify these plants," she said to Kelton.

"Even your oh-so-proper businessman husband?"

"I'll oh-so-proper you!"

Angie looked around at the camp. "Everybody done? Gather in." She ushered the twelve students to a central area where a couple of fallen logs made seats. "We need to set up a few ground rules and discuss tomorrow's plans."

As she outlined cooking and bathroom policies, Kelton moved in behind her. She leaned into his embrace, but continued speaking: "We'll start with a preliminary survey in the morning—identification of common plants, data entry, and such. After lunch we'll begin frequency sampling. Four teams, three people each. You'll each get a chance to set up a grid, map, count and identify." She noticed the professor beside her. "Did I leave anything out, Dr. Stoker?"

"No, that's fine. It's late enough now, you can all relax for a while, start your dinners. Some of you enterprising sorts might like to get a jump on identifying a few plants. . . ."

When she got back to the tent, Kelton had lit the little back-pack stove. Water steamed in the pan over the flame. The valley was quiet—just the murmur of wind through the branches, hushed voices, and the distant splash of the creek. *Still no birds or squirrels scolding trespassers; perhaps we scared them off with our noise.* So why did she feel watched?

"What's that?" Someone called out, away in the forest—a girl's voice, startled but not frightened. Angie listened, but heard nothing else. Still, unease shivered down her back.

"I'm going to check on the students," she told Kelton. They'd set up their tent away from the others for privacy.

The straggle of tents was a beehive of quiet activity as people prepared dinner. One girl—Colleen—stood looking into the forest, a dripping cooking spoon forgotten in one hand. Helen sat in her tent doorway putting on socks and boots.

"Everything okay?" asked Angie.

"Laurie went between those trees, said she'd only be a minute," said Colleen. "I fixed our dinner, and she's still not back. We were just going to look for her."

"I thought I heard someone out there," said Angie. "Let's call her."

"Lau-rie," they chorused.

No answer.

Other students gathered around. "Maybe she slipped and fell," someone suggested.

"Let's go look." Eleven students scattered into the trees.

"What's all the noise?" Dr. Stoker poked his head out of his tent, then crawled out completely when he saw Angie was alone.

"One of the girls took a walk, and hasn't come back. Everybody went to look for her."

"While they're doing that, let me show you the database I'm setting up for the valley." He took her arm.

"Um, well, Kelton's almost got dinner done, and you know how quickly food cools at this altitude." She pulled away and hurried back to their tent.

"What's going on?" asked Kelton.

"Laurie's missing. Cover the stew and we'll help look."

"What about Stoker?"

"He's busy with his database. But he's made *me* responsible for the students."

"Okay. Grab a flashlight, it'll be dark soon."

They started at the end of camp closest to the waterfall and followed the stream up the valley. All around them among the wide-spaced trees people talked or called, their feet swished through the grass, and a breeze whispered through the leaves. But every time Angie felt someone behind her and turned, she saw nothing.

"Angie?" It was Colleen, Laurie's friend. "Can you come here?"

Angie and Kelton—and most of the other students—followed Colleen's voice, found her staring at the base of an aspen. A little pile of clothing lay there, torn and dirty."

"My God," said Kelton.

"They're Laurie's." Colleen's voice broke, and she started sobbing.

Angie pulled Colleen against her shoulder, let her sob until she was calmer. The other students talked in shocked whispers.

Kelton knelt to look at the clothing. "Anj—there's no blood." He pulled at the shredded jeans, found them trapped beneath the dirt. "Anybody got a trowel?"

George handed him one; Kelton dug around the tree's base. "There's nothing there—just roots, and I can't dig through them."

"So she's not . . . ?"

"Nothing buried here but clothing."

Angie looked around. Only nine students. "Let's get people together." She straightened, took a deep breath, and yelled, "Everybody back here." When no one came, Angie called again—and again.

"So, that's three people missing?" said Helen.

Angie's head ached. *My responsibility.* "Let's go back to camp and discuss this intelligently," she said. "Stay together." Everyone nodded and set off slowly through the trees. As Angie turned to follow them, helping Colleen along, she seemed to feel eyes on her back.

They settled on the logs, and Kelton built a fire pit, then lit a fire. He'd gathered dry wood while searching. *My well-organized executive,* thought Angie.

The headache eased when she realized she *didn't* have to accept full responsibility for this—it was *Dr. Stoker's* class, *his* field trip. "I'll get Dr. Stoker; then we'll decide what to do."

"Unless it's him that did it," said Helen, her voice dry.

"Ah, c'mon. He's never done anything but touch. . . ."

"That *we* know of."

* * *

Dr. Stoker sat cross-legged in his tent, entering data into his laptop computer by lantern light.

"We're missing three students," said Angie without preamble. "Laurie, Cory, and Steve."

"Damn," he said. "How'd that happen?"

"There's more. We found Laurie's clothing, all torn up and half buried under a tree. But no Laurie." She watched his face carefully, Helen's words ringing in her mind.

It was hard to tell, in the harsh light of the lantern, but she thought he paled. "This can't happen to me. It could ruin my career. You've *got* to find those kids." He turned off the computer, zipped it carefully into its case, then followed her to the campfire.

Colleen and Helen huddled together, as close to the fire as they could get. Behind them, George brandished a stick like a sword. Ed and Flora had brought their dinners into the circle of firelight, but the plates were still full. Malcolm, the football player, sat pounding one fist into the other palm.

"There *wasn't* any blood—I looked, too," said Brad, "But man, it looked like some *maniac* tore her clothes up, then buried them; tried to hide them?"

"Didn't do a very good job," said David.

Dr. Stoker brushed off one end of a log and sat down. "I don't want you panicking each other with this talk. There must be some explanation of all this."

"They're *gone,* and we haven't heard screams or anything," said Helen. "You think they ripped off their clothes to run around naked for a joke?"

"I didn't say that."

"We need to get back out there and find them now," insisted George.

"And lose more people?" asked Dr. Stoker.

"I'd suggest that most of us stay here, by the fire, and send out parties of, say, four people at a time to search," said Angie. "We can rotate *until* we find the lost students."

"You'd better have ideas. You're as much responsible for these students as I am."

Angie stiffened, and Kelton, beside her, stepped forward. She grabbed him and said, "No, don't cause trouble," so softly that only he could hear. His hand tightened painfully on hers, but he stayed where he was.

"I'll take the first party out," she said. "Um, George and Helen, come with us?"

"Let me know if you find anything," said Dr. Stoker, and went back to his tent.

"I'm never taking another class from him," said David. "You're cool, Angie, but he's an uncaring old bastard."

The group headed into the twilight between ghostly white aspen trunks. Voices whispered among the leaves as a breeze picked up, and the tiniest noises made Angie jump.

"What do you think happened to them?" she asked Kelton, after flinching from nothing for the fifth or sixth time.

"I don't have any ideas yet. All we ever heard was a surprised exclamation—no screams. We found clothes, but no blood, no bodies. . . ."

His flashlight beam illuminated a red fannypack resting against the base of an aspen. A few tatters of torn shorts and underwear rested beneath it. Pieces of shredded T-shirt hung from the branches.

"That's Cory's," said Helen.

Angie tried to pick up the fannypack; it was buckled around the tree's trunk. She popped the buckle with trembling hands and turned it over; CORY MITCHELL.

"Kel, this is just too weird. What the hell is going on?"

He shook his head, face a pale blur in the darkness. "All I can think of is some maniac out here in the woods." He bent to tug at the shorts, but they were half buried under the tree. "I don't like this at all."

Angie's group returned to the campfire, and she sent out other search parties, but she and Kelton couldn't sleep. They huddled together on a log, sipping tepid chocolate and throwing branches into the fire, staring over the flames into the forest. Toward dawn, when David, Ed, Flora and Colleen returned with news of finding Steve's clothing half-buried at the base of a tree, Angie made a decision.

"Start packing; we're leaving," she told the returning search party.

"Hey, we still want to go out and look," said Malcolm, from across the fire. "I can't just turn tail and run, and leave those guys out there somewhere."

"I think we ought to let the cops deal with this," said Angie. "There must be a maniac out there. We can't deal with something like that."

"Why don't we search—it's starting to get light—while everybody else packs? If we don't find anything, we'll leave with you."

"Okay, but be careful." Angie swirled the chocolate dregs in her cup, made a face at it, and set the cup down. "I'll wake Dr. Stoker."

The professor answered her call immediately, but kept her waiting until he crawled out of the tent dressed in clean clothes, blond hair neatly combed.

"What news?"

"They found Steve's clothing, same as the others. I've told everybody to pack; we've got to leave, let the cops deal with this."

"God, I hate that—it makes me look incompetent. I'd rather we'd search again, in daylight."

"I sent out another party just now, but when they come back in, we're leaving."

"Isn't it a little high-handed of *you* to make that decision?" he asked, grabbing her shoulders.

"*You* made me responsible, last night. *I* stayed up all night to search. I think I have the right to make this decision."

A man's voice called, panic scaling it to falsetto, "My God, Angie, Brad's gone!"

Angie pulled away from Dr. Stoker. "Come on, Kel." They ran into the trees, found Malcom and David standing back to back, pale and trembling.

"What happened?" said Kelton.

"He was over there," said Malcolm. "He said, 'What's that?' and I went over to look—but he wasn't there."

She turned to look where Malcolm pointed. Three slender aspens grew close together, and she bent to examine the base of the farthest one. The grass had been pushed up from below, with dirt clods and small rocks littering the ground beneath the tree's roots. A gopher? She was a botanist, not a zoologist. "Malcolm, come look at this." She heard an oddly pleasant buzz and a gasp. A breeze rustled aspen leaves behind her, but Malcolm didn't answer. "Malcolm?"

Hair raised on her neck and arms; she turned to look. Malcolm wasn't there. Kelton, face pale, stared at an aspen. "Kel, where'd Malcolm and David go?"

Kelton shuddered and shook his head. "I ... I don't know. They were here ... and then ..."

"Kel?" She looked a question at him, but he shook his head. "Not now. Let's get *out* of this valley."

* * *

When they got back to camp, they found Dr. Stoker had sent out another search party.

"You're crazy!" yelled Kelton. "Something out there is snatching your students, and you send them into its jaws—or whatever?"

Angie took her husband's arm and said, "Kel," in a quiet warning voice.

He shook off her hand. "Three more missing. We can't fight this; let somebody else find out what's going on. Let's leave while we can!"

"Mr. Lindstrom," said Dr. Stoker in a frigid voice. "You are only here to accompany my TA; you have no authority. I made this decision. . . ."

"Then can Angie and I leave? You want authority; you can take full responsibility for your students disappearing, and we'll go for help."

Helen stumbled into camp, face pale as aspen bark. "They're turning into trees! I saw it."

Dr. Stoker turned on her. "What kind of nonsense is that?"

"I was talking to Ed. He looked past my shoulder—and got this puzzled look." She closed her eyes, took a deep, wavery breath. "I asked him what was going on and he . . . changed. He stretched up, tall and skinny, and his arms lengthened and branches came out of them, and leaves, and his legs grew roots. It all happened so fast. Flora saw it, too, but she was standing by Ed looking at me. And . . . and her eyes got big and then . . . she changed too. I didn't dare look around. It was aw-wful!" She started sobbing.

Dr. Stoker slapped her. "Helen, you're hysterical. Too much excitement. Overactive imagination. Go lie down in your tent." She staggered off, still sobbing.

Kelton's hand tightened on Angie's; he pulled her away. "Angie," he said softly into her ear, "she's right."

"What do you know, Kel? Why didn't you tell me?"

"I didn't believe what I saw. I couldn't tell you—let alone Dr. Stoker—that I saw Malcolm and David turn into trees."

"But Kel. . . ."

"Angie." Dr. Stoker beckoned her over. "I admit we need help. I don't want to send out search parties if they come back with stories like that. But I need you here. Could Kelton. . . ?"

"I'm not leaving Angie." Kelton had that stubborn look on his face. No one had ever changed his mind when he got stubborn.

"Then what can we do?" Dr. Stoker grabbed her shoulders. "I

could lose my career over this mess! We've got to think of something."

Angie pulled away from Dr. Stoker, stepped back to put Kelton between them. "Is that all you're worried about—your career? There are eight people missing!" She turned to go. "Come on, Kel, let's get the last search party." She started into the forest.

"Angie, wait!" Kelton took her arm. "I've got an idea." He led her to the tent, pulled her inside. They faced each other cross-legged on the rumpled sleeping bags. "Do you believe we saw people turn into trees?"

"I . . . I don't know. I know you both saw *something* awfully disturbing."

"Anj, we've got the minicam! We can record this whatever-it-is. . . ."

"And turn into trees ourselves?" She couldn't help herself.

"Listen, Angie. People are *seeing* something. And it's the *seeing* that does . . . whatever it does. Remember the myth of Perseus and Medusa? He looked into his shield—used it like a mirror—so he wouldn't get turned to stone."

"So you think the minicam. . . ?"

"Through the minicam you're looking at an image, not the thing itself. And I'll use one of our metal survival mirrors. That way we'll be safe."

"Kel, at this point I'll try anything. Because . . ." her lips started to tremble, and she caught her lower one between her teeth, "because dammit, I'm terrified."

The forest was still in the midday heat; occasional insect noises made Angie jump. She turned on the video camera, patting her pocket to assure herself the extra battery pack was there. "Got your mirror?" she asked Kelton.

"Yeah. Wish I had a bigger one. I'm gonna fall over my feet trying to look into this thing as I walk."

"I'll trade you."

"No."

Angie looked at him out of the corner of her eye; he had that stubborn look on his face.

They walked over the sparse grass under the trees for a long time. Angie swung the camera from a clump of Oregon grape to an oddly twisted aspen, trying to still her trembling hands. Her stomach knotted with fear. *What if this doesn't work? What if something really is turning people into trees?*

Kelton made a strange, choked noise in his throat, and she swung the camera to focus on him. He stared into his mirror, an intent look, half surprise, on his face. "Those eyes!" he said.

Even as he spoke, his mouth twisted, his face lengthened. The mirror dropped from fingers that elongated, sprouted twigs, leaves.

"No, oh no, oh please." Angie didn't lower the minicam even as tears dripped down her cheeks. She recorded her beloved's entire metamorphosis; roots digging into the soft earth, branches tearing through his clothing and rising from his brown hair. Her stomach lurched and her knees shook with anguish—but she kept the camera focused.

It was over. An aspen swayed slightly without benefit of breeze, torn clothing half buried beneath its roots. Thousands of coin-shaped leaves winked like semaphores sending a message in an unknown language. "Kelton, Kelton, no," she sobbed. She slowly turned, camera running, panned past every tree, wildflower and low-growing bush. Somewhere on this tape should be the answer. If not . . . She couldn't finish the thought. Life without Kelton?

Angie huddled in her tent, watching the minicam's tiny black-and-white screen. She rewound the tape again, began the sequence. Kelton's face, intent and surprised, his mouth moving, then twisting. Nothing there. *He* was looking at it, *she* was taping him. Whatever it was, she hadn't taped it.

No, wait. The thing was *behind* him—he saw it in the mirror! She rewound, watched slender trees bob through the field of view. The picture shifted to Kelton's face. And behind him—a flash of movement. A bush stirring in the breeze? But there was no breeze.

Rewind again, switch to slow motion, move frame by frame. *Not* a bush behind Kelton. A thing, as if a pile of autumn leaves had humped into vaguely human shape, with twiggy teeth, and bleached branch horns rising from its temples. Its eyes glittered even in the tiny black and white replay. 'Those eyes,' he had said. It was real, a monster that turned people into trees.

Angie wanted to close her eyes and scream and scream. Her hands trembled as she switched the minicam off and laid it on her sleeping bag. What now? Hunt the thing down? What would kill it—fire? Chase it with a torch, like a villager in a Frankenstein movie?

"Angie?"

Oh, please, not now, Dr. Stoker. "Yes?" She was pleased that her voice was steady.

"Where's Kelton?"

I can't tell him. He won't believe me. He'll laugh. I have proof, but I don't want to show it to him. . . . "He decided to go for help after all."

"Can I come in?"

Every fiber of her being screamed *no,* but she had to be polite. And after her lie, she could hardly tell him she was mourning her lost husband. "Sure."

He slid through the zippered door-slit, settled on Kelton's sleeping bag. His presence made the hot, close air even more oppressive. Angie bit her lips to keep herself from ordering him out.

"I'm glad Kelton decided to go for help. I just don't know what to make of all this. There's no sign of violence or struggle—just torn clothing to hint at what's happening." He leaned forward and patted her knee. "I know you've done your best—I'm sorry I barked at you earlier."

"Yeah."

"Listen, Angie, I know you're a newlywed, and Kelton is a very attractive man, but I could help you a lot if you'd just be a little more . . . friendly."

Angie couldn't believe it. To come seeking sexual favors at a time like this! The *nerve* of him.

"I've never been unfriendly," she answered, struggling inwardly. *If I slap him, he'll be my enemy forever.*

"Don't play naive, Angie. You know what I mean. You won't even call me by my first name." He reached forward, stroked one finger down her arm.

"Sir, I *am,* as you mentioned, a married woman. I don't feel any need for other . . . companionship." She looked him straight in the eye.

"I can make it very pleasant for you." He smiled, smoothed his hair, and reached for her breast.

This had gone beyond nerve. Something snapped inside her. "Listen, you . . . bastard! All the grad students know about you. Can't keep your hands off the women! Well, this is one student you'll not touch again."

"Why you. . . ."

"And don't threaten me about my dissertation. I'll finish, with or without you. There's a law against sexual harassment, and I'm not too shy to engage a lawyer."

"If you ever get out of this valley." His smile turned ugly, and she felt a twinge of purely physical fear. He *was* much bigger than she.

"You try anything, and I'll squash you like . . . like a *weed.*"

Light burst in her mind. A *weed.* That thing had looked like a heap of leaves—would the herbicide harm it, kill it? She scrambled past Stoker, avoiding his reaching arms, and rolled out of the tent.

Herbicide, that was it. The cans lay in the boulder heap where Kelton had dropped them yesterday afternoon. First lose Stoker. She ran behind a tree, crouching in the low-lying brush. *He'll probably think I'm so upset I'll run blindly into the woods.*

Stoker surged out of the tent, glanced around, then stalked through camp, looking into tents. Angie's heart pounded. The camp was deserted. Were they the only two left?

When he disappeared behind a tree she wasted no time. Keeping under cover as best she could, she ran for the west end of the valley. There, the herbicide. She checked the little backpack sprayer, heavy, sloshing—Stoker didn't want to miss a chance to exterminate his noxious weeds. She pumped the handle to pressurize it. Now, back to where she had left . . . Kelton. That's the last place she had seen the creature.

Where had they been? *There, that's the low-lying mountain-ash, and that clump of columbine. I taped them.* Then what?

Landmark by landmark, she wandered through the forest. Then, a group of trees, familiar from her replays on the minicam. A tremor ran through the Kelton-tree when she walked past. *I didn't bring the minicam. It's back in the tent—where Stoker might be waiting for me.* What should she do? She dared not go back.

I'll have to be very, very careful. I know what it looks like. Glory, a motile plant. If only she could study it! How in the world did it turn people into trees—and why? She would love to get it into a lab, find out where it got the energy to move so quickly. *It can't be just "solar-powered"—maybe another source of nourishment? There* are *carnivorous plants. . . .* No birds or small animals in the valley. She shivered.

Something crashed through the brush. The creature made little or no noise—so this had to be Stoker.

"What are you doing out here?" he called as he approached her. "You know it's dangerous."

"Doing *your* job," she said. "Trying to kill the thing that's been trapping our students."

"What?" His mouth stayed open, his eyes bulged. Angie heard it this time, a sweet, seductive sound, compounded of wind through leaves, cricket chirrs, and the endless buzz of cicadas.

It's behind me.

Stoker raised his arms, tried to take a step. Again, she saw it, watched in horror as his fingers elongated, grew leaves, his body slimmed and elongated, roots grew through his shoes, burying them, to seek the nutrients beneath the soil. . . .

She turned, ready to spray, eyes averted. *If it gets me, I'll only have a few seconds,* she told herself. *Don't hit the trees, just the creature.*

Where? She saw something move, sprayed it—and met its eyes, golden-green and very alive, like flame. Music swelled around her, soothing, welcoming. Then the creature faltered, drenched with herbicide, and the sprayer fell from her lengthening fingers.

Dizzy, disoriented, looking down at something very small and odd from a great height. Rush of wind through leaves—like voices.

There *were* voices. *So many people this time,* one of the old aspens sighed.

Not really words, but emotions—thoughts. They moved slowly, while clouds sped by; dark, then light again. Rush of energy from sunlight on leaves.

Much emotion from the next tree—no, not tree—Kelton! *Why? Why? Angie should have run!*

Her thousand eyes, looking up, down, around. Don't think about it all at once—too much, too much! Focus on that tree—no, it's Stoker. As handsome a tree as he was a man—the bastard—but Kelton was more attractive . . . slender, graceful, his leaves a distinctive silver-green.

Angie has the loveliest bark—smooth, white, Kelton thought at her.

Nearby, other emotions pulled at her. *Lust,* its thoughts insinuated into her being. *Submit to me. Pleasure me.*

She trembled in horror, hunching her branches away from the Stoker-tree.

Something moved—a flicker, she should know what. Yes—the creature. As the sun sank quickly toward the close horizon of the valley's edge, the creature crawled toward the grove, drawn by lust. It embraced the Stoker-tree's base, and lay quiescent, pulsing.

No! Leave me! Rape!

The stars wheeled overhead, day came, and the creature stirred, moving quickly away from the professor's trunk.

I didn't kill it. A wave of regret, horror, anger from Angie.

It ... hard ... kill. A huge old aspen; she could just glimpse its crown across the valley. *I ... make it. Guard valley ... years long past. I seek ... knowledge. It too ... strong. Changed *me.**

You not-tree that time? Another old, thick-trunked tree, its thoughts almost as foreign as the ancient creature-maker.

I ... man ... then.

The conversation lasted all day. As darkness fell, the creature crawled back to the professor-tree, who moaned. *It is *poisoned*. I feel the poison.*

Ssssslowwwwly. It ssstronnng, the ancient tree thought.

Angie thought, *If it dies, have I killed a species?*

I ... made it. Not ... natural ... being. Mistake.

Angie spent days tracing Kelton's branches and admiring the angles his twigs made. She basked in warm awareness of his tree-gaze on her bark, but also felt Stoker's lustful pull and trembled, her leaves agitated. Would she have to endure this for centuries?

In the dark time Angie's thoughts slowed. But she knew when the creature crept, ever so slowly, to drop at Stoker-tree's roots. *Don't touch me. Pain,* his anguished thought crawled into her mind.

The first welcome rays of sunlight warmed her, and with her thousand eyes she saw the creature, its scalelike leaves pale, brown at the edges. It writhed, scratching at the ground. Then it stopped, collapsed in on itself. Stoker-tree rejoiced.

But she mourned. *I'll never study it now.*

Pain began. Her sap dried, her roots and branches withered. *We die with the creature!*

Other plant-people screamed, trembled. Trees twisted as if a capricious whirlwind meandered through the grove. And not just trees; a waxy white flower convulsed near her roots.

She could no longer see, could barely communicate. She hoped she would fall across Kelton's tree body when her roots gave way. *Kelton. I love you.*

Angie, my love.

Her mind twisted with pain.

Angie uncurled, stretched, looked down at her scratched and naked body. Something furry brushed her arm—a rabbit, dazed and blank-eyed. So it didn't eat the animals, she thought in near hysteria. It changed them, too.

I'm alive.

Kelton.

He lay curled nearby, eyes closed in a face drawn with the agony of tree-change. "Kel, sweetheart." She massaged his back, rubbed his arms and legs. "Wake up."

He stirred finally, sat up. "We didn't die after all."

"No." She leaned against him, soaking his chest with tears.

"Where are the others?"

"I'm sure they'll wake up soon. I want to enjoy *you*." She snuggled against him, and his arms tightened around her.

"What happened to the creature?" he said into her ear.

"The herbicide finally killed it."

"I know. But is the body still about?"

"Hey, that should have been my question, mister business executive. I'm the one with the overwhelming scientific curiosity." She sat straight up, looked around. Stoker lay nearby, barely breathing. Seeing him made her remember her nakedness. She looked for her clothing; found rags mixed with the dirt where she had stood for—how many days?

The creature lay like a drift of crisp autumn leaves, already disintegrating. She slid her tattered shirt carefully under the remnants. This much, at least, she could study.

Kelton reached over and squeezed her hand. "Let's get back to camp. We've got to get dressed, find the others, and . . . and sort out this mess."

"I have a feeling there's a lot more mess than we expect. What about the guy who made that creature? And those other old tree-people? Who are they?"

Back at camp they pulled on shorts, T-shirts, sandals. Subdued, shivering students wandered in from the forest. Laurie talked incessantly about the tree next to her; Colleen clutched at her and sobbed. "Told you so," said Helen—Angie and Kelton nodded.

Something inside Angie's head drew her up-valley. She led Kelton with her into the forest. Trees shivered around them, though there was no wind, as something tree-tall and not human emerged from amongst them. Branches and leaves crowned an almost-head, grasping limbs angled below, and long root-toes writhed forward, sank into the ground and drew it forward in an oddly fluid stride.

"Little-one. You ... free us ... from my ... folly." The voice whispered and boomed all at once.

Angie clutched Kelton's hand, then relaxed. After what they'd been through, a walking tree was nothing to be afraid of. And she knew "who" this was. "Where are the other people we heard? All I see are the ones who came with me."

"Too ... long ... they ... be tree. Now ... like me. Stay. Care for ... children."

"Children?" she asked.

All about, aspens shook and writhed in no-wind. "Few ... trees here ... once men. Others ... we seed. Children. ... We ... free to ... nurture ... now."

Pollination—natural reproduction, for trees. Seeds growing into trees—children of changelings. They'd lived so long as trees, they were more tree than human. *How long were we trees? Weeks, at least. Guess I've got roots here too.*

"I wish you—and your children—well," she said. "I must care for my own now."

"You ... may ... return." Trees rustled again and the aspen-man was gone.

I will.

They went back to the students—to *her* students.

"George, Steve, get Dr. Stoker, help him back to camp. We don't want to leave any noxious weeds in the forest. Pack up, folks; it's time to go home."

Benbow

by Nancy Etchemendy

Nancy Etchemendy lives and writes in the San Francisco Bay area. Her short stories and poems have appeared in F&SF, The Year's Best Fantasy and Horror and a number of other anthologies and periodicals both here and abroad. She has also written three novels for children.

I never would have guessed the boy had a thick crop of green, shiny leaves on his head. He wore an Oakland A's baseball cap pulled low, so he looked pretty ordinary, maybe a little young to be hitchhiking, thirteen or fourteen I thought. He carried a maroon duffel bag, stuffed full, but with no signs of wear. I've been around enough teenagers to know a runaway when I see one. He was a textbook example.

"Thanks, mister," he said, as he climbed onto the seat of my pickup.

I had been to Garberville for grocery shopping, something I try not to do more than once a month, so the truck was full. The back had twenty heavily loaded bags in it, plus my old Labrador retriever, Scratch. The overflow of two or three bags had ended up in the cab with me. I watched as the boy carefully moved them to make room for himself and his duffel as far away from me as possible. A package of lamb chops poked up from the top of one bag, and he eyed it as if he wouldn't mind ripping it open and wolfing them down on the spot. It seemed likely that he hadn't eaten in a while.

"Just call me Chet. Glad to be of service," I said. "Where are you going?"

"Benbow," he replied. "You know where that is? It's supposed to be around here somewhere."

He had a pleasant voice, still fairly high, but rich and even, not squeaky as is common among boys his age. I couldn't see much of his face because he hunched down and turned away as if he were trying to hide. What I glimpsed of him was dirty, like his clothes, which were stained and specked with dead leaves. He had clearly been sleeping outside. All my old instincts as a teacher, a school principal, and a repentant absentee father rose to attention.

I pulled onto the pavement and started slowly down the winding road, wondering what I should do. "Yeah, I know where Benbow is," I said. "You know, there's nothing there anymore. The last of the hippies left four or five years ago, and they didn't exactly build to last. It's just a few empty shacks in the middle of the woods. Nobody lives there but raccoons."

His shoulders went practically rigid. "I know," he said. He was a bad liar, which was a very good sign as far as I was concerned.

"Sure you still want to go there?" I asked.

"I have to. It's important. *Real* important."

"Okay, whatever you say."

I drove on in silence for a while. I had the window on my side open. A summer day just like this one first convinced me that the northern California coast was the place to retire. The resinous smells of deep forest filled the mild air. The road meandered among oaks, pines and even the occasional redwood. Bird songs mingled in a pleasing cascade. We crested a hill, and I sighted the Pacific Ocean. I knew if I parked and stopped the engine, I'd hear the surf like a distant whisper. The big cities and their troubles lay far away. I didn't even bother to lock my doors at night, and it felt deeply good and right. Not everything between Garberville and the sea was perfect. We had our own kinds of problems in the coastal woods. But they didn't usually include lost, hungry runaways.

"What's your name?" I asked the boy.

"Birk," he said without looking at me, still hunched forward, his shirt collar turned up and his hat pulled down.

"Got a last name?"

He did look at me then, though he said nothing, just turned his head. His eyes were dark and full of pain, his face pale and worried. I noticed for the first time that his hair, though I couldn't see much of it, was full of leaves. The sight made me shiver, though I couldn't have said why. Maybe I knew, in the back of my mind, that there was something strange about him. It didn't hit me till later that the leaves were green and fresh-looking. I thought he must have gotten them from sleeping on the ground, and that triggered in me a powerful urge to help in any way I could.

I shrugged and said, trying to sound nonchalant, "None of my business anyway. Well, Birk, there's a café in Whitethorn just down the road from here. We have to pass it on the way to Benbow. How would you like to stop there for a sandwich and a piece of pie?"

He licked his lips, and a little smile skittered across his face. But it was soon gone, replaced by the look of strain and worry. "Thanks, but I can't."

"Why not? If it's a matter of money, it can be my treat. I'm a rich old geezer anyway." Which was a long way from the truth, and I could see he knew it. After all, what would a rich old geezer be doing in a twenty-year-old pickup truck with 150,000 miles on it? I just didn't want him to think I was making some kind of big sacrifice by inviting him to lunch. It might have hurt his pride.

He hunched even further forward, and tugged his shirt collar up higher. "I just can't, that's all."

I knew if I said the wrong thing, he'd be out of the truck like a jack rabbit as soon as I slowed for the next curve. Why would a starving kid shy away from a café? I had offered him a free handout and he had turned it down, so it couldn't be money. What was it then?

"You've got to eat," I said. "A growing person can get sick and weak pretty fast without food."

"I know," he said for the second time since I'd picked him up. There was a tremor in his voice. I had the impression he would have said more, but he didn't want to risk crying in front of me.

He was a hard one to reach. If I wanted to find out anything about him, I would have to hurry, because the window of opportunity was going to close at the turnoff to Benbow.

I tried to remember the contents of the three sacks of groceries beside us. I had bagged them myself because that's how it's done at the Garberville Discount Food Mart. I'm a sixty-five-year-old man with high blood pressure. I don't buy much in the way of snack food. But I had picked up a package of granola bars, and I seemed to remember tossing them in with the lamb chops. I rummaged through the bag with one hand, a challenge on a road so curvy it takes an hour to go 23 miles. I found the granola bars and slid the package toward Birk.

"Try some of these. They're nothing compared to Milky Ways, but they're all right if you're real hungry."

That got me a little grin. He wasted no time tearing them open and shoving two bars into his mouth practically whole.

"There's milk in there, too, if you want it," I said. "It's skim, and I don't have any cups, but you could drink it from the carton. It's okay."

He pulled the quart container onto his lap, opened it, and gulped it down greedily. Out of breath, he beamed and swiped at a milk mustache.

"Thanks, mister," he said. For the first time since I'd picked him up, he had a little color in his cheeks.

"Chet," I said.

"Okay, Chet. Thanks."

It was the first time he'd called me by name. I allowed myself a smile.

The Benbow turnoff was now about ten minutes away. I had no time left for finesse. "Look, I hope you don't think I'm trying to butt my nose in where it doesn't belong. But there's something you ought to know about these woods. They're not safe unless you know exactly where you're going."

He frowned and turned away again.

"I don't mean dumb stuff, lions and tigers and bears, that kind of junk. I don't even mean getting lost, exactly. I mean drug dealers."

"What?" he said, looking at me from the corner of his eye as if to say, *How stupid do you think I am?*

"No, I mean it. I'm not just making up stories to scare you. There are a lot of marijuana growers up in these hills. Believe me, they want their operations kept secret. They don't take kindly to trespassers. The woods look real peaceful, but they're full of shotgun snares and bear traps. You can get yourself in a pile of trouble if you wander down the wrong path."

"So are you letting me off at Benbow or not?" he said, eyes slitted.

"If that's what you want, I'll do it, but I don't have to like it."

We traveled on in silence for a few minutes. We passed through Whitethorn and I waved to Milt Perry at the lumber yard. The woods closed around us again, quieter now, dimmer. In another hour, the sun would set.

Coming up on our right was a rickety hand-lettered sign that

said "BENBOW," with an arrow under it. I pulled over and set
the handbrake. "Here is it," I said. "You have to walk a couple
of miles down that trail. I'd take you in there, but I'd probably
need four-wheel drive and a chain saw."

He rolled down his window and looked out. The undergrowth
was fierce. Ferns, briars, and poison oak formed a matted wall
through which the path delved like a deep wound. The trees
above it shut out most of the remaining sun. Something rustled,
and the hoot of an owl wafted out of the twilight. In the back of
the truck, Scratch growled deeply and continuously.

Birk reached hesitantly for his duffel. I could see this was
something he did to save face, not because it was really what he
wanted anymore. He had hoped to find people at Benbow, someone he knew, or someone who could tell him what he needed to
know. But the place was deserted, an ominous ruin. *Carpe diem,*
I thought.

"Maybe you'd rather wait till you have some daylight. I could
bring you back up here tomorrow. I've got a little place down the
road at Shelter Cove. I built it myself. It's not much, but you're
welcome to the spare bed. Lamb chops for dinner, and a hot
shower. If you want a way to pay me back, I could use some
help in the garden."

Relief washed over him, visible as rain, loosening his muscles
and his troubled heart. He trusted easily, which meant that, whatever was wrong, he might heal easily, too. I had won a chance
to help him. It was one of those moments of great atonement that
I have sought since I left my own children half-grown and went
off to do things I thought were more important than being their
father. If I had stayed home with them, my son might well be
alive today. It's a hard thing to live with, even though it happened years ago.

When we arrived, Birk jumped out of the truck and started
carrying groceries into the kitchen. I didn't even have to ask.
Somebody had taken the time to civilize him beautifully, somebody who loved him and was probably worried sick about him.

He stopped briefly to watch me lift Scratch down from the
back. "What's the matter with him?" he asked.

"Oh, he's just old. I've had him eleven years. He's got cata-
racts and rheumatism. It hurts him to jump down, and he can't
always see where he's going to land."

He held out his hand, and Scratch licked it, wagging his tail
enthusiastically. "He's great."

I nodded my agreement, and helped carry in the last few bags. I showed Birk where to put his duffel, and I hung fresh towels in the guest bathroom. When I claim it's not much of a place, I'm being modest, if I say so myself. I took early retirement and came up here to do one of the things I'd always dreamed of, design my own house and build it myself from the ground up. It's not huge, but it's done right, snug and solid even in the worst storms. It's two bedrooms and two baths, bigger than Scratch and I really need, but we like having company. It gets too lonely without people around, and they're more likely to come if there's plenty of space. I probably would have built closer to my daughter if I could have afforded it. I never give up hoping she'll come here someday and bring my grandkids, but so far, no luck. She tends to act like I'm dead except when she needs money. I can't blame her. I just wish she'd forgive me.

Birk said if it was all right with me he'd wait till bedtime for his shower. He asked if I needed help getting dinner, and when I said, "No, take a load off," he said he'd like to fool around out in the yard a while. I said that sounded fine. I expected him to go out and throw a stick for Scratch or something. I was busy putting the groceries away, and I didn't think much about it till I glanced out the window and saw him down on his hands and knees in the vegetable garden. He appeared to be weeding, a very odd thing for a boy his age to do voluntarily.

About the time I put the lamb chops in the pan, he tapped at the kitchen door and walked in with his arms full of produce. He had harvested several tomatoes, some green onions, lettuce, peas, and a few small zucchinis. It was more than the two of us could eat and I felt a little irritated about it.

"You get all that from my garden?"

He nodded, grinning.

"That's great, though I kind of wish you'd asked first."

The grin disappeared and he stammered, "Oh ... oh, I'm sorry. I didn't mean to ... it's just they won't be nearly as good tomorrow. They're ready right now, and it's always best to pick things at their peak. Better for the plants, too."

I helped him load the stuff into a basket. "Where'd you learn so much about growing vegetables?"

"I dunno," he said. "Seems like I've always known how. My mom ..." His voice caught and he looked at the floor. "My mom says I have a green thumb."

I thought about asking him if he didn't think maybe his mom was a little worried about him right now. But I could see he didn't need the reminder. He knew very well she was worried. I wondered yet again what he hoped to find at Benbow, something so important that he would run away from home and face a frightening series of hitchhikes for it. My curiosity shortly overcame my tact.

"So where is your mom? Where do you live?" I asked. I flipped the lamb chops over and sliced two of the tomatoes into a little salad. Birk wandered to the sink and washed his hands, slowly and thoroughly. I thought maybe he was never going to answer.

"San Francisco," he said finally.

He was much farther from home than I'd thought. It's a couple hundred miles from here to the Bay Area, much of it on narrow mountain roads. I had him pegged as a small-town boy. Maybe it was his interest in growing things that made me think that, because it didn't seem to fit the profile of a city kid.

I motioned him to the table and set a loaded plate in front of him. "So what's so important about Benbow?"

He gave me that look, the same one I'd gotten when I asked his last name. He didn't say anything, just went about the important business of cutting his meat.

I shrugged. "Don't mind me. Sometimes I'm too nosy for my own good," I said. Which was an understatement.

Things might have been all right if I had just left them at that. But I didn't. Maybe my feelings were hurt because he wouldn't open up, or because he knew more about vegetables than I did. Maybe I was just worried about how much trouble I could get into for picking up a stray and doing anything except driving him straight to the nearest authorities. Maybe he reminded me too much of my own son. Whatever the reasons, I said, "Oh, I forgot to tell you, no hats at the table. It's a house rule."

He dropped his knife and fork on his plate and said softly, "I need to keep it on."

"No you don't," I said. "You just *want* to keep it on. There's a difference."

He got to his feet and started for the door, then after a second's hesitation came back and picked up his plate.

Without a word, he walked out to the porch, leaving me with a piece of lamb halfway to my mouth. I heard the groan of a deck chair and the renewed scraping of his cutlery. I was lucky he didn't run off into the night.

After dinner, he helped with the dishes. He did this silently, in spite of my best efforts to start a conversation. A thin, clammy fog had rolled in off the sea, and I threw a log in the wood stove to keep Scratch's joints warm. Birk said he was tired and excused himself. I was astonished to see my dog abandon the hearth and follow him to his room. A few minutes later, I heard the water running in the shower. I sat alone in the firelight a while, mentally kicking myself for letting something as silly as a baseball cap take me back to square one with this gentle, frightened boy. Sometimes it seems to me that we are doomed to make the same mistakes over and over again, no matter how hard we try to change ourselves.

Eventually, I got tired, too, and I went off to my own bedroom. On the way, feeling tender and guilty, I tapped on Birk's door, which stood a little ajar. There was no answer, so I opened it further and looked in. Scratch snored on the rug at the foot of the bed where Birk lay in the open-mouthed sleep of an exhausted child. Half the blankets had fallen to the floor. He wore partially buttoned pajamas that looked freshly laundered. The grimy Oakland A's baseball cap was firmly settled on his head.

I shivered, as suddenly and inexplicably as I had earlier beside Birk in the truck. Chiding myself for this groundless skittishness, I pulled the covers over him and tucked them around his chin. Gently, I removed the hat. For a moment, what I saw simply left me confused. He looked and smelled freshly showered, and what I could see of his hair was clearly damp as if he'd washed it. But the leaves I had noticed earlier in the day still clung there. I went to the hall light and flipped it on so I could see better without waking him. Hundreds of leaves mingled with his dark curls, small and slender as if from a miniature willow—not dry, but green and healthy looking. I pinched one between my fingertips and tugged experimentally, but it wouldn't come out. It seemed quite firmly attached. I eased the baseball cap back onto his head and rushed out of the room.

I stood in the hallway for a moment, unable to quite believe what I'd seen. I tiptoed back into the room and took another look. The leaves were still there. I lifted the elastic waistband of his pajamas and peeked southward. He had leaves there, too. Shaking, I made my way to the kitchen and did something that's rare for me. I poured myself a short bourbon and drank it straight. I sat by the fire a few minutes, then went back to Birk's room. The situation remained unchanged. I thought of my mother, who died of Alzheimer's a few years before I retired. She used to have conversations with people long dead. She be-

lieved that her sister lived on the moon, and that my shoelaces
were garter snakes. Maybe this was how it began.

Hours passed before I came anywhere near sleeping. The
whole situation shook me badly, and stirred up ghosts and memories that made rest impossible. I wondered if Birk's parents
knew why he'd gone. The leaves were small and bright, like a
tree's new spring growth. Maybe they were a recent develop-
ment, something he'd hidden from them until it became impossible.

I knew what it was like to sleepwalk through three days and
nights, wondering where your son was and imagining the worst.
My daughter called me one evening, frantic, to say her brother
had run away from home and she was afraid he might kill himself. She didn't know where her mother was. I did my best to fix
things, but it was too late.

I remembered the phone call from the police—professional,
detached. "Are you the father of Robert Marston of 1750 Washington Street . . . a person matching your son's description was
struck and killed by a Southern Pacific Railroad train near the
Center Street crossing at 1:55 a.m. . . . we're unable to find the
boy's mother . . . could you meet us at the hospital . . ." Neither
of us was ever there when Bobby needed us. Why can't people
listen to their children? Why can't children tell us what they
need?

Eventually I dragged myself from my chair by the fire and
made my way to bed, where I spent the rest of the night dozing
and dreaming of my children with leaves instead of hair, who
called to me through the bars of my mother's room in the Alzheimer's ward.

When I woke up, a wide swath of midmorning sun warmed
my blankets, and Scratch was whining to be let out. I knew immediately that I had overslept.

I crawled out of bed feeling stiff and old, struggled into my
bathrobe, and opened the door for Scratch who bolted like a
stone from a slingshot. This was unusual, though I wasn't awake
enough for it to sink in till later. I guess I thought he must feel
the same way I did—that nothing else in the world was quite as
important as peeing. On my way back from the toilet, I peeked
into the guest room. Sunlight danced cheerfully over the neat bed
and the spotless floor, no wrinkled sheets, no dirty clothes or
damp towels. The canvas duffel and its owner had disappeared,

leaving no evidence of their existence except my memory of them, which suddenly seemed inadequate.

I hurried into jeans and a shirt and combed my hair with my hands as I rushed out the front door. I was in for another shock. The yard looked incredible. The grass seemed freshly mown, every blade crisp and vigorously green, though I had no recollection of having heard the mower. The leaves of each tree and shrub gleamed with health. Flowers that had previously brought forth only anemic foliage now drooped with lively blossoms. The vegetable garden was a canner's dream. Plump beans and ripe tomatoes had developed overnight, and the corn swayed with heavy, sweet ears. Bird calls and the whisper of bees filled the air. If I needed evidence of Birk's visit, here it was in profusion.

Scratch ran back and forth between me and the pickup truck, barking at nothing I could see. The message was clear.

"All right, pal," I said as I helped him onto the seat. "We're going to Benbow."

It was one of those days when bright sunlight burns away all subtleties, leaving only brilliance and deep shadow. The smells of warm pine sap and seawater filled the air. Everything seemed clear. Birk must have risen early and gone off to finish his quest as he had begun it, alone. When you're fourteen years old, you think your biggest problem is conquering your fears. You have no way of knowing that sometimes fear is a good thing, that it can lead to survival even if it makes you desperate. My daughter blames me for not having been there to make Bobby understand that before it was too late. And she is right.

I knew the road well, and I pushed the old truck to its limits, squealing the tires on the curves and praying the brakes held out. Scratch glared at me in baffled surprise as he slid back and forth on the seat, unable to connect our hurry with the rough ride. We reached the Benbow road in twenty minutes, probably a record.

I let the truck idle a minute while I got out and scouted the overgrown trail that led to the old commune. There were washouts and fallen trees everywhere. Decomposed forest debris made the soil spongy. It was impossible to tell whether anyone had walked on it recently. Taking the pickup down it would have been crazy. I knew I'd be stuck within a hundred feet.

Scratch whined and barked from the cab of the truck, trying to squeeze his big black body through four inches of open window. He was no bloodhound, but he thought the world of our leafy-haired friend. If Birk had walked down this road, Scratch would know.

I reached in and turned off the truck's engine, pulled a leash out of the glove compartment, and clipped it to Scratch's collar. If his arthritis was bothering him, he was too excited to think ahead about it. He almost dislocated my shoulder as he leaped down from the truck. He landed with a yelp, but was up again in a moment. I let him tug me down the dim forest tunnel that was once the road to Benbow.

We walked fast, almost trotting. We forded shallow streams and ducked under deadfalls. All the while, apprehension swelled inside me like a toadstool. I couldn't keep my mind off bear traps and homemade mines and the glazed dopiness I'd occasionally seen in the eyes of known growers. There was something else, too. The forest felt strange here—"powerful" is the word I'd choose. And I wondered yet again who or what Birk was, and what had brought him here.

We were hot and out of breath by the time we reached what was left of the commune. I hadn't seen it in two or three years, since the time a neighbor gave me a guided tour of the ruins. It looked perceptibly less human now than it had then. The hippies of Benbow had never had electricity or a sewage system or running water, just a misguided sense that they could live as the Indians had and the earth would take care of them. Now slugs, flies, and green things went about the business of reclaiming the hills of garbage. Wasps and wood rats nested in the sagging rafters of the shacks.

The place had the feel of a battle lost. Redwoods and oaks watched darkly over the place from rare heights, as they always had. Even in the spots the residents had cleared, first briars then baby trees and madrone had reestablished themselves. The plank walls sank into the green earth. Grass grew on the roofs. There was no longer a trace of human scent, just the damp smell of earth and mushrooms. Scratch, however, disagreed. Whining with excitement, he followed his nose to a place among the ferns and snowberries where we discovered the burgundy duffel.

As I knelt to examine it, I heard voices. Scratch lifted his nose toward them, silent for once, almost apprehensive. It wasn't a conversation exactly, nor a song. A windy murmur drifted through the forest, like people praying in a language I'd never heard before. It made Scratch's legs tremble, and my empty stomach burn.

"Birk!" I shouted. "Birk, where are you?"

I got no answer, just a flood of imaginary horrors, the boy maimed and unconscious from a shotgun snare, or gagged and bound by paranoid pot growers. Almost at once I regretted having called to him. Now the owners of the voices knew I was here. I had no way to defend myself, just carpenter's muscles and an old dog. I thought of running back down the road to the truck, driving somewhere in search of a sheriff. But anything could happen between now and the time I returned.

An insidious thought crept up on me, familiar and reprehensible. Technically, Birk wasn't my problem. But then, that's what I'd thought about Bobby. Had I learned anything at all since then?

The voices continued undisturbed, and I, realizing there was only one course of action I could live with, moved toward them carefully. This time, my role and Scratch's were reversed. I did the tugging.

We walked a quarter mile deeper into the woods before the voices surrounded us. I still don't know exactly when we stumbled into the grove; maybe the grove engulfed us. Suddenly the trees looked different—unlike anything I'd seen in this forest or any other. They had drooping branches and narrow, silky trunks, a little like aspen or birch. A pale golden haze enveloped them, like sunlight shining through dust. Their leaves were small and slender, as if from miniature willows, exactly matching the ones in Birk's hair.

The boy stood with his back to me. His clothing, including the beloved baseball cap, lay in a neat pile beside him. His leafy hair stood out in otherworldly dreadlocks, and a fine down of leaves ran along his spine from neck to buttocks. He grasped a golden tree trunk with his hands, head thrown back, eyes wide but unseeing, and his whole body shivered as if he were caught in an electrical current. I could hear his teeth clicking, and it looked and sounded horrible.

Before I knew it, I had my hands on Birk's, trying to pry him away from the whispering, luminous tree. A feeling bubbled up through my arms, like a bath of tepid honey, and it kept going. First my shoulders, then my neck, my spine, the tops of my thighs, loosened and warmed. It reminded me of sliding into sleep as a child—that drowsy comfort of blankets in a cold room, the perfect hum of a thriving young body, knowing that Mother is near.

I've never taken any drug stronger than aspirin, except once when I had a tooth out and they gave me nitrous oxide. The part of me that people know as Chet the retired principal with both feet on the ground hates to even think about what happened next, because it sounds so irrational. I never mention it to other people, but privately I take the memory out and relish it now and then. It's important to me, though I still don't understand it completely, and probably never will.

When the warm honey feeling reached my head, I realized that I had become the forest. I felt the movements of every animal and bird and leaf, every rivulet of water; I stood as tall as a mountain and when I looked up I could feel the light of the stars pulsing through me. I dipped into the day of Birk's conception. I watched his human mother make love with the trees in this very grove, lithe, glowing, impossible. "She lived in Benbow a while, you know," I heard Birk say as if from the mouth of a cave. "My tree father says I'm not the only one."

After a while, I realized Scratch was licking my face. I sat up among the ferns, frightened and disoriented. Moisture from the forest floor had soaked through the back of my shirt, and I ached as badly as I had after my first day of framing the house. Birk and his clothes were gone. I dragged myself to my feet, much to Scratch's delight, and made my way back toward the old compound. In the trampled place where Birk's duffel had been, I found a note written in pencil on a scrap of binder paper.

"Dear Chet," it said. "Thanks for trying to help. You can see I have to look for the others. I'll be okay, and I appreciate everything. I'm asking a favor. Please don't follow me. Sincerely, your friend, Birk."

The loneliness of the ordinary young is a terrible thing. For a boy like Birk, it must have been beyond imagining.

I thought about Birk all day, and for many days afterward, wondering if I should have gone after him, or told the sheriff I'd seen him. I mulled it over while Scratch and I fished for smelt on a deserted beach, while I worked alone in my transformed garden, while I methodically cooked dinner for myself and my dog. I wondered where he was, and hoped he was safe. A long time later, I drove back to Benbow and looked for the grove of strange trees, but I never found them. In the end, I kept Birk's secret in return for the gift he gave me: the certainty that life is full of unlikely possibilities.

Not long ago, after a series of regular phone calls, I drove up to my daughter's house in Washington state for a visit. It feels like springtime, like ice is melting, and anything might happen. Who would have thought I'd have Benbow and a boy with leafy hair to thank for that?

INHERITANCES

Different dances to a single tune

The Prism of Memory

by Jo Clayton

Jo Clayton lives in Portland, Oregon with a calico cat named Tigerlily who functions as monitor sitter and a seal point Siamese named Owl who has a habit of levitating into small high places. While listening to the rain and laughing at the cats, she manages to write science fiction and fantasy novels and a few short stories.

One summer day when Jenny was four, she put the sandwiches her mother had made for her lunch in the pocket of her dress, took the thermos with the milk in it, crawled through the hole the dog dug under the back fence, and went into the Forest.

A squirrel went rippling along the ground, and she trotted after it.

When it scrambled up a tall scraggly pine and disappeared into a hole, she stopped to look round. She was in a small glade with a pool not much bigger than a bathtub but round like a silver dollar. And there was a big old rock taller than she was and covered with moss. It had two deep holes like eyes and a crack for a smiling mouth, and the moss was like short green hair.

Jenny put the thermos down and curtsied to the boulder. "Grandma Mossy," she said. "You have a very nice house."

The tree rustled at her with that whisper pine needles make.

"Aunt Piney, I di'n't forget you, but I di'n't know it's your house, too."

She took the crushed and grubby sandwiches from her pocket, shared bits of them with the boulder and the tree and poured a little milk in the boulder's mouth crack and on the pine tree's roots. She was a lonely child. The house on the edge of the forest was miles from the nearest farm and even farther from the small town that was the shopping center for the area. When her mother wasn't painting or on the phone to her agent, she played wonderful games with her, read to her, or just talked with her, but those times were scattered among the many more days when her mother's smile was there only because she forgot to take it off and her eyes had a glaze that told Jenny she was only seeing what was on the inside of her head.

Grandma Mossy smiled at her and her hole eyes squinted with good humor as the sun shifted the pattern of shadow. Aunt Piney rustled her needles in a friendly, chatty way. The sun was warm and the clumpy grass next to the pond was soft and warm and it was time for her afternoon nap. Jenny yawned, curled up and went to sleep.

She woke to the ripple of music, sat up, rubbing her eyes, prepared to be afraid. She saw a small goatboy on the far side of the pond. He grinned at her and lifted a funny thing like a harmonica made of twigs and played a giggle for her. She hugged her arms close to her chest because it was beginning to get chilly out here, then giggled back at him.

He played some more and a white doe came from the shadow under the trees. She circled the pool, touched her nose to the hand that Jenny held out to her, then she walked a few steps away, turned her head and fixed her brown eyes on Jenny. As clearly as if the doe had said the words, she heard in her head, *It's time to go home.*

She went to the pool often that summer, chatted with Aunt Piney and Grandma Mossy, shared her lunch with them, played with the goatboy, and watched in awe and wonder as a golden man with branching antlers danced with a pure white woman. The man wore brown heavily encrusted with embroidery and a long brown velvet cape lined with gold satin. The woman wore a white silk dress embroidered in silver. Her hair was her cape, ice white, long, and fine enough to float on air.

They were wild and strange and made the hair stand up on Jenny's arms, but they were also eerily lovely and touched that hunger for beauty she'd gotten from her mother.

The woman beckoned to Jenny, calling her to join the dance, but she was shy and shook her head.

The summer when Jenny was six, the Man came to live with them. He had shaggy brown hair and a roar of a laugh that made everyone who heard it laugh with him. He made Jenny nervous, but she didn't know why until she saw his eyes never joined the laugh. And she started to hate him when she saw her mother glowing with happiness and letting her paint go dry while he wheedled money out of her and bought things they didn't need.

Fall came and her mother's eyes went absent again. She started spending most of her days and sometimes much of the night in her studio. The Man grew restless. He bought a gun and went hunting in the forest and shouted at her mother when she wouldn't clean and cook the game he brought back.

He threw the dead things outside the back fence and they rotted. The stink they gave off came into the house, and Jenny felt that rotting, too. She went still and silent like a killdeer chick, hoping that if she stayed hidden the danger she sensed but didn't understand would walk past and miss her.

The Man came round the kitchen table, bent over Jenny's mother, and whispered to her. His face was red and there was a sheen of sweat on his skin. Jenny could hear the urgency in his whisper even without knowing the words he said.

Her mother pushed her plate away, shook her head.

He whispered longer, caught hold of her hand, and nuzzled it.

She pushed him away and got to her feet. "Not tonight, Ned. The dance figure isn't working. I've got to find something else to balance and comment on the blue flow."

His face closed in. It was a minute before he found his usual smile. "Ah, you did warn me, Elena."

He came back in the kitchen and watched Jenny as she stood washing the dishes. After a minute, he pulled her away from the sink. "If your mother won't, you'll do."

The pool was bright and silver in the moonlight. Jenny grabbed a handful of grass, tore off the old dress which was the first that had come to her hand, plunged into the chill clean water and scrubbed at herself, trying to scrub away the smell of the Man.

The water went very cold; it numbed her and seemed to push away the bad thing that had happened. When she was shivering so hard she couldn't stand up, she crawled out, wrapped the dress around her and lay beside Grandma Mossy, sobbing out her fear and outrage. "If I tell, he'll kill us both like he kills the squirrels and things. He said it. He said it lots of times. He's going to do it again. He said I was pretty and sweet and soft. He said he knew I wanted it. He said I wasn't like my mother. He's going to do it again."

The goatboy came and patted her shoulder, then played her a song on his pipes that started soft and ended fierce. She heard the promise in it and lay still.

Cold touched the back of her neck. It was the white doe, nuzzling her. Beyond her, on the far side of the pond, the horned man stood. He lifted his head, opened his mouth, and cried out without sound at all, yet Jenny heard the terrible wild sound of it. Then he went away.

Aunt Piney rustled. The sound comforted her, it was so homey and ordinary. Clutching the dress around her shoulders, she got to her feet, looked down into Grandma Mossy's deep dark eyes, and drew a long breath. She didn't say anything more, just put on the dress and started home through the forest, her hand on the shoulder of the white doe.

The Man went hunting in the morning and he didn't come home that night. He never came back.

At the end of the summer when Jenny was twelve, she came sad and angry into the Forest. She spread out a dishtowel on the grass and set out the picnic she'd made for herself. Grave and silent, she broke off bits of sandwich and laid them on Aunt Piney's roots and in front of Grandma Mossy, then she poured a dollop of lemonade on the bits, gave another to the pool, the ritual she'd followed through the years though she no longer really believed in it.

She poured lemonade into the thermos top, sipped at it, then sat holding the cool silver cup in her hands. "I'm going away," she said. "Mother says I have to. I'm supposed to live with my father back east and go to school there. She says I should go on with my clay stuff and I can't do that here. I think she's just tired of having me around, not that she really notices me much. Jake says I can learn by myself, but she tells him to shut up, he just fools with words, he doesn't know what he's talking about when it comes to working with his hands. Well, that's true. He can't sharpen a pencil without nearly cutting his finger off. But he's a good guy. He teaches me things and doesn't fuss. I don't even know my father. I'm afraid he won't like me."

The afternoon was hot and dry and very still. Once or twice she heard a snatch of birdsong and the bark of a fox, but they were far off and very faint. The boulder was only an old rock with patches of drying moss, the pine tree was only an ordinary tree, the pool had dust on the surface and a spiral of tiny black bugs buzzing around it. She finished her sandwiches, drank the last of the lemonade, cleaned up after herself, and went away.

When Jenny was thirty-two, Jake hired a private detective to find her, then paid her way so she could come back for her mother's funeral. Twenty years since she'd seen the house, twenty years since she'd heard a word from her mother. She'd heard about her, at least after she walked out of her father's life, seen her on TV, read about her in magazines and newspapers, but never heard a word from her.

Hard years.

Stupid years.

Coming back here showed her just how stupid they were, all the days she'd wasted looking for ... something. ...

She stopped thinking. It was one thing she was really good at, not thinking.

Jake had almost vanished behind bushy white whiskers and eyebrows fibrous as dead lichen. His eyes were red with grief, but when he looked at her, they turned cold. After the funeral and the session with the lawyer, he drove her to the house and took her inside. She didn't want to go into her mother's studio, but he took her by the arm and walked her there. "Your mother wanted this," he said. "I would've let you go to hell your own way."

There was dust on everything which told her more than anything else how long a time her mother had spent dying. "It was her sent me away."

He walked to a corner of the room to the slotted case where her mother kept her drawing portfolios, counted along the slots, and drew out a shabby black folder. "Because your father threatened to haul the both of you to court and get her declared unfit; there was me and the other men and what happened the time Ned disappeared, she knew how fighting it would turn out." He fished in the slot, drew out a sealed envelope, brought both across the room and set them on the palette table. "She wrote to you every day the first year. Not a word from you. Then she said 'if she wants to talk to me, she knows where I am.' You know her, she put the hurt away and went on with her work."

"I never got any of those letters."

"Ah." He brushed at his eyes, turned away. "Even so," he said, not looking at her. "Even so, you should have written at least once."

"I did. I took the letters down and gave them to the clerk to mail; that's what you did in that place. I took them myself. I didn't trust him. He must have paid off the clerk. He wouldn't let me go out by myself, he said the streets were too dangerous." She sighed. "In a way he was right. When I left. . . ." She picked up the letter, looked at it, saw the blob of red wax and impression from the goatboy seal she'd made her last summer here. She set it down as if it burned her fingers.

"You should have come back here."

"Yeah. Well."

Jake had scrubbed down her mother's room, got it ready for her. He was staying in town these days. Shrugged when he told her. Said it just seemed the best thing to do.

Because she couldn't deal with the stench of sickness that lingered in that room, she cleaned out her own and lay staring at the stains on the ceiling whose patterns she'd never forgot. Same old bed, grown too short for her now. Smells of ancient turpentine and oils. Her mother was a practical woman in unexpected ways and had used this room to store paint cans and old easels. It was like trying to sleep in the middle of ghosts.

The light from the full moon came in through curtains held together by cobwebs and dust; it fell across the bed, across her face. Her mind went round and round. Round and round like a squirrel in a wheel. Round and round and getting nowhere.

She left the bed and wandered about the house. It seemed smaller than she remembered. The long narrow kitchen was full of light now and dancing shadows as the wind fluttered the leaves on vines that had grown across several of the windows. She opened the door to the studio and looked in, decided she didn't want to go in there and wandered into the small living room with the fireplace that took up half a wall. Her room was on the other side of that fireplace. Winter nights she pushed her bed against its backside and snuggled against the warm bricks.

She only had the one black dress she'd worn for the funeral, so she went into her mother's room, opened the closet, and pulled out what came to hand, a pair of ancient twill slacks, one knee torn, smears of dried paint stiffening the folds, an even older sweater and a pair of boots worn so limp she didn't know if she could get her feet in them. She threw the clothes on the bed and it was like standing by her mother's coffin, looking down at her before they closed the lid and sent her to the fires, seeing the strong bones that were always there though never quite so stark as now with the masking flesh gone from between bone and skin.

She remembered her mother as a big woman, with broad shoulders, heavy hips and big strong hands that were always gentle and always smelling of oil and turpentine. Usually a bruise on a thumbnail where she hit it with the hammer when she was building one of her stretchers. Pencil smudges on her fingertips and along the resting side of the hand. And charcoal smudges everywhere.

She pulled the sweater over her head. The shoulders were all right, but the arms were too long and the body hung in bunches about her narrower torso. On her way out she passed through the kitchen to collect the bottle of wine she'd seen in the refrigerator. She found an unbroken wineglass, rinsed it out, and dried it with a forgotten dishtowel drawn through the towel loop beside the sink.

The pool glimmered like molten silver. She'd tried so often for that particular effect in her glazes, never remembering where she'd first seen it. "Easy for you," she said, and laughed until she heard a too familiar edge to the sound and broke it off.

The old boulder was smaller than she remembered, but the eyes and the smile were still there. The pine tree had got taller and scragglier, but the rustle of its needles was as welcoming as ever.

Creakier in the joints now than she'd been as a child, she bowed to them both, gave them a libation from the wine bottle, and added a dollop for the pond, the small ritual bringing back a flood of memory. Wishing she'd brought a blanket as the chill rose into her bones, she settled on the dew-damp grass and poured herself half a glass of the wine. Before she drank, she lifted it to the moon floating overhead through shreds of cloud. "To dreams and madness."

She emptied the glass, set it beside her. "I wasn't a drunk, in case you think that's what this is about. It wasn't cool, being a drunk. You know, I must have damn good genes. I'm still alive. Maybe broke. Maybe thirty years wasted. Maybe the guy I thought loved me kicked me out when I started getting straight. That's a hoot, isn't it. Long as I was a mess, he adored me. But I'm still alive."

Legs drawn up, arms crossed on her knees, she sat gazing into the mirrored water, watching the face of the full moon glide slowly across it, remembering her mother.

Remembering how desperately she'd loved her. How much she'd wanted her approval. How sad she'd been when her mother's absorption in her painting took her so far away in mind, if not in body.

She thought about the portfolio of sketches Jake had given her. Hundreds of them, some of them finished drawings in the minimal style of her mother's early period, achingly lovely, simple lines, some of them quick studies that were barely more than scrawls on scraps of paper. All of them her. As a baby, a toddler, a young girl. Her. Yet she'd never posed for her mother, not once. And the ones that touched her most deeply were the messy, labored sketches from her mother's last days, attempts the dying woman had made at extrapolating the adult from the child.

She cried a little, more for herself than her mother. And for all the wasted years. The stupid years.

"Maybe Jake was right," she said. "Maybe I should have come home long ago. Maybe a lot of dross would've been cleared away. Maybe not. The mess I was. . . ."

She leaned on the boulder; it was warm against her back like bricks of the fireplace. "Grandma Mossy." She smiled. "Jake's the writer," she said, her voice drowsy and dragging a little with weariness. Above her, pine needles rustled a gentle reproof. "Aunt Piney. Well, if you don't mind, why should I."

All her mother's money, more than she'd expected actually, was in trust to the land. A lot of land. An old grant the lawyer said. *Your great-grandfather got firm title through Congress. I wish I knew how. It's yours now, along with the income from the trust. You have to live in the house for five years, though, and if you sell any land, the trust money stops immediately and the remainder of the grant goes to the Nature Conservancy.*

Through half-closed eyes she watched starlight glitter on the wind-wrinkled water of the pool. "I own you. Isn't that funny."

She'd been furious then, feeling trapped, wanting to scratch and bite, wanting to go on a tear that would make the tears she'd been on before she'd gotten clean look like the games of a child. Her hands had curled into claws.

The lawyer wouldn't meet her eyes and fidgeted nervously with the papers on his desk. She chuckled a little when she remembered how uneasy he was, how relieved when she left. Stupid man. What did he expect? That I'd jump him and bite his throat out?

This place was doing it again. The anger was draining out of her, the urgencies, the need to move and keep moving so something . . . whatever . . . wouldn't catch up with her. She drowsed for a while, aware of the sounds of the night but not really there to notice them until a thread of music came from the shadow under the trees, breathy, simple music, clear and clean as drops of water falling on water. She sat up, aware that Grandma Mossy had grown warmer behind her.

On the far side of the pond a golden man with antlers branching from his head danced with a pure white woman, gliding and turning in time with the music. The man smiled at her and held out his hand as if to say "come join us." They turned and the woman held out her hand and beckoned with a sinuous graceful gesture.

Jenny rose, walked round the pond, and stood while they moved round her, touching her. The woman's hand was cool and smooth, ivory rather than flesh, the man's hand was golden brown like polished oak, cool and smooth. Their eyes were cat eyes, shiny and shallow; their faces up close were even more beautiful than she remembered, but stranger now, eerier. As she moved into the dance, their smell enveloped her, musky and wild, their breath was sweet on her face. . . .

She woke stiff and chilled when the morning sun touched her face. Groaning as her body protested every twitch, she pushed up, sat yawning and rubbing her eyes. A sometime breeze teased at her hair, sent wisps tickling across her face. It was going to be a warm day.

An emerald dragonfly darted in zags across the pond, eating the small black biters swarming there. Somewhere a long way off a bird sang a few notes alone, then another joined it, another and another.

There was a rustle in the brush and weeds at the far side of the glade. In the shadow under the trees, she caught a glimpse of a pointed face, a glint of sunlight on black glass horns. She got to her feet, bent, and picked up the wineglass and the bottle. When she straightened she looked down at Grandma Mossy. "Don't worry. I understand now. Mother may be gone, but I'm here and I know what to do."

Feeling the Forest come alive around her, she moved briskly along, thinking of breakfast and how much cleaning the house needs. Go into town. Pry money out of the lawyer. Order supplies. Buy a car. See a contractor to dig a ripening pit for clay under the studio and reinforce the floor so it would hold the weight of a kiln. A backup generator. She remembered poles going down, lines breaking when limbs fell across them. They wouldn't have gotten better, just older.

She was whistling a cheerful tune and almost running by the time she left the shadow of the trees.

The Force That Through the Green Fuse

by Mark Kreighbaum

Mark Kreighbaum has published short fiction and poetry in a number of anthologies and small press magazines. He and Katharine Kerr are collaborating on the science fiction novel, Palace, *due out from Bantam in 1996.*

She dreamed of Yggdrasil again, of the father of forests.

Again, she hung by the neck from an ash limb of Yggdrasil. A spear pierced her side. The pain was immense, worse than anything she had ever endured in the waking world. Ratatosk scurried close, carrying the dragon Nidhogg's insults to the noble unnamed eagle in the crown, his endless task. His presence frightened away the crows that tormented her.

"Help me," she said to the squirrel. It had taken many dreams before she learned that she could speak. Every word cost spikes of pain in her throat.

Ratatosk paused, his great red eyes alight with mischief.

"Do you know the First Rune, my lady?"

"No." Always the same question, the same taunt. "Teach me, please."

"Fool. You sip at the well of the world and tell me you are thirsty."

"Please." She wept. Her throat burned as if she were swallowing shards of glass. "Oh, please, dear Ratatosk."

The squirrel cocked his huge gray face at her.

"You are the daughter of Odin, lady. Too great a matter for the likes of me." His voice seemed slightly regretful, and that was new. She allowed herself to hope, a little. Ratatosk climbed closer to her. She could smell his breath, sulfurous from his journeys under the world where dragons gnawed at the roots of Yggdrasil. His red eyes were echoes of the flames of his dragon masters. "But I have never been called 'dear' before. It has a fair sound. A fair sound, indeed."

"You're my only friend, Ratatosk." And she meant it, in the waking or dreaming world alike.

"Ah, you *are* a miserable fruit, then, hanging so friendless on the Tree."

"Will you teach me?"

"Dream deeper, poor fruit. Teach yourself."

"I don't understand."

"Neither did the All-Father. But nine years of hanging taught him much. Farewell, fair fruit. Do not despair. The Twilight comes, I am told." With a high mocking laugh that shook the leaves, Ratatosk departed on his eternal errand.

"No! Please come back. Don't go. Don't go."

But it was too late. She hung in silence, within sight of burning Bifrost, the rainbow bridge of the gods, alone with her agony.

Clare awoke to a coughing fit and pressed her fingers to her throat until it subsided. She was always surprised that no rope encircled her neck.

"You all right, honey?" Her husband reached over to touch her. She flinched.

"I'm fine." She pushed his hand away and got out of bed before he could reach again. The bedroom was dark, but she could guess his expression—bewildered hurt. She'd seen it often enough these days. She wrapped herself in her bathrobe. "I'll make breakfast."

"You don't have to—"

"I'm working late tonight," she said. "Don't wait up."

He muttered something. Clare waited, ready to fight, but he didn't push the matter. He never pushed.

The classroom was empty. She liked it this way, just before classes started. Clare had her lesson plan open before her on the desk, but she wasn't really reading it. After twelve years of teaching English to seventh graders, she could recite whole chapters of *The Grapes of Wrath* by heart. In any case, today was scheduled for tests, a simple matter of passing out papers and watching for cheats.

Clare went to the window to water the plants there, thyme, lilac, and sage and others. One of them was a cactus, given to her by her sister for her birthday. She'd called it Yggdrasil in the birthday card. She wondered what Gail would say if she knew that her older sister was having nightmares about the mythical Yggdrasil. Probably insist that she see a psychiatrist. That would be the smart thing to do. But Clare couldn't do it. Lately, she'd begun reading every book she could find on Norse myths, the legends of Asgard, the Eddas. They all came to her like echoes, as if she had heard them sung to her long ago. Gail would never understand.

Clare stared out the window of the classroom. Spring was struggling with the end of another Minnesota winter. Frost clutched the fields outside the school, and snow scarred the ripple of forest on the horizon. She remembered all the camping trips into those woods that she, Gail, and her father had made when they were young. The forest held endless treasures, but they were also a green curtain guarding secrets. It had been many years since she'd spent time in the forest her father had taught her to love.

Someone knocked on the door and opened it. Terence Finch, the physics teacher, sauntered in.

"Jesus, Clare, why are the lights off?" He flipped them on. Banks of fluorescents flickered into life with a hum and a snap.

"They give me a headache," she said. She put away the watering can. "What do you want?"

He shut the door. His face had the sallow look of a man who spends too much time indoors and the cruel light of the fluorescents only emphasized his pallor. Still, he had a good body, the legacy of his years in the Marines. He shoved his hands in his pockets and shrugged.

"Well, I just wondered if we were still on for tonight?"

He grinned. It wasn't exactly a leer, but close enough to make her muscles tense. Clare's hands clenched into fists. How had she gotten involved with him again? How could she have been such a fool?

"No. I have errands to run. And Dave is expecting me home early tonight."

Finch slumped a fraction.

"Oh. Okay. No problem." He flashed another grin at her, but this one was nicer, somehow. "You okay, kiddo? Never see you smile these days. Anything I can do?"

"Terry ..." She stared at him. *Can you teach me the First Rune?* Clare felt a flare of bitterness and hurt. It prompted her to say something she'd been putting off for too long. "We have to stop seeing each other."

"What? But why? Does your husband suspect, or something?"

Clare sighed. "No. And it wouldn't matter if he did."

"Then why? Have I done something wrong?"

"Wrong?" She heard her own voice, the edge of sarcasm that she was never able to fully sheath. Lately, she didn't seem to want to. "I don't know. Do you consider adultery wrong, Terry? Hm?"

"Now wait a minute, Clare. You were the one who wanted to—"

"Just go, Terry."

"Can't we talk about this?"

"There's nothing to say." Clare stared him down. His face took on the same look of bewilderment that Dave showed most of the time when they fought. She wanted to hurt him, as if he were the eagle that lived in the crown of Yggdrasil and she the bearer of insults from the dragons gnawing the roots. But she held back, barely. "You better go."

He scowled, but was there also a glimmer of relief in his expression? She thought there might be. He shut the door softly behind him.

Soon after, the first period kids started to arrive. She handed out the tests—a quiz on parts of speech. Then she settled behind her desk and watched the children work. She didn't expect to catch any cheaters. They knew better than to try anything on her. She knew all the tricks.

After a few minutes, though, her mind wandered back to the dream. For four months, she'd been suffering the same nightmare, since she and Dave had come back from visiting her mother over Christmas. She and Gail were her only family, and though all three lived within an hour of one another, they seldom came together. Her mother had been so sad, losing Daddy just before the holidays like that. She could see her, gray hair uncombed and eyes always restless, trying too hard to make conversation. Gail had spent most of her time bragging about her new therapist and flirting with Dave.

It had been a miserable vacation. Clare fought with everyone. Dave kept trying to make peace, and her mother fussed over Gail constantly.

Since that vacation, Clare hadn't been able to keep her temper under control, as if a dam of fury had burst in her heart. She kept hurting Dave whenever he tried to help, and she hadn't spoken to her sister in months. She'd started up with Finch again. She couldn't bear to let Dave touch her—

"Mrs. Lenahan?"

Clare came alert with a start. One of the boys—Simon Cherney, last row, third seat—had his hand raised. Frail, with black hair, he reminded her of a crow.

"Yes? What?" She looked around the room. The children were all staring back. She glanced at the wall clock and felt a chill. The period was nearly over. She'd lost track of herself for almost an hour. "Is everyone done?" They all nodded, too solemn. It took an effort for her to keep her voice steady. "Please pass your papers forward."

After the tests were returned, most of the students rushed out ahead of the bell, but Simon hesitated. He hung back by the window, as still as the trees framed in the glass behind him, and in a sense, further away. Clare had to wrench her stare from the view of the woods.

"Yes?" The boy reacted to her tone as if he had been slapped. Clare was ashamed. She softened her voice. "What is it, Simon?"

But whatever he had been about to say, the moment was lost. He mumbled something and fled.

The rest of the day dragged on. Clare lowered the blinds over the windows. She caught Maryanne Cray copying during third period and was proud of herself for not screaming at the girl. Instead, she sent her to the principal's office with a calmly worded note.

The parking lot was filled with cars, their exhaust pluming in the air, as parents came to pick up their children. The battered yellow buses were also loading students. Shouts and squeals filled the air like soprano thunder. Clare moved quickly to her car, hoping to get out ahead of the buses before they clogged up the two narrow access roads. While she was cranking the old Escort's engine, she chanced to see Simon again. He was getting into a station wagon, driven by a man, his father if the raven black hair was any indication. His father leaned toward him, resting one large hand on the back of the boy's thin neck.

Just then, someone knocked on her driver's side window and she whirled around, eyes wide. She reached into her pocket and her hand closed around the handle of the knife she always carried with her. But it was only Finch out there, bundled up against the chill of April in Minnesota. She rolled the window down part way.

"Hey there," he said. She was about to snap something at him, but he held up a gloved hand. "No, look. I thought about what you said. We did agree it was just a temporary thing. It's okay. Just wanted you to know, I'm not going to give you a hard time about it, like before. Friends?" He reached a glove through the partly open window. For a moment, the briefest moment, she saw herself stabbing him through his palm, creating stigmata. Instead, she unclenched her fingers from the hilt of the knife and reached up to shake his hand. He smiled and left. Clare sat in her car for a long time, trembling.

The air around Yggdrasil was filled with flakes of snow. They kissed her cheeks, leaving icy tears. Clare wondered if she could die from the pain in this dream, but the thought brought no fear, only a vague curiosity. It wasn't the pain that frightened her so much as the loneliness. At least Ratatosk would speak to her now.

The squirrel sat back on his haunches and regarded her with his crimson eyes. He chased the crows away with absent flicks of his great tail.

"Do you know the tale of Skadi?" he asked.

"Sure. She went to Asgard to revenge her father's death and found a husband instead."

"Foolish fruit." But his voice was not unkind. "That is not her tale, but only the glance of it."

"What do you mean? I don't understand. Please tell me why I'm here, dearest Ratatosk. Please."

"Poor ornament. Do you know the First Rune yet?"

Clare tried to recall the story of Odin's winning of the runes. All her studies in the waking world seemed infinitely far away. More and more, it was only Yggdrasil that mattered. It was hard to think as the rope twisted against her throat and the spear bit into her side like a serpent. There were eighteen runes. Runes for unlocking, unbinding, for confounding witches, but what was the first?

"Help," she remembered abruptly. "Help is the First Rune."

"So it is," said Ratatosk. "Wisdom is an empty bowl, until filled with need." And with that the squirrel whisked away up the trunk of Yggdrasil.

"Don't go! Please don't go. Don't leave me alone. Don't leave me." Her voice rasped like a knife against bark. "Please don't leave me."

But he was gone.

She fell silent at last. A great peace stole over her. Snow continued to fall until she was cloaked with it. She watched the crows, the fragile crows, dance above the flames of Bifrost.

Dave was waiting in the kitchen for her the next morning. He was making breakfast. She sat on one of stools by the counter and watched him. Skinny and tall, his graying hair fell to his shoulders in a tangle. His hair was the exact color of Ratatosk's fur.

"You'll be late for work," she said.

He turned away from the pan in which he was clumsily scrambling eggs. His face was so open. She remembered how she had loved the clarity of his expressions, and even now the honesty of him pierced her, like a spear.

"I called in sick," he said. "I want us to talk, Clare. I want to help."

Help, she thought. *The First Rune.*

"I have to be at school early. I didn't finish grading the tests."

"Please, Clare. Let me help."

"There's nothing wrong."

He stared at her, then turned back to the eggs. Without looking at her, he spoke softly.

"I talked to your sister last night. I told her how worried I've been about you. She told me about your father, Clare, and those trips to the woods. She made me promise not to tell you that I knew, but I can't keep that promise." Dave's voice started to shake. "There was nothing you could have done, honey. It wasn't your fault. Gail doesn't blame you—"

"Is this some kind of nineties male nurturing bullshit?" She jumped off the stool. Her fists were clenched at her side. The nails dug into her palms. "It's none of your business."

He faced her. "I love you, Clare. God, I love you. Things haven't been so good between us, but I'm your husband. Please let me try to help."

"Help? What are you going to do, build me a time machine so I can save my sister from that bastard? That's the only help I want from you. If you can't do that, then I don't need it."

"Maybe some kind of counseling—"

"That's everybody's answer for everything, isn't it?"

"It's been good for Gail. She thinks it would be good for you, too."

"Just leave me alone, Dave. I don't need you."

He spread his hands in a gesture of helplessness. She hated him for not being angry. She hated him for just standing there, loving her.

"Don't wait up," she said, and left.

She didn't go to school.

Instead, she drove aimlessly, following the tree line out away from everything, driving as fast as the old Escort could go.

After hours of skirting the verge of the forest, she surrendered to it. She found the old deer track her father had used so often to take them, like secrets, into his green home. Soon, she was parked on the hill her father had named Asgard, looking down on her childhood joy and horror.

She sat in the car, staring out at the expanse of cottonwoods, and farther away the sweep of maple, elm, and ash that cloaked the rolling hills. A majestic rack of storm clouds crowned the forest.

She leaned forward and squinted through the windshield. There was a tree out there that was huge, with branches that reached impossibly high into the clouded sky. It was an ash. She was sure of it.

Clare left the car by the side of the road with its doors open and the key in the ignition. She entered the forest without looking back.

She slogged through sloughs, her eyes marking the frogs and wood thrushes. She recognized box elder, jewelweed and sweet flag and the seedlings of silver maple and hackberry under the cottonwoods. Somewhere, a wood duck squealed and she heard the warbling call of a vireo. Her father had taught her all the names of things, showed her the nests, found the hidden treasures. He had made her love the forest as much as he did. She stumbled through the trumpet creeper, tears blurring her vision. Gail had hated the father-daughter trips, but Clare always convinced her to come. How could she have failed to hear Gail's silence and fear? How could she have been blind to the lantern in the night? Had she really not known that those cries were not owls? And if she had known, if she had allowed herself to know, what then? The forest and her father would have been lost. And Gail. Gail was always his favorite.

It took a long time for her to find the ash she'd seen from the road. It rose, straight and tall as a column and its bole was dozens of feet wide. She knew instantly that this was no ordinary tree. Slender green ash saplings grew around it like pale children. Its top was hidden in the lowering sky. She reached out a hand to touch the ancient bark of the trunk. A gray squirrel chittered at her from a nearby clump of bur cucumber.

"Ratatosk?" she murmured. The squirrel cocked its head at her and skittered away.

Sinuous vines of trumpet creeper grew thick all around. Clare put her hand in her pocket and found the knife that she had almost used on Terry. She spent a sweaty hour hacking vines free until she had enough to weave into a rope. Then she went hunting for a piece of wood that could be whittled into a spear.

The storm clouds had begun to send a warning drizzle when she was finally ready to climb. She'd always been an excellent climber. The ash gave her few holds, but she was patient and determined. Scattered drops of rain had begun to fall by the time she found a branch. She rested there, trying to decide whether to climb higher. A grim little smile touched her lips. Maybe the eagle was waiting in the crown. The great noble eagle was fated to suffer the insults of Nidhogg the dragon until Ragnarok, the Twilight of the Gods, released him. She wanted to see him, just once.

She kept climbing, the spear tied to her back with the vine rope. The intermittent rain mingled with the tears on her face.

Time passed. She couldn't tell how much because the driving rain had stolen away the sun. Her arms ached and trembled with strain and still the top of the tree remained out of sight, unreachable.

Clare slumped into a wedge between the trunk and a branch and let the storm drive into her and wash the scrapes and cuts that covered her hands and face. Her clothes stuck to her skin.

Her mind brought back the memory of the day many years ago when her sister told her the truth about the camping trips. They were in the garden section of some supermarket and Clare was showing off by naming all the plants, when Gail broke down, screaming. And the worst of it was that Clare guessed the reason almost before Gail said it aloud. Clare had always known, somewhere.

Clare realized that her throat was raw from screaming. For a long time, she simply crouched against the trunk of the tree, shaking, unable to weep.

At last, she took out her vine rope and began to fashion a noose. She wasn't sure how she would manage the spear, but she'd think of something. Her father had taught her so much. The ground below was lost in the storm's darkness.

"Even Loki did not go willing to the stone."

Clare looked up and saw a shadowy bulk perched a few feet away on the branch. The figure blinked red eyes as large as plates.

"Ratatosk?" She smiled. "Ratatosk, my friend."

"Do you feel the waters of Urd, precious fruit? The Norns have come." The great squirrel let out a mocking sigh. "Recall the tale of Skadi, little one. She surrendered revenge for love, but failed to keep her husband close."

"What do you mean? Oh, please, dear Ratatosk, no more riddles."

"Very well, my lady. Did you believe that Odin won Help, and all the others, for his own solitary glory? Do you believe the master teacher desired no students?"

"I don't—"

"What use is wisdom, unless shared?" Ratatosk's flaming eyes steamed in the rain. His voice was cold. "You are not alone on the Tree, lady. But you, at least, have won the runes."

Before she could reply, Ratatosk leaped up and vanished into the upper branches. Faintly, his voice came to her.

"The dragon hates the eagle, because the eagle does not hate him."

Clare stared up after Ratatosk. Her last and best friend was gone. But at least the crows were gone as well. The crows. That reminded her of Simon. Clare closed her eyes, seeing the boy and the look in his eyes, that broken look.

"Oh, no." It couldn't be. "God, no."

Clare rested her head on her knees. She thought she'd been emptied of tears, but there were some left, after all. Was the boy suffering what Gail had? She didn't know. But she couldn't get his face out of her mind. And Dave's face was there, too. She had left him to hang on another kind of Tree. It was enough to make her consider again all of Ratatosk's words. The teacher must teach. Suffering must be made into meaning. The First Rune. The lesson of Yggdrasil.

After she climbed down from her perch, Clare stood before the tree, soaked by the rain and chilled to the bone. She touched the trunk again with the palm of her hand. The stories said that Yggdrasil cared for all its children and suffered for them.

"I'll try," she whispered.

She left the spear and rope behind, and never again dreamed of Yggdrasil, the father of forests.

My Soul Into the Boughs
A Gothic Tale

by Teresa Edgerton

Teresa Edgerton's most recent book is her eighth fantasy novel, The Moon and the Thorn. *Before she wrote "My Soul into the Boughs," she spent some months reading fairy tales and Victorian horror stories which could account for a certain spookily hybrid quality in her story.*

There are owls nesting in the rafters over her bed. Lying trapped under the covers, her limbs weighted with sleep, Laurel cannot see the birds, but she knows they are there. She can hear a dull fluttering of wings, a harsh scrape of talons on the heavy oak beams, and she can picture the owls vividly in her mind: great white predatory birds with ominous yellow eyes.

At the same time, she realizes there is something very strange about her bedchamber, the broad, pleasant room that appeared so ordinary by daylight—no sign of owls or nests among the rafters then. But now there seems to be a stream running through, a slow, steady trickle of cold water over her feet that is just as unaccountable as it is chilly.

To make matters worse, every time the owls become particularly active, she feels a sharp, painful tug on her scalp, as though the hairs of her head have somehow grown to an incredible length and become entangled with the branching rafters overhead. With a sudden wrenching shock, she realizes all at once that this is literally true: her hair has grown and involved itself with the leaves and branches . . . at the same time that her toenails have anchored her to the footboard.

In a panic, she opens her mouth to scream, but the only sound that emerges is low and tortured, like a creaking of tree limbs during a storm.

"The most extraordinary dream," Laurel tells her grandmother, over the breakfast table. "I actually believed I was turning into a tree. I'm afraid there is something about the position of this house and the way the trees grow in so close, that has made a remarkable and rather unpleasant impression on my mind."

Mrs. Windbourne reaches out with a hand as pale and skeletal as the birches and the aspens surrounding the ancient manor house, and pours herself a second cup of tea. "You find the situation oppressive? It is true we have very few visitors and none of them linger very long. But I hoped you would be different, that you would love the house . . . and the forest as well." Her voice trails away on a deep sigh.

"Because my mother was born here?" Laurel considers that, as she raises her own cup of tea to her lips. She and her grandmother are eating their breakfast in a dim sitting room attached to the old lady's bedchamber. The room is dim because there is no light except a beam of weak sunlight which has somehow managed to creep in through a leaded glass window partly obscured by vines; the sitting room is also damp and smells strongly of earth, but the reason for this is less apparent. In one shadowy corner a blotch of moisture has spread across the wall, under a rogues' gallery of miniature portraits done in oils. To a fanciful mind, an unfocused eye, the irregular stain might appear as a frieze of leering foliate heads, created as an obscure jest on the family pictures.

Laurel, however, is a practical young woman, and she only sees a spot of damp. Besides, she is otherwise occupied, pondering the question at hand: Should she feel some particular affinity to a particular location, merely because her mother and who-knows-how-many of her more distant ancestors were born on the spot? It is not as though her mother ever regaled her with stories about the place, not as though Laurel was reared with any sense that the history of this decaying mansion on the verge of a primeval forest is her own history as well. In fact, her mother never shared any family history or childhood memories with her at all.

"It really is hard to know what I should or shouldn't feel," Laurel says out loud.

And not just about the house, she adds silently. What is she to think, for instance, about the faded little creature in musty, rustling autumn-colored silks, who sits on the other side of the breakfast table, still a stranger for all the ties of blood that bind them? "It is such an amazing set of circumstances, to suddenly discover I have a grandmother I never even knew existed, and in less than a month after that discovery to find myself staying with you here."

Mrs. Windbourne smiles. Despite her great age, her teeth appear very strong and even; it is the strange quality of the light, probably, that gives them a greenish cast. "Laurel dear, you must have suspected there was a grandmother somewhere in your past. Or did you suppose your mother came into existence in anything other than the usual way ... brought forth out of the womb of the earth itself in some monstrous cataclysm, or else ripped out by force like a mandrake root?"

Laurel laughs uneasily, because it is such an odd and improper remark, especially considering the source. She takes another sip of the tea. There are bits of bark floating among the tiny black leaves, and the flavor of the tea is not like anything she has ever tasted before. However, it *smells* of mushrooms and cellars.

"Let us say, then, a grandmother I supposed unalterably estranged and probably long since dead," she amends. "And you never did tell me what my mother did to offend you so badly, that you and my grandfather refused to see her ever again."

Mrs. Windbourne sits up a little straighter in her carved oak chair. The carvings consist of owls and ivy in a highly involved pattern. Laurel wonders if some brief glimpse the night before was the source of her nightmare.

"Is that what your mother told you?" the old woman asks indignantly. "But it was Linnet who turned her back on *us,* who ran away from home after a trifling quarrel and never made any attempt to communicate with any member of the family afterward." She subsides a little, brushes one hand over her eyes. "Perhaps both sides were equally to blame. We were each too proud to even think of making the first move. And now it is too late for your grandfather and for poor Linnet ... but how fortunate that you and I somehow managed to find each other before the end."

It makes Laurel feel hot and uncomfortable under her light summery dress, how frankly the old woman speaks of her own imminent demise. It was one of the first things mentioned in her letter—that remarkable document which arrived so unexpectedly to announce Mrs. Windbourne's existence and her desire for reconciliation—and the spreading cancer was also one of the first things they discussed when Laurel arrived at the house. Under

other circumstances such openness might make everything easier
and more natural, since it frees them both from so many eva-
sions. But again, Laurel is left not knowing how she ought to
feel. Should she grieve for this woman she hardly knows?

*I can grieve, anyway, for the time that has been denied us.
Feel disappointed I have so little opportunity to get really ac-
quainted with her, or to learn how to love her. Life can be so
beastly unfair sometimes!*

"Grandmother, do you feel well enough to go out for a walk
this afternoon?" she asks, on a sudden conciliating impulse. "I
would so like for you to show me the garden and a little of the
forest."

"And I would like that also," Mrs. Windbourne answers. "But
the doctor has warned me against too much air or exertion, and
I doubt I will ever leave these rooms again. However, do please
feel free to wander about as much as you like on your own."

Now Laurel thinks she has caught her grandmother in a lie.
There is a crust of mud on the soles of the old lady's shoes—
Laurel noticed it as soon as she came into the room—and a frail
leaf skeleton caught in the wispy white hair over one ear. It
seems obvious Mrs. Windbourne has already been out for a walk
in the early morning air. But the old woman looks so frail and
tired, the younger one feels a guilty disinclination to call her to
account.

The garden is really nothing more than a patch of overgrown
ground between the back of the house and the ragged edge of the
encroaching woodlands. There is a stable, a thicket, a stagnant
fishpond, and beyond a tumbled drystone wall, what appears to
be a ruined chapel and a graveyard right in among the trees.

The weather is pleasant and not too warm, but everything
looks dull and lifeless: grass, trees, brambles, and a few scrubby
bushes over by the stable—everything limp and sapless. On the
trunks of some birches up ahead, the white bark is peeling off
like tissue paper. The oaks and the elms farther on are already
losing their leaves, and they look ugly in their semi-nakedness,
all contorted into shapes of agony. Laurel wonders if there has
been a drought in this part of the country, or if the forest and the
garden have been infected by some invisible blight. Remembering the dampness inside the house, she decides a drought is out
of the question.

Raising the hem of her white batiste skirt, she climbs through
a gap in the drystone wall and wanders among the gravestones.

One of them, a little taller than the rest and draped in vines that look somewhat greener and fresher, catches her eye, and she bends down to examine the chiseled inscription more closely. "NICHOLAS WINDBOURNE," it proclaims. And below that, in smaller and rounder letters: *"Nicholas Perrin."*

Standing by her grandfather's grave, Laurel again realizes how little she knows of her family history. When and why did her grandfather change his name? It seems an extraordinary, even a slightly disreputable, thing to do. *Like a man with a secret,* she muses.

At this moment, something sharp pierces her ankle. Glancing down and lifting the hem of her skirt a chaste few inches off the ground, Laurel discovers she has somehow blundered into one of the thorny vines. Her ankle, under its delicate white silk stocking, is scratched and spotted with blood. And now something truly appalling begins to happen: the vine writhes, constricts, and begins to *crawl* up her leg with a sinuous, sensuous movement that is just as indecent as it is terrifying.

Laurel screams, tries to pull away, and in doing so, unintentionally steps backward onto the grave . . . only to learn that the soil there is so soft and so loose that she instantly starts to sink. Within seconds, she is trapped in the devouring earth up to her knees.

But a hard hand catches hold of her shoulder, a strong arm encircles her waist, and someone lifts her bodily out of the grave and deposits her safely on solid ground.

Still gasping, Laurel turns to confront her rescuer.

He is a rough-looking fellow and her first impression is all in shades of brown: shaggy russet hair; tawny face; amber eyes flecked with something darker; a pair of broad shoulders under an earth-colored coat. Further impressions are more complex: He smells of smoke and autumn leaves. He is not much older than she is herself, and rather attractive—in a crude, unfinished sort of way. She likes the way his hand rests at the small of her back, the pressure of one muscular, leather-clad thigh, felt through her skirt and petticoat. He is holding her much too closely.

Before she can act on any of this, he steps back and releases her. Robbed of both her breath and her dignity, Laurel seeks to restore both by smoothing her skirt, tidying her hair. It works tolerably well, and she is finally able to address him with a fair degree of equanimity.

"I suppose I ought to thank you," she says primly.

He regards her solemnly, yet Laurel thinks she detects a flicker of something . . . arousal? . . . curiosity? . . . resentment? . . . in those amber eyes.

"You'll be the granddaughter," he states flatly, in a deep, countrified burr.

Glancing down, Laurel sees that the entrapping tendril of vine has withdrawn, disappeared; could it be that she only imagined its astonishing, provocative behavior?

Feeling once more in control of the situation, she smiles graciously. "Yes, I am Laurel Springer, Mrs. Windbourne's granddaughter. But who are you?"

He waves a square brown hand in the direction of the stable and on toward the house. "Josiah Marten. But you open any window and call out 'Joss.' That usually fetches me."

"Joss, then." Laurel permits her gaze to wander back to the grave. Though she is well on the way to convincing herself that she imagined the vine was making indecent advances, there can be no doubt of what happened afterward. The signs of her mishap are still there, clearly imprinted in the soft dirt, and she can feel the grit inside her shoes. "Perhaps you can tell me just how long it has been since my grandfather *died* and was buried here?"

Young Marten appears to make a quick mental calculation, standing there with his hands in his pockets, the afternoon sunlight bringing out all the colors of autumn in his russet hair. "Must've been twenty, twenty-one years ago," he finally ventures.

This takes Laurel completely by surprise. "Then why," she demands indignantly, "has the earth on his grave been so recently disturbed?"

Joss Marten shrugs a burly shoulder, and this time it is easy for Laurel to identify the expression in his eyes: amusement, tinged with insolence. "Not just the old man's grave," he says. "You want to watch where you go, Miss Laurel. They do say the land around here is unreliable, and you wouldn't be the first pretty girl to get herself eaten alive."

Dinner is served that night, not in Mrs. Windbourne's sitting room, but in the dusty though still magnificent banquet hall on the first floor. This is because, as the housekeeper informs Laurel, her grandmother "took a bad turn" during her afternoon nap and so feels inadequate to rise from her bed.

Determined not to pick up the manners of a rustic, no matter how long she remains in the country, Laurel has dressed herself in a shoulder-baring gown of black satin, fastened a cool string of pearls around her neck. So now she dines in solitary splendor, off cracked china plates weirdly painted with a pattern of carnivorous-looking flowers and nervous butterflies. The food tastes gritty and coarse, and the wine is flavored with berries, leading Laurel to suspect that *she* is sharing the servants' dinner, while Mrs. Windbourne feasts royally on the floor above. Of course, she realizes almost at once that the idea is unworthy and immediately abandons it.

Before she retires for the night, Laurel pays a visit to her grandmother's bedchamber, where Mrs. Windbourne—propped up in bed by numerous pillows and bolsters—receives her in a dingy nightgown and wrapper. In her decaying linens and laces, with her white hair unpinned and frizzled around her face, the old lady already looks like a ghost . . . or a madwoman.

And the bedroom, like the sitting room, smells damp and unhealthy. Laurel wishes she knew her grandmother well enough to take charge and make some changes in the way the household is run, but she is afraid to make any suggestions for fear the old woman will take offense. She does, however, resolve to speak with Mrs. Windbourne's doctor at the first opportunity.

Gingerly taking a seat at the foot of the bed, Laurel listens politely to her grandmother's account of her most recent symptoms: shortness of breath, a sudden giddy sensation, a dull pain in one side where the cancer is growing. For just a moment, Laurel experiences a terrifying impression that *she* cannot breathe either, that something is squeezing all the air out of her chest. But the sensation passes quickly, leaving her shaken yet strangely moved by this unexpected sympathetic reaction to her grandmother's suffering. *Perhaps I am learning to love her after all.*

It is not, however, an experience she wants to repeat. To change the subject, she mentions her visit to the graveyard. "And I was nearly swallowed alive . . . at least, that was how your stableboy described it. A horrid turn of phrase, and I think he was positively enjoying my discomfort."

The old woman chuckles indulgently. "You must excuse poor Joss. Being fatherless and of half-gypsy blood he could hardly be expected to cultivate a polished manner, though he was raised right here in the house. He is not, in fact, a stableboy, and his duties more nearly approximate those of . . . a gardener and gamekeeper."

Here Laurel decides that she does not want to *know* what her grandmother means by "fatherless." So she asks instead about the unstable ground down in the graveyard. "He said that the land was unreliable. What could he possibly mean by that?"

Mrs. Windbourne begins to fuss with the mildewed bed linens. "I believe there are springs and underground streams that are constantly changing course, under the property. What ancient scientists and philosophers must have meant when they spoke of 'a radical moisture.' But you needn't worry. Though the ground does cave in from time to time, no one has actually been killed."

Now Laurel thinks she has learned something interesting about her grandmother, from that phrase about *radical moisture:* the old woman has been reading nasty old books on magic and alchemy, and that would explain some of her more shocking statements.

"I won't worry, then," Laurel answers coolly. "But there is something else that puzzles me. Why did my grandfather change his name from Perrin to Windbourne?"

Her grandmother sighs and settles back against the pillows. "Because the house and the land and all the other property belonged to me. The Windbourne inheritance always descends in the female line. And because we could not marry unless he agreed to take the family name and ... certain obligations ... and pass them on to his own descendents." The old woman smiles, faintly malicious, showing the green teeth. "The Perrin family is nothing. Prosperous yeoman farmers with very little breeding. But the moment I saw Nicholas—so stout and strong and virile as he was—I knew he was the one for me. And as my mother was dying at the time, and my father never could deny me anything, I eventually got him."

"How very interesting," says Laurel, not sounding interested at all. But in fact she is interested, though somewhat repulsed. Because she suddenly realizes that *she* may be heir to all this moldering grandeur ... as well as the unwomanly freedom and independence that seem to be a part of the Windbourne inheritance.

In the morning, Laurel cannot remember her dreams, but she carries a vague, uneasy presentiment through the rest of that day and the days which follow. She is much occupied during that time with nursing her grandmother, who has most decidedly "taken a turn" for the worse.

Mrs. Windbourne's pain is heart-wrenching. And there is really very little that Laurel can do for the dying woman—certainly not anything that the housekeeper and the other servants could not do as well. But her company seems to be particularly wanted, so Laurel spends practically every day from first rising until bedtime at her grandmother's side.

Until one day when the walls of the house begin to feel too close and confining, the sickly, oppressive atmosphere in her grandmother's bedchamber becomes unbearable, and Laurel escapes for a walk in the fresh air. This time, however, she avoids the graveyard, and follows a narrow path leading into the heart of the forest.

The trees are ailing; there is no longer any question about that. Though it is still early summer, the oaks and the elms have dropped the last of their leaves, and the fragile skeletons crunch under her feet as she walks. The birches have shed so much bark, they look raw and vulnerable. And there is a faint odor of decay that reminds Laurel of the sickroom.

The bushes to one side of the path rustle and stir, and Joss Marten appears on the trail about five feet in front of her. Laurel greets him with a catch of her breath, a faint tingling of pleasure—after so many days with the invalid, she is irresistibly drawn to his virile good looks.

But pleasure turns to irritation as he stares at her with dull hostile eyes and growls, "Still here, are you?"

Laurel tosses her head. "And why shouldn't I be here, Josiah Marten? I have been invited to stay for as long as I wish."

Joss shrugs a broad shoulder. What he has been doing off by himself in the forest, Laurel does not like to guess. There are clods of dirt adhering to his clothes, and fragments of leaves and moss in his russet hair. He *looks* as though he has been burrowing under the earth like a rabbit or a badger. "Thought you might have sense enough to go before your grandmother dies . . . you won't find much opportunity afterward."

So . . . Laurel thinks, her mind beginning to whirl with interesting possibilities . . . *it would appear that I* am *the heir. And if I am, he is probably correct: I daresay everyone expects me to take charge at once and get the house in order, and that will certainly be a formidable task.* It is a task, however, which appeals strongly to her passion for organization. *Assuming of course, there is any money left to accomplish all the things that have to be done, that everything here has gone to rack and ruin simply because my grandmother is too old and too ill to care anymore, and not because the family fortunes are decaying along with the house.*

She would like to ask Joss what he knows about this, but of

course it would be improper to discuss her grandmother's finances with one of the servants. Besides, she does not entirely care for the way he is looking at her.

But when she turns aside to take another path, he reaches out with a big rough hand to stop her. "You don't want to go wandering off into the woods alone. There's snakes in them bushes, and spiders, too. And the foxes and the weasels run mad in the hot weather—didn't no one ever tell you that?"

Now Laurel would like to pretend he has not frightened her, but in fact he has, and she cannot entirely conceal her dismay. Although she can just tolerate dogs, cats, and horses, she has an unreasoning fear of brute creation—the kind of fear that leads to panics and to cold sweats—instilled by her mother at an early age, and as for creatures that have too many legs or not enough . . .

She swallows hard, glances back over her shoulder to reassure herself that there are no rabid foxes or weasels anywhere in sight. Yet she manages to keep the panic out of her voice when she speaks. "It is difficult to imagine anything living amidst all this withering. Why are the trees dying . . . or don't you know?"

His hold on her wrist relaxes, his arm drops. "There's a story the old folks tell, but maybe you don't want to hear it."

Laurel gives a false little laugh. "Of course I do . . . though I certainly don't promise to believe everything you tell me."

Again he gives that annoying shrug, again she detects an ambiguous expression in his amber eyes. "Well enough, then, since you insist. In the ancient times, they say, the forest would begin to fade once every thirty, forty years. Then the priests they had in those days would take one of the village girls—she had to be a virgin—and carry her off by force into the woods, where they had built themselves an altar to their heathen gods. Once they had her there . . .'" He makes a quick expressive gesture with one hand across his throat. "They do say, also, that the trees and the beasts and even the earth still remember that time."

Now Laurel is simply furious. *He is deliberately trying to scare me!* Suddenly, a great many things begin to make sense. His questionable antecedents, his being raised right in the house . . . he is undoubtedly some bastard of the Windbournes or the Perrins, and perhaps he is foolish enough to suppose that gives him some claim to the house and the property? It is clear by now, anyway, that he resents Laurel and that he is trying to get rid of her. Perhaps resentful enough to rig up a trap in the graveyard, in order to give his wild pagan stories some credibility?

Enough to start digging another pit somewhere in the forest and to almost get himself caught just now in the very act?

"You are despicable," she tells him, between her teeth. "Utterly beneath contempt." And she turns on her heel and leaves him alone on the forest path.

Much to her relief, he makes no effort to call her back or to follow after her.

Returning to the house, Laurel discovers that Mrs. Windbourne's doctor has *finally* put in an appearance. He is a wizened little man in tweeds and a pair of dark spectacles, not particularly prepossessing, but as he is the first medical man to set foot inside the house since her arrival, Laurel takes him into one of the dim parlors and launches into a detailed account of her grandmother's suffering.

Halfway through the conversation, she realizes that he is not a physician at all—just a country apothecary who dabbles in herbalism on the side. But Mrs. Windbourne, he assures Laurel, will not admit a regular doctor into her bedchamber . . . perhaps because she retains some outdated notions about cupping and bleeding.

"But surely," says Laurel, growing a little desperate, "there is something you can do to make her more easy. She is in so much pain! Laudanum perhaps, or even morphine?"

"No," the apothecary answers with a mournful shake of his head. "Either of these would cloud her mind, and she desires to stay lucid until the very end, no matter the cost in pain and suffering."

At this Laurel feels a twinge of guilt. At the same time, she is deeply moved. It is obviously for *her* sake that Mrs. Windbourne wishes to remain alert and aware, not wishing to waste a single precious moment of their remaining time together. *And I have been too cold and selfish to return the half of her affection.* Yet if she has been cool and distant in the past, she can at least resolve to be warmer and more receptive in the future.

When she goes upstairs to visit her grandmother, a half hour later, Laurel is still feeling chastened. Because of that, she decides not to mention her encounter with Joss Marten down in the forest, decides not to speak of anything that might cause her grandmother the slightest distress.

Laurel comes to herself in the darkness. She cannot see, she can barely breathe. A great stifling weight is pressing her down, and her arms and legs have gone as cold and lifeless as clay.

"I am sorry," says a gentle voice inside her head. "But the forest and I were dying. You must understand, you were the heir, and there was nobody else that was at all suitable."

With a thrill of horror, Laurel understands that she is under the ground. There is dirt in her eyes and in her nose and her mouth; she can hear the dull thud of more clods descending. But a strange thing happens to Laurel: she does not die, she simply changes. Her flesh becomes earth, her bones become roots, her hair grass, her eyes—

Laurel wakes to feel a hard pair of hands dragging her out of her bed, a strong pair of arms lifting her up. For a moment, all is darkness and confusion, mixed with the scent of woodsmoke and autumn leaves, before she begins to comprehend what is happening.

"How dare you, Josiah Marten. How *dare* you accost me in my grandmother's house, my own bedchamber," she rages, struggling in his grip.

But he only laughs and crushes her more painfully against his chest as he carries her out of the room, down a dim hallway, and finally to the top of a long pair of stairs. "You was warned, Miss Laurel, but you was too stubborn to listen. Didn't I tell you that you had to go away while you still could? Couldn't you see plain enough, down in the graveyard, that the forest wanted you? But you, you chose to stay in spite of everything, and that was enough to satisfy the old woman."

Laurel continues to rage and to struggle, but to no avail. And she does not really listen to what he says—or rather, the meaning of his words only penetrate her conscious mind when they finally reach the bottom of the steps and she finds her grandmother waiting there.

Mrs. Windbourne is paler than ever and so unsteady she must lean against the newel post for support, but she is smiling triumphantly.

In that moment, Laurel realizes that her common sense has betrayed her. All this time, she has been trying to come up with rational explanations for the events surrounding her, never stopping to think that the other people involved might be utterly irrational.

"You are simply insane," gasps Laurel, as Joss lowers her to the floor. He allows her to stand on her own feet, but he still keeps a strong grip on both her arms, holding them securely behind her. "Do you really believe that you are dying just because some trees and bushes and vines are withering away at the same time? It is the cancer ... the cancer is killing you, and you can't save yourself by sacrificing *me*."

"I am in full possession of my senses, Laurel dear," the old woman replies calmly. "And of course the cancer is killing me. I told you that myself; you never heard it from anyone else."

Laurel lets out her breath in a long sigh, shakes the hair out of her eyes. "Then what on earth is this all *about?* Why have you sent this man to pull me out of my bed in the middle of the night, and what was that nonsense he was telling me? Maiden sacrifices and the forest wanting me, and my having to make a choice? And why ..." she adds tremulously, because her slightest movement causes Joss to tighten his hold, and she can feel that his fingers are going to leave bruises on the tender inside flesh of her arms. "... why won't he let me go, if nobody means me any harm?"

"As to nonsense," her grandmother answers, "I am afraid that it's all perfectly true. In ancient times, they did shed the blood of the occasional maiden—until a better way was found. Really, my dear, you disappoint me. I was sure you would be clever enough to guess the truth by now. *I* am not dying because the forest is ailing, the forest is dying along with *me*."

Mrs. Windbourne smiles, making an obvious display of the strong green teeth. "And no one means to kill you, Laurel. On the contrary, I mean to confer on you ... a kind of immortality."

The trees are beginning to revive down in the forest. Trees, bushes, vines ... where all was weak and flaccid before, a vital tension has been restored. A pulse of life passes through the earth, leaving a greening world in its wake.

From her vantage point at Mrs. Windbourne's latticed bedchamber window, the woman behind the veil can see it all changing from moment to moment. It is, at the same time, terrible and wonderful to behold.

But when Joss Marten appears down below—unusually neat and precise in a black suit and a white collar—crosses the garden, and slips out of sight again in the vicinity of the entrance to the house, she forces herself to turn away from the window. With a rustle of satin skirts, she glides over to the great four-poster bed and looks down at the body that is lying there.

Death has turned Laurel's grandmother into a wax figure: pure, changeless, serene. No sign remains of her recent suffering. If the signs are to be seen anywhere, they are on Laurel's face behind the veil, as if something passed out of the old woman at the moment of death and into her granddaughter.

There is a light scratching at the half-open door, and in response to Laurel's invitation the housekeeper enters. "Time for you to go down. The guests have all arrived." Her glance slides past the corpse lying on the bed but never quite reaches Laurel. "You wouldn't want to keep them all waiting on such an important occasion."

"Yes, I can hear them."

It would be difficult not to. From the rooms on the ground floor came many sounds: grunting, growling, squeaking, hooting, the occasional scrape of moving furniture, the thud of something carelessly knocked over. Yet Laurel takes a few moments to smooth out the skirt of her pale silk gown, to adjust her white lace veil.

Then, with a mixture of joy and trepidation, she begins the long walk down to the banquet hall where the wedding guests and her bridegroom are waiting.

THE SCARS OF WAR

Echoes in flesh and wood

These Shoes Strangers Have Died Of

by Bruce Holland Rogers

Bruce Holland Rogers has been published in F&SF, Ellery Queen's Mystery Magazine, Quarterly West *and many other periodicals. A story of his, "Enduring as Dust," was nominated for an Edgar. His work has also appeared in a number of antholgies, including DAW's* Witch Fantastic.

Nineteen forty-two was the first summer of the war bond campaign. After the newsreels and before the feature, a government clip showed a Japanese soldier bayoneting a Chinese baby. The voice-over said again and again, "Buy a bond. Kill a Jap. Buy a bond. Kill a Jap."

The rifle with its bayonet rose and fell. People coming out of the theater later would look at me, a young man old enough to shave. Some of them asked me outright why I hadn't enlisted.

"I'll be old enough in September," I'd say.

After the theater was empty, I'd sweep the aisles and then sit in one of the middle seats, the popular ones even on slow nights and matinees. I'd close my eyes and grip the wooden armrests. Beneath my palms the joy and fear and anger and relief that others had felt in this theater moved in the wood grain like a nest of animals, stirring.

Buy a bond. Kill a Jap.

Feelings like a knot you can't begin to untie.

"Kill a Jap. Be a Jap," I said to the curtained screen.

The house I live in now was built to my own design on the north-facing slope of a canyon where the trees grow dense and dark. The first floor is half buried so that the second floor won't rise above the trees, won't too easily reveal the house. To drive here, you must follow a pair of wheel ruts that turn off from the gravel road five miles distant. Unless you know where to look, underbrush hides the way. I stay put in winter. For five months of the year, the snow between house and road lies undisturbed.

On the second floor is a corner room without windows. There's a deadbolt on the door to that room, and a padlock. Inside, a Nazi battle flag hangs on one wall alongside photos of the camps. Black and white photos of the living and the dead. The far side of that wall is devoted to wartime posters of buck-toothed Japanese. There's a photo of me as I was in 1943, a new-minted soldier, posing with fixed bayonet and glaring at the camera as if the lens were Tojo himself.

Buy a bond. Kill a Jap.

The war, my war, is limited to that wall. The other walls are papered with photographs of skulls stacked in Cambodia, bodies swelling in the sun of Burundi or Rwanda, mass graves opened like ripe fruit split wide to spill their seeds. Some of the newspaper images have yellowed. Some are fresh.

Nina, my agent, has seen the locked door, but has never asked what's on the other side. She has other things on her mind. "Build a studio in Boulder or Denver," she says to me twice a year. "You'd be close to the galleries. All of this would be so much *easier.*"

She wants me out of the mountains. If I had a heart attack, a stroke, no one would know unless I radioed for help myself. Park County Rescue would have to travel the same pair of wheel ruts that Nina's hired truck negotiates, spring and fall, when it comes to take my work to the galleries.

"I can hunt deer from my front porch," I tell her. "Could I do that in Denver or Boulder?"

In the closet of the locked room, I keep the shoes, the boots, the uniforms.

The shoes are flattened, sun-cracked—a right shoe hidden among high weeds in El Salvador, a left shoe I stole from Bergen-Belsen, a right that I dug from the rotting mud of Cambodia. Shoes strangers have died of. Shoes that fit me. I only keep the ones that do.

Some of the boots are like the shoes—dry-rotted, split-seamed. The others go with the uniforms, patent leather boots hand-polished until they gleam like black glass.

A full-length mirror hangs on the inside of the closet door.

Several of the uniforms are simple: fatigues of the Ugandan security forces, the Khmer Rouge, Brazilian or Chilean troops assigned to domestic duty. Khaki is interchangeable with tan, with gray, with blue.

It's the black uniform that I prize above the others. It's the black that I dress in to stand before the mirror. On the World War II wall, young men in dress uniforms like this one smile easy smiles.

I smile their smiles for the mirror, feeling what is natural to feel in such a uniform. Invincibility. Pride. The twin lightning bolts on the collar have everything and nothing to do with history. The death's head in the band of the cap is timeless.

To my smiling reflection, I say, "What are we to do with you? What is to be done?" The question is no abstraction. It's a practical matter. It's the question I must ask each day before I begin to carve.

Today, though, it's more practical than ever.

Downstairs on my couch is a young man, bound and gagged.

What am I to do with him?

The silver skull insignia gleams.

I hang the uniform and dress for work.

Snow covers the studio skylight. The shadows are soft, deep, and blue. Before turning on the lights, I run my hands over the rough-hewn block.

When I begin a new piece, even when I can feel into the wood and know exactly what I'm cutting down to, the first hours of work are always a struggle. The wood resists. Chisels skip off, and saw blades twist out of shape as if I were trying to cut my way through granite. I have to prove myself each time, coax the echoes from the grain.

Then, once I have the shape roughed out, the heartwood softens, yields, invites me in. My blades melt through crosscuts as if I were carving butter. The wood guides the tools, and the face, the shoulder, the hand emerges.

For the piece I am working on today, the early stage lasts a long time. The wood is green. Ordinarily, I cure the wood before I work, but in this case, I don't have the time. Resin sticks to my tools.

After two hours of work in the studio, I brush the sawdust from my coveralls and come downstairs to have a look at him. His eyes are wide, but it's hard to say if what I see in them is fear. He's young. Young, but old enough to shave.

Hanging near the stove where I put them out to dry are his black jeans, black T-shirt, and motorcycle boots. He wears the jeans and work shirt I dressed him in, a size too large.

His hands, tied together, rest in his lap. The knuckles of his left hand are tattooed with F-U-C-K, and the right with K-I-L-L. Though his feet are tied together, he has kicked the books from one of my shelves, the only damage he's been at liberty to do. Shirer, Arendt, Camus. History and philosophy in a little pile at his feet.

I say, "If only you had a match, right?"

He glares. I watch him breathe.

It seems to me as if the wooden faces in the room are watching him, too—the teak faces locked in screams, the anguished expressions in pine or spruce or ebony. All the hollow wooden eyes take him in.

Untying the gag is like breaking a dam. Obscenities flow from him like water.

"I wouldn't have to gag you," I tell him, "if you could keep a civil tongue."

"Fuck you."

I remind him that I saved his life.

"Fuck if you did," he says. "They'd have come back for me."

"I told you. There have been no new tracks in the snow. They haven't been back."

"Fuck you," he says, but he must know his confederates, must understand the truth as I tell it to him.

"You'd be frozen solid without me," I say, "so whatever I do to you now, it's better than that, right? It's better than being dead."

I force the gag back into his mouth before he can answer. If I don't, he'll shout his lungs out and I won't be able to concentrate.

I go back to work.

I earn more for Nina than all of her other clients combined. If she worries that I will have a heart attack, it is only because of the money.

She is not without compassion, but some of the things she has done for me have hardened her. The Auschwitz crossbeam was one.

I grant few interviews. Shouldn't the work speak for itself? But sometimes an interview brings its surprises. I once regretted aloud that there was no wood from Auschwitz for me to carve.

A month after my words were in print, Nina had a call from the Israeli government. They'd have preferred a Jewish artist, but no one else achieves my effects.

The crossbeam came from one of the barracks torn down after the war. It had, for a time, supported the roof of a Polish barn.

When they flew me in to inspect it, I did not ask how the beam had come to Israel, to a warehouse where it lay in a military truck bed like a missile.

The Deputy Minister of Culture, standing before the truck, waved some documentation under my nose. I stepped past him and touched the wood. Even after forty years, it was alive with ghosts.

"We will give it to you," he said, "on the condition that you cut it in half and produce two finished works, one of which you will return to us. For the memorial."

I agreed.

They could not know how dense the wood was with tortured faces, with gestures of pain and despair. Back in the States, I cut the beam in half, as agreed. Then I split each half lengthwise and carved four pieces instead of two. Let the Israelis imagine that I'd had to carve deep to find the images I gave them. Let them think the missing wood littered the floor of my studio as chips and dust.

All four finished pieces were a tangled knot of victims.

Nina told me, "You can't sell the extras. You'll give yourself away."

"We will sell them," I said. "Sealed bids. Secret bids. We'll give slides for Hauptmann to circulate among likely buyers."

Nina's arms were crossed. "Not Hauptmann. I won't go through Hauptmann again. Even talking to him on the phone, I feel dirty."

"So write him. Mail him the slides."

"But the bidders he will bring us . . ."

"It's what I want, Nina."

"This is the last time I go through Hauptmann."

I said nothing. No one else knew the people Hauptmann knew.

A month later, Nina flung the list at my face. "Do you see where these bids are coming from? Do you *see?*"

I picked up the loose pages from my floor, looked at the names and offers. "Here," I said, and pointed at a bid from El Salvador. "This can only be Rosado himself. It's not the highest bid, but I want you to sell it to him."

"If we weren't using Hauptmann's list, I could find someone

else," Nina said. "A collector. An investor who would put it away in a vault for his heirs. The money would be better, and—"

"Sell it to Rosado."

"In God's name, why?" Nina said. "Why do you want some-one like him to have it?"

"If I'm lucky," I said, "he'll install it over his bed."

Nina's face was pale.

"Sell it to him, Nina. In a way, it's his already."

Then I picked another bid, one Nina liked no better.

The last carving we sold openly to the Museum of Modern Art.

Once or twice a year, I look for trees in the killing fields. Some are old fields. Some are fresh. I walk around the tree trunks, touching them, feeling for the echoes. Then I direct the cutting of the logs that will be shipped to the States, trucked from Denver to the house and studio in the mountains.

Usually, the freshest sources are the hardest to get to. Not al-ways, though. Not always.

A logging road runs parallel to my canyon, on the other side of the ridge. If I have unwelcome visitors, that's usually where they come from.

The night I found my guest, I was reading. I heard the crack of a rifle shot.

I turned my lights off, shut down the generator.

Snow was falling. It had been coming down for hours in a fine powder, the sort of snow that continues, steadily, all through one day and into the next.

When I stepped outside, I could hear their voices at the top of the ridge.

There was another shot. Youthful laughter. Raised voices.

Then silence.

When at last I heard one of the voices again, there was no mirth in it. Indistinct words. Then another voice, pleading.

Again, silence. Enduring silence.

I waited a long time before getting the kerosene lantern out and putting on my boots. Ordinary boots. Sorels. I had no way of knowing that something special would be waiting for me at the top of the ridge.

Lighting my way with the lantern, I found my way up the slope to a small clearing. Fresh snowfall hadn't yet covered the shell casings and beer bottles that appeared in the lantern's circle of yellow light.

A shadow caught my eye, and I extended the lantern toward it. Stretched out on bloody snow was a body. The bald head was uncovered. Vapor clouds of breath rose from the face. The eyes were closed.

An old man, I thought. Lantern light is tricky. It took a moment for me to see that, no, his face was unlined. He was young. Stepping closer, I saw the swastikas tattooed on his arm.

When I leaned to see his face, my hand fell upon the trunk, and I paused, taking it all in.

I got my first taste of fighting in the fall of '44, in the Hürtgen Forest. The trees of the Hürtgen were still just trees to me then. I had the same feelings for them any infantryman would. When they gave cover to my unit's advance, I loved them. When German shells exploded among the branches over our heads, they rained down limbs heavy as stones, splinters sharp as shrapnel. We grenade-felled trees to clear booby traps, to build an instant bridge over tangles of barbed wire. Trees were obstacles, trees were useful. The tang of fresh resin filled the air.

I paid more attention to the Germans.

Up close, as I stepped over them, the German dead in the Hürtgen could have been my cousins. Even after news of Malmédy, I didn't hate them. I understood what had to be done. I did it.

Buy a bond. Kill a Jap.

Kill a Jerry. A Nazi.

The swastika tattoos on the kid's arms are sharp-edged and very black. He hasn't had them long.

"Do you know what I think?" I say to him. I haven't removed the gag this time. His eyes bore into me.

"I think," I tell him, "that when a victim isn't handy, one needs to be manufactured. Am I right?"

His eyes narrow. His gaze shifts to the deer rifle by the door, but even if he unties himself while I'm upstairs, he'll find that it's unloaded.

"I'm lucky that you and your companions didn't know I was here—an old man living alone. An artist with shelves of history books. I'd have been a more interesting victim, don't you think? I'd have been perfect. You might be drinking a beer with them right now, remembering, laughing. Instead, you had a little surprise. Like Rohm's surprise. You know about Rohm, of course, about what happened to him. You know all about the turn things can take."

His lips work around the gag, but he's only trying to swallow. There's no question, no understanding in his eyes.

"Ah. Never heard of Rohm. Well. It's an old, old story. Your friends, your compatriots, they really did surprise you, yes?"

He doesn't nod, but emotions play over his face like shadows. He was surprised. He still doesn't understand it.

"Your strength is that you might do anything." I lower my voice, lean toward him. "Anything." I smile. "But that's the danger, too. Do you understand? Hitler purged his lieutenants. You should know that. You should know what history can teach you about yourself."

From the books on the floor, I select Shirer's *Rise and Fall*. "We could start here," I say hefting the thick volume. "Shall I read you a chapter? Shall we begin at the beginning?"

Oh, the hate in his eyes.

"No," I say. "That's not the right sort of history for you. You need something tailored to you, yes? Something more personal, more relevant to your present situation. In fact, let's not call it history at all. Let's call it a crime story, set in the winter of '44. A crime story. A puzzle. I'll give you the crime. You tell me the motive."

The snow was deep, and in places the wind was piling it deeper still. Here and there, it came up to my belt.

I held my rifle at port arms and kept a good ten feet between myself and my prisoner. I doubted that he'd try to jump me for the gun—his own lines were far away, now, melting back into Germany—but SS soldiers were a cocky lot.

I wished for tire ruts to walk in. Even with the prisoner blazing the trail, wading through the snow was wearing me out, and we were still a long hike from Battalion HQ.

I heard, like an answered prayer, the sound of engines. A couple of jeeps emerged from the forest below and turned toward us. The paths left by their churning wheels invited me, and I thought, *Hallelujah!*

Planning to wait for the jeeps to pass, I said to the prisoner, "Hold up. Halt."

An explosion belted my gut like a sucker punch. I hit the deck, but the German remained standing, hands still clasped calmly behind his head. He smirked at me.

"Nur eine Landmine," he said in a voice that might be explaining thunder to a child. *"Nichts befürchten."*

Memory is tricky. That probably isn't exactly what he said. I did not learn German until after the war.

One of the jeeps was upside down, and the snow had been blown clear for ten feet around it.

I stood up and let my rifle point more emphatically at the German while I brushed snow from the front of my jacket with my other hand.

Around us trees swayed in the wind.

"Okay," I said as deeply as I could manage. "Now march!"

A third jeep had pulled up behind the other two, then turned around to go back for medics. Running down the opposite slope of the valley, churning snow before him like a plow, was some GI who must have popped out of a foxhole. He was shouldering an aidman's bag.

I didn't have to hurry my prisoner. He waded forward resolutely, as if eager to draw closer.

One of the jeep's passengers, an infantryman, was lying facedown in the crater. He had no legs. Another guy was lying beside the tree trunk he'd been thrown against, and nothing but his mouth was moving. He said, "Jesus, sweet Jesus," again and again.

The third man, a lieutenant, lay on his back with the jeep pinning his chest. The aidman leaned close to see if he was breathing.

He wasn't.

Clicking his tongue as we passed, my prisoner said, and this I'm almost sure of, *"Daß ist also das Kriegsglück."*

The aidman looked up. There was an 82nd Airborne patch on his shoulder. "What did he say?"

"I don't know," I admitted. "I don't speak German."

From the other jeep, a man said, "Thinks he's clever, don't he?"

It was true. The German was smirking as he surveyed the scene.

The dead lieutenant looked asleep, eyes half closed, mouth slack. He was young, a ninety-day wonder.

"You take that Jerry son of a bitch into the woods," the aidman told me, "and you shoot that grin off his goddamn face."

The prisoner shook his head very slightly and clicked his tongue again. I prodded him with the gun barrel. "Stop that shit. Keep moving."

The aidman crouched beside the man who'd been thrown against the tree, but over his shoulder he said, "If you were Airborne, you'd take my advice."

It was easier to walk in the tire ruts.

A while later, the jeep that had gone back for help came rolling through the snow, ferrying medics to where the mine had blown the first jeep. They drove slowly, staying in the tracks, wary of another mine. We stood aside to let them through.

Very quietly, the prisoner started singing, bobbing his head in time with the song. It was a march. It was a true believer's song.

"Knock it off," I said to his back.

He stopped, but before long he had started it up again.

"Come on," I said. "You've made your point."

He stopped singing, but he still bobbed his head from side to side, and he turned slightly, awkwardly because his hands were still clasped behind his neck. I saw enough of his face to see the smirk again.

"What is it with you?" I said. "Halt!"

He stopped and turned full around to face me.

We stood, watching each other.

His eyes were the color of ice, of winter skies.

"Let's take a detour. Up there." I gestured with my head, up the slope, away from the tire ruts.

He unclasped his hands and pointed, tentatively, over his head.

"You got it," I said. "Let's go."

As we walked, wading again through deep drifts, he began once again to sing. Loudly. This time, I didn't shut him up.

The farther we went, the more densely the pine trees crowded around us.

Remember, this is a mystery. Why was I doing this? I can tell you, it wasn't the Malmédy massacre. And all the rest, all the rumors, smacked of propaganda.

I made him stop, then turn to face me.

The trees circled us like witnesses.

I brought the M1 to my shoulder and pointed it at his chest.

"Doctor's orders," I told him, "courtesy of the 82nd Airborne."

I watched where I was aiming—the center of his chest.

The rifle report echoed from the surrounding hills.

He pitched back and hardly kicked. It had been a clean shot, a hunter's shot. His back arched for a moment, then fell.

Then, when it was too late, I wanted to know what his face

had been like before I had shot him. Was he surprised? Was he smirking?

I couldn't tell. Dead, his face was a mask.

My knees got weak. I knelt next to him in the snow.

There was a secret here.

The smell of blood was like copper in the cold air. I thought of hunting again, of killing and dressing out deer, spilling their steaming guts onto the snow.

I detached my bayonet, opened his coat and shirt, unbuckled his belt. A bayonet is not a hunting knife. It's made for stabbing, not slicing. The blade is too long for good leverage. But I made it do, opening him up, spilling him out, looking for clues. Blood up to my elbows.

Months later, when we began to liberate the camps, I told myself that there was justice in what I had done. But the killing preceded the motive. Even though I had heard the rumors, I only believed in the camps when I saw them myself.

"So," I say to him, "it's a mystery, isn't it? Why did I kill him?"

He had listened intently. I pat his leg, and he doesn't try to kick me.

"And here you are, another mystery. Another Nazi, delivered into my hands. But things are different. I didn't kill you, I saved you. What for? What happens next?"

His eyes are wide.

There is more. After I dressed out the SS trooper and strung his unreadable entrails across the snow, I pulled off his boots.

My hands were sticky. I washed them with snow, then undid my laces with numb fingers.

I had to stamp down hard to get his boots to fit my feet.

I walked around him, in his own boots, searching. Then I happened to rest my hand on the trunk of a pine tree.

And I felt him inside.

If the bayonet was a bad hunting knife, it was even worse for carving. At best, I could only strip the bark in the place where my trembling fingers detected him. But he was there. If I could free him of the wood, I would know what his face had looked like in his last moment.

But I lacked the tools.

For the rest of the war, I kept finding other faces in other trees. At Stavelot, where the SS had shot Belgian children, I found a face in a garden birch tree. In broken French, I explained. A farmer lent me his hand ax, and I did the detail work with another man's pocket knife.

The farmer, watching me work, watching the face that emerged, shed quiet tears. The face, I was made to understand, was his niece's.

Many times since the war, I have searched the Ardennes forest. I have never been able to find the spot where I killed the trooper. I have never been able to find the tree.

I remove his gag.

He says nothing.

I say, "That's better. That's much better."

He is looking at the wooden faces, shaking his head. "It's bullshit," he says at last. "I don't fucking believe you."

"What part don't you believe?"

"Ghosts," he says. "I don't believe in ghosts."

"Not ghosts," I tell him. "That's not what they are."

I go back to the studio to work, to finish what I have worked on all the time that he's been here.

Really, it is necessary to wear the uniform, to pull those shining boots over your calves and pose and smile. I have the Luger that matches the uniform. It is not a heavy gun, but without the weight of it in its glossy holster, the uniform and its truth are incomplete.

The commander of SS troops at Malmédy, at Stavelot, was Lt. Col. Jochen Peiper. Sentenced to hang, confident of reprieve, he called the war "a proud and heroic time. Wherever we stood was Germany, and as far as my tank gun reached was my kingdom."

The boots are proud and heroic.

The holster is proud and heroic.

The insignia gleam.

When I come downstairs again, he has freed his hands and is working at the ropes that bind his feet. He hears me coming, but seems unconcerned until he looks up and sees the uniform.

I unholster the Luger.

He hardly seems to notice the boots and canvas bag I carry in my other hand. All his attention is on the gun.

"Isn't it beautiful?" I say, but I mean the uniform, not the gun. "Go on." I wave the muzzle at him casually. "It's time for us to go. Finish untying yourself."

He doesn't move.

"Come on," I tell him. "I haven't got all day."

"What are you going to do?"

"Shut up," I tell him, "and get those ropes off your feet."

When he has freed himself, I tell him to stand. He grunts and holds his side where he must have taken a kick to the ribs. I make him strip and dress in his own clothes. All but his boots.

"Wear these," I say. I toss the boots—very much like the ones I am wearing, only these ones do not shine. They are boots that have seen the battlefield. They are scarred. The leather is cracked.

I say, "You can't get them on by staring at them."

He had no coat when I found him. I tell him to bring the blanket from the couch. It's an old woolen one that I won't miss.

"Now out," I say. "Back to where I found you."

"I'm thirsty," he says, "and hungry."

"If you had the gun and I were the one who was hungry, would you feed me?"

He thinks about it. "Yes."

"All right." I herd him into the kitchen. Without taking my eyes from him, I get down a box of crackers. At the sink, he drinks water from his cupped hands. Then he eats a handful of the crackers.

"That's enough," I say. "Take the box. Eat them later."

The snow has gone on falling almost all the time he's been with me. I can find no tracks. The snow is up to our knees.

We need a tune for marching. I whistle the regimental march of the *Liebstandarte Adolf Hitler*.

Very quietly, he says, "Please."

I stop whistling.

We march.

He says, "What will happen?"

I say, "What are we to do with the killers, with the people who are filled with hate?"

"I never killed anyone," he says.

"But you have hurt people. Don't ask me to believe that you haven't done that."

I start to whistle the march again. Then I stop to say, "Do you know that in Germany, that music is illegal? They'll throw you in jail just for carrying the tune. There's a long list of forbidden music. What do you think of that?"

He says, "I don't understand you. Who *are* you?"

By which he must mean, *Whose side are you on?*

* * *

Once I was at a gallery opening of my recent work. This set of sculptures had been especially demanding. Like the Auschwitz crossbeams, each piece incorporated a score of twisted faces, a hundred twisted limbs. Drawing them out had exhausted me. I could hardly stand to look at them.

The wood had come from Cambodian trees.

The gallery was full. Patrons had wineglasses in their hands as they went from one piece to another. Sometimes an art opening is noisy as a cocktail party. Mine tend to be subdued. This one was silent.

Nina and the gallery owner had already seen the pieces, and I was relieved to find, as I stood in the middle of the room with them, that they, like me, were in the mood for something else, anything else. We managed to hold a conversation in the middle of the room, focusing on each other, ignoring the little wooden hells that were all around us. And it worked. Before long we really did forget ourselves.

The gallery owner said something that struck me as funny. I laughed. I put my head back and roared.

A woman wheeled from one of the sculptures and shouted, "How can you laugh in here? How *can* you?"

It is easy for me to find the spot on the ridge where I had found him. There's the stump of the pine tree that I felled while he was still unconscious.

"Stand there," I say. "Right where I found you."

He doesn't move.

I wave the pistol and say, "Come on."

He looks at me, hesitates, then steps sideways to the spot.

"I don't know about you," I say. "I don't know how far gone you might be, how you got started down this path."

"You won't—"

"Shut up," I say. "It doesn't matter whether I know or not. I only have one answer. There's only one thing for me to do about you and others like you."

I toss him the canvas bag. Catching it, he drops the box of crackers.

"Open it up," I say, and he does. He takes out the sculpture of the hand, and he doesn't know what to make of it until he turns it the right way, can see the meaning of the outstretched fingers, the unmistakable gesture.

Please. I'm hurt. I'm down. No more. Please.

"I took it out of the tree," I tell him, nodding at the stump.

With his free hand, he touches his side where his ribs still ache. His expression seems more angry than sad, more vengeful than softened with wisdom. But who knows?

He opens his mouth, begins to form a word.

"No," I say. "It doesn't matter. We're finished already."

He looks at the boots on his feet. The boots strangers have died of. When he looks up, I'm pointing the pistol at his chest. I watch his face. His expression is impossible to read.

I turn away, begin to retrace my steps. I, too, wear boots. The lustrous leather clings to my calves like a second skin, and melting snow beads up on the blackness to glint like the stars coming out. One point of light. Then another. Then one more. Soon, they will be numberless as the dead. And as cold.

The Clearing

by Lois Tilton

Lois Tilton has recently completed her fourth novel, Ac-
cusations, *set in the universe of the television series*
Babylon 5. *More than forty of her short stories have appeared in magazines and anthologies featuring the genres
of science fiction, fantasy, and horror.*

The forest's breath was cool and damp, with a scent of old, decaying leaves. Cat moved silently through sunlight-dappled
shade, soft-footed like the striped forest hunter he was named
for. Pigment streaked his bare arms, and two broad lines of it
across his cheekbones to below the corner of his eyes: a cat
mask.

There were others with him: his brothers, the men of his tribe,
all armed as he was with short bows carved from the striated
heartwood of the yew and stone-tipped arrows. Cat could see the
movement of his brother Leaping Hare through the trees ahead
of him on his right, and behind him the shadow of Wolf-the-
Hunter on his left. The rest, unseen and unheard, followed, intent
on their path.

Suddenly, as the breeze shifted slightly, Cat caught the scent,
halted, raised a hand to signal to the rest, and they all paused at
the thin, acrid taint of woodsmoke in the air: fire, which the
forest-dwellers always feared.

Now the faces of the men were grim as they advanced through
the dense, old-growth trees, and their bows were in their hands,
arrows ready to be nocked into the string, for Cat had warned
them what he'd seen. As they went forward, the smoke hung

more thickly in the air, until it obscured vision and made the hunters' eyes sting. There was a repeated sound also, like a woodpecker's beak striking a tree, but dull and echoing. Then, ahead of them, even though the smoke, the glare of bright sunlight was visible, sunlight unfiltered through the translucent leaves of the forest canopy, a light bare and raw and harsh to the eyes.

Leaping Hare, closest to the clearing, spoke a curse of anger and disbelief. And Cat, creeping forward, saw again what he had seen before and clutched the catskin bag that hung around his neck. It held the teeth and claws and polished bone of the striped forest cat that had come to him in his naming-dream. It was his most potent protection, for with it around his neck, the cat walked with him, his spirit-brother: shadow-stealth, quick-striking.

And he felt the need for protection now, for what he saw—what he had brought the others to see with him—was an enormity so great it passed all comprehension. A man might cut a tree, for wood, to make a bow. A man would make a fire for warmth in winter, and to cook his meat. But what kind of men would lay a whole hillside bare so nothing was left but haggled stumps and bare dead ground? What kind of men would heap the hacked-off branches into a pile as high as their heads and light a fire to send black smoke rolling up like stormclouds?

But they were men, of that there was no doubt—dark-skinned men, their bare muscular backs gleaming with sweat as they swung their axes into the trees still standing. That was the sound the forest tribe heard now, the bite of axes into the living wood. Chips and wedges of it flew, then one of the men gave a cry of warning, and a great tree swayed, its fibers cracked and snapped, and it fell to the ground like a crash of thunder.

But elsewhere on the hillside, other men continued their labor, other axes chopped on, the sound of their blades striking wood and ringing off the denuded slope. It made Cat shake inside to see it.

The forest men were familiar with war, when one tribe would encroach the hunting territory of another: quick raids, swift strikes, sometimes an enemy's head to show as a trophy, sometimes widows scarring their faces in mourning. This, though, this was war on the forest itself, killing it tree by tree, so no animal could live, no hunter stalk, no woman gather the nuts that fell from its branches.

None of them questioned what they must now do, so they

withdrew to prepare, and Cat and Leaping Hare both took paint
and renewed the totem marks on each other's face and body.
Then each man went apart by himself, and Cat took the catskin
bag from around his neck and reverently laid each object out in
front of him on the ground, praying to the spirit of the cat: *Walk
with me, brother—give me your quickness, give me your strength.*

It would be his first war, the first time for him to face another
man with intent to kill. He was the youngest of them, only come
into his name this spring. If he died, his mother and sisters would
cut their faces with their skinning knives, but he had no wife to
bleed for him. He glanced through the trees to where his brother
was praying to his own spirit-brother. Leaping Hare had two small
daughters. If he died tonight, it would be up to Cat to provide for
them, to move into the widow's tent, since he had no wife of his
own. Cat thought that it might be better if he were the one to die,
and he felt shame that he hoped it wouldn't be so. He almost
wished now that he'd never come to the edge of the forest, or
smelled the smoke, or seen the ax-blades flashing in the sun.

As dusk fell, the hunters gathered, looked down again on the
strange men, who had finally ceased their work of destruction
and gathered around a high, leaping fire. They had meat roasting
there—the scent of it made Cat's belly twitch.

They attacked from three directions, creeping silently toward
their enemies under the cover of darkness. Their arrows fell
on the woodcutters, who bellowed in rage and pain and snatched
up their axes to defend themselves, charging their enemies. The
two forces closed, and then there was no more room for bow-
work.

But the woodcutters had the advantage at close quarters with
their axes and their other weapons, great knives as long as a
man's forearm. Cat watched in horror as one of the blades
slashed across his brother's belly, and blood gushed and entrails
swelled out like a gutted deer's. Leaping Hare staggered, still on
his feet, arms clutching his life, until an ax took him from behind
and he went down. The enemy turned on Cat next—Cat, armed
with only his stone knife, and he couldn't make himself face that
terrible blade. He took the first step backward, then another, but
the axeman cut him off, swung his weapon, and the crushing
blow sent Cat to the ground.

When it was all over, they found him, still trying to crawl
back to the safety of the forest. A hand wrenched his head back
by the hair, he felt a sharp blade at his throat, but someone
barked sounds that were words, and they dragged him back to

their fire, tied him hand and foot, and left him to his agony alone.

In the morning, they pulled him to his feet, struck him, tried to make him stand, but he could not, and they left him again. All that day he suffered, tied and staked under the naked, open sun. His fair skin burned, his limbs had passed from torture to numb lifelessness, and the effort of every breath cost his broken ribs terrible pain. But the worst misery was the thirst, as the sun beat down on his unprotected head, baked him like a fire, cracked his lips, and dried his throat to ashes.

All throughout that day, the sound of the axes filled the hillside, blow after blow, bite after bite into the bleeding sapwood of the trees, pounding, ringing, echoing against the ache in his head. On and on and on, unceasing, relentless. When would they ever stop? In his anguish, Cat felt the catskin bag still tied around his neck, and he prayed to his spirit-brother for help, for the strength to break away, to escape into the cool familiar safety of the forest, to his tribe.

But when the sun fell low in the sky, the sound of the axes ceased. Once again the loggers built up a roaring fire, so great that Cat could feel the heat of it licking his sunburned skin. He could smell flesh cooking, and he wondered if they meant to spit him over the fire like a deer and burn him alive, if that was why they'd kept him tied all the long day, to save him for the ordeal.

Someone kicked him to make him move, but he couldn't, he could only moan in his pain and thirst. He heard voices quarreling above him, opened his eyes enough to make out a man with a long blade, gesturing with it, and Cat understood that he wanted to cut his throat or gut him, like Leaping Hare had been gutted. But another man, with an ax, struck his fist to his own chest angrily as he argued back. A moment later he was back, with water in a clay bowl. He splashed it onto Cat's head and face and made him drink the rest, and soon after that, Cat could lift his head and see what was happening.

They were throwing the bodies onto the fire. No, there were two fires, and the bodies they were throwing onto the larger one were the dead of his tribe. So many of them! Cat wept for his brother and all the rest of them, killed so horribly and now denied the burial rites to free their souls from the dead flesh. There were corpses burning in the other fire, as well, dead limbs writhing in the flames, but Cat could take no joy in the enemy's losses, not in the face of his own.

They kept him tied again that night, but in the morning his

bonds were cut, and when he could finally move, the man with the ax threw him a chunk of meat, but Cat couldn't eat it, not knowing what kind of flesh it was. The axeman swore at him, then pushed him and gestured that he was to work, and he did, all that day, hauling the brush to the fires that burned constantly, fouling the air. When he stumbled, they beat him until he got back to his feet. But though the smoke stung his eyes, he could still see the forest, the trees so close, if he could only reach them, and he clutched his spirit-bag in one hand and prayed for the chance.

The axeman, he learned, was named Tagh. Tagh made it clear by beatings and gestures that he now belonged to him, his slave, but Cat refused to submit to being owned. He made himself force down the meat they gave him this time, and again in the morning when he was untied, to give him strength. He watched and he waited with the patience of a stalking cat, and when he thought their eyes weren't on him, he broke and ran for the safety of the trees, knowing he could disappear if he could make it into the forest, knowing they could never find him there. But he'd underestimated his weakness, the pain in his broken ribs slowed him down, and one of the loggers tackled him, brought him to the ground. Then Tagh stormed up, furious, snatched up a stick and beat him until it was broken, while Cat lay curled up on the ground trying to protect his broken side from the hardest blows.

From then on, his feet were tied, although the leather thongs cut into this ankles, tripped him and made him clumsy at his work. Tagh beat him well and kicked him up to his feet again to make him keep working. Some of the others advised him to kill this slave, that he was more trouble than he was worth, but the axeman was stubborn. Cat understood this without knowing their words.

But he was stubborn, too, and when he found a broken arrowhead, he hid it in his belt, saved it till night to saw cautiously at his bonds. He didn't dare try to bolt, not with the ribs that stabbed him with pain at every step. Stealth it would have to be, to crawl unseen and unheard from the loggers' camp, to steal like a shadow into the trees, and away. Stealth like a cat's, and he prayed again to his spirit-brother for a cat's silent feet.

But Cat hadn't known that the woodcutters were posting a watch around their camp now at night, to guard against another attack from the forest tribes. He was close, so painfully close to the trees when the sentry spotted him, gave the alarm.

Tagh cursed when he saw the severed bonds, and then he spotted the catskin sack around Cat's neck, tore it off, although Cat screamed and fought for it, even with the loggers holding his arms behind his back. Tagh spilled the teeth and claws on the ground, then tossed the sack into the fire, and Cat felt the loss as if it was his heart being ripped open, his protection gone, his spirit-brother lost to him. It was a worse pain than the beating, and the beating was hard, Tagh grimly smiling this time as he brought the stick down on his slave's back, knowing that he'd stripped away his spirit-power.

Not many days later, though, the woodcutters packed up their camp and deserted it, leaving the fallen logs stacked on the bare, dry, ash-covered ground. Cat stumbled under the weight of a pack, his ankles still tied, in growing despair as each step took him farther and farther from the forest, from the only world he knew. The sun overhead glared down like a malevolent spirit of heat, with a single burning eye. The distant horizon made him reel with vertigo. So much empty land, all cleared of trees! Why so much mindless destruction, with such effort?

But after a while he could see that there was a purpose to it, that the cleared lands were full of tall, waving grasses and other lush strands of vegetation, men and women at work in them, bent over the crops. Dark-skinned men and women like the woodcutters, who greeted them cheerfully, as if they were returning from a long hunt, laden with game.

There was no glad welcome for Cat, only stares of misgiving, though he was given food, at least, by the women of Tagh's house. It was fear that made him run that night, fear of spending his life in such a place. But he was caught again, and dragged back, and Tagh beat him again, grimly, relentlessly, until the blood ran down his back and legs.

When are you going to learn? Or do I have to kill you first?

Cat understood the question from the tone more than the words. He shook his head weakly. They were both stubborn men.

He's too wild, like a forest animal! What use is he as a slave if you have to beat him half-dead every time he runs? That was Tagh's wife, arguing with him.

The priest will tame him for me.

The woman held her tongue, but her doubt was visible in her eyes as she cleaned the blood from Cat's back and pouticed it with a salve that stung like nettles.

The next day, Tagh took Cat to a house in the village that was darker inside than the rest, and filled with the scents of smoke

and burning herbs. Cat struggled when they bore him down to
the ground, thinking this meant more than just another beating,
that they were going to hamstring him or geld him like the oxen
he'd seen in the fields. Tagh had threatened as much. *I won't run
again,* he wanted to beg, knowing it was a lie, his fear speaking.

But when the priest bent over him, his fear took a new form
and the protest froze in his throat, because this man's eyes were
wide-dilated, even for the darkness of the house, and Cat could
see the spirits looking out of them—spirits like the ones that possessed the shaman of his own tribe in a holy trance, or when a
spirit-dream came over a man and he spoke with their voice.
Those eyes took hold of his own and held them, and Cat was
powerless to resist, alone as he was, with his brother-spirit torn
away from him and lost.

What followed was like an evil spirit-dream, because Cat was
held helpless by the priest's eyes and by his voice. He couldn't
move or speak or even cry aloud when the priest took a knife
from the fire where it had been heating and put the white-hot tip
of the blade against his leg, just above the welts the thongs had
made, and slowly drew a mark there, branding it into his flesh.
Cat could feel the pain sear him in all its burning intensity, he
could smell the singeing of his hair and flesh, but he couldn't
pull away or even scream. Then the priest took another knife
from the fire and branded him again on his other leg.

The incantation suddenly ceased, releasing him, and Cat cried
out in reaction. But Tagh looked satisfied, and he thanked the
priest and his apprentice in respectful tones. Then he pulled his
slave to his feet and sent him out to the fields.

The work was hard. Cat had never known anything like the incessant grinding toil under the sun, hacking at the weeds in the
fields, bending all day until he thought his back would break and
his head burst from the heat. But gradually his muscles grew accustomed to the work, his fair skin stopped blistering and turned
a darker brown, and he learned to plait a hat from grass to protect his head. He discovered that he wasn't the only slave in the
village, not even the only one who was branded. But they had all
submitted to their condition, or had been born to slavery, and that
frightened Cat, that he would grow to be like them, dull-eyed
and resigned.

He ran again, of course. Not the first day, or the second. He
meant to get his strength back this time, to wait till his broken
ribs had healed. Tagh wasn't ungenerous with his food, and Cat
wasn't tied at night any more. In fact, it almost seemed as if

Tagh was watching him, waiting for him to make the attempt, even eager.

Cat was wary, but he waited, he judged his time, and finally, he ran. His escape would be easy, as he conceived it, for the stream that ran past the margin of the village, fouled and muddied by their animals, flowed from the north, out of the forest. All he had to do was follow it back. So he made his escape on a moonlit night, following the streambed, but when dawn came he saw with horror that he had run all night downstream, in the wrong direction, and was now even further than ever from where he wanted to be. Desperate, he tried to retrace his steps, but he ran directly into the search party from Tagh's village, who dragged him back.

"The sooner you learn you can't get away, the easier it'll be on your hide," Tagh told him as he flogged his runaway slave with a thick strap cut from the ox's harness. There was a distinct tone of satisfaction in his voice. "You don't have your own magic anymore, and the priest's is stronger."

"Pigheaded," his wife said, poulticing Cat's raw back, not too gently either. He wasn't sure which one of them she meant, or possibly both. "He'll run again, all right. He'll be thinking about it as soon as the scabs heal. And you'll strap the skin off his back again, and how much work will we get out of him then?"

"He may run, but he won't get anywhere," Tagh insisted. "His feet will bring him back, no matter where he tries to go."

Could it be true? Cat rubbed the red brand marks above his ankles, the symbol that the priest had burned into his flesh. Memory of that ordeal made him shudder, and he reached instinctively for his spirit-bag, but of course it was gone, and with it his power to resist. He prayed, at night, for his spirit-brother to return to him, to guide him from this place, but there was no answer. The cat was a forest spirit, and there was no place for it here.

He tried once again that fall to escape, at the harvest festival, on the night when the priest called for blessings on the crops and the whole village celebrated with beer they'd brewed from the last season's grain. Tagh was soon reeling from the beer he'd poured down his throat, and Cat took his chance. He ran all night, guiding his steps by the moon and the stars in the sky overhead, but in the morning he found he was still in sight of Tagh's village, that he had run in circles all that time, like the ox tethered to tread out the grain.

"He'll learn," Tagh said to his skeptical wife as she brought out her jar of poultice and waited with impatient resignation to use it. "He's not stupid, just stubborn." Then he paused a moment, as if to rest his arm. "Aren't you, Khagt?"

But Cat kept his face turned away and made no reply.

"Pigheaded," the wife muttered.

Then came winter, the first snows fell, and the rhythm of work in the village fell off. Cat wore a shirt of wool now, instead of his deerhide kilt. That was the incessant toil of the house's women, to spin the coats of the sheep and goats into yarn and weave it into cloth. They were Tagh's wives and daughters, Cat thought at first, but later he learned that the younger woman with the covered hair of a wife was in fact Tagh's widowed daughter, returned to her father's house under some kind of disgrace. And, to Cat's surprise, the smallest brown-skinned girl was also a slave. But Margha, the wife, beat her no more or more often than the rest.

With the approach of spring, though, half the village uprooted itself, packed up its possessions, and hauled them north to the land cleared out of the forest the summer before. The ashes were already spread over the earth, the logs stacked, seasoned and ready for building.

Now Cat began to realize the true scale of a farmer's labor, from the earliest light of dawn to dusk, clearing and planting the land, constructing shelter for men and animals—unceasing, wearying toil that left him at night almost too exhausted to eat. Why did men wish to live this way when there was the forest, with game to hunt and food to gather freely from the ground and the trees?

There was no moment of the day now when he couldn't look up from his work and see the forest, cool and dark-green, beyond the boundaries of the new village. The air held the cool, familiar scent of the trees. At night, when the ache in his overworked muscles kept him from sleeping, he thought he could hear the voice of the forest calling to him, the rustle of the breeze through its leaves. He would close his eyes and try to dream, hoping for a vision of a striped cat who would speak to him and lead him away, but the dream never came. Their spirit-bond had been broken, and the fading brands on his legs, the magic of the terrible old priest, kept the cat from coming to him.

"He'll run again," Margha warned her husband, scowling at Cat. "It was a bad idea to bring him here. See how he stares off into the woods whenever he thinks no one is looking?"

"He may run, but he'll have to come back," Tagh said with grim confidence, but he greased the harness leather strap with pigfat, to keep it supple.

Cat did run, because the nearness of the forest was a constant torment, a near-physical pain to see it every day, bent over a hoe in a half-cleared field where the stumps still stood out in the earth, under the relentless sun that made the weeds grow more quickly than the crops. And the old hope grew again, that he knew the forest and the farmers didn't, that once he made the shelter of the trees, they wouldn't ever be able to find him. And even, possibly, that once he was in the forest its spirits would be stronger than the priest's brands, or that he could find a shaman to help him break them.

He had to try.

He was strong now, with work and adequate food. His ribs had long since healed, and his back, from Tagh's last beating in the fall. And if there was any pursuit as he fled into the trees, he quickly left it behind. His heart rose, there beneath the familiar trees, inhaling their scents, feeling the cool damp breeze against his sweaty skin. He tore off the sweaty wool shirt and cast it aside.

But the forest was not quite as he remembered. The familiar trails were overgrown, and in some places faded away altogether. He came after a day of wandering to the bank of the swift-running creek where his tribe had been camped, but the site was deserted now, deserted. With difficulty, he found the remains of a campfire and sifted through its cold, damp ashes. Nothing remained.

He reminded himself that the tribe moved more often than the farmers' village, at least two or three times a season. All he had to do was follow the trails and he'd find them eventually, or possibly some other tribe who might welcome a hunter, because it was possible that his worst dread had come to pass, and his tribe no longer existed, wiped out in the raid on the logging camp.

But the trails had been too long abandoned, and the overgrowth had come up in the months since he'd been gone. He could spot no sign of any hunters, no fresh tracks on the ground or the remains of recent campfires. But the longer he walked, the more often the paths through the trees faded away, or led him to the edge of a swamp where no swamp had been before, or doubled back on themselves to bring him back to the same landmarks, only from a different direction.

He'd been too long away, that was all, he tried to tell himself at first. Soon he'd find the right trails, and everything would be all right. And he searched, desperately, for any sign of a striped cat, its tracks or scat or clawmarks on the trunk of a tree. If only his spirit-brother would come to him.

But the forest was empty, as if all its spirits had fled, and finally Cat had to admit the truth to himself, that the priest's power was more potent even here, that the brands on his ankles fettered him as securely as chains, and that the trails would continue to bend and twist and turn back on themselves until they led him back to Tagh's village, no matter how long or how far he tried to run.

There was another choice, which he considered now, instead of going back—to find a sharp flake of flint and cut his own throat like an animal's, to bleed out his life, in the forest where he belonged. But the thought of rotting here unburied, with no rites to free his soul, and the crows pecking out his eyes and the wolves cracking his bones, was too much. The farmers burned their dead to release their spirits, or so they claimed, and it was better than no rite at all.

So at last, weary and beyond despair, he followed the trail, let it take him back to the clearing with the naked sun overhead, and the crops and the weeds, and Tagh with the greased harness leather—back to all the bitterness of slavery.

Tagh was an ambitious man.

In the new village he was a chief, and his new house, when it was built, was one of the largest, to hold all his sons and daughters and livestock and slaves. His sons were just now beginning to come into the size of men, to do a man's work, and Tagh planned, as they grew, to clear even more land from the forest and expand his farm.

Much of the work still fell on Cat's scarred shoulders, except for one thing. Tagh thrust the ax at him one day and ordered him to start to work clearing the trees at the east border of the farm, but Cat refused to take it from him.

"A taste of leather on your back will change your mind," Tagh warned, but Cat met his eyes.

"Flog me or not, I won't."

They stared at each other. "We'll see about that."

But in the end it was Tagh who took the ax and called to his oldest son that it was time for him to learn to clear the land, since it was going to be his land, when he was a man. Since that time, he had let the leather grow hard and cracked.

Tagh's youngest daughter was ready to be married, which would bring in a bride-price but deprive the household of her labor at the loom. But there was the little slave girl, Erla, to take her place, although she was very recently no longer a child. Cat wasn't the only one who had noted the fact. Margha began to keep a closer eye on the girl, and on her sons. "I don't want that kind of thing going on in the house. First one of them is at her, and then the rest, like a pack of dogs fighting over a bitch."

"She's ready to breed," Tagh observed.

"Best give her to Khagt, then. He can keep the rest of them off her."

"Hm," Tagh grunted noncommittally, for he'd been looking at the girl himself.

Cat heard the exchange, for there were few secrets in the crowded household, and he supposed that Erla had, too. She'd been looking at him lately with dark, shy, but interested eyes. Cat lay on his pallet at night and thought of how it would be to have her next to him there, to have a woman. It was hard to be alone and have to listen to the vigorous grunts of Tagh mounting his wife, though she was old for child-bearing.

After the wedding there was only one more woman in the house, the widowed daughter, Kharra. Cat knew more of her story now, how the dead husband's family had demanded the bride-price back, which stubborn Tagh refused to pay. The ill-will had been one reason behind his move to the new village.

But it was no simple task to hack new farms out of the wilderness, even with every man and woman working themselves to exhaustion, sunrise to dark. And there was bad fortune. Even the young priest with all his sacrifices could not avert a murrain among the sheep. The feast of thanksgiving at harvest-time was sober that year, as the villagers laid up their stocks and grimly considered the winter to come. Tagh reluctantly decided to waste no grain in brewing ale.

Cat had never known so hungry a winter. The little girl Erla sometimes wept in her bed at night with the pangs of an empty belly, for Tagh's pack of growing sons left little in the kettle for the women and slaves. Time and again Cat would pause in his tasks to look across the snow-covered, stubbled fields to the darkness of the forest, where deer browsed beneath the trees, and wild boars rooted, and a hunter could follow the tracks of a hare through the snow.

There came a day when Tagh stood staring long and hard at his breeding sow, then went into the house to take out his whetstone. Cat waited for him to come out again. "I could bring back meat," he said.

Tagh looked hard at him, then at the forest.

"Deer," Cat said. "Venison and hare and other game."

Tagh thought for a moment. "What would you need?"

"You'll never see him again," Margha warned.

"Oh, he'll be back. With meat. He came back today, didn't you, Khagt?"

Cat said nothing in reply, not looking up from his place at the hearth where he worked on his bow, planing the yew-wood down to its heart with Tagh's sharp bronze knife. It had taken him all day to find the right wood, and for a long moment he had stood alone in the silent woods, staring into the trees, the trails that led ever deeper into the forest. But then he had turned his back and returned to the barren fields and the close, smoky atmosphere of Tagh's house.

The finished bow would be a crude thing by the standards of his tribe, but he was a skilled wood-worker, and the bronze knife made the work go so much more quickly.

"Maybe I should send one of the boys with him, though," Tagh said thoughtfully.

Now Cat looked up from his work. "No. They don't know how to walk in the woods. Their noise would scare away the game."

"Mmgh," Tagh grunted.

But it was alone Cat went, back into the forest, a hunter again, if still a branded slave.

The woods had receded away from the village by this time, and the familiar trails had disappeared, but once away from the margin of the trees, the unmarked snow made the tracking easy. Cat stalked the deer slowly, silently, content to pause and simply breathe the fresh, chill forest air. He found a small herd sheltering in the windbreak of a grove of firs, and his first arrow found a yearling buck. It wasn't a clean kill, for he had no points to his arrows, but he followed the blood-trail and brought his prey down.

By then it was near-dark, and he built up a fire in the shelter of a cleft in the rocks. Gutting the buck with Tagh's bronze knife, he cut out the liver and roasted it over the flames, letting the rich, fat juices run down his chin as he gorged himself on the half-raw meat.

During the night, while he lay wrapped in the deerhide, he

could hear the growls and snarling of scavengers as they tore at the offal he had cast aside. He held quiet, waiting to hear the distinctive cry of a forest cat, but after some time, he fell asleep.

When dawn came, he cut poles and branches and wove them into a crude sledge, onto which he loaded the carcass of the deer. He paused then, looking out into the snow-covered, trackless wilderness for a long time. But then he turned and followed his tracks back toward the village.

Tagh's household ate well for the rest of the winter, with plenty of venison, even for the slaves. But Tagh kept the deerhides and tanned them as he had learned in his tribe, to make boots and a coat for himself instead of the wool the villagers wore.

Then the snow melted, the earth warmed, and the village began to prepare for the sowing. This was always a solemn rite, after the last, thin, hungry days of winter, while everyone waited for the thaw and the first shoots of green and the moon to turn his favorable face onto the land. On that sacred night, the priest stripped naked and went out to the waiting fields to couple with the new-plowed earth. He was possessed by the moon's spirit then, which spread among the whole village. Men hardened and women softened, and they joined together in the act, rutting openly in the same fields where they would sow their crops.

Cat found himself possessed by the spirit along with the rest, and his body ached with the pressure of his unsown seed. He thought he saw Erla the little slave girl, who hadn't yet been a woman at the last sowing. But it wasn't Erla who stood at the edge of the fields, alone and away from the rest, although she was almost as small and as slender. He snatched his hands away as he realized his mistake, that this was Kharra, Tagh's daughter. "Sorry, I . . . thought you were . . ."

"Someone else."

But he paused to look at her. "Why aren't you . . . ?"

"In the fields with the rest?" She shook her head. "They're afraid."

Seeing his reaction, "But you don't know? When I was wed, the omens were very bad. They wanted the bride-price back—his people did—but my father wouldn't. And he—my husband—still wanted me." She paused. "Three days after the wedding, he died, in our bed. They say that I'm cursed, or a witch. So, you see, no other man would dare take me."

The spirit of the night was very strong in Cat, and she was beautiful in the moonlight, and the scent of the spirit was on her.

He couldn't fear her, or anything that would happen. Not quite believing what he was doing, he uttered the words: "I would . . . dare. If you would."

Without more words, they fell together, onto the waiting earth. The spirit moved in them both—him to discharge his seed, her to accept it.

Then each of them began to consider the consequences of what they'd done. Cat wondered nervously, "Do you care? That I'm a slave? Your father . . ."

She stroked his hair, murmured, "A slave and a forest savage. With straw-colored hair. I remember when he first brought you home—how wild you were." Then she looked hard at him. "What about you? Aren't you afraid I might be a witch?"

"Did you hate your husband so much that you'd kill him in his sleep, then?"

"No," she said sadly, "He was a good man, I wanted to be his wife. Those three nights—I dream about them, still." She paused, and her hand moved to the root of his manhood. "I've missed . . . having a man."

"Ah," said Cat as the spirit rose in him again.

The next day, he looked at her whenever he could snatch a chance, and it seemed to him that her face had a glow in it, her eyes a warm light that he'd never noticed before.

Her parents observed it, too. "She had a man in the sowing fields, I'm sure of it," Margha announced.

"She should marry again. I could still get a decent price for her."

"Everyone knows."

"Not everywhere. And if she's breeding, it proves there's no curse. Like I said all along."

"Unless some man in the village drops dead tomorrow."

Tagh made the sign to avert evil. "Watch her, then. If she breeds, maybe we can convince the man to take her."

"She's useful here," Margha argued.

But Tagh snorted. "That's why I bought the girl, to take over the work. Kharra's my daughter, she should be married."

A month later, the wife brought Kharra to him, looking defiant. "I was right, she had a man. She's with child."

"Who was it?" he demanded. "If some man's gotten a child on you, then he can pay the bride-price for it."

But Kharra was his daughter, and as stubborn. "It was sowing night, and all men had the face of the moon."

"I won't take that, girl. You have eyes! I want his name!"

"For what? Do you think any man in this village will pay you your price, after the last time?"

"Then I'll marry you outside. There are plenty of men who don't know what happened."

She looked at him with eyes like hard, dark stones. "Not after I tell them, there won't be. Not if I say I'm a witch, and I can shrivel their balls up with a curse, and that my father won't ever pay back their bride-price. Find a man to marry me then!"

"I'll thrash the name out of you," Tagh threatened, but the daughter stood her ground, and Margha scowled at them both, muttering, "Pigheaded."

Cat had heard it all—by then half the village had heard them—but when he saw Tagh raise his arm, he stepped in front of Kharra, reached one arm around her to put his hand on her belly, still flat and firm, but holding a child inside it—his child. It seemed as if there was a strange spirit moving him when he told Tagh, "You can thrash me, then, because I'm the one who had her."

Tagh's eyes bulged. "You?" And to his daughter, "With a slave? A forest savage?"

"He's the only man in this village who'd dare to touch me," she said defiantly. "And the only one I'll allow, so you can forget about your bride-price."

But the spirit inside Cat insisted, "I'll pay your price for her. I can."

Tagh bellowed terrible threats, but in the end he could do nothing to stop the child from growing in Kharra's belly, no more than he could change her mind. "Making the best of it," was what Margha called it when he finally challenged Cat to produce the bride-price if he thought he could. "The damage is done, and at least she'll have a husband."

Cat's way of tanning deerhide, the way of his vanished tribe, had already earned the envy of the villagers. Now he went back to the woods to find more oak and tanbark. As much as the forest had changed, the scents were the same, and the cool shadows. For a moment, as ever, he could forget the brands on his legs, and think, "I could disappear. They'd never be able to find me." But Kharra was waiting, and his child.

The leather he made was good, the villagers wanted more, and by the time his daughter was born, Cat had paid Tagh his price and taken Kharra openly to his bed as his wife.

"Healthy," Tagh muttered, staring at his grandchild. "And her hair is decently dark, at least. She ought to fetch a good price when she marries."

But Cat watched his daughter nursing at his wife's breast, and he made her a cradle of leather and wood, as it was done in the forest tribes. When he came in from his work at night, he would lift her in his arms and make her laugh. Then Kharra's belly grew big again, and she had a son. When he was born, Cat stared at him a long while, remembering. In secret, he carved a small bow for the boy, no longer than his arm, but he put it away without showing it to anyone.

The work was still hard, clearing more and more farmland as one by one Tagh's sons found wives, and now it was Tagh who had to find the bride-prices. The house was soon filled with women and children, and he was respected as the owner of the largest farm in the village.

When the old man died suddenly, in the middle of an argument with a neighbor who disputed his boundary-rights, Tagh's sons divided up their father's lands among themselves. The slave girl Erla and her children were sold for a good price. But Kharra confronted her brothers with stone-cold eyes and claimed Cat for her own portion of the inheritance, since her father had kept the bride-price from her first marriage. They looked at her and agreed, afraid to cross a woman who still had a reputation as a witch.

Cat's tannery prospered in a small way, and he taught his craft to his sons. Each year he had to travel farther and search harder to find the right barks in the forest. At first he taught the boys; later, as they grew, he gave over the task to them.

One day his oldest son came to him with the girl he meant to marry, if he could meet her father's price. She was a pretty thing, with dark brown eyes. Like Kharra's eyes when they were warm, Cat thought.

The young man was excited. "Father, look at this fur! I traded for it from a village north of here, near the forest. Do you think we could tan furs like this? So soft and warm, I'm sure people would pay well for them!"

Cat's mouth had gone dry. Wordlessly, he reached out for the dried skin of the forest cat, stroked its striped fur. He closed his eyes and called out to the spirit in his mind: *Brother!*

He opened his eyes. No. It was only the pelt of an animal, killed and skinned and brought by strangers to this place so far from its forest home.

VICTORIAN VARIATIONS

New shoots from an old trunk

How the Ant Made a Bargain

by Karawynn Long

Though Karawynn Long missed reading the Just So Stories *as a kid, she was delighted to discover them as an adult. She won the Writers of the Future Grand Prize in 1993 and has stories forthcoming in* Full Spectrum 5, Alternate Tyrants, *and other anthologies. At this time she is living in Seattle, where she is working on more short fiction and a novel.*

Now I shall tell you a story of the hot and humid days at the beginning of the world, when the Queen of all the Ants lived in the dark damp bottom of the forest with her many daughters.

The Queen was a very wise Ant, for she knew many secrets, and was a little bit magic besides. All the same she was often bored, for her Principal Occupation was egglaying, and if you have ever tried laying eggs, Best Beloved, you will have discovered that it is a tedious task, rather like washing dishes. But without eggs there soon would be no daughter Ants to burrow and build and forage and fight, so she tried to make the best of things by thinking up new and interesting ideas.

One uncomfortably stuffy day the Queen noticed that some of her daughters were 'sclusively strong and fierce, and these she instructed to become soldiers and guard the colony from harm. For the Tamandua and the Pangolin and the Angwantibo all thought Ants were 'specially tasty delicacies, and would eat them right up whenever they could.

Then the Queen noticed that some of her daughters were 'sclusively sturdy and industrious, and these she instructed to become workers and gather new foods for the colony. For the Calliandra and the Heliconia and the Banisteriopsis all had an unfathomable preference for not being eaten, and so grew thick and tough and tasted of noxious toxins.

And in this way the Queen Ant invented Specialization (which is, Best Beloved, only a fancy way of saying that different people do different things). And the Queen laid eggs and thought wise thoughts in her nest in the dark damp bottom of the forest, while her specialized colony grew prosperous and large.

One indisputably humid day the Queen called her strongest, fiercest soldier daughter to her and said, "The sun is high and it is time you made your own way in the world. But first I will give you one magic and tell you one secret."

And the fierce soldier daughter replied, "O my Mother and O my Queen, I am angry that the Tamandua and the Pangolin and the Angwantibo all think that we are 'specially tasty delicacies, and will eat us right up whenever they can. I should like to lead a platoon of ants, all as fierce as ever could be, so that I and my daughters will never fear being eaten."

"Then so you shall," said the Queen, and she touched the soldier daughter with her antennae. And the fierce soldier daughter grew a gigantic stinger that she could move in and out like a needle. "Now you will be Army Ant," said the Queen, "and your fierce daughters may march right under the noses of the Tamandua and the Pangolin and the Angwantibo, and even eat them right up if they don't move quickly out of your way."

"O my Mother and O my Queen, that would be most gratifying, but however shall we build a nest if we are continually marching?"

"That is the secret I shall tell you," replied the Queen. And she told Army Ant how her daughters could hook themselves together by the ends of their spindly legs and so make a nest out of their own bodies wherever they happened to be. And Army Ant went away satisfied to make her own way in the world.

And the Queen laid eggs and thought wise thoughts in her nest in the dark damp bottom of the forest, while her specialized colony grew prosperous and large.

One particularly sticky day the Queen called her sturdiest, most industrious worker daughter to her and said, "The sun is high and it is time you made your own way in the world. But first I will give you one magic and tell you one secret."

And the industrious worker daughter replied, "O my Mother and O my Queen, I am frustrated that the Calliandra and the Hel-

iconia and the Banisteriopsis all have an unfathomable preference for not being eaten, and so grow thick and tough and taste
of noxious toxins. I should like to direct a plantation of ants, all
as industrious as ever could be, so that I and my daughters will
never worry about being hungry."

"Then so you shall," said the Queen, and she touched the
worker daughter with her antennae. And the industrious worker
daughter grew enormous jaws that she could open and shut like
scissors. "Now you will be Leaf-Cutter Ant," said the Queen,
"and your industrious daughters may cut the leaves of the Calliandra and the Heliconia and the Banisteriopsis, and carry them
away over their heads and down into the ground."

"O my Mother and O my Queen, that would be most gratifying, but however can we digest them when they taste of noxious
toxins?"

"That is the secret I shall tell you," replied the Queen. And
she told Leaf-Cutter Ant how her daughters could chew the
leaves up and place a drop of spittle on them to cultivate a de-
licious fungus. And Leaf-Cutter Ant went away satisfied to make
her own way in the world.

And the Queen laid eggs and thought wise thoughts in her nest
in the dark damp bottom of the forest, while her specialized colony grew prosperous and large.

One utterly muggy day a third daughter Ant approached the
Queen. She was neither the strongest, nor the sturdiest, nor the
fiercest, nor the most industrious, and indeed the Queen could
not remember her particularly out of the thousands of daughters
she had engendered since the beginning of the world. But you
should know, Best Beloved, that this Ant was most scintillating
clever. "The sun is high," said the daughter Ant, "and I would
like to make my own way in the world."

"Very well," said the Queen, "I will give you one magic and
tell you one secret, for that is only fair, but I warn you that I've
already given the most valuable magics and told the most useful
secrets to your sisters Army Ant and Leaf-Cutter Ant."

"As you say," said the clever Ant with a shrug of her antennae. "But they do not have the ability to converse with all the
plants and animals of the forest, and that is the magic I would
like."

"Then you shall have it," said the Queen, and she touched the
daughter Ant with her antennae. If you had been watching most
spectacularly close, Best Beloved, you would have seen nothing
happen to the Ant at all. Only the Ant herself could tell the dif-

ference, for suddenly she could comprehend what the birds and
bugs and bushes were saying to each other, all above and around
and beside and beneath her.

"Now I will tell you a secret," said the Queen, but the daughter Ant didn't let her.

"I can find my own secret," said the Ant, for she knew very
well that she was scintillating clever, and this made her more
than a little proud. "And choose my own name, too," she added,
and went away satisfied to make her own way in the world.

Before long the Ant came upon the Paper Wasp, sucking rainwater from her paper nest and spitting it out over the side. Paper
Wasp certainly knew how to build a nest, thought the clever Ant,
and set herself to bargain.

"O my Friend," she said, waving her antennae high. "You
have the most beautiful nest I have ever seen, but I could not
help noticing that it is almost empty. Perhaps you could use
some assistance in guarding it? I have a fine sharp stinger that I
would wield in your defense."

"O my Enemy, you think to trick me," said the Paper Wasp,
"but I have seen your sister the Army Ant, who marched her
daughters over my nest, all as fierce as ever could be, and killed
my poor helpless brood and carried them all away. As for sting-
ers, I have a 'scruciating one of my own, as you will learn if you
come any closer."

At that the Ant's antennae drooped, and she went hastily on
her way. Before long she came upon the Passion Flower, tilting
her broad leaves to catch glimmers of sunlight. Passion Flower
certainly knew how to make nectar, thought the clever Ant, and
set herself to bargain.

"O my Friend," she said, waving her antennae high. "You
have the most beautiful flowers I have ever seen, but I could not
help noticing that some of them have been eaten. Perhaps you
could use some assistance in guarding them? I have fine sharp
jaws that I would wield in your defense."

"O my Enemy, you think to trick me," said the Passion
Flower, "but I have seen your sister the Leaf-Cutter Ant, who
marched her daughters over my petals, all as industrious as ever
could be, and cut out immense semicircular pieces and carried
them all away. I have had enough of jaws, and so I am making
a pernicious poison, as you will learn if you come any closer."

At that the Ant's antennae drooped, and she went hastily on
her way. And so it went with every plant and animal she spoke
to, until she began to think her choice of magics had been a fool-

ish one after all. Still she walked on across the dark damp bottom of the forest.

The Ant walked far and she walked wide, she walked low and she walked high, until one day while climbing a cloudy mountain she came upon the Resplendent Quetzal sitting on an Avocado tree and ruffling his emerald-and-scarlet feathers. She didn't have a bargain to make with the Quetzal, so she kept walking without bothering to speak. But as she passed she heard him say, "What manner of animal do you suppose that is?" From the Avocado's trunk his wife replied irritably that she hadn't the faintest idea, since the only thing she could currently see was the interior of a tree.

Aha, thought the clever Ant to herself, *the Quetzal has never met any of my sisters.* And she thought perhaps her luck was about to change.

Indeed it was the very next day that the Ant discovered the Acacia. He was a tattered tree, a bedraggled tree, and nearly all of his leaves had been chewed right off their stems. But the clever Ant looked at the thick prickly thorns that grew all along the Acacia's trunk, and she thought of the Quetzal's wife, and she set herself to bargain.

"O my Friend," she said to the Acacia, "those are impressive thorns that you have grown all along your trunk. But I cannot help noticing that they have not kept the Grasshopper and the Caterpillar and the Katydid from chewing nearly all your leaves right off their stems. Perhaps you could use some assistance? I have a fine sharp stinger that I would wield in your defense."

"All right," said the Acacia, who had never seen an Ant of any sort before.

So the Ant climbed high in the bare branches of the Acacia to the very tiptop, where the last little leaves were stretching toward a sliver of sunlight, and waited. Soon enough the Grasshopper landed on the leaves and widened his mandibles to take one incisive bite. But he never got even a taste because the Ant ran right up to him and stuck her stinger into the Grasshopper's foot. When he lifted that foot out of reach, she stung another one, and when he lifted that foot up, she stung a different one, until finally the Grasshopper had no feet left to stand on, and he flew off in a huff.

"Well, that takes care of him," said the Ant to the Acacia. "I'll be on my way now. Best of luck." And she started climbing back down along the bare branches.

"O my Friend," replied the Acacia in something of a panic, for he knew that as soon as the Ant left the Grasshopper or the Caterpillar or the Katydid would come back and chew his last little leaves right off their stems. "You must have been traveling very far. Why don't you crawl inside one of my hollow thorns and rest for a while?"

"That sounds splendid," said the Ant, "but I shall be hungry soon, so I really shouldn't stop until I've found something to eat."

"Oh, you needn't worry about that," said the Acacia. "I'm sure I can manage to feed such a valiant Ant as yourself."

At that, the Ant (you remember she was scintillating clever) gave a little fillip of her antennae, which was her way of smiling to herself, and chewed a round hole in one of his thick thorns. Then she crawled right inside, curled up, and went to sleep.

Then the Acacia concentrated *very* hard, until he had grown a nubby little knob at the base of a nearby stem, and filled it with nectar. When the Ant woke, she took one sip and vibrated with delight, for it was the sweetest nectar she had ever tasted.

"O Acacia," said the Ant, "I will make a bargain with you. I and my daughters will live inside your thick thorns for always and always, and defend your tender leaves from the Grasshopper and the Caterpillar and the Katydid, for always and always. In return you will provide me and my daughters with as much sweet nectar as we need, for always and always."

"Agreed," said the Acacia. Whereupon the Ant crawled back into the hollow thorn and began to lay her eggs.

Now as you recall, Best Beloved, egglaying is a tedious task, especially for someone so scintillating clever, so the Ant did a lot of thinking besides. And what she thought was this: that sweet nectar is all very well for grown-up Ants to eat, but that young Ants need something rather more highly-nutritious, or they will not be very clever Ants at all when they are grown-up. Her bargain was not yet done. She clambered back out of the hole in the thorn.

"O my Friend," said the Ant to the Acacia, "your leaves are looking ever so marvelous, but I cannot help noticing that clingy curly vines have twined around your stems and are stealing the light from them. Perhaps you could use some assistance? I have fine sharp jaws that I would wield in your defense."

"All right," said the Acacia.

So the Ant climbed high among the leafy limbs and crossed over onto one of the clingy curly vines where it spiraled around a branch. Then she opened her jaws and bit into the vine, just at the base of the leaf-stem, and chewed and chewed until she chewed clean through it and the leaf fell off. Then she bit through another leaf-stem, and another, until the clingy curly vine was as bare as could be, with no leaves at all to gather light.

"Well, that takes care of that," said the Ant to the Acacia. "But I am far too tired to bite any more vines for quite a while." And she let her antennae sag in a most exhausted fashion.

"That's all right," said the Acacia. "Soon your eggs will hatch and you will have many daughter Ants to help you."

"They'll be far too stupid for that," the Ant replied sorrowfully. "You see, sweet nectar is all very well for grown-up Ants to eat, but young Ants need something rather more highly-nutritious, or they will not be very clever Ants at all when they are grown-up."

"You needn't worry about that," said the Acacia. "I'm certain I can manage to feed the daughters of such a loyal Ant as yourself."

At that the Ant (you remember she was scintillating clever) gave a little fillip of her antennae, which was her way of smiling to herself, and crawled back inside her hollow thorn to tend her eggs.

Then the Acacia concentrated *very* hard, until he had grown highly-nutritious globules at the tips of the leaves on one branch, all of them a radiant orange color. When the eggs began to hatch, the Ant detached one of the orange globules and clambered back through the round hole in the thorn, where she fed it to her own first best beloved daughter.

"I will make a bargain with you," said the Ant to the Acacia. "I and my daughters shall live in your thick thorns for always and always, and with our sharp jaws protect your juicy stems from the curly clingy vines, for always and always. In return you shall provide me and my daughters with as many of these highly-nutritious globules as we need, for always and always."

"Agreed," said the Acacia.

"Surely this is the best bargain anyone has ever made since the beginning of the world," said the Ant. "I shall call myself Acacia Ant in recognition of it." And she gave a little fillip of her antennae.

Before long the Tamandua and the Pangolin and the Angwantibo all trundled through that part of the forest, hunting for 'specially tasty delicacies, but the Acacia's thick thorns pricked them every time they came close. Finally the Tamandua snuffled his long nose, and the Pangolin curled his sticky tongue, and the

Angwantibo blinked his round eyes, and they all went away hungry.

So even today, Best Beloved, if you look at the dark damp bottom of the forest, you can see the strong fierce daughters of the Army Ant hooking themselves together by the ends of their spindly legs, and the sturdy industrious daughters of the Leaf-Cutter Ant carrying semicircular pieces of leaf away over their heads.

And if somewhere in the forest you see a tree with a wide space around it that no plant nor animal dares to encroach upon, then you will know that it is an Acacia. For the daughters of the Acacia Ant are valiant and loyal and (so long as they eat their highly-nutritious globules when they are young) most scintillating clever, and they keep the bargain the Acacia Ant made for always and always and always.

In Fear of Little Nell

by Gregory Feeley

Gregory Feeley, whose novel The Oxygen Barons *was nominated for the Philip K. Dick award, here assembles a tale around a famous character from Charles Dickens, a writer best known for his urban settings. But the dichotomy between city and countryside is present in much of Dickens, which allows Feeley to take a fresh look at a very different nineteenth-century story.*

"She needs rest," said the old man, patting her cheek; "too pale—too pale. She is not like what she was."

"When?" asked the child.

—*The Old Curiosity Shop*

Garlic grows poorly in Shropshire; the strings of bulbs that the four men dropped around their necks had come on a boat from Calais. Dalton fingered a clove, and found it soft: would its efficacy, like the bloom of a cut flower, fade after the first day? The question did not bear thinking on. He tried to stuff the reeking necklace into his shirt, got it tangled with the cross on its cord—a bit of papistry he was ashamed to wear, but afraid not to—and pulled both free with a curse.

"Like a stinking censer," growled Burke, the sweat of fear mingling with garlic as he bent to break open the crate. Burke had traveled as far as Silesia and seen much, but spoke of nothing more specific than his disdain for Romish practices. And what if their quarry was no Catholic? wondered Dalton, unable to halt the runaway train of his thought. Should the superstitions avail them then?

The top split with a crunch, and Burke tossed aside his iron to pry up the spintered boards and peer with his companions into the crate. A dozen wooden stakes lay like carrots, each symmetrical as a geometer's cone. Dalton lifted one and felt its unnatural smoothness, then discovered with a finger the indentation at the base where the lathe had held it. The stakes had been machined, probably in a Spitalfields mill. He held it up, and saw Burke's eyes narrow in recognition.

"By God," he swore, "it's one monster hunting another." He seemed ready to recoil from the stake, as though it had transformed into his prey.

"Mind your language," said the parson, spectacles glinting as he raised his chin. "This is a holy business we are about."

"It's a dirty business, and don't you forget it."

"Burke," Dalton interjected firmly, "will a stake turned on a lathe serve our purpose? Or need it be carved by human hands?"

Burke glowered and considered. "Not that I know," he allowed. "If a stake cut by gypsies proved worthy, as I have heard tell, then its making matters not. It could be machined by a Jew on Whitsunday, so long as it is driven well home."

The journalist had said nothing, as was customary, and Dalton would not have been surprised to see him recording this exchange in a memorandum. Instead, he was crouched before the crate, rummaging through its contents with a bony rattle. "A baker's dozen," he said, looking up. "Perhaps not a propitious number. Are we likely to need so many?"

"Heaven forbid," cried the parson.

"If the first try fails," Burke said, "ye shan't get another."

"Perhaps the Professor expects us to split up, each taking three?" Dalton asked. But that made no sense, as well as begging the question. He didn't mention his next apprehension: that the Professor had feared their quarry was not one, but many.

"Hullo," said the journalist, "here's something." His fingers had merely touched the bottommost stakes as he counted them, but now he brought one forth. He raised it like a candle, and they stared. It was less than half the length of the others, although shaped to the same proportions. The stake was a perfect miniature, as though fashioned for a—

The thought struck them all at once. "Sweet Jesus Christ," exclaimed Burke. And this time the parson did not rebuke him.

* * *

"We know it's a child," Dalton said, more for his own benefit than for the journalist's. "The professor said that the examination *post mortem* showed clear—"

"We know," said Burke shortly. He stood and crossed the deck, to take up his station against the far railing, looking out over the dark water.

The journalist looked mildly after him, then back down at his notebook. "Have you ever read *De masticatione mortuorom in tumulus?*" he asked.

Dalton shook his head. "Something about the biting dead?" he asked. "I haven't studied Latin since grammar school."

"I don't read Latin," the journalist said, "so do not know the volume. Nor have I entree to the Bodleian Library, so have not seen Calmet's *Dissertation on the Vampyres of Hungary,* evidently on a like topic, although I paid a tipsy undergraduate to abstract it for me, and learned for my trouble that I 'would not like it.' A similar book, however—the *Travels of Three English Gentlemen*—was made available to me at a lending library in Greenwich, and dates from 1734, the same era as the earlier tomes."

"And what does that volume have to say?" asked Dalton wearily.

The journalist turned a page and held it so to catch the light of the barge's lantern. "Travels from Venice to Austria," he read, "including the Carnian Alps, Hamburgh, and the Duchy of Siria. Local superstitions, including vampyres, an apparently Servian word. 'These Vampyres are supposed to be the Bodies of deceased Persons, animated by evil Spirits, which come out of the Graves, in the Night-time, suck the Blood of many of the Living and thereby destroy them.' "

Dalton shivered suddenly, and drew his coat more closely about him. "And how are they hunted?" he asked.

"The grave of a suspected vampyre is opened, and if the corpse be rosy-cheeked, bearing no evidence of decay, it is a vampyre."

"And how killed?"

The journalist said mildly, "By those means already familiar to us."

Dalton thought of something. "But the corpses are still undisturbed in their graves. How do they come to plague the living?"

"I believe the creature is thought to be a ghost or spirit, which drinks living blood while its body yet lies underground. The

vampyre of Slavic imagination seems as much a superstitious
fancy as a banshee or goblin."

"I wonder what Burke knows of this," Dalton mused.

"Burke," said the journalist, "is not talking." As he spoke, the
barge bumped softly against something below the water line.
Dalton looked over the railing to see that the towpath had drawn
closer; two figures stood by a wagon in the false dawn, the tiny
glow of a pipe showing briefly in the darkness. The team drawing the barge had been halted and were cropping placidly as the
vessel drifted to a stop.

"Banbury?" asked the parson, looking confusedly at the empty
crossroads.

"We're not going that far," said Dalton, who reached for the
crate. One of the barge hands was lifting a long plank, which he
shoved over the rail until its far end touched the shore. The journalist steadied Dalton as he stepped over the railing, the crate un-
wieldy but light in his arms, and onto the swaybacked plank. He
dropped the crate with a rattle on the wet grass and waited as his
colleagues joined him. One of the figures climbed down from the
wagon and came toward them.

"Reverend?" the man muttered, low.

"Just say yes," said Burke, as the parson made to extend his
hand. He lifted a burlap sack with a clank and threw it over one
shoulder.

Dalton felt in his pocket and produced silver, which he handed
to the bargeman and his companion holding the horses. In seconds the bargeman was back across the plank, which withdrew
with a small plash, and the barge had resumed its journey with
no sound greater than the creak of ropes and clopping hooves.
"They think we're smugglers," said Dalton in sudden surmise.

"Just as well," answered Burke. He followed the others back
to the wagon, whose driver turned his head away at their approach. Clouds were beginning to brighten to the east, a filthy
umber that Dalton had never seen, even in London. He climbed
into the back with the others and fell asleep within ten minutes,
lulled by the jouncing bed where the barge's smooth glide had
only spooked him.

He woke at midmorning when the driver pulled up at a brook
and everyone climbed out to piss. A yellow haze tinctured the
sky in the direction (Dalton thought) of Birmingham, but a wood
lay some miles ahead, a green smudge beyond open fields. Dalton felt his chest constrict, and a horror arose in him that he
could force down only by turning away.

The young man, evidently the driver's son, had climbed back into the seat, and was looking curiously at the crate and sack in the back. When he saw Dalton watching him, his face went rigid, and he turned his back with unmistakable contempt. So we are your *Untouchables,* thought Dalton with a grim smile. We'll do your dirty work, but you won't acknowledge us.

They entered the wood an hour later, and were quickly among trees so tall that they leaned over the narrow road like curious specters, and at last met overhead in a green vault. The wagon still clattered so loudly as to make speech impossible, and the four men simply looked at each other or lapsed into abstraction; but the leafy canopy had an immediate effect on Burke, who stared up at it in a kind of terror. Patterns of light and shadow ran across his upturned face, which drained of color as though through his opened mouth.

The journalist reached into his pea-jacket and pulled forth a stoppered flask, which he passed to Burke without a word. Twelve hours earlier, thought Dalton, Burke would have disdained the offer, but now he grasped the bottle and drank off half in a draught. When the journalist (who seemed slightly unnerved by this response) offered the remaining spirits around, Dalton took a swallow himself.

The road narrowed, and in mid-afternoon turned sharply downward, descending on a narrow pathway into a woody hollow. The houses of a small village appeared fitfully between the trees, already in shadow although the summer sun would linger for hours.

The four men looked at each other warily. The journalist twitched alertly as a hare sensing danger, while the parson tried to put on a brave face, and Burke looked as though he were riding a tumbrel to execution. Dalton wondered at Burke's nerves; did he expect the vampyre to drop from the trees like a leopard?

With a pull on the reins the driver drew his horse to a halt. The wagon came to rest at an overgrown switchback, the village unseen below them. "Far enough," he said shortly, not turning.

They climbed out stiffly and lowered their gear to the ground. "We'll be needing to speak to the vicar," Dalton told the driver.

"Nay," he replied, and lifted his reins.

"Wait!" Dalton cried. "I appreciate how we cannot ride into the green like a pack of rat-catchers, but we shall have to interview—"

The horses started forward, and the wagon rattled down the path without either occupant turning his back. The four men watched it disappear around a turn, then stooped to pick up their equipment.

"Better get off the road," said the journalist. "Don't want that one's cousin coming round the bend to wonder at us."

They pushed into the wood like Spanish *guerillas*, taking care to make as little noise as possible. Dalton worried about encountering a village boy hunting squirrels, who would run back and raise an alarum. Eventually they found a footpath and followed it, although it increased the chances of encountering someone. The crate rattled and was difficult to carry down the slope, so they stopped and untied the rope that held down its splintered lid, and shoved the thirteen stakes into their belts.

"Look at Burke," muttered the journalist as he and Dalton bent over the crate. "You would think he'd been drinking a week." And indeed the shorter man was pallid and sweaty, his thin hair plastered to his brow. "And do you know why? It came to me a minute ago: this landscape looks like Bohemia, at least to judge from engravings. Burke is reliving his last journey to Europe."

From the last stand of trees they studied the village. At the far side of the green, oddly empty for a late summer afternoon, stood a small Norman chapel beside an overgrown churchyard. Taking care not to be seen, they crept around to the vicarage, where they composed themselves before knocking at the back door. When the door opened and a wizened sexton peered suspiciously out, it was the parson who spoke, and gained them entry.

"A horrible business," the man muttered as he conducted them along the rear passageway. Whether he meant the village's troubles or the strangers' presence was uncertain, for when the parson ventured to reassure him, the sexton only hunched his shoulders and rapped on a door before disappearing, leaving the vicar to look out in bewilderment at the four strangers that crowded his hallway.

"Mr. Palor," said the parson, "I am Reverend Coburn. Professor Spode has told us of your crisis."

The vicar stared, then cried, "Thank God," at once anxious and nearly faint with relief.

He led them through the churchyard, as though too agitated to fit them into his small study. The parson elicited the man's story, which added only incidentally—the names and particular virtues of the victims; local horror and alarm—to what they already knew. Dalton had hoped that the Professor had explained matters, but finally decided that he would have to ask the pertinent questions himself.

"Reverend Palor," he said. They were walking in high grass, scuffing their toes against sunken fragments of stone that might have marked graves in the last century. "Has anyone come to the village in the past year?"

The vicar gave him a confounded look. "No, no one. We have not even had a new schoolmaster since the last one left the past year. Mr. Burdock, who was a solicitor's clerk in London as a young man, has attempted to fill Mr. Marton's shoes, but he is really not fit for the position. It is a shame that Mr. Marton left us, but he never really recovered after poor little Harry wasted away and died."

Dalton, who had only half-listened to this disquisition after the first word, looked suddenly up. "Wasted away and died?" he asked.

"Indeed, it was a sad business." Mr. Palor gazed dolefully to a corner of the churchyard as the other three men glanced sharply at Dalton. "The Little Scholar, he called him. The schoolmaster visited him every day, but the lad faded like a cut lilac. And truly, the village has not been the same since."

Dalton looked hard at the parson, who spoke up after a moment. "Do you suppose you could show us the grave of this young unfortunate?"

The moon was not full that night, and would moreover be late in rising above the wooded hills. Dalton sat smoking, one hand shielding the pipe's glow from the eyes of any villager glancing uphill at the ruined cottage they inhabited, while the journalist stood looking over a collapsed wall into the rustling darkness. The sexton had sullenly led them to the place, which looked upon the village and the slopes beyond; and after establishing that the monster had not made its nest there, they had fallen upon the ground directly after making plans and slept till dusk. The parson yet breathed in the rhythms of sleep, while Burke, invisible in a far corner, was utterly silent.

"What did you think of the grave?" asked the journalist very softly.

"Of little Harry? Just what I expected—a disordered plot, frequently dug up for the graves of new children, so the fact that the ground had been disturbed troubled no one. And the coffin, I'm sure, had been laid no more than three feet down. It would be interesting to disinter it, but some things aren't done by day-light."

"Care to try now?"

"Why bother? If he's what we're looking for, we'd find an empty kist, broke open from within and the loose earth above it pushed out then carelessly replaced. But we're not gathering evidence, or a story—" here he looked sharply at the journalist, "—we're hunting the creature. We catch him, we don't need to poke further."

"The story may go further," the journalist noted mildly. "There was that boy down in Kent, the fat sluggish fellow. 'I wants to make your flesh creep'?"

"You weren't there," said Dalton firmly. "I don't think he was a vampyre at all. He seemed in some ways a victim—assuming some monster was keeping him as a cow instead of simply slaughtering him—but we never found anything. You are multiplying entities in pursuit of a story."

"Perhaps. But what was that name the vicar gave us?" The journalist sang softly:

> Up the airy mountain,
> Down the Dingley Dell,
> We dare not go a-hunting,
> For fear of Little—

"Shut up!" Burke cried hoarsely from the darkness. Both men jumped. Burke lurched to his feet in the darkness. "Speak the name of one, and you think its fellows can't hear?" His breath puffed sourly in Dalton's face.

The journalist made to answer, but Burke shoved past, and was over the threshold and out amid the underbrush, where he could be heard thrashing for a minute before the sounds faded. Dalton stood still, wondering whether the parson would wake, but after a minute heard only the journalist sigh.

"Burke is a riotous man," the journalist remarked. "Did he grow up in Europe?"

"Hardly. His father was a Luddite, and came to a bad end for it. Burke lost a sister to some fever, of the sort that goes sweeping through mill towns when men are out of work and children hungry. I suspect he went to France a fugitive, and traveled east to put more distance between himself and England. Until he saw a vampyre, I doubt he ever met anything he hated so much as a foundry."

"And Spode engaged him for the same reason he did you? For his acquaintance with unnatural phenomena?"

"I do not know the particulars of Professor Spode's arrangements," Dalton said rather stiffly. "I work with him because I would rather assist in first-rate researches than mount second-rate ones. Burke plainly considers his work here important."

The journalist, unfazed, looked after Burke speculatively. "I bet he's thinking what I am," he said after a moment.

"And what is that?"

"How many there are, of course. Don't all the accounts state that the vampyre's victims turn vampyres themselves?"

"That's nonsense, else the living would be outnumbered by them. Only a few must succumb to the contagion, or else only a few escape their graves, while the rest remain buried, to die for a second and final time."

"But you think you've got one here," the journalist stated.

"That may be so," Dalton admitted. His gut was certain: it contracted at the thought. "Spode saw the evidence, and he doesn't jump at shadows. And he sent up that box of stakes, after we had set out. I wonder why he did that?"

"There's something on 'em," the journalist said. "Can't you tell? Keep one under your shirt long enough and it starts to get ripe. He has some poison on the tips, I warrant you."

"Really?" said Dalton, turning round.

"Take care not to be jabbed. I have the points of mine impaled on bits of strap leather, and recommend the same to you."

Dalton was about to examine his when a thin shriek cut through the night. Both men started up: it sounded like a vole being struck by an owl, but came from one of the whistles Burke had handed out. They scrambled outside, Dalton pausing to shake the parson. The night air sang with crickets and soughing leaves, and the sound of their own hard breathing.

"The path," the journalist whispered. The two men started down it, Dalton (without intending it) in front. A wooden mallet thrust in his belt banged hard against his hip as he blundered down the narrow trail, striving to combine haste with silence but managing (he was certain) neither.

They nearly ran into Burke, who crouched in the path with an arm upraised. "Listen," he murmured. The two men stood there, trying to still their heaving chests as the parson came up behind them, and strained to hear something as a low breeze rustled through the hollow.

A faint keening—was it the wind bending a laden bough?—

seemed to waft from the ground ahead. Dalton tried to order his thoughts: Burke had laid garlic across every footpath leading to the village but one, which they hoped to compel the creature to use. But was this the path? He hadn't thought so.

The wind shifted, and for a second Dalton could hear it plainly: a thin wail, like a cat in heat or mewling puppy. He pushed past Burke, who had gone suddenly nerveless, and advanced slowly on the path, achieving at last a measure of stealth as his night vision grew stronger.

The child was standing before the post Burke had driven into the ground, balked like a waif who can't manage his way past an obstruction. Its shoulders were shaking slightly as it sobbed, and Dalton could see that its garments were torn and dirty. As he stepped forward, the child turned and looked up at him.

Its dirty face white beneath the filth and smeared with tears, the child—it was a boy, Dalton noted, hair knotted with twigs— opened his mouth in a forlorn wail. He looked at Dalton for a moment, then raised his arms in entreaty and took a few halting steps forward.

Dalton bent down, and someone shoved him aside. "No!" cried Burke as Dalton fell against a tangle of brush. There was a scuffle and a sudden high scream. The others were crowding past, and Dalton had trouble recovering his footing. A struggle was taking place on the path, curses and thrashing branches. Dalton scrambled to his feet. "For the love of God, Burke!" someone cried.

The sound thrilled his blood: the unmistakable thud of a mallet pounding wood. The three men were bent over something, falling against each other. Suddenly there was a light, and they all stood back, aghast.

Eyes watering in the glare, Dalton pushed forward and looked over their shoulders. The child, eyes livid and mouth gaping in rictus, lay spread upon the flattened vegetation, a great stake driven into his chest. Blood was everywhere: matting his hair, rimming his distended mouth, soaking his shirt so wetly the torchlight gleamed on it. "Good Christ," Dalton whispered. Behind him, someone was being sick.

"Do you realize what you have done?" Dalton couldn't tell who was speaking. "Can you see now what you *did?*"

"I've killed a monster." Burke's voice was flat beyond exhaustion. "Look at the blood around its mouth: it's long dried."

Dalton looked, but the surrounding details were beginning to come clear to him, even as the horror at their center beggared notice. The journalist had ignited the scrap of leather on the tip of his stake, which he now held point down so that the flame licked over the wood, producing a vile stench. Burke stood panting, his leather apron slick with blood. The parson, face white as a sheet, was in tears.

Dalton looked down again. "He's right," he said after a moment. "God help us." The child's lips, drawn back in agony, disclosed teeth black with old blood. His clothes, filthy and blood-soaked as they were, were churchgoing best: nothing to wear while wandering at night. A white scrap was caught on a trouser button, which Dalton numbly recognized as material from a winding sheet.

They stood staring for a second. Then Burke said, "Right, then. Let's be about it."

With the journalist scribbling and the parson mumbling prayers, Burke brought out a palm-sized block of paraffin, then cupped one hand behind the creature's neck. "Mind those teeth," he told Dalton, who had gingerly grasped the jaw. The flesh was cold, and felt like the skin on old oatmeal.

Carefully they took an impression of the child's dentition. This body was lain in the grave, Dalton thought, and felt the skin of his fingertips creep.

"Got it," muttered Burke. He raised the block to the light, then frowned. Somewhere below a dog was barking. Suddenly afraid of discovery, Dalton grasped the child's shoulder and tried to pull him off the path. The small body twisted before encountering resistance, and with a sudden nausea Dalton realize that the stake had pinned it to the ground.

"We must get out of here," the journalist said.

"We have to dispose of the body," Dalton replied. Hands shaking, he grasped the stake and tried to pull it free.

"We will take it down for Christian burial," said the parson, his voice quavering.

"Like hell," said Dalton, suddenly angry. "It's had a Christian burial. Spode wants to see it—"

"Oh, Christ," said Burke.

"—But I wouldn't transport it for a peerage. We're going to saw off its head and bury it in the woods."

"Oh, Christ."

"What is it?" cried Dalton.

Burke held up the paraffin block, as though it were a page from Revelation. "This isn't the same vampyre," he said.

* * *

Birmingham glowed at night like coals in a grate, scattered orange and red in the smoking darkness. Licks of flame appeared atop smokestacks, and the tall windows of factories blazed like lurid canvases hung against the night sky. The highway ran past districts governed by mills and foundries, which flared through the carriage windows like seeping fissures in the earth.

Dalton had expected the journalist to be up studying this spectacle, but it was the parson whose eyes were open, dim whites unblinking in the dark interior. Although they had all slept most of the day, Burke and the journalist were slumped in the far seats, as though fled from the jagged shards of consciousness into Morpheus' enshrouding fog. Dalton wondered if he would ever sleep again.

"What are you thinking of?" he asked the parson.

"Eternity," the man replied, surprising him. "That child had died—I acknowledge that now—and been brought back, or his release hindered, by the curse of vampyrism, whatever that be. Did we deliver him in destroying his body?"

"Reverend, I am a naturalist, or once was. I don't think that spiritual corruption is spread by contagion, like the plague. If it makes you feel better, I believe that there is a scientific explanation for what we saw last night, and all the Slavic stories about crosses and holy water are but superstitions."

The parson shook his head. "I appreciate what you're trying to say, but I know enslavement when I see it, and it is not something suffered by nature. That child had been enslaved by something evil, and we must think as much of his slaver as of its other victims. You must have thought of this."

Dalton sighed. "Something made little Harry into what we saw. It is no longer in that village, else we would have seen a vampyre scare like those in Hungary in the last century. So we have a mobile agent."

"A traveling vampyre."

Dalton winced. The image of an undead monster ranging through the Midlands, perhaps taking the same highways as they, felt worse the more he thought of it.

He ordered his thoughts before speaking. "An adult vampyre, a canny one, could feed without making the kind of attacks that attract attention. Feed upon helpless victims, like the infirm . . . or children."

"And if he fed carefully?" the parson asked quietly.

"They would not die quickly. But if they were children, they would . . . waste away."

The two men were silent.

From the opposite corner the journalist spoke. "The school-master, Mr. Marton. Who moved to the village of Tong."

"Yes," said Dalton.

"Who took a solicitous interest in that itinerant girl, whose name I should not mention."

"Yes."

"We are riding to Wolverhampton, because of an old report there, but you intend to continue to Tong, now, don't you? Because he is there. Where he has charge of a school full of children."

"Yes," said Dalton. "This is so."

"Mister Marton remains schoolmaster, but has given up his other duties as clerk," the clergyman told them. "He has led a retired life since the unhappy events of last winter."

The parson nodded politely as he walked beside his colleague through the ruin of a church, which seemed to have been decaying steadily since its construction sometime during the Crusades. Dalton, who had been introduced as a student of church architecture, followed a step behind them, pausing frequently to peer about at the recesses and crannies of the chill stone pile.

"You mean the death of the little girl, Nell," he said.

The clergyman sighed. "Although she lived in our parish for but a few scant months, she won a place in the hearts of the townspeople that may never again be filled. Those last weeks—when it was clear she would not live to hear the birds sing—cast a pall on the hearts of all who knew her."

"It must have been a terrible blow to Mr. Marton," the parson observed.

"It was hard—very hard," the clergyman admitted with a melancholy air. "But he has responded by throwing himself into his work, and has shown such devotion to his duties that the child's memory must shine in the light of heaven. To some of his students he has grown especially close."

"I see." The parson did not glance back. "And the poor girl—I assume her body was returned to her original home?"

"Oh, no. It rests within this very church."

"Indeed?" Dalton looked up at this. "Within the church itself?"

The clergyman led them into a tiny chapel, where the statues of medieval knights rested supine atop stone coffins like Egyptian sarcophagi. Dalton looked about him in bewilderment: clearly no one had been interred in this chamber in centuries.

"Nell is laid to rest beneath this pavement-stone," said the clergyman, looking down upon it. Several lines had been carved into the stone, unreadable in the dim light.

Dalton looked down with interest. The stone, and an adjacent one, had plainly been taken up recently, while the mortar lining the others bore the undisturbed grime of decades. "You buried someone beside her?"

"Her grandfather," the clergyman explained. "He survived her only by a few months. After her death, he would come and sit right here, all day long, alone with his beloved granddaughter."

"I see." Above the clergyman's lowered countenance, the two men exchanged a long stare.

Burke had spent a night and a day in Wolverton, and was of dangerous countenance when he met them at the inn a few miles from Tong. "Children dying every day," he said, raising his tankard and glowering at them. "Tiny bundles laid on wagons. A vampyre could live forever in a mill town and no one would ever suspect."

"Never mind that," the journalist told him. "We found our Mr. Marton."

The three men listened as the journalist described his interview with the schoolmaster. "His hand is cold, and he withdrew it quickly from mine, which I had rubbed with garlic juice. His garden is small; villagers say he gives away many of his vegetables, I think he gives them all away. He keeps his cottage dim, but can see well in it; he avoids daylight as an owl does. And one of his students is ailing."

"He never died and was buried," the parson interrupted. "The clergyman, who hired him, has letters of recommendation from his school days."

The journalist shrugged. "A victim may die alone, and lie neglected until he rise a vampyre. He may, indeed, not know himself for what he truly is."

"We will tell him ere we strike off his head," Burke said.

Dalton spoke up then. "No, that we cannot do," he said as the other two started in alarm. "It is one thing to decapitate a monster that everyone thinks in its grave; it is another to kill a schoolmaster. I have written the Professor this evening, and we will wait on his reply. I suspect he will want the schoolmaster taken alive—if that is the proper term."

Burke actually growled. "A vampyre is not a Bengal tiger to be caged and studied," he said. "If you will not act, I—"

"Stay," said Dalton, raising a hand. "We shall have our answer in two days. If you want to hunt monsters tonight, we have scented another." And when the journalist turned to stare at him, Dalton added, "The girl, your Little Nell. She is in the church itself."

They picked the sexton's lock silently, then stood within the softly-closed door for long minutes, letting the stillness return like a startled animal. Only after ascertaining that nothing was moving within the church did they begin to advance, in single file, slowly up the aisle.

They entered the old chapel as cautiously as if it were a bear's cave, though Dalton was certain that their quarry did not sleep here. He satisfied himself by putting one foot on either side of her pavement-stone (as he could not do when the clergyman was present) and shifting his weight back and forth. After a minute he nodded at Burke, who was standing with his stake gripped like a butcher's knife: the stone was not loose in its setting.

They had slowly filed out of the chapel and stood uncertainly in the darkness when Dalton heard it. A faint scratching, oddly amplified, echoed in the dim expanse, its point of origin unknowable. The four men froze. Dalton raised his face, like a blind man seeking the sun's warmth, and sought its source.

It's echoing off the chancel ceiling, he thought. *So it is not at this end of the nave.* He slowly began to step down the aisle, straining so hard to hear that his arched eyebrows began to ache.

The parson touched his sleeve. "Where is it?" he whispered into Dalton's ear. "The belfry?"

The thought of the creature being above his head was almost too horrible to entertain, but after a second's reflection Dalton shook his head. The tiny belfry lacked space for concealment.

The scraping came a bit louder, distorted by its own echoes. "Sounds as though it's coming from the bottom of a well," the parson whispered.

"Good God," said Dalton, softly but aloud. "The well!"

He ran toward the narthex, and was slowly pulling open a heavy oak door when his colleagues caught up with him. A musty exhalation breathed forth from the crypt below, and the sounds grew immediately louder.

"The well is old, and dry at the bottom," Dalton said. "It's covered by a few boards. What a fool I've been."

Burke was unshouldering his canvas bag. With a scratch, a lucifer flamed into life in the journalist's hands. "Can she see
that?" whispered the parson, glancing down the stairwell to see
how far the weak light penetrated.

"If she's still in the well, it won't matter that she knows we're
coming," Burke answered.

The stone steps did not creak, but Dalton grimaced at each
footfall as they hastened down. Burke held a lantern, its lamp
hooded so that only a single beam fell onto the steps before
them. The low ceiling of the crypt prevented the diffusion of
light.

The sounds were coming through a low vaulted arch, built in
an age when men were smaller. They were louder now, and had
taken on definition: a sliding scrape, a pause, some tiny fidgety
sounds, and then another scrape.

Slowly they stepped through the arch. At the center of the
small chamber, a trestle with a bucket hanging on a cord stood
over a circular hole three feet across. The sounds were echoing
off the low ceiling directly above.

The irregular oval of lantern light, which had advanced to the
edge of the well and then circled it like a cautious dog, slid suddenly to a far wall as Burke thrust the lantern into Dalton's
hands. Slowly he advanced to the edge of the well, where he
stood looking down for several seconds.

He's going to kill her, Dalton thought in alarm. *He's going to
cosh in her head.* In the dim light, he could not see whether
Burke's arms were raised. He wanted to call out, but didn't dare.

Then he saw a hand rise out of the blackness and grasp the lip
of the well. He didn't see Burke's reaction; his gaze was fixed on
the dim white shape clutching the stone's edge. A second later
another hand appeared, and a small head rose above the level of
the floor.

Its face was turned away, but Dalton could see the head tilt as
it noticed the dim light in the chamber. Then it turned, and a
dead white face—white even in the faint hooded lamplight—
turned and saw Dalton, then looked up at Burke.

"Have you come for me, then?" it asked in a little girl's voice,
scratchy with disuse. "I have been waiting so long."

A low moan filled the room, and Dalton realized with horror
that it was Burke. Something metal fell from his hands and
clanged against the stone floor.

The girl was pulling herself out of the hole. A funerary gown,
streaked with dirt, hung from her slender frame. The lantern

beam fell as if of its own volition onto the girl; she blinked once when it crossed her face.

She rose unsteadily to her feet, like one stiff from labor. Her crown scarcely reached Burke's elbow, and the legs beneath her ragged hem were thin as a doe's.

She held out her open arms, as though inviting the blow. "I have been so cold and so lonely," she said in a quavering tone. "I did not mean to be like this."

With a cry Burke bent over her, and her tiny arms closed around his neck. Dalton shouted, or started to, but things happened too quickly for the sound to escape his throat.

Whether she pulled Burke down or slipped backward Dalton could not tell, but the two fell together, with a terrible cracking sound that must have been Burke's skull striking the far side. Like a nut clattering down a rain spout, they knocked against the sides going down, falling not freely but impeded, and hence for far longer. Dalton thought he heard a scream, but it might have been his own.

Dust flew through the beam as it swung wildly through the chamber, then settled once more upon the well, now horribly silent. Heart pounding, Dalton advanced to its edge, then leaned slowly—he had to force himself for the last inches—over the well's mouth, and shone the lantern downward. Rock dust boiled up, obscuring the beam before it had penetrated a yard. It would, he realized, be hours in settling.

No sound from below. Somewhere behind, the faint call of voices.

She could not have survived the fall, Dalton knew. Thin-boned and emaciated, the poor monster had surely perished, breaking (to some degree) the large man's fall. Even Burke, hale and burly and aproned in cushioning leather, must lie unconscious at the well's dry bottom.

Dalton tugged at the rope, which he found too thin to trust, and pushed the bucket aside. He set the lantern next to the edge, and unhooded it: the light cast a half-circle of pale illumination through the dust-swarming chamber, but none fell into the well.

She is dead, he thought. *Burke, perhaps, is alive.* With trembling hands he planted his palms upon either side of the well, then swung his legs over the edge. Bracing each foot against the rough stone was easy, and Dalton gingerly lowered his weight below the level of the floor, disappearing at once into darkness.

If anything brushes my foot, I shall kick, he thought. *I can climb quickly, if need be. It is, moreover, a long way down.*

The image of the girl's pipestem arms rose before him, and a puff of invisible dust made his eyes sting. "The poor girl," he murmured, too intent on maintaining his footing as he slowly descended the narrow shaft to direct his train of thought. "She should not have ended thus."

He coughed as the dust coated his throat, and hawked in a racking sob. "I'm coming," he said softly, as he let his soles slip several feet before regaining purchase. The stone was not as chill as the crypt itself had been; a few feet further, and its temperature was the same as his own flesh. "Poor helpless thing, I'm coming. . . ."

And when the hands reached up for him, he fell into their embrace with a cry of exhausted relief. The smell of moist earth rose about him, a puff of warm breath, and Dalton fell into unconsciousness with the release of his overstrained limbs.

He woke when something prodded his shoulder, paused, then bumped against his knee. Dalton was lying in a tangle of limbs, some his own. He reached out, every muscle aching, and felt a tiny smooth arm, cool as a root. He jerked his hand back.

Something was bumping about in the darkness, striking the wall every few seconds with a metallic clang. He suddenly guessed it: the weight at the end of a dangling cord. With an effort he recalled the coil of hemp slung over the journalist's shoulder. He grabbed at it, but snatched only air.

He looked up into the darkness, and saw it quickly brighten to gray. A burning lucifer fell through the dust and dropped before him, illuminating the surrounding carnage for an instant before snuffing out. Both Burke and the girl lay motionless, a disordered salad of outflung limbs and loose hair.

Dalton stirred with difficulty in the cramped space, and squeamishly felt their lifeless persons. Both were extensively bloodied, as (he came to realize) he was himself. Numerous bones were broken: he felt them through the girl's thin gown, and even Burke's heavy clothing. The weight brushed his neck and he grabbed it, pulling down hard once. A muffle shout reached him from above. Wrapping the cord around his bloodied knuckles, Dalton tugged to ensure it was secure, then began to climb. After a moment he could feel the cord being slowly drawn up.

"Good God!" the parson cried when he neared the top. Dalton blinked at the lantern as his head crossed the plane of the floor, and he felt hands pulling at him. The journalist's face, frightened and alarmed, swam briefly in his vision.

"Are you all right? Burke is—?"

"Down there. Dead." He found it difficult to speak. "Both of them," he managed to add.

They laid him on the stone cold floor, smoother than the well. "You are hurt," the parson said.

Dalton touched the side of his face. It was raw, and stung dully. He wondered if he were in shock.

The parson spoke of going for help; footsteps retreated up the stone stairwell. Dalton felt a bundled jacket placed beneath his head. The lantern was set nearby, and he could see the journalist in the harsh shadows.

"You have been hurt," the journalist observed.

Dalton nodded.

"Scrapes, from the look. From cascading down the well."

Dalton said nothing.

"It must have been nasty, in that hole," the journalist said after a moment. "Especially at the bottom."

"I feel as if I am still there," Dalton said.

The other man nodded, not looking at him. "She must have been ... hard to resist. Going to all those children who loved her, and none of them ever complaining, not one report from this village. These angelic young girls, sometimes I think they spend their lives training to be dead."

Dalton closed his eyes. When he opened them a moment later, the journalist had met his gaze at last.

"We'll take you to the Professor, and he'll look at you, and wait. And then we'll see, won't we?"

THE NEW WORLD THAT NEVER WAS

Branchings from history

Wood Song

by Kate Daniel

Statistics say most people today will have three careers in their lifetime. As a writer Kate Daniel is on her third right now, having already been a teacher and a computer programmer. She has six YA mystery novels in print, the most recent being Babysitter's Nightmare II, *along with several fantasy short stories.*

At certain times of the year, late at night, the Coaster Grove on Coney Island seems to sing softly to itself. Those who walk beneath the trees at such times feel a sense of awe, as though they walk in a holy place. The grove has stood for over a hundred years, immune to the twentieth century, wrapped in the peace of an older time, and some credit the sensation to age. But even they do not know how deep the years are that twist around the young trees, or how far their roots extend. Like so many dreams of the new world, the dream that is the Grove began in the old, in a promise and prophecy given to a young girl as old as the Attic hills. . . .

"Go; you'll feel better. See what a wonderful place this country is!"

The landlady's shrill voice grated on Daphne's ears. At least the woman spoke Greek. It wasn't a musical sound, but it carried the accents of home, here in this new world of foreigners where Daphne was trapped by bricks and streets. And Mrs. Kontos meant well. She was kind. Kind, but she'd never heard the delicate song of a breeze dancing among spring leaves, never tasted

the silence when trees hold their breath. . . . Daphne never should
have left her grove, no matter what the laurel had promised.

"You're so thin," Mrs. Kontos went on. "And pale as well. Go
on, let the salt air put some flesh on you. A body'd think you
was consumptive, to look at you. You couldn't go alone, it
wouldn't be proper, what with you not married yet and at your
age, too, but the Pappadeases want to take you."

"Are there woods there?" None of the trees in this new land
spoke to Daphne. She had tried to call them with her powers so
many times, in the park near the tenement, on the tree-lined
paths of Central Park. There was never a response, and she had
almost given up hope of finding the grove the laurel had promised her. But at least the scent of green helped her stay alive
amid the noise and crowds of this great city.

"Woods! What do you need with woods? There's people there,
good people—well, some others as well, but Mrs. Pappadeas will
watch out for you." Mrs. Kontos nodded as she looked at
Daphne. "Your aunt is a decent woman, Miss, but she should
have found a proper match for you before now."

Daphne said nothing. Mrs. Kontos meant well, but Daphne
feared her. The tiny woman was a tireless matchmaker. Next she
would again hymn the praises of the Pappadeas' eldest son,
Nikkolas. He was past twenty and reckoned a good catch, with
dark good looks. For weeks now Nikki had pursued her, confident that the eldest son of a prosperous family would never be
refused as a match. Mrs. Kontos would be outraged if she knew
how little interest Daphne had in him. But she had watched
many young mortals such as Nikki fade with age, brittle as autumn leaves in as little time. Daphne shivered. Nikkolas
Pappadeas was mortal, but she feared him even more than the
landlady. She feared the autumn he would bring to her eternal
spring.

Despite her misgivings, the next Saturday found Daphne
standing with Mrs. Pappadeas on the deck of an overcrowded excursion steamer as it cast off from the pier and started down the
river toward the ocean and Coney Island. The Atlantic wasn't the
wine-dark sea she longed for, any more than Coney Island was
one of the Kikladhes. But the Atlantic led to the Middle Sea and
the home she'd never see again.

She tried to shut her ears against the horrible din of the
"band," a small group of musicians who seemed determined to
force payment from the crowd by playing till they yielded their

silver dimes. Money was a mortal concern, but mortal concerns were hers now as well. Glaring at the nearest player, a sweaty German man puffing on a brass horn, she clutched her reticule with its precious coins. The pittance she earned at the florist's wasn't enough to support her. But her "aunt," Mrs. Zanos, still regarded Daphne with a trace of old reverence and paid for her lodgings at Kontos' Boarding House.

Eleni Zanos had been a young bride when Daphne came to the village near Olympus, driven from her grove by a prophecy of wars soon to come and a promise of a new grove in a new land. When Eleni's family left for the New World, Daphne had followed, searching for her promised grove. Now only Eleni knew what Daphne was, and she was beginning to forget. If she forgot entirely . . .

". . . much nicer, isn't it, Miss Dendrophilos?" For once, Mrs. Pappadeas waited for an answer and Daphne realized she hadn't been listening. So did Mrs. Pappadeas; after a moment she repeated herself. "I said, this is much nicer than the tenements, isn't it? Manhattan may be an island, but it's not like home." She looked wistful. The Pappadeases had been in the United States for over a decade, but a tiny island in the Aegean was still *home*. Her broad face tightened as she added, "I shouldn't complain. It's not Greece, but we don't starve, and we don't have the Turks." She made as if to spit, but refrained.

"Yes, thank you, Mrs. Pappadeas. It's very pleasant." As the flood of words resumed, Daphne privately thought the excursion boat not much better than steerage. It was as overcrowded, and to her nose almost as smelly. And if anything, it was noisier: the German band was still creating a racket that made her head ache, and there were screaming children and scolding parents and rude remarks in the half-comprehended English tongue and. . . .

People. There were too many people. Mrs. Pappadeas was still speaking, her voice lost in the din. Daphne nodded without meaning. Mrs. Pappadeas was another one like the landlady, her voice loud after years spent among red bricks and mortar. It clacked endlessly, like the rattle of wheels and the clanging bell of the horse-trolley and the shouts of the teamsters that kept Daphne from sleep during the noisy nights.

Nikkolas stood beside his mother, smiling past her at Daphne. When he caught her eye, the smile widened. She shivered and turned back toward the sea, focusing on the open water at the horizon and trying to ignore the crowded bay. Despite the smells of a busy harbor, there was the fresh smell of salt, of Poseidon's realm. She whispered its name, *"Thalassa."* The sea. It eased the home-hunger a little.

Demigods had become mortal, mortals had been transformed, gods had died or vanished over the long years. Always Daphne had remained alone in her grove, speaking to the laurel. Even leaving her grove for the village of Florterini had not changed her, other than teaching her a more modern tongue. Her transformation had begun in the marble building she had mistaken for a temple, there on Ellis Island. Uniformed officials had filled in forms naming her Daphne Dendrophilos, niece of Eleni Zanos. At the time, she had thought little of taking a name in the fashion of this land. It had amused her to choose the name Dendrophilos, *lover of trees.* The officials had accepted it as a human name, and written it on their forms.

She realized now that had been the first step toward mortality, the question after question asked by the officials with their forms. Words had always held power, but only in this land did men weave words onto pieces of paper to capture souls. Once the final words were spoken by the *papa,* the priest at the Orthodox Church, binding her to a mortal man, the transformation would be complete.

As the boat docked at West Brighton, Daphne gazed on the swarms with dismay. Despite eight months in New York City and the crowds on the excursion steamer, she had expected Coney Island to be an island such as she had known in Greece, with hills and perhaps a few trees, rocks and places where she could slip away and free herself, if only for a while. But this! A short distance from the water's edge, beer bars and oyster bars were jammed in between sideshows, while farther back hotels sprawled their way down the sandspit island. Instead of rocky shores, there was sand, almost hidden by the endless crowds of people. Hundreds splashed in the waves, shrieking with laughter, wearing costumes Daphne thought even more hideous than those she was forced to wear daily.

She let herself be urged down the gangway to the iron pier by a still-talking Mrs. Pappadeas. The younger children clung to their mother's wide skirts and chattered with excitement. Nikkolas followed silently, his eyes never shifting from Daphne. She could feel them on her back, as hot as the sun overhead. Behind them all, Mr. Pappadeas carried the basket with their lunch. Once they reached the beach, they trudged along until they found a likely spot. Mr. Pappadeas set down the basket and looked around with a satisfied air.

"It's good, getting out of the city," he said, making one of his rare comments. He spoke in heavily accented English rather than Greek, and for a moment Daphne struggled to understand the words. She wasn't sure she had: they hadn't escaped the city, they'd carried it with them.

Mrs. Pappadeas, shooing the youngest children away from the water, replied in a more familiar tongue. "A pity we can't live here, Stavros. You could fish again."

He scowled. "And how would I get a boat, hah? I don't fish another man's boat. No, the fish-stall makes good money and that's what I am now. A fishmonger."

A fisherman, a man of the sea, son of generations of the sea. Selling fish caught by another. Nothing was as it had been. Daphne spent her days in a cramped shop, surrounded by flowers that were as far from their home as Stavros' fish were from theirs. Almost as far as she was from her own.

The day wore on, as tiring as a day in the shop. Nikki continued to follow her with his eyes. He tried to catch her alone, but Daphne was too old a hand at that game. She ignored him, as she had always ignored hungry-eyed young men. But she was afraid a match would soon be arranged. Eleni was her only "relative," responsible for Daphne in the eyes of the world. The longer they stayed in this country, the less Eleni remembered the village. Once she forgot the truth, marriage would be inevitable, and Daphne would never again dance with the trees.

The family sampled the pleasures of the island, spending their dimes on cheap trinkets and the sideshows. They bought oysters and Saratoga crullers, and the younger children played at the water's edge with the wooden buckets that every child on the beach carried. Daphne stared out over the waves breaking on the shore. She wanted to change herself into one of Zeus' eagles and fly toward the horizon, fly till wings gave out. But that power had never been hers.

"Would you care to bathe, Miss Dendrophilos?" Nikki's voice broke her thoughts. It was polite enough, pitched low so his mother wouldn't hear. "You can rent a bathing costume for only a quarter. I'd be happy to go in and keep you safe." He moved closer and smiled at her possessively. As though she already were his mortal wife.

Careful as he'd been to speak softly, his mother overheard. "Nikkolas! She's a good girl, not one of those shameless creatures." She nodded sharply out toward the rope, where several young ladies in bathing costume clung, squealing as the waves broke over them. "No *lady* would dress that indecently. Leave her alone."

With a muttered apology, Nikki drew back, his face sullen. Daphne was grateful for his mother's intervention. The water was tempting, but she refused to don one of those bathing costumes. She didn't find them immodest, but they were ugly. The heavy black wool clung to the limbs, hampering them as much as the voluminous skirts of the dresses she wore at the shop. Modern clothing was as graceless as the shape of their buildings. Daphne turned her back on the ocean. There was no answer there.

As the time drew near for the return trip, Daphne again felt the pull of the sea. If she could throw herself over the rail—but that would be cruel repayment to the Pappadeases, and useless besides. She was no child of Nereus. They would steam upriver and return to the swarming tenements, and soon she would forget the hills of Thessaly and accept the arranged marriage.

As though to confirm her fears, Nikki once more tried to draw her apart from the others. "Before we leave, would you like to ride the *roller coaster?*" The final words were in English, and she had no idea what they meant.

Before she could ask, Mrs. Pappadeas shrieked. "Nikki! That devil's road? Here we give our guest a day to enjoy and you want to scare her half out of her wits." But she was beaming as she spoke; she obviously approved the idea.

"What is this *roller coaster?*" Daphne asked. The Church's devils held no terror for her, but this new world was full of other fears.

"A new thing, they just built it last year," Mrs. Pappadeas said. "There are cars on little wheels and you roll over hills made of wood. They used to call it the sliding hill."

"Please—I would be honored," Nikki said, his dark eyes hot on her.

Daphne didn't want to go anyplace with Nikki, but the phrase "hills made of wood" intrigued her. "Perhaps if you would like to, Mrs. Pappadeas," she began.

Nikki's mother shook her head violently. "No! It's for you young people. But maybe the children . . ."

They walked down the beach toward the new attraction, suitably chaperoned by Nikki's younger brothers and sister. As they drew close enough for her to see the hills in question, Daphne regretted her impulsive yes. The structure was just a flimsy lattice-work of wooden beams and cross-braces, like a railway bridge grown wild. Closer, it looked even more like one, for there were twin rails to carry the cars. It wasn't as shaky as it appeared at a distance; the beams were solid wood and the rails were supported at every point. As Mrs. Pappadeas had said, the top of this bridge to nowhere was sculpted into dips and crests. It was an impressive piece of American engineering, but it wasn't a hill of wood. Daphne had grown tired of American engineering.

There was a line of people waiting to ride the amusement. Nikki spoke firmly to the children. "You will ride in a different car. I will ride beside Miss Daphne." He took her arm as calmly as he had assumed the right to use her name.

For once, she hardly noticed his arrogance. The understructure, as regular as Arachne's weaving, drew her. Uprights stood like sturdy trunks, regular and strong. Beams crossed the way the branches of trees that danced in her grove had done. Daphne moved closer to the supports. It was cut wood, dead and separated from the living trees, yet it called to her as no living tree had called her yet in this land. She stretched her hand out and touched the wood with reverence. Under her fingers, it felt alive, warm from more than the heat of the sun. This was the promise of the laurel.

The touch of Nikki's hand shocked her back to awareness of her surroundings. His arm had slid around her waist while she stared in fascination at the web of wood, and he now took advantage of the children's shrieking excitement and the holiday atmosphere to pull her closer. "My father has said he will speak to your aunt next week," he murmured, his mouth almost brushing her hair. He said no more, and there was no need. She knew what he meant: arrangements for their marriage. Her reluctance was ignored, as no more than the proper modesty of a decent girl.

One of the children tugged at Nikki's sleeve, demanding his attention to settle a squabble, and Daphne carefully pulled away from him. Her fingers stroked the wood once more, savoring its warmth. The tree-longing was stronger than it had been since she had left her grove, but it could do no good here. Dead, dry lumber. If it were a tree—but she knew better. Goat-footed Pan had never held his revels in this strange land, and the trees locked her out of their heartwood. Still, this wood spoke as her own grove had, calling her name.

They reached the head of the line. While Nikki fished in his

pocket for enough nickels to pay for them all, Daphne whispered
a prayer in the old tongue to the gods that were gone. If they
proved as dead as this wood, she would accept her new world
and life, let the past slip from her. She glanced around. Crowds
clustered around the sliding hill, but for the moment no one's
eyes were on her. Moments before, a cloud had covered the sun.
Now it slid aside. As the sun shone forth again unshielded,
Daphne called on Phoebus Apollo and reached one last time for
her long-unused powers.

At first nothing happened. The crowd pressed close around
her, jostling and sweaty and cheerfully noisy. Again she called
on the god, straining with her heart toward the wood and the life
she could feel still deep within it. Then the sun's warmth flooded
her, renewing life in her clothing-hampered limbs. Under her
seeking fingers, the wood quivered, alive. The crowd-noise
changed, fading and becoming the sound of a chant to the god.

"Yes." She whispered the word over and over, as the wood
opened its heart to her, waking under her hands. The ridiculous
heavy costume she had worn in deference to the strange customs
of this land thinned and faded. Faintly, in the distance, she heard
a mortal voice calling her name, but she did not turn. She had
left poor Nikki far behind her.

She began to sing, the song of spring and new leaves, the song
of trees, and spread her open hands flat against the wood. Wood.
It was no longer dead wood, it was living tree, many trees, a
grove interwoven with many branches and crowned with iron
railings. "Soon we will dance," she promised them, and stepped
forward, merging into the now-living wood.

At the front of the ticket line, there was confusion as a young
man looked around for his companion. Confusion gave way to
panic, and later to an organized search. Long after a sobbing
family of Greek immigrants had been sent home by the frustrated
police, the search continued, but even under the roller coaster itself, there was nothing to be found.

The sensational press took up the story quickly. Rumors of
white slavery circulated, as always. The Pappadeas family found
themselves briefly famous, and the fish-stall thrived. The missing
girl's landlady defended her honor. Miss Dendrophilos was a
good girl, almost betrothed to that nice young man, Nikkolas
Pappadeas. In the newspaper, the betrothal became a settled
thing. A young lady who was merely *almost* betrothed wasn't as

tragic, or as newsworthy, as one who had attained that happy state.

The girl's aunt was interviewed, but she spoke so little English the reporter gave it up as a bad job. Anything she might have said would only have added to the confusion, since she no longer remembered much about her niece. Eleni Zanos had confused memories of a sacred grove near Olympus, and a young girl older than the oldest man in the village. She put it from her mind, retreating into Greek and timidity in the face of the reporter's questions. He went away satisfied. He had enough, with the romantic Mrs. Kontos and the broken-hearted Nikki.

Long before the last echoes of sensation died away, before a new lodger moved in to Kontos' Boarding House, months before a suitable bride was found for Nikki Pappadeas, the newsmen returned to Coney Island. No one thought of the missing immigrant girl when the supporting structure of the roller coaster, made of seasoned wood, began to sprout. At first the owners were accused of trickery. But the cross-pieces continued to put forth twigs and leaves, and the uprights sheathed themselves in bark.

The roller coaster became the most famous thing on the island, surpassing even the Iron Pier and the Elevator. Slips were taken from the living wood and nurtured, growing into a new species of tree. The popular fancy at once dubbed the trees coaster-trees, and it was noted that trees planted near one another would grow together, connected by branches resembling the cross-pieces of a railway bridge. Science had no explanation for the new species. Members of the Royal Society crossed the Atlantic to visit Coney Island, and the newly-formed National Geographic Society published an article about the living artifact. Darwinists claimed it as clearly evolutionary, while pulpits around the country praised the miracle.

But even miracles grow commonplace. The story slipped from the front pages to the back ones, then quietly vanished as an item of interest. The scientists adjusted their theories to account for it, then accepted it just as the public had done. However impossible it was, it had happened.

The roller coaster at Coney Island has never lost its popularity, and the picnic grounds in the Coaster Grove are still the most popular at the resort. Neither the picnickers nor the occasional scientist, still hoping to solve the old puzzle, ever see the beautiful young girl watching from within the trees. Daphne, no longer tied to mortal form, welcomes visitors to her grove with soft breezes and the scent of green leaves. Sometimes she slips from the wood and wanders past groups of young men near the shore, teasing them as she never dared tease poor Nikkolas. She had been mortal then, or almost. But her spirit has been given back to her, and she is home.

At certain times of the year, late at night, the Coaster Grove on Coney Island seems to sing softly to itself. Those who walk beneath the trees at such times feel a sense of awe, as though they walk in a holy place. Beneath the metal tracks of the old roller coaster, a nymph dances praise to the ancient gods of Greece. The laurel, the original Daphne of legend, had prophesied truth for her namesake. In a new land, in a new grove beside new seas, the dryad Daphne sings to her trees.

Virginia Woods

by Janni Lee Simner

Janni Lee Simner has sold more than a dozen short stories, including those in Mike Resnick's Alternate Outlaws *and Susan Shwartz's* Sisters in Fantasy 2. *Although she grew up surrounded by East Coast oaks and maples, she now lives among the cactus forests of the Arizona desert.*

As always, the Indians came at night. Eleanor had known they would. When she saw the fields of trampled maize, gold beneath the morning sun, she couldn't even bring herself to cry. She just stood there, staring at the broken dirt. Already it seemed that weeds were moving in, growing over the battered corn. The Indians had destroyed their crops once before this spring. She didn't have enough seed to plant again, not if she wanted to eat as well.

The man set out on guard duty the night before was missing. A search party—her husband Ananias among them—had gone out to look for him. Eleanor drew her arms tightly around herself. The last guard had been found just inside the forest, his chest riddled with arrow holes. No arrows, though—the Indians must have pulled them out before leaving the body.

Eleanor shivered, looking toward the edge of the field. The trampled soil gave way to grass and scrubby bushes; the bushes, in turn, gave way to dark trees. Their branches intersected at wild angles; their leaves blew fitfully about.

The colony was surrounded by those trees. In the morning light, their shadows stretched across the field, like the claws of some wild beast. Eleanor stepped back, away from the dark shapes.

Somewhere within the forest, the Indians were hiding. Only Savages would hide in a place like that. The settlers had chased them off the island, over and over again, but they always returned. The last time the Indians had fled, the settlers' muskets had been loud behind them. Still, the Indians had come back; the ruined crops were proof of that.

With a whole continent to live on, surely the Savages could leave Roanoke Island alone.

Eleanor sighed, brushing a loose strand of hair from her face. She turned and looked back toward the village. The distant houses seemed small and vulnerable, huddled together in a sweep of farmland. Beyond them stood the walls of Fort Raleigh. The fields closer to the houses and the fort were never damaged as badly as those further out; perhaps they would bear enough seed that the settlers could plant again.

"Mama!" Eleanor looked down to see her daughter running toward her. The girl tripped over her own short legs and fell, face-first, into the mud. Eleanor hurried over and scooped her off the ground.

"Virginia Dare! I told you to stay inside."

Virginia squirmed in Eleanor's arms; soon she'd be too heavy to hold at all. "Didn't want to stay inside." Virginia stuck out her lip. Her face and long shirt were covered with mud; her hair was plastered to her forehead. Eleanor scowled, and Virginia giggled at the fierce look.

Eleanor sighed. Nothing upset that child, and even less scared her. It was unnatural, almost. Eleanor wondered, sometimes, whether Virginia's being born on the island, rather than back in London, had anything to do with it. But Margery's boy, Hugh, had also been born here, and he was nothing like Virginia. He was a quiet, frightened boy, always clinging to his mother's skirts.

Virginia broke free of Eleanor's grip, sliding with a laugh to the ground. She ran across the field and through the grass, Eleanor close behind.

The wind picked up, carrying with it the smell of spring rain. Clouds gathered over the forest. The wind blew them across the field, toward the village.

Eleanor caught up with Virginia at the edge of the forest. "Windy trees!" Virginia giggled and continued forward.

"No!" Eleanor grabbed her. Virginia squirmed, but Eleanor tightened her grip.

The branches swayed wildly, green leaves bright against the gray sky. The neat, tended trees in London parks didn't have that wildness; neither did the trees in any other civilized place Eleanor knew. But then, this wasn't a land for civilized people. It was a land for Savages.

What would the Savages do to Virginia, if she wandered into the forest?

Eleanor didn't want to know. Tightening her hold on her daughter, she hurried back toward the village.

By the time she got inside, rain had started to fall. It leaked through the roof, muddying the dirt floor.

Eleanor dipped a rag in the washbasin, then sat on the edge of the bed and washed Virginia up. She peeled off the girl's damp shirt, scrubbed the mud off her face, ran fingers through her tangled curls. Outside, thunder rumbled; flashes of lightning lit the gaps in the log walls.

"Bright light!" Virginia laughed. Eleanor just kept washing off the mud. Thunderstorms scared her; they made the house seem even smaller and more vulnerable than it was.

Her gaze darted around the room as she worked. A table and wobbling chairs stood against one wall, a chest of drawers against another. Battered pots hung from the ceiling; empty jars were piled in a corner. A clothesline stretched across the room, damp clothes draped over it. Oil paintings hung on the walls. The paint had begun to flake away, and the canvas beneath was spotted with water stains. Ananias thought Eleanor was crazy to hang her father's paintings here. He was probably right.

Eleanor stared at a painting in which tall, thick trees—oaks and cedars, mostly—stood neatly side by side. Their trunks were straight, leaves set like clouds of carded wool among the branches. Sun shone between them, casting bright swatches of light onto the ground.

All of her father's pictures were like that: bright, cheerful, unreal. Sometimes Eleanor wondered if he'd really looked around him at all, when he painted. Then again, if he'd shown the colony as it really was, with all its dirt and dark places, would she and Ananias have agreed to come here? Would anyone?

Eleanor pulled a dry shirt over Virginia's head, set her down on the bed, and walked over to the painting. She ran a finger along the signature. *John White, 1586.* The paint fell away at her touch.

"You should have stayed with us," Eleanor whispered, then pushed the thought fiercely aside. As governor of the colony, it made sense for her father to sail back to London for supplies. He'd return as soon as he could.

After three years, Eleanor was one of the few settlers left who believed that.

Outside, she heard voices, arguing as they approached the village. Virginia tugged at her skirt. "Want to go out," she said.

"No." Eleanor tried to make out what the voices were saying, but she couldn't. If she wanted to learn what had happened to the guard, she'd have to go outside. She picked up Virginia and sat her in a chair. Reaching for a thick length of yarn, she started tying the girl down.

Virginia screamed, "Don't want to be tied!" But Eleanor had no choice. She couldn't leave Virginia alone otherwise, not after the way she'd run out that morning.

Eleanor knotted the ends of the yarn together. Then she went outside, her daughter's yells still loud behind her.

Within the huddle of houses was a small open space, the closest thing the settlers had to a village square. Most of them were already there, talking in small groups. Once, the square wouldn't have had enough space to hold them all. But three winters, without supplies from England, had taken their toll. Half the houses were empty now, their walls beginning to rot.

Eleanor hurried across the square, looking for Ananias. Light rain still fell, but the wind had subsided. Off to one side, Eleanor saw a wet deerskin on the ground, with a lump beneath it that had to be a body. The guard had been found then—but not alive. Eleanor's throat felt dry. How many more would the Savages kill? She turned quickly away and kept walking.

She found Ananias by one of the deserted houses. His hair and beard dripped rainwater; muddy brown curls fell into his face. He argued with Manteo. Several other colonists stood around them, listening. Eleanor moved to Ananias' side.

"No wild animal did that!" Ananias' voice was fierce. He gestured toward Manteo. "The hole in our man's chest was made by an arrow. An Indian arrow."

Manteo shrugged; the gesture looked wrong on his wiry frame. "I said nothing about wild animals." His English was perfect, but his voice held an accent that flattened the words, twisting the meanings in all the wrong places. He wore the same English wool as the others, but his beardless face was too thin, his eyes and straight hair too dark. The time he'd spent in England, the fact that he'd been baptized once he returned to America—none of that mattered. He was still a Savage. Eleanor didn't understand why the others trusted him at all. If it were up to her, he'd be in the woods with the other Indians, not living here in the village.

"You're the one who mentioned animals." Manteo's dark gaze fixed on Ananias. Neither of them seemed to notice Eleanor at all.

"You said—" Ananias measured each word, "—that your people didn't do this."

"There are things besides Indians and wild animals that can kill a man. Surely you know that by now."

"Don't complicate this with fairy stories." Ananias' voice turned suddenly low, threatening. "If your people did this, they won't go unpunished. If the Indians are hiding in these woods, or anywhere else on the island, we'll find them. You can be sure of that."

"The *Croatoan* are gone." Manteo stared at Ananias, as if he expected some answer to that.

Ananias ignored him. He turned to Eleanor, as if seeing her for the first time. "Why aren't you repairing the damage the Savages did to our fields? It's bad enough that one of us had to be away."

Eleanor looked down, away from his sharp gaze. When Ananias spoke like that, the gap in their ages felt much larger than the decade it really was. "I wanted to see what you found."

"We found a dead man," Ananias snapped. "Did you expect any differently?" Eleanor just shook her head.

Margery Harvie walked up to join them. "We'll all be dead before this spring is through." As always, Hugh stood by his mother's side. His straight yellow hair fell neatly into place; his blue eyes were serious in his small face.

Margery wiped a hand across her forehead. "Our only hope is that our governor stops tarrying in England and spares some time for the colony in his care." She cast a long look at Eleanor, as if she were to blame for all the colony's problems.

Eleanor measured her words, afraid she might yell if she didn't. "My father will return as soon as he can."

Margery laughed at that, and Hugh echoed the sound. Then he turned away, suddenly embarrassed, and hid behind his mother.

Eleanor's cheeks felt red. "Many things could keep a man in England. Spring storms, or lack of funds to hire a ship."

"A gentleman of his rank, lacking funds?" Margery laughed again.

"It's hardly unheard of," Ananias said, his voice suddenly mild. Whatever the others thought, he still believed that Eleanor's father meant to return.

The conversation drifted; Ananias and Margery began discussing other reasons the governor could have been delayed. Shipwrecks, trouble with the Spanish—Eleanor had heard all the reasons before.

Her attention wandered. She watched Manteo drift away from the small group, watched as he and several settlers carried the dead man's body from the square. Hugh released his hold on his mother and walked off as well. Eleanor almost called Margery's attention to the fact, but decided against it. Hugh never went very far, after all.

She began to think that Ananias was right, that it was time to start repairing their fields. She needed to check on Virginia, too, to make certain the child had calmed down.

Ananias and Margery were still talking when she left. She walked past them, walked past the small knots of settlers still talking throughout the square. There were a few other women, and somewhere an infant cried, though most of the colonists were men. Eleanor walked past wooden houses, some sturdy and well-kept, others crumbling into the dirt. Two chickens scratched the ground beside one house; a boy herded several sheep by another. Like all the colony's animals, these had been brought over from England; there were no tame animals in the New World.

Eleanor walked up to her house, pushed the door open, and stepped inside. Then she stopped, stone-cold, in the doorway.

The chair was empty. Yarn trailed, untied, to the floor. Virginia was nowhere in sight.

Eleanor slowly untangled the yarn from the chair, twisting it around her hands. How could she have been so foolish? She should have known Virginia was old enough to untie herself.

Behind her, the door creaked open. Eleanor turned around.

Margery stood there, hands on hips. "Where's my boy?"

"Hugh?" Eleanor thought he would have returned by now.

"After you left, I looked down, and he was gone. He was with me until then. What have you done with him?"

"I did nothing. Virginia's gone, too." As she spoke, Eleanor felt a cold lump in her chest.

"I'd expect that from your child." Margery folded her arms across her chest. "Not Hugh. If they're gone, it's Virginia's fault."

Eleanor opened her mouth to say something, then closed it again. She didn't have time for idle talk; she had to find her daughter. Maybe Virginia hadn't left very long ago. Maybe she hadn't had time to get very far. Eleanor pushed past Margery, through the door. Margery followed her out.

In the mud outside Eleanor's house, they found tiny footprints. The footprints led around the house, through the village, and across the fields. A second set of footprints, even smaller, joined the first. Margery took this as proof that leaving had been Virginia's idea, and that Hugh had only followed.

The footsteps stretched to the edge of the field, and the grass beyond was trampled. "Windy trees," Virginia had shouted, only hours ago. Eleanor had been able to stop her then. This time, she'd been too late.

The rain stopped. Sun broke up the clouds, letting bright blue patches show through the gray. Between the trees, though, Eleanor saw only darkness.

She didn't dare enter that darkness alone. She turned back toward the village. Margery followed, but Eleanor hardly noticed her.

She thought of the wet deerskin, of the guard's still body beneath it. She followed Virginia's footsteps back home, praying that this time the search party wouldn't be too late.

Eleanor found Ananias beside the house, hooking an ox to the plow. She explained what had happened, as quickly and calmly as she could.

Ananias ran a hand through his hair, splattering water in every direction. "You should have taken time to tie her properly, instead of chattering outside." His voice was harsh, his face taut with concern.

"I did tie her properly." Eleanor twisted her hands together. "She figured out how to untie the knots herself."

"She should have been raised to know better."

Eleanor couldn't argue with that; she wished, more than anyone, that Virginia was a tamer child.

Ananias' face tightened. "I'll gather a party together." He turned abruptly away, starting toward the square without another word.

He gathered the searchers quickly, twelve men in all. He in-

sisted Manteo join them. "This way," he said, "if the Indians attack, they'll have to take one of their own, too." The men lit the
wicks on their muskets before leaving, to make certain they
could fire on a moment's notice. Assuming, of course, that the
gunpowder stayed dry.

Eleanor didn't ask whether she could go with the men; she
simply followed. Ananias glanced back at her once, his gray eyes
telling her that she should return home, but so long as he didn't
speak aloud, Eleanor didn't have to listen. She didn't bring a
gun, though; seeing her armed might have been enough to make
Ananias send her back after all.

Margery also followed. But then, her husband had died during
the colony's first winter; there was no one to tell her what she
should or shouldn't do.

Manteo led the way, through fields of ruined maize toward the
edge of the woods. The search party crossed the trampled fields,
following Virginia and Hugh's small prints. The smell of their
sweat mixed with the smell of muddy weeds and wet wool.
There should have been larger footprints, too, Eleanor realized,
from the Indians who'd destroyed their crops last night. Or had
the morning rain already washed those prints away?

Manteo crossed the scrubby grass to the edge of the forest.
The men fanned out on either side of him as they entered the
woods; Margery followed close behind. For a moment Eleanor
just stood there, watching them disappear among the twisted
trees. Then she hurried after them. Whatever she feared in those
woods, she didn't fear it half as much as she feared finding Virginia's lifeless body in the mud.

At first, the trees were still. No wind blew; light shone through
the gaps in the forest and cast bright patches of sun onto the
ground. Eleanor thought maybe she'd imagined the wild
branches and deep shadows. Maybe her father had known what
he'd painted after all.

But the trees grew thicker and more twisted as she walked.
The light thinned, until it barely penetrated the leaves at all. Twilight settled early over the forest. The space between the trees
was crowded with bushes and vines. Eleanor's shoes kept getting
tangled in low branches; thorns tore at her skirt. Dead leaves
were everywhere, heavy with the smell of decay. Animals rustled
beneath them. Eleanor shivered. Animals could attack children,
too, and do as much damage as Savages.

The wind picked up, shaking water down from the branches.
It cried with a high animal sound as it blew, at odds with the rus-

tling Eleanor expected. Her skirt blew around her ankles, and wisps of damp hair came loose into her face.

The others slowed their pace. Their low conversation faded to silence. Whatever Eleanor felt, maybe they felt it too.

All but Manteo. He continued steadily forward, as if he didn't even notice that the others had slowed down.

Margery screamed, a high, hysterical sound. Eleanor froze; a chill ran down her spine. She saw Margery collapse to the ground. Several of the men raced to her side. Eleanor ran after them, into a small clearing. Her foot caught on a vine, and she tumbled to the ground. Scrambling to her feet, she kept running.

The smell hit her first—like fresh-killed meat, heavy with blood. What she saw on the ground beside Margery looked like meat, too, all torn flesh and bloody tatters, bright against the grass and leaves. For a moment Eleanor was all right; so long as it didn't look like a child, she didn't have to believe it was real. Then she saw a shredded piece of linen. Following it, she found a hand—a tiny child's hand—clutching the fabric through the blood. Eleanor's stomach rolled; she fought to keep from vomiting.

The hand was too small to belong to Virginia. Eleanor felt relief, then guilt. Margery's child lay dead on the ground in front of her. Eleanor knelt by Margery, putting an arm around her shoulders to offer what comfort she could.

Margery flinched as if touched by fire. She pushed Eleanor roughly away. "Your child did this. Hugh would never—" Margery's voice rose, then cracked. She leaped forward, shoving Eleanor into the brush. "You killed him!" The men pulled Margery away, but she kept yelling. "Your daughter killed him! He never would have come here, if not for her!"

Eleanor sat up, staring numbly at the crying woman, at the mangled body by her side.

Ananias walked over to her. "You should go back now." His low voice was firm, turning the words into a command. "Take Margery with you."

Eleanor couldn't go back. Not with her own daughter still missing. She opened her mouth, searching for words that would make Ananias understand.

Somewhere, a twig snapped—close enough that Eleanor froze at the sound, far enough that she couldn't quite tell where it came from. Ananias whirled around, gun raised.

"Show yourself!"

The bushes in front of him rustled—a wild rhythm, not in time with the wind—but no one answered. Ananias stepped back, bracing the musket against his shoulder. The end of the wick glowed orange. The other men raised their guns, too.

Manteo stared at them, his eyes wide. Then he dropped his musket and fled into the woods. Eleanor wondered whether the other Indians waited for him. Had he already betrayed the settlers to the Savages?

For just a moment, Ananias hesitated. A strange, worried look crossed his face. Then he fired into the bushes. Smoke filled the air, heavy with the smell of gunpowder. The forest went suddenly still.

And Ananias fell slowly backwards, making no sound as he hit the soft earth. Eleanor screamed.

Suddenly everyone was shooting at once. Smoke burned Eleanor's eyes; the acrid smell of gunpowder clogged her throat. She buried her head in her hands, praying the Savages would spare her.

The shots cut off abruptly. The smoke drifted slowly away, too gentle for the noise that had made it. When it cleared, every last man had fallen.

Eleanor stared at the bodies, splattered with blood, but she couldn't make herself believe they were real. She felt as if she were in a dream that she couldn't shake off. Her thoughts were as slow as the tendrils of smoke rising through the trees. She expected the Indians to come for her, too, but they didn't. There was only the wind, crying as it blew through the leaves, and the soft sound of Margery's sobs. Eleanor saw Manteo's abandoned musket on the ground; she reached for it. The musket was splattered with mud, but somehow, the wick had stayed lit.

Finally, Eleanor crawled to Ananias' side. There was a ragged, bleeding hole in his chest, the sort an arrow might make. Around it, his shirt was stained bright crimson. There was no arrow, though, not in the wound and not on the ground nearby. Ananias' face held a wide, startled look, as if even now he didn't understand how he'd died.

Eleanor should have started screaming. But she just sat there, feeling strange and cold, watching her husband's blood trickle onto the dead leaves. The forest twilight deepened, but she barely noticed. Did Virginia lie on the ground somewhere too, her skin slowly growing cold?

Eleanor froze at the sound of soft footsteps behind her. Clutching the musket, she slowly stood and turned around.

Manteo's dark eyes stared back at her. "I did not think English men were so easily frightened." His voice was strange and somber, even flatter than usual.

"You killed them." Eleanor felt hot rage, bitter as the gunpowder that lingered in the air. "You warned your people before we ever arrived!" She aimed the gun at Manteo. Manteo stepped sideways, but Eleanor followed, keeping him in range. She wanted, more than anything, to shoot that gun, to watch Manteo fall screaming to the ground. She held her fire, though, praying that in turn the other Indians would hold theirs.

"I did nothing." Manteo's face twisted into a frown. "The *Croatoan* are dead. They died the same way as the English."

Eleanor braced the gun against her shoulder. How dare he deny what he'd done?

"Listen." Manteo took a deep breath, his eyes on the musket all the while. "The men expected an attack, so they got one. That happens sometimes in these woods. I've tried to warn them, but they never listened. My people died the same way—only they feared musket shots, not arrows."

"People don't die of fear," Eleanor said. Had Manteo gone mad?

"That may be true in England, where you've cut down your forests and scrubbed clean your dark places. Not here."

Eleanor thought of the arrows that should have littered the ground. She thought of the startled look on Ananias' face. But she knew she'd go crazy if she believed Manteo's words.

"What about our crops?" Eleanor's voice came out higher and more frightened than she expected.

Manteo shrugged, but his eyes were still on the musket. "The crops near the forest were hit worst." He lunged forward, reaching to grab the gun out of Eleanor's hands. Eleanor pulled the trigger, praying she was fast enough.

Nothing happened. The gunpowder must have gotten wet; it wouldn't ignite, no matter how long Eleanor held the trigger in place.

But Manteo's hands went to his chest, as if the musket had fired after all. He tumbled, face first, to the ground.

Eleanor stared at him, not believing what she saw. If she rolled him over, would she find a bloody wound in his chest? No, she told herself. People didn't die of fear, no matter what Manteo said. They died of arrows and gunshots.

Yet she couldn't bring herself to turn Manteo's body over, no matter how long she looked at it.

The wind brushed her cheek—had it ever stopped? It whistled through the leaves, high and sharp, crying like an animal in pain.

Not an animal, Eleanor realized. Ice trickled down her spine. A child. *Her* child.

"Virginia?" Eleanor looked wildly around. The wind continued to cry. "Virginia, where are you?" Eleanor started forward, in the direction of the voice, then stopped when she felt herself trembling. Would she really find her daughter? Or just another mangled body, nothing human left to it? She looked past the fallen men, to where Margery lay sobbing on the ground. Beside her, Hugh's torn body still bled.

Eleanor took another step. For a moment she wished she were like Virginia, too wild and foolish to be afraid.

Too foolish to be afraid. The thought hit Eleanor like ice. Virginia didn't fear anything—and her body hadn't been found.

The men had feared Indian arrows, and Manteo had feared the musket she held. Eleanor glanced once again at Hugh. What fear could tear a child apart like that? Eleanor drew her arms tightly around herself; she didn't want to know.

"Mama?" Virginia's voice, low and uncertain, but still very much alive.

For a long moment Eleanor stared at the dark trees. What did she expect to find, when she followed her daughter's voice?

She heard footsteps, too light to belong to a man, too awkward and heavy for an animal. Only a child walked like that. Eleanor shivered. The day had grown cold, and clouds had moved in once more, dimming the few ribbons of light that reached the forest floor. The light only grew fainter further in.

Eleanor closed her eyes and thought of her father's painting. She thought of his bright colors, of the light between the trees. She tried to imagine the forest around her like that—green and soft, branches swaying gently back and forth.

Maybe Manteo wasn't mad after all. Maybe what Eleanor found was up to her.

She took a deep breath, opening her eyes once more. The she followed her daughter's call, deeper into the woods.

And she tried not to be afraid.

IMPOSSIBLE LOVES

Joy comes in many shapes

Ties of Love

by Lawrence Schimel

Lawrence Schimel, 22, has sold stories and poems to over forty anthologies, among them Weird Tales from Shakespeare, Phantoms of the Night, *and* Friends of Valdemar. *He lives in Manhattan.*

My father and I hardly spoke when he picked me up at the train station, nor during the long drive out to the farm through the snow-covered landscape. He'd recognized me instantly among the sea of young men who disembarked, waited patiently as I threaded my way to him through the crowd, pack slung over my shoulder. "Welcome home, son," he'd said, shaking my hand firmly, and I could tell by the tone of his voice and the force of his grip that he was real proud of me, and real glad to have me home alive once more. He didn't push at all, as we drove, no questions about what I would do now that the war was over, if I had ever killed a man, or how I felt to be home. All the questions I had been dreading during the long train ride from New York, when I wasn't thinking about her.

Staring at the bare trees that lined the road I couldn't help worrying about her. Would everything be the same? So much might've happened: lightning, loggers, fire . . . I tried not to think about it, almost wished my father *did* ask me questions, anything to keep my mind from forming disaster scenarios.

But when we pulled up to the house, my worst fears were realized as I stared at the acres of barren furrows that stretched into land that before I left had been forest. I stepped out of the car, staring at all the missing trees. I was about to go racing off into the woods to make sure she was still there, make sure she was all right, when my mother saw me from the kitchen porch, came rushing out into the cold in just her apron to throw her arms about me. I kissed her, of course, took one last look at the forest over her shoulder as I hugged her tight, then dutifully followed her inside. But I couldn't help thinking about the forest the entire time, couldn't help worrying. I was quiet all through dinner, and even my sisters were subdued by my silence, noticeable since in all the letters I got from home Mother wrote how they were at that age when they could talk a hole through a wall. I could feel my mother casting worried looks to my father. They thought it was the war, I knew, and were dying to ask me what was wrong. But they were afraid to. My mother wanted to take away my pain, make me her same happy boy I was before I left and I loved her for it, but how could I tell them?

I wasn't thinking about the war at all. I was thinking about a tree, and the woman who is its spirit; a woman whose eyes are filled with starlight; a woman whose hair is green in spring and summer, golden and red in fall; the woman who held my heart.

I kept my silence, letting them think it was the war that absorbed my thoughts as I bided my time until I could rush out into the woods and see her.

As I ran along the familiar path after dinner, I couldn't help wondering if she had missed me as much as I had her, if she had missed me at all. I couldn't write her, as the other guys had done with their loves. She couldn't read, had never learned because she was so pained by the trees it took to make paper. And even if she could, I'd no way of getting a letter to her. Where was I to send it, 14th oak behind the McLeran's farm, General Delivery, Pine Plains, New York? I kept to myself and, when the other guys got letters from their loves, read them aloud to the rest of us and showed off the locks of yellow, red, brown, or black, I thought of the four leaves I kept pressed between the pages of a book of poems by Wordsworth. I made whistles from the hats of her acorns, played slow and lonely songs on them in the evenings, as I thought of her.

Snow crunched under my feet as I ran beneath the bare, skeletal trees. Their long, moonlit shadows cut across my path like solid bars trying to prevent me from reaching her. I ran faster, desperate to see her again. I knew I couldn't really see her now, that she was dormant until Spring, but I needed to at least see her tree. I needed to see if she had left a sign of some sort, that she was still safe. That she still loved me.

My heart pounded with the exertion and anticipation as I ran along the last curve of the path before her tree. I cried out with relief when I saw that it was still whole and upright. I paused to catch my breath after my run and, standing in the snow as I stared at her tree, I felt warm with love. Her branches were covered with hundreds of yellow ribbons, fluttering like leaves in the moonlight.

The Heart of the Forest

by Dave Smeds

Dave Smeds has written two fantasy novels and numerous short stories which have appeared in magazines and anthologies here and abroad; he has also been a graphic artist and a typesetter and holds a third degree black belt in Goju-ryu karate. He lives in Santa Rosa, California, with his wife Connie and children Lerina and Elliott.

Though the rain had passed hours ago, the trees dripped, creating an ominous whisper among the freshly fallen autumn leaves. The loam gave up a fecund aroma—a primal breath as old as the land itself. In his fifty-three years, Oxal had intruded beneath these boughs only twice. This time felt no more familiar or welcome. The Forest of the Old Ones did not lightly tolerate the presence of humans, certainly not a company of fifty armed soldiers, some with axes.

The rider ahead tugged his beard, nervously eyeing a raven that watched from a tall, leafless spar. Saddle leather creaked as he reined back and leaned close to Oxal.

"This is a fool's quest," he murmured.

Oxal raised an eyebrow. "Yet here you are, Yram. Are you calling yourself a fool?"

Yram scowled and nudged his mount back into formation.

Oxal regretted his curtness. Yram's skepticism was warranted. Other men—good men—had failed at this search. Yet the pikeman should not have spoken so. It was disrespectful of the lord who led the quest. Oxal would not be party to such criticisms. He considered it vital to behave as a proper soldier, playing the role right down to the ancient practice of going beardless so that an enemy would have less to seize during combat—though Ayana teased him with spousal good will that he shaved only to hide the gray in his whiskers.

The company halted as they came to a large meadow. Here the woodland presented a choice of obvious paths—either along the stream that fed the expanse of peat, or over a hill strewn with rock outcroppings.

Oxal favored the former for its flatness, its proximity to water, its promise of fresh game for the night's cookfires. The scree draping the hill could slide underhoof.

At the head of the procession, a tall figure in blue and gold dismounted. Oxal had never been one to admire the physiques of other males, but he did so now. Prince Rahnnic radiated the lithe, angular beauty of the Arith. In an ordinary human, his aspect might be called delicate, but in him the smooth complexion and subdued musculature somehow conveyed the impression of virility and strength.

Yet this prince was a stranger, unproven in many ways. Handsomeness mattered little here. If Rahnnic could not determine which route to take from the meadow, he had no business leading a mission into the forest.

Oxal watched keenly as Rahnnic knelt and lifted a handful of soil. Sniffing it deeply, the Arith royal scanned the treetops. He tilted his head, as if listening. Finally he began to walk. Stopping periodically, he repeated his odd ceremony until he had wound past both the stream and the hill and come to stand across the meadow next to a dense thicket. Three pikemen and the standard bearer clung to his heels, guarding him vigilantly.

With sudden confidence the prince waved for the remainder of the column to join him.

The main knot of riders started forward, tracing their lord's route along the fringe of the clearing. But the rider just ahead of Yram chose to cut straight across the meadow. Yram, Oxal, and the rest turned as well.

Halfway across, the hair on the nape of Oxal's neck began to stiffen. The grass, toughened by a long dry summer, gave good purchase for the horses' hooves, yet as a mass it seemed to wobble, as if the layer of turf were suspended over liquid.

Prince Rahnnic turned from his examination of the forest and saw his riders in the open. Shock blanked his features. "Go back!" he shouted.

The echo had not yet faded as the ground gave way beneath five of the horses.

Oxal's mount dropped from under him. Boggy soil poured in from every side, submerging the animal and burying Oxal to his shoulders. Caught like the victim of an avalanche, only a desperate surge of strength freed his arms. From the waist down, his body was trapped.

Enveloped in the muck, his mount thrashed frantically. Just in front of Oxal's the ground trembled. Oxal dug quickly, uncovering the gelding's face. The beast snorted, eyes rolling in terror.

"Easy, easy," Oxal murmured, knowing that if the horse struggled too much, it would die. Broad, gentle swimming motions would keep them from sinking further, but rapid wiggling would draw them under.

Oxal had cared for his roan since it had been a day-old colt. Though terrified, it obeyed him and grew calm. Only then did Oxal have the chance to look about him.

Yram and his mount were nowhere to be seen. Of the other victims, the head of one companion remained above the surface.

Ropes landed among the stricken warriors. Oxal grabbed one. Meanwhile from the periphery of the meadow unmounted men, their armor and heavy gear shucked, crawled across the uncollapsed area with digging implements. Valiantly they dug where their comrades had vanished, trying to create breathing funnels.

Prince Rahnnic sat cross-legged, entering into a spellcaster's trance. Oxal wasn't certain what sort of magic could help— perhaps an enchantment to harden the ground—but he did know it would be too late. Sorcery was a sluggish affair; otherwise soldiers would be obsolete.

Before the spell took effect, the diggers uncovered Yram's upper body. He had suffocated.

"This is how the Forest of the Old Ones greets intruders," muttered a veteran sourly as the last body was pulled onto solid ground. Three men were dead. That it could have been worse did not lessen the sense of gloom.

Oxal, brooding over his last words to Yram, occupied himself brushing the mud from his gelding's coat. His was the only animal saved. Four mounts and a pack mule would remain part of the bog forever.

For the dead riders there would be a pyre. The captain raised an ax toward a sapling, glaring defiantly at the forest as he did so.

"No," declared Prince Rahnnic. "Killing trees will not bring him back, and it will only anger the guardians of this place. Gather fallen limbs."

Reluctantly the captain nodded, though he made it a point to have the pyre built at the very edge of the woods, where the flames would lick at the tips of extended branches.

The company watched with tightly pressed lips as the fire burned. Many faces turned back toward Irithel, toward home.

"Do any of you wish to leave?" asked the prince.

The company stirred. Here and there, a man muttered under his breath. Yet Oxal knew that no archer, pikeman, or horse soldier would wish to return to the capital wearing the badge of cowardice.

However, it was a good strategic move of Rahnnic to ask.

"For those who would come, this is the way," Prince Rahnnic said, pointing into the thickets at the meadow's edge. His statement was unequivocal. As the prince threaded between the close-set trees, a narrow trail appeared where no passage had seemed to exist. Everyone followed.

Perhaps, thought Oxal, the quest could succeed after all.

As dusk neared they came to a spot where a year earlier a brushfire had cleared the terrain. The prince announced they would camp there, beyond the reach of living trees.

When his chores were done, Oxal declined to join his comrades at the cookfires, preferring a few moments alone to mull over his narrow escape from death. He found a granite slab worn smooth by untold seasons of rainwater and sat, regarding the forest. An old oak, its trunk charred from the fire, drew his attention. Had the tree shifted closer to its neighbor since the company had camped?

"Sprites are moving the trees with their songs. They will play such music all night."

Oxal stood abruptly, bowing to Prince Rahnnic.

The Arith lord waved his soldier back down, and joined him on the slab. "You are Oxal, are you not? You were cool-headed in the meadow. I would not have cared to lose another man."

Oxal inclined his head, acknowledging the sincerity in Rahnnic's tone. "You did what you could, Your Highness."

"I could have sensed the trap earlier had my attention been on the meadow, rather than on the route away from it."

"Hindsight," Oxal said.

The prince shrugged, unwilling as yet to let himself off so easily.

Oxal nodded at the trees. "How far can they move?"

"No farther than their major roots can stretch. They are trees, after all, and are moored to the earth. But they will strain far enough by morning to disguise the existing trail, leaving a new path to lead us astray. I have to be vigilant to keep ahead of such tricks, if we are to find Lady Arameth." Rahnnic's gaze seemed to penetrate deep into the woods, as if he were already fathoming which way to travel in the morning.

He had finally mentioned her name aloud. "They say she was the most beautiful princess of her generation," Oxal said.

Rahnnic smiled in a melancholy way. "It would please her to hear such words. A hundred years ago, it was her voice that folk complimented. To hear her sing to our children—every father should have such an experience."

Oxal found it odd to hear someone talk of bygone days with such immediacy. Odder still to sit next to a legend. For all Oxal's life, the story of Rahnnic and his bride had been told at the hearthfires: How Theron raiders had attacked the capital without warning, hidden until then by the most simple of illusions—fog. How Rahnnic's defense of the palace allowed his grandfather, the king, to escape and, with reinforcements, recapture the city that same year. Such tales of valor had been what drew Oxal to a martial career. He would often visit the shrine in the old throne room of the palace, where Rahnnic stood like a statue, frozen in time within the ward he had formed in the last desperate moments of battle. Everyone knew that someday the ward would burst and Rahnnic would rejoin the world, but when it happened at last, Oxal was not the only one who had to make a pilgrimage to the shrine and see it empty before he would believe the hero lived and breathed once more.

The prince's voice fell to a whisper. Oxal averted his glance. Obviously, it pained Rahnnic to speak of children gone to the grave. After ninety-seven years suspended in time, the prince had lost nearly everyone he had known. His grandson now ruled Irithel, and for the sake of political stability Rahnnic had agreed not to seek the throne, accepting an honorary role as adviser to the crown.

But the story was not yet over. There was a chance that Arameth, wife of Rahnnic, still lived. She had not been able to bear living out her life without her prince. She waited ten years, until her children were of an independent age, and then she vanished into the forest to give herself to the dryads. As a dryad, she would be nigh immortal, and survive until Rahnnic's release.

The talespinners always spoke of how Rahnnic and Arameth would one day be happily reunited. But in truth, no one knew if that could happen.

"Your Highness . . ."

"Yes?"

"How can you be sure the lady is alive? The search parties her father sent found no sign of her. How is it you know where to look?"

To Oxal's relief, Rahnnic took no offense at the question. "In truth, I have no way of knowing if she lives. But if the sylvan folk accepted her pledge to become one of them, they would have taken her to dwell in only one place—the Heart of the Forest."

"But no one knows where that is," Oxal protested. "Some say it does not exist."

"It exists. I can find it."

Rahnnic seemed to glow in the numinous way of the Arith as he spoke. Oxal was reminded of passions he had felt at one glorious moment of his youth when, in the span of three seasons, he won the city wrestling tourney, was accepted into the palace guard, and came to know the favors of the potter's fine, worldly daughter. Oh, to feel such a fire again.

"Are you married, soldier? Do you have children?" the prince asked.

Oxal shifted uncomfortably. It seemed a sacrilege to speak. His had been a marriage of convenience. His cousin's foster sister had needed a husband; he had needed a companionable woman to make a home. It had been a suitable match, with few arguments over the years, but how could his situation possibly compare to that of legend? "My wife's name is Ayana. Four children. The youngest still lives at home," he mumbled.

Rahnnic nodded respectfully. "I am sure you miss them. With luck, this task of mine will soon be over, and you will soon be with them."

"I think of little else," Oxal lied, and felt relief as the prince returned to his pavilion.

In the morning, the sprites had indeed altered the trail. Rahnnic forged on, leading the column through brambles and around thickets. Often he was forced to meditate in order to divine the correct path. They could have made better time, but the Arith lord refused to allow his men to cut living branches, even when it meant a considerable detour.

The latter courtesy did not seem to temper the forest's animosity. Pines dropped heavy green cones. Twice hornets attacked, forcing Rahnnic to lay a charm to keep them away. The more the men progressed, the more the trees seemed to moan in protest.

Something *was* moaning, Oxal realized. A faint, keening chant drifted on the wind. It was fascinating.

"Hold!" cried Prince Rahnnic.

Oxal stopped. He and several other riders had turned away from the column and were edging toward the lip of a ravine. The prince had to cut off the lead pair of soldiers and drive them back before they would turn away.

"The willows in the ravine are singing a siren melody to make us tumble into the rapids," Rahnnic explained. "Plug your ears. Watch each other carefully. We must leave *now*."

The men obeyed. Eventually the trail turned away from the ravine, and the call faded.

"By the gods," grumbled the old fletcher behind Oxal. "A man can't void his bowels in this forest without fretting that a snake will jump into his undergarments."

Camp was made near a lake in a spot clear of trees. The men preferred to brave the resident hordes of mosquitoes than sleep in the shadows of the wood.

Rahnnic retired early. Oxal noticed bags under the prince's eyes and a stoop to his shoulders. The continual use of magic was taking its toll.

Oxal needed rest, too, yet two hours after bedding down, he woke. Sleeplessness was the bane of his middle age. After another hour of tossing, he gave up the struggle, put on his boots, and relieved one of the sentries.

The frogs had fallen silent. Sibilant whispers seemed to filter from the groves of pine and ash. Oxal shivered. To ease his nervousness, he paced back and forth along the stream bank.

Well after midnight, as the waning moon approached zenith, a scream roused the camp. Oxal whirled. A sentry, who had been perched on a fallen log for most of his watch, was frantically trying to lift his feet from the ground. Oxal rushed over.

Surely, he thought, the moonlight was deceiving him. A mesh of pallid root tendrils poked from the humus and into the leather seams of the sentry's boots.

"They're in my skin!" cried the man as if in the throes of a nightmare. In fact, Oxal was sure that the soldier had been dozing at his post. He sliced through the tendrils with his knife. The man lifted his feet.

Screams were now radiating over the camp. Soldiers struggled in their bedrolls. Oxal saw an archer claw at his feet.

"It has everyone," the sentry moaned.

An hour later, Rahnnic set down the foot of his afflicted captain. A pale nimbus of sorcery faded from the prince's hand.

"I can do nothing," he announced. He dragged his gauntlet across the ground, disturbing the network of vines that had emerged from the soil of the camp. Thin as capillaries, they were tough and sticky, like spider web made of plant matter. At the juncture of each branching lay a thorn as narrow as a mosquito's snout.

Oxal shifted self-consciously from foot to foot, worried that he might yet be stung. He and two of the sentries had escaped because they had stayed mobile while the vines had done their evil. All the other men in the company had been punctured by a least one thorn, save the prince, who would have sensed the encroachment.

"These vines must be woodcutter's bane," the prince added. "Once they poison a man's blood, roots will grow from whatever part of his flesh is closest to the ground. The cure takes weeks to administer. You must return to the city and convalesce in high stone towers. Go quickly. Do not let yourselves become thoroughly rooted or you will never be able to move again."

He pointed to Oxal and the two unafflicted sentries. "You men have charge of their safety. Watch them carefully. Within a few hours, they will begin to *wish* to take root."

"You aren't returning with us?" Oxal asked.

"No."

"Take me with you," Oxal said.

The prince raised his hand to protest.

"You'll need someone to watch your back, someone to share the watch at night. A single attendant is far better than none."

Rahnnic let his hand fall. "You are right. If I wish to succeed, I must not refuse aid."

The captain of the guard spoke. "Your Highness, how are we to find our way out without you?" His tone implied shame at seeming weak.

"Follow our path in reverse. The forest will not hinder you as long as you ride for its borders."

Oxal did not begrudge the captain his fear. Any sensible man would abandon the quest. He found a place away from the patch of woodcutter's bane and waited for the prince.

The next three mornings began at first light after hasty gulpings of cold rations. They rested each midday, making up for nights spent peering anxiously into shadows. Oxal was reminded of a campaign across the Far Dunes. The regiment had risked ambush for days on end crossing the sand. This trek did the same things to his mind. Alert to every mouse scurry and every sigh of the breeze, the soldier lived for the moment, storing little in memory.

Yet they were not attacked. The prince, with only one extra body to protect, managed to keep peril at a distance. Once, Oxal was forced to put an arrow in a rabid wolf that appeared in their wake. Otherwise, the only visible hostility was the forest's continued attempts to lead the men astray.

Rahnnic spoke less and less. Though his gaze remained alert, he slouched in his saddle. He sat listlessly beside the fire each night, leaving the care of the horses and other essentials entirely to Oxal. His cheeks grew gaunt. By late on the third day afternoon, Oxal was beginning to worry that his lord would fall from the saddle.

Abruptly, Rahnnic straightened up. Oxal followed his gaze. Across the path lay a row of unusually large trees of many types. They seemed to be part of a huge circle.

"We have arrived," the prince stated.

Abruptly the massive walnut directly ahead of them swung its branches, flinging its hard fruit. The horses, stung, reared back. Only quick hands on the reins kept the animals from bolting.

"Dryad trees!" Oxal yelled, cupping a bruise on his forehead.

"Yes," replied the prince. "The greatest of all. We dare not approach. The branches are nigh as supple as our own arms, and nearly as fast."

As if to prove Rahnnic's point, the walnut and a neighboring juniper reached out, shaping their outer branches like great claws. The men were only a few paces from the closest twigs.

"What now?" asked Oxal.

The prince dismounted, shaking a nut from his cuff. He led Oxal and the horses out of the range of more such missiles. "We wait for moonrise."

* * *

As twilight arrived, the forest's numerous murmurs grew clearer. Oxal heard the thumping of log drums and the trill of reed pipes. Gone was the oppressive air of enmity. The soldier felt as though he'd sampled a fine ale, sipping just enough to loosen his muscles and dissipate anxiety, but not so much that his senses were dulled.

"Is this a trick?"

"The music is not intended for us," Rahnnic explained. "Have you not heard the tales? This is the anthem of the forest, sung here every night."

The fey symphony grew louder until it was all Oxal could do to resist seeking its origin. This was not like the siren call of the willows. That had been a sinister compulsion. This urge came from within him. He knew he could stifle it, but had no wish to.

Rahnnic stood. He pointed at the moon, which had risen above the treeline. "Now we can proceed."

Leaving the horses tethered, the men approached the guardian ring. The trees swayed menacingly, but Rahnnic raised his arms, palms open to the sky. He caught the moon's light and fashioned cords of glowing silver. When he had accumulated two huge coils, he flung the strands forward. They wrapped two of the trees, pulling their branches to either side, opening a passage.

"Quickly," the prince said.

Oxal sensed the frustration of the trees. The limbs trembled. A single walnut sailed feebly through the air, off target. No sooner had the men sprinted through the gap than the ropes of moonlight snapped, the fragments growing dull and gray as they fell.

The men stood on the lip of an earthen amphitheater. At the center a troupe of women danced around a brightly shimmering pool. They ranged from young to old, from thick to willowy, some as dark-skinned as hill oak, some as fair as aspen. Yet all shared a grace that set them apart from human dancers. When their feet lifted, the grass sprang up as if untrampled, rich with wildflowers and herbs. Each time their soles landed, the ground shook with a vibrant, life-giving pulse that traveled outward into the far reaches of the forest.

Oxal found himself swaying to the rhythm of the instruments—where the musicians were, he couldn't say. He only wanted to partake of the joy and vigor bathing the amphitheater. Here was a treasure barely hinted at in the myths. This could only be the sanctuary where sap was taught the joy of flowing, where antlers learned to sprout from the heads of stags, where

the streams learned their babbling. The spirit of the forest
reached out from here, giving every sapling and brush finch its
purpose.

The forest had not attacked the soldiers out of an evil nature,
but out of the need to preserve this nest from which its essence
sprang.

The women began to chant. As the melody wafted into the
treetops, Oxal was unable to contain the upwelling of celebration
inside himself. He cried out.

Instantly the music ceased. The women spun toward the men.
Their eyes widened and they fled toward the limits of the amphitheater. As each reached the bole of one of the great trees, they
were swallowed up as if they had melted into the bark.

Oxal's cheeks grew hot with embarrassment. "I . . . I . . ." he
began, and turned helplessly toward Rahnnic.

The prince's gaze clung to one of the last of the dancers. Oxal
saw a glimpse of supple legs in flight, auburn tresses waving behind, and then she was absorbed into a tree unlike any the soldier
had ever seen. Only when she was out of sight did Rahnnic turn
and face the pool.

"Forgive our trespass," he said. "We mean no harm."

The dryads did not answer him. Waving away Oxal's mutters
of apology, the prince skirted the pool and began to approach the
tree that had engulfed the auburn-haired woman.

While he was still many paces away, the oldest, hoariest member of the ring contorted and groaned. From its bole emerged an
ancient crone. Oxal, who had been moving to join his lord,
stopped and retreated. Though the apparition had assumed the
general shape of a human, she seemed half made of earth, roots,
and grubs, with hair of twigs. The soldier had no doubt she commanded the obedience of every plant and creature of the forest.

"Few of your kind have stood where you now stand, magician," said the goddess.

"I know, Mother," Rahnnic replied. "Few have had such
need."

"I know your need. You seek to take the brightest sapling of
my grove. How can you ask me to surrender that which I love
so much?"

"Before you had ever seen her, I loved her. Can you tell me
that you love her more? Or can you find a place for me here?
Show me that either is true, and I will accept it."

The great mother of the forest leaned forward, staring. Off to
the side, Oxal shivered. The crone's eyes glazed over, seeing

something more than the moonlight could show. Oxal sensed that
were she to turn his way, she would peer right into him, uncovering every memory, every quirk of his character, every true
emotion he had ever felt. Even the edge of her glance was
enough to make the soldier sink to his knees as if reduced to in-
fancy. Yet the prince stood firm.

Gradually the mother's head bowed.

"Yours is a pure soul, Rahnnic of Irithel. Would that there
were a place for you here. But you are of fire and air, a rider of
the sun's rays and seducer of the moon's light. I cannot alter
your nature enough to find you a place here. Nor can I stand
against the light blazing in you now. It must be given its moment
to shine.

"Take her, then. Take her quickly, while I can keep from
reaching to snatch her back. Take her with my blessing. Promise
only that if your passion should ever dim for her, you will return
her to me."

"I so promise," Rahnnic replied.

The mother turned. Like a baby being born, Arameth emerged
from the trunk of her tree. She seemed dazed and almost unconscious, except that when Rahnnic reached for her, she rushed into
his arms.

Oxal climbed unsteadily to his feet, almost ashamed to be
watching, as if he'd stumbled over a couple making love.
Arameth seemed only slightly older than Rahnnic. The gambit
had worked. The decades ahead were theirs to share.

It was only as he handed the prince a blanket with which to
cover his wife that Oxal realized something was wrong. Rahnnic
had already seen it, and the blanket fell nerveless from his fingers.

"She is not as you remember her," the mother of the forest
confessed. She held out a round, polished acorn as big as a hen's
egg. "Take this. In time you may have need of it."

Rahnnic's hand shook as he accepted the acorn. Stricken, he
led his princess from the amphitheater.

The end of the quest was not as Oxal would have imagined.
True, hordes of onlookers lined the streets of the capital. Musicians played, clowns distracted impatient children, and decora-
tions hung from shop lintels and street lamps. But the gaiety
faded at the first glimpse of Arameth.

The princess frowned at the structures of brick and tile and
lumber as if she had never seen them before. The people she ig-

nored altogether. She demonstrated only one sign of intentional thought—occasionally she grasped Rahnnic's hand.

The somber discussions within the palace were the worst ordeal. Since the prince was reluctant to speak, it fell to the soldier to describe the liberation of the princess.

"She seems to know Rahnnic," he said, intimidated to be speaking to so many royals, "but gives no other sign that she remembers her life as Arameth. It's been too long. The human part of her has withered. All the way back she would sit in silence, listening to the babble of streams, raising her face to the sun, swaying as the breeze stroked her. Like a tree."

The royal family could see for themselves the truth of the account. Rahnnic and Arameth retired to private quarters. The king tripled Oxal's pension as a reward for his fealty and granted him permission to leave.

Though he was a palace guard, Oxal seldom saw the prince over the next few seasons. Most of that was at a distance, as Rahnnic guided his mate through the gardens or along the ramparts, viewing the seashore where, in an earlier life, they had shared many walks.

The princess remained wordless, though occasionally she voiced sounds that mimicked the rustling of leaves in the wind. Only a few sights made her smile, chiefly the arrival of birds, who would perch on her and sing. Sometimes on moonlit nights she would dance, and Oxal heard it whispered that it was not such a dance as the proper ladies of the court would dare attempt.

One day in autumn, Rahnnic came to the barracks where Oxal had just completed his round of duty.

"It was a year ago today I took Arameth from the wood," said the prince. "Come. You were my witness then. Be my witness now."

With Arameth at his side, Rahnnic guided Oxal to a secluded area of the royal gardens where a large tree had recently been removed. Soft soil, wet from that morning's storm, filled the cavity where the stump had been dug out. There the prince planted the acorn given to him by the mother of the forest.

Scarcely had he stepped back than a sprig emerged from the soil. It swelled within moments into a full-sized evergreen bright with waxy leaves and amber flowers. It stopped growing only when its bole was thicker than a man could wrap his arms around. It vaguely resembled a laurel, but its bark was a smooth tan and tiny clusters of acorns hid in the centers of the blossoms.

Arameth stepped forward, smiling radiantly. She slid hastily from her garments, fluttered to the evergreen, and vanished.

Rahnnic sighed, tears hovering on his lashes. He pointed at the ground on which he stood. "She was becoming ill. Though she has left the forest—willingly—the forest will not leave her. This will give her time to remember herself."

"How much time will that be?"

"Who knows? I will have a bench made so that I may sit in her shade. I have memorized her dance, and will perform it with her. Perhaps that is all that I can hope for."

"I am sorry, Your Highness, that things have not gone better."

"Do not be sorry for me, sir. I have her again. That in itself is greater fortune than I had a right to expect. I waited a century for her companionship. I can wait another, if need be, to see her fully restored." A branch of the tree reached downward, stroking his cheek with soft leaves. "You see? She knows that I love her. Surely the rest is worth a bit of patience."

Oxal quietly took his leave. The prince remained, hand tenderly pressing the tree.

The soldier made his way down the familiar cobbled streets to his modest house. Ayana was waiting as he stepped across the threshold. She took one look at him and said, "It is done, then?"

"Yes." Oxal coughed. "Yes."

Over supper he described the scene at the garden. "The legend is fulfilled," Ayana replied. "For better or worse, they are reunited. It makes a mighty tale."

Oxal nodded absently. He was watching his daughter. His baby, Fihelia, now fourteen years old. She was placing the screen in front of the hearth for the night, looking for all the world like a grown woman tending to the duties of her own house.

Gradually his aging, scarred features eased into a smile.

He and Ayana had shared these walls for over thirty years. Quietly, with harmony. Passion had not blazed for them as in legends, but they had grown accustomed to each other in ways that soothed the soul. He had never truly appreciated that fact until he had returned from the forest. And now, more than ever, he wondered how it could have been that once he had been envious of Rahnnic, Prince of Irithel. It had not been a fool's quest. A prize had been waiting, after all.

Holy Ground

by Thomas S. Roche

*Thoms S. Roche has published fiction in several antholo-
gies and a number of magazines such as Truth Until Par-
adox and The Splendour Falls and Marion Zimmer
Bradley's Fantasy Magazine. When not working on his stories, he has been a bus driver, a temp and a medical
writer.*

We came out of the hills screaming bloody murder, our horses
lathered and choking, Rajni's shoes striking sparks, the lightning
flashing around us. The Enemy was behind us, their pale skin
glinting in the lightning flashes, longbows spread out like wings,
armor black as death. Their arrows cut past my ears. The edge of
the forest was only minutes ahead of me, and it loomed like
damned salvation.

"Have you gone crazy? We can't go into the forest!"

I drew rein as my dozen-and-a-half companions did the same.
"It's our only chance. You know the Enemy won't go in there!"

"We've got to stand and fight! No one but the priests—!"

"Go to hell, then!" I turned and spurred Rajni toward the forest. As the Enemy grew closer, the men turned to fight. I lost
sight of them under the sound of clashing metal and screams of
battle. If they wanted to die defending their city, that was fine
with me, for all the good it would do anyone. Forget them.

A party of the Enemy branched off to pursue me over the open
field—perhaps two dozen. I did not doubt that my companions
would soon be dead, or in chains.

I pushed my head down farther, my hands grasping Rajni's

reins. Lightning hit the ground nearby; the explosion made Rajni stumble and throw me. It was pure luck that I landed on my feet.

Realizing that I had disappeared from his back, Rajni slowed to a trot, just slow enough for me to catch up. The Enemy closed in. They were almost upon me. I raised my hands to Heaven.

The lightning came down between me and them, exploding a tree stump, and the party drew rein, their horses spooked. I saw one rider go flying, but then I didn't look back.

Despite myself, I closed my eyes and said a prayer.

The sounds of pursuit grew closer. They were much more heavily armored than me, but they knew I was trying to reach the forest. Their arrows grew fewer, and suddenly I was at the forest's edge.

The light of the world seemed to go right up to the edge of the forest and stop. Past the border, the edge of the forest, what light cut through the storm clouds seemed absorbed by the black trees, swallowed by darkness. It was as if those trees thrived on light as demons thrived on blood. A thick black liquid dripped from the black leaves and twisted branches. Dark shapes moved within the forest. My stomach quivered slightly.

The sky darkened in the few moments I hesitated. Flashes of lightning lit up the edge of the wood and were similarly engulfed. The Enemy drew rein some hundred yards off and readied their bows, knowing my fear.

I spurred Rajni, and on we went.

We passed the wall of shadow and the sky exploded. Sheets of rain came down, drenching me in seconds even under the cover of the trees. The black sap from the trees washed onto me. A few feeble arrows passed me, but they were poorly aimed and half-hearted. When I looked back the Enemy had disappeared and I could barely see past the forest edge. I knew they would wait for me.

Now that I was in, it was black as midnight. The branches over me grew thicker. I could hear the rain overhead, and rivulets dribbled down on me through the thick forest cover. Rajni had to pick his way between the trees at first, and then, later, I had to lead him. Before long it was impossible to see where I was going. Dark shapes moved in the wood.

I kept moving, knowing my only hope was to make it deep enough into the forest to reach a Shrine. In this forest, that could be forever.

The forest deepened, and I could hardly pick my way out among the twisted vines and bushes. The dark shapes continued to move, and I thought I saw glowing eyes. The rumbling and flashes of lightning gradually illuminated small, black furry things.

Finally, I reached a tiny clearing, perhaps ten feet across, where I could crouch and try to work enough charm to light my pipe. I was still breathing very hard.

After the fifth try, I managed to get the pipe going. My cloak was almost soaked through, but I huddled into it just the same. I was desperately hungry, not having eaten in days. I wondered if the Enemy had taken the city yet. A few days ago my eyes would have filled with tears at the thought of those gleaming spires of Laure in the hands of the pale ones. But now, it caused only a twinge of fear to contemplate it.

Rajni made an uncomfortable noise, snorting and looking around nervously. I drew my blade and set it across my knees.

Rajni's discomfort seemed to increase. I covered my glowing pipe with my hand, though I was quite sure any creatures around could see adequately in the dark. I squinted into the shadows, listening carefully.

The chill drew up my spine, starting at the base, slowly moving up to spread across my shoulders. The creature slowly became visible, and I knew it had been staring at me for some time. As I watched, the beast's eyes began to glow a bright red. I could just make out an enormous snout and a set of fangs.

"You disturb my sense of harmony," I said absently.

To my surprise, I received an answer. The voice rang in my ears: harsh, ancient-sounding, half-disembodied, dangerous. "That is not my intention. I am more interested in your mount than in you."

I moved in between the eyes-and-snout and Rajni, who had grown visibly uncomfortable and was pawing the black-mossed ground. "I don't blame you; I don't have much meat on my bones. But I'm afraid I have need of my mount."

"So have I. You will kindly stand aside?"

I shook my head sadly. "Afraid I can't do that. Look, Creature, I have no desire to come into your house and start a fight here in the middle of a rainstorm."

"The name's not Creature, but forget it. Stand aside?"

"No."

As it leaped out of the shadows, I got my first look.

The moment seemed frozen in amber. The creature was like an enormous wolf, as if I really cared. The body was bigger than mine, and he had the advantage of a nasty set of claws, and those enormous fangs. He was upon me, and I had to admit I deserved what I got for not being ready. He avoided my sword and landed on my chest, slamming me into the ground. The wind rushed out of my lungs.

I managed to work the edge of my sword up against the beast's furry throat, trying to cut in, but the skin seemed impenetrable and I didn't have the free hand to work a charm. The fangs snapped shut three times, inches from my face, as the claws raked my leather garments. Then, in a second, he was gone, and I lay there gasping for breath like a beaten child.

I heard the horse's terrified bleating, and the nightmare scuffle. I had been lucky to catch the beast with the flat of my blade, or he would have done to me as he was now doing to Rajni. I got to my feet.

"I wish you hadn't done that," I said, making a sign with my left hand as I raised my sword.

The beast looked up at me across the clearing, his mouth full of living flesh. Rajni's legs kicked pathetically. A sound like a laugh escaped the beast's full mouth, as my sword began to glow.

"I'm sure you do," said the beast. "But I did, so why not be moving along. I have taken what I wanted, and I will leave you unmolested. Get out of this place. I've no more quarrel with you than you do with me—horse flesh is much more to my liking."

I said: "I'm fond of wolf, myself," and leaped, the glowing sword cutting a path of light into attack position. The speed of the beast was incredible, but I was helped by the charm. The sword sought its mark without me, dragging my body as a matter of carry-on luggage, and as I landed, the blade's point drove deep into the creature's mouth and down into its throat and out the back.

As I had anticipated, it severed his spine. A howling scream escaped his lips, and the light in the eyes grew brighter. The lips did not move as the voice echoed in my brain.

"Human, you have spilled blood on holy ground. You have ensured your doom. I rule this place."

"I'm sure you do," I said. "And I do apologize. But I'm not exactly a welcome guest in the first place."

The light went out of the eyes, and I hacked off the head, just to be sure. My heart was still pounding, and I would have vomited if I had food in my stomach. Rajni was not quite dead and I had to finish him off and, as is the custom, eat his heart. I suppose the beast's spirit was envious. There are times when beasts are kinder than people.

Rajni's heart sustained me for some time, long enough to wander through the forest and become desperately lost. I had the saddlebags slung over my shoulder. The shapes continued to move in the blackness of the forest, but for now they left me alone.

The night passed, and faint shafts of light streamed through the dense cover here and there. I finally found space in a small clearing to rest with my back to an old blasted tree stump crawling with insects.

Later, I was surprised to find a hollow in a giant tree, a tree big as a house. The hollow was more than large enough for me to sleep in—it resembled a cave. A large field of ancient, melted candles on boards was set up before the tree-hollow, indicating that this place had once been a shrine. I struck a light and found that the hollow was relatively clean, and didn't seem to be home to anything carnivorous. I crawled in, wrapping myself in my musty-smelling cloak, and curled gratefully up inside the tree.

It had been weeks since I had slept a full night. Ever since the defenses broke and the Enemy approached the city, I had been among the defenders. Until we had been routed at the border, and I had taken off with the small party. I might call myself a deserter . . . but there had been no choice.

And thus, into the forest. The sacred forest, the holiest of places, the place where the irritating priests kept their Shrines and forbade any nonclergied citizen to enter. I had never been much on religion, and I figured an eternity in hell for trespass on holy ground was probably about equal to the fate the Enemy would dole out if they captured me. The forest was that most feared of sacred places, the place where the heart of the world was kept, where my race had (perhaps) been born from the trees, the place the Enemy feared more than anything. And the place I, as a secular magician, and one who particularly tended toward irreverence and blasphemy, was most forbidden to go.

Sleep took me like a forest fire.

The spirit came to me as I slept, and I realized the enormity of my transgression. In my confusion, I had stumbled upon my own Mother; in my exhaustion I had used her as if she were a conveniently-placed cot. I should have guessed she wouldn't appreciate that much, or maybe that she would appreciate it greatly.

The sleep was like nothing I had ever experienced, sweet and deep and peaceful. I had no visions of my city's spires set on fire, my people murdered, my country's fields burned and the ground salted. I felt only a oneness with my own existence, or perhaps nonexistence. I felt peace. I came out of sleep with her face in front of me and her hand upon mine. She had a look of vague concern.

"You do not seem well," she said.

Crossing the line between sleep and waking, several times in each direction, I looked at her, and finally managed to croak an answer.

"I am *not* well, lady. I'm afraid I've been fleeing."

"You've trespassed."

"I'm sorry. I didn't realize the tree was already rented."

I considered her through my half-closed eyes, since I was afraid to open them all the way. She shimmered with a faint spray of light, and her flesh was of the whitest white—the color of a corpse drained of blood. Her hair and lips were blacker than coal, with the slightest blue tinge to them, and her eyes were a phosphorescent green. She was naked. Her face looked ageless, an eternal, androgynous youth.

"You killed Fenris," she said. "He really meant you no harm."

"I apologize," I said, "but I had no way to know he wouldn't get hungry for a snack, later, something with more white meat on it."

She shook her head. "He wouldn't have done that. Perhaps you could apologize to his spirit?"

"Sorry, I've never been very good at communing with nature, lady."

"The name is Alaura. No hard feelings—yet." Her blue-black lips twisted into a dark smile, and I shifted uncomfortably. "Fenris' time had come, anyway, so you performed a necessary function—thank you. Why have you come to the Center?"

A bolt of lighting went down my spine. It was not possible that this was the Center of the forest. The being crouched between me and the entrance to the hollow. My sword was still in my hand. I slowly sat up and then got to my knees.

"The Center?"

"Not of the forest, of course. There is no center to the forest. But this is your Center. You must have known that, to sleep here."

"I don't quite understand what you're getting at."

"Certainly you noticed the candles?"

"Notice them? Yes. But I don't subscribe to the religion that placed them there. . . ."

"And so you ignored the fact that this was a holy place. Well, that's reasonable. It seems to have been a mistake. But you're still part of the race."

I considered it for a moment. "Pretty much. I suppose so, yes—Alaura."

"Then you've still found your center."

"I don't understand."

A smile crossed her corpselike face, in a wave of ephemeral but terrifying beauty. She laughed and changed the subject.

"Tell me, what was the meaning of that storm?"

"I'm afraid I caused it. I was trying to cause trouble for the ones who pursued me. But these things have a way of getting out of hand."

"So they do. Your pursuers did not follow you into the forest?"

"No, they were afraid."

"And why are they afraid of the forest?"

"Superstition, mostly, and hatred of my own race. They know it is our sacred place, the supposed center of my people, the place where our nation was born—according to legend. It is a place of great power and terror to my people, and therefore to the Enemy." Despite myself, I felt a tear forming in my eye, and it ran down my cheek. My voice caught when I continued. "They've done horrible things to my people, and want to exterminate them from the world. They invaded our country and confined its people to camps where they were murdered *en masse*. The atrocities these beasts have performed . . ." My voice caught, and I shook my head. I added, as an afterthought, "And they seek to destroy this forest."

"Nothing can destroy this forest."

"They are able to ride the skies on giant birds, powerful birds that carry huge containers of poisons, much like the poisons used against my people. These compounds can destroy foliage. . . ."

"Nothing can destroy this forest," she repeated. "It is the heart center. You are safe here."

"I don't feel very safe," I said, moving away from her. "I'm quite uncomfortable, to tell you the truth, though your company is quite charming and your countenance supernaturally beautiful, believe me. Just the same, I think I shall leave now, if it's all the same to you."

"I'm sorry, but I must insist that you stay and talk with me for just a little longer. Were you afraid, too? Do you understand what I said about your center?"

"Yes, and no. I was very afraid. And rightly so, from what happened with—Fenris, was that his name?"

"Is," she said. "He has been reborn, albeit in a somewhat different form."

"Damn," I said. "My troubles have a way of doing that."

"It was the least I could do for him. You should not be afraid of the forest. Or of me."

I gripped the hilt of my sword. "Why not, lady? I've already been attacked by a giant wolf named Fenris and had my horse killed. I am now, apparently, trapped inside a tree with its guardian spirit."

Her hair seemed to blow in the wind. "You have reached your center. It is therefore impossible for you to be trapped here, since by your race's very existence you are part of the forest."

I frowned. "But if I interpret your actions correctly, you are not willing to stand aside to let me crawl out of this tree?"

"I'm afraid you cannot leave, without my help."

"Why is that?" I looked down, and slowly came to the realization that she was correct. My calves and thighs had taken on a strangely wooden appearance. My boots seemed to have disappeared, and I had sunk several inches into the soft wood of the tree. I felt strangely dispassionate about the whole thing, having traded one oblivion for another.

I lifted my sword. "If you will not be so kind—"

"I'm sorry," she said, as my sword-arm stiffened and the sword came clattering to the floor of the hollow. My arm stretched back, entangled in what seemed to be vines, and my clothing crumbled to dust and rotted away. I felt my hair, now black leaves and vines which smelled like the black forest, tangling about my face.

"Please," I said. "I am not really ready for communion with nature."

"But commune you must. You may be the last one left," said Alaura. "What was your name again?"

My lips had become wooden by the time she bent to kiss me, so she gave me a name of her choosing, in a language I did not understand, spoken in a way I could no longer speak.

She has transplanted me to a new Center, a place where I can grow as a creature of the forest.

Black birds come to roost in my branches, carrying the remnants of eyes they have eaten from the heads of my people, miles away, outside the burned cities. They build nests with the hair of my comrades. But in my branches these ravens thrive.

Alaura comes to me sometimes, but despite her appearance, she is very old. The beauty of her lustrous blue-black lips is deceiving. Her hair sways in the breeze which bears the far-off odor of burning flesh.

Alaura's people have met their end. But my lover lays a darkened death bed of moss on holy ground, and the sun rises like a holocaust above the cleansed earth. Alaura is with child.

Ghostwood

by Michelle Sagara

Michelle Sagara writes fantasy because she loves the genre, whether it is novel-length as in the Books of the Sundered, *or short work. Twice nominated for the Campbell Award (and now a two-time member of the Campbell Loser's club), she expects to continue writing for a long time.*

It was winter in a forest that had forgotten spring.

Ice was on the trees, and although sunlight glittered through it, lacing the shadows with sharp, perfect light, it never melted. Silence reigned; even the breeze moved nothing. It was serene and calm at the heart of the woods.

Justin woke up slowly. His back ached and his arms were sore from the previous day's work. The winter air had been dry and cold enough that splitting logs for the fire was easy. For the first two hours, at any rate.

He never quit when it was smart to.

"Justin?"

"I'm out cutting wood." He groaned as the door to his room opened.

"You sleep too much."

"You don't sleep enough. Show a little pity, won't you?"

"How much pity do you want?"

"Any. Which is obviously not what an older sister worth her salt is capable of giving." He lifted a pillow and hurled it at her; she ducked.

"I'm capable of some. There's coffee on the burner, and it's fresh. Is that stubble I see?"

"On my face or on your legs?"

She shrieked, laughed, and threw the pillow back at his face. "That's it—you fend for yourself at breakfast!"

The coffee was good; Chris always made a good cup of coffee. Almost good enough to wake up early for, but not quite.

"I can't believe you're twenty-five and you still can't wake up in the morning—it must be the city air." She put a plate of sunny-side-up eggs under Justin's nose and added a few pieces of bacon to it.

"This isn't exactly rural," he replied. "You've got electricity, you've got septic tanks, you've got paved roads and phones—"

"And they cost a lot more than you pay in Toronto."

"I guess that's why you haven't bothered to turn on the heaters."

She smiled at his ill-humor. "The heat's about as on as it gets. Go sit in the solarium; sun's strong through the windows."

"You mean go out and join the rest of the vegetation?" He picked up his plate and his mug, dropped his fork on the floor, and fished around on hands and knees trying to find it before she turned up another one.

"Justin?"

"What?"

"I love you, you idiot."

The solarium was bright with sun, but the light was a cold light, and frost covered the lower half of the full-length windows. The doors, ostensibly sliding ones, were frozen in their tracks. Too much humidity.

Plants lined five sides of the small hexagonal room. Justin shook his head as he looked at the yellow-brown leaves of a withered wax begonia. The cacti were extremely sorry looking; there was a green patina on the soil's surface that looked suspiciously like algae. An amaryllis was in bloom, and of all the plants here, it looked most healthy, although its flowers were paler than usual.

"Chris?"

She came through the door with a steaming mug of tea. "Don't give me a hard time."

"We both know you've got a black thumb. I just didn't realize the rest of your fingers were that color, too." He ducked as he said it, and she laughed. "These—it almost looks like someone gave you all of my plants—and then you killed them."

Her face froze for an instant; she looked outside, to the snow across the grassy hills that rose gently on either side of her home. Then the shadow passed, and she smiled. "You aren't the only person in the world who knows something about plants, you know."

"Yeah, but you're one of the seven that doesn't."

"Great. My brother still laughs at his own jokes."

"No one else will." He finished the yolk of his second egg and started in on the bacon.

"Justin!"

"Yes, Mother." He never liked the whites, and didn't usually eat them when he was on his own. "You're going to have to let me do something about these plants, you know."

"Do whatever you like to them—they're officially your responsibility now."

"Where are you going?"

"If I can figure out how to tie these damned tennis rackets—"

"Snow shoes."

"—tennis rackets on, I'm going for a walk."

"It's—it's really cold out there. You're sure you want to go out?"

"I didn't come all the way up here to be cooped in a house; I could've saved time and money and just stayed in Toronto."

"You want company?"

"If you want, but I'm not going to get lost."

She was already putting on an extra sweater. "I don't trust you," she said. "Here, give me those."

There wasn't another track in sight. Even the path to the house was remarkably pristine; if Justin had trudged through the knee-deep snow, no sign of his passing remained.

"How much snow do you get here anyway?"

"Not much." She shrugged; her breath wreathed her face like smoke in a crowded bar. "The last fall was really heavy for this time of year. Shouldn't get much more."

He nodded absently, catching half of what she said. It was better than he often did, especially when he was thinking. "You know, Chris, I've never seen the sun look so cold." He pointed to the sparkle of light across the winter landscape. "I mean, if it weren't so cold, I'd say this place looked like a . . . a desert."

She shivered and drew her coat more tightly around her broad shoulders.

"You cold?"

"A little."

"Go on home, then. I want a little more air before I turn in for the day."

Justin wasn't used to the forest; he was a city person with the barest touch of the country wilderness in his heart. He liked to visit the wild woods only when he had the comfort of modern conveniences directly behind him; even camping was a discomfort that he had only put up with for Chris' sake.

Chris, now *she* could forage, cook, build and—more impressive—start a fire. She could tell you what the flora and fauna were, even if she did kill the occasional bits of flora she tried to pot.

It was her forest in some ways. She loved the oaks, she loved the pines, she loved the spruces and the funny silver-barked trees. But she best loved the rowans. Justin couldn't stand rowans. Their smell at the height of summer was strong and unpleasant. That made no difference at all to Chris.

In fact, she'd bought this patch of hard-to-reach land because it had a circle of rowan trees that were, in her words, ancient. They made him uncomfortable, although he wouldn't have ever admitted it, and whenever Chris could coax him to visit, he went out of his way not to look at the circle that was her pride.

So he didn't understand how one moment he was shaking the deciduous spines of a spruce, and the next, he was bumping into the periphery of that very circle. But he decided that his subconscious hated him. He took a deep breath, shook his head, and turned to leave the rowans.

Something blocked his way.

It was thin and gaunt, and rags clung to its elbows, shoulders and waist; its skin was gray, its lips so stretched they were almost nonexistent. It had a thatch of white hair over a patchy skull.

Justin cried out in shock and took a step back, followed by a second, larger one. He had seen, in museum displays, the mummified corpses of ancient Egyptians. He had never seen one walk, until now.

He could not take his eyes off the creature as it shambled toward him. But he knew that he stood in the centre of the rowan circle. Something caught the corner of his eye; he was afraid to look, but he did. Another creature. And another. And another.

There was no escape; they approached the circle from every possible direction. He began to turn wildly, first in one direction, then in another. He ran to the east, stopped short, and scuttled back to the west. The forest was filled with walking shadows.

Oh, God, he thought. *Chris!* He listened, but heard nothing; the forest was silent.

And then they stopped. Magically and in unison. They threw themselves forward, but seemed to hit an invisible barrier. The circle.

I don't believe it. Numb with cold, he let his knees buckle. *They can't get in. Dear God, get me out of here alive and I'll never avoid rowans again, I swear.*

They moved, these creatures; they circled like hungry jackals. But they couldn't reach him, and after a while, he huddled, knees to chest, and waited. It got cold, and colder still, as the night fell. His cheeks began to tingle with pain as the cold bit in.

He sat and watched them, until he could no longer distinguish them from the shadows of nighttime winter woods. And then his eyes grew heavy. He knew it was dangerous. He tried to wake up.

"Justin!"

He screamed, bolted from the security of his bed, realized, in mid-jump, that he wasn't in the snow anymore, and fell flat out on his stomach. Winded, he stared down at the rag rug underneath his nose.

"Justin!"

He looked up, saw his sister's feet, and got to his own. "What?" He touched his chest; it was covered in red, plaid flannel. His grandfather's pajamas.

"You were screaming."

"I was—" He walked over to the window, yanked the curtains back, and looked out into a clear, cold sky. It was dark now; moonlight glittered on the snow, the sun's ghost. He pulled the curtains back into place, cutting the outside world off.

He turned to stare at his sister. Her eyes were ringed black; they always were when she wasn't sleeping well. She was dressed in her housecoat and her old slippers, and she was tying knots in the belt as she watched him, her face full of open concern.

"It was your cooking," he said at last. "Tomorrow, I make dinner. Got it?"

That does it. Next time, Chris cuts the wood. Any responsible person would've built up enough of a stockpile for the winter instead of making their younger brother freeze. Even though he was in boots that practically topped his knees, he could feel the sting of the ice and snow. Chris was going to give him hell for not strapping his feet into snowshoes. Again.

How the hell was I supposed to know it was all this deep? His breath was condensing on his face, and the drops were crackling into ice. Time to go home.

There was a shadow across the snow—long, thin and skeletal. Not an ounce of blood moved in his veins; it was frozen solid.

Taking a deep, icy breath, Justin Larkin turned around. Five feet away, bony claws attached to the snow-covered bark of an oak, one of the creatures stood watching him.

At this distance, it looked a little less like a creature out of nightmare, and a little more like something out of a bad B movie. Except for its eyes. The eyes were like slate; colder than the winter, gleaming like the soul of the ice itself.

Justin took a step back, and then turned suddenly; the forest was empty, except for this one walking skeleton. It made him feel slightly safer. But only slightly.

The circle, he thought. *I'll just head back to the rowan circle. Either that, or I'll wake up. Come on, sunshine.*

"So, uh, come this way often?" Justin took a step back; the creature stayed anchored to the tree beneath its claws. "Uh, I'd like to stay and talk, but I, uh, have to be going now. That all right with you?"

Its lips stretched wide over rotten teeth. "The sssssssssspring."

Before Justin could faint or run, he was suddenly very much alone. He waited a moment before he dared to look around at the ground where the creature had made its stand. It was untouched.

Great. I'm losing my mind in the middle of nowhere, with only my sister for company.

He was certain that he had never felt a winter so cold, and he longed for the city. It was big, yes, and dirty; there were all the usual signs of urban decay on select downtown street corners; there was too much traffic, too much hostility, too much stress. But there was also life, warmth, motion; there was a sense of things being done, of connectivity, of purpose.

He had come to Chris' place to escape all of that, but found that emptiness, the vast expanse of untouched wilderness, perversely reminded him of the things that it wasn't.

That, and his nightmares in the city were profoundly more mundane. He might wake up in a sweat from dreams of a tax audit—he was not completely organized for a self-employed man—but he didn't wander around the ice and snow looking over his shoulder for walking cadavers who made the coming of spring sound like a dire threat.

He had mastered the art of walking in snowshoes, and so no longer tripped on his feet. He wore an undershirt, a shirt, a sweater, a coat, a vest, a scarf, a hat, thin gloves and thick mittens, as well as two pairs of socks and moon boots. He carried a flashlight, just in case he was stupid enough to be caught out after sunset.

Sunset, across the expanse of untouched snow, should have been beautiful. The sun's rays, tinged crimson and orange, seeping across the horizon had always been one of the sights that he valued when he came to visit his sister.

But tonight, for some reason, it was cold. Just cold.

He watched it, waiting for something to click.

Something snapped instead. He turned slowly, flashlight in hand, to see the creature of his daytime nightmare. This close to the boundary of night, Justin should have been terrified.

But the creature looked less skeletal, somehow. A little less gaunt.

"You again," Justin said, through clenched teeth that he hoped resembled a smile.

The creature said nothing, but rather stared at the horizon with unblinking eyes. He pointed straight ahead, to where sun met ground, and as Justin followed his long, bony finger, he saw blood, rather than light, across the crust of ice.

"Sssssspring."

"What's wrong with winter?" Justin asked, half-expecting the vision to be gone again when he turned from the dying sun. But the creature remained, staring at him with eyes that were still colder than the season.

No answer was offered, but suddenly, none was wanted. Justin knew that the winter here had lasted too long.

"Diiiiiiie."

He took a step back, and then stood his ground. The creature stared at him for a moment, then turned slowly and began to shamble off through the trees.

Justin stared down at his flashlight, and then looked up at the stiff, emaciated back of the winter creature. I am an idiot, he said to himself. A complete fool. An utter moron. He carefully clicked the on switch of the flashlight—which, through two layers of wool was no mean feat—made a prayer that the batteries weren't as old as he thought they were, made another, quite different, prayer, and then began to follow.

The creature made no noise as it walked. It wore no snow-shoes, but seemed to move through the ice and snow as if they were liquid. No evidence of its passing remained.

Not so with Justin; he kicked up a spray of snow-dust that his flashlight shimmered off, snapped the occasional brittle twig as it caught on his scarf, and walked into the lower skirts of snow-covered pines. But he followed.

Once or twice, the creature looked back, its icy eyes unblinking. But, seeing Justin, it nodded, and continued to walk.

He had no idea how much time passed; he was barely aware when twilight slipped into night. The moon was bright enough to see by; it made a mockery of battery power as it glinted across sheets of thin ice and thick snow. Justin held the flashlight tightly anyway. It had become a talisman of sorts.

He listened for the sound of night creatures, but there were none. No owls, no winter birds, no animals. *They're sleeping,* he thought, as he drew the light closer.

No, they're dead.

He didn't know why he thought it, but once thought, it was hard to forget. Like the verse of a song that somehow managed to cling to his mind, he replayed the words over and over. They felt right, but they felt wrong.

He was so intent on them, that he almost walked into the back of the creature; it had stopped suddenly, and pivoted, without making a sound. Justin lifted the flashlight and saw that the creature was no longer alone. Others of its ilk were gathered by the trunks of bare trees, glaring at him in silence.

He studied them, let the light skim their faces.

In his first nightmare, they had seemed of one kind, but now, he could see differences. Their cheekbones, their foreheads, their heights—each was unique, as people were. Some, in fact, seemed to be so different in build—broad and short and stocky, rather than tall and delicate—that they might have been different species.

Had they been alive.

As if aware of his appraisal, they stood and endured it. And then, as the light left the face of the last one—although he couldn't have said how many there were—they all turned as one person and looked toward the center of their gathering. He followed their vision.

He thought to see something magical, something poetic, something deadly.

He saw a car instead.

The fender was bent, and rust spots were slowly devouring the paint job at the edge of the trunk. "What the hell?" He began to walk toward it, and the creatures made way for him, opening their ranks to let him pass unhindered. But they began to chant a single word.

"Sssssspring."

He barely heard it. The back of the car was fine. But as he began to circle the car, he saw that something was very, very wrong with it. The passenger and driver's seats were gone in a press of metal and broken glass. The engine had been crumpled with the hood; the front tires were completely flattened.

The light began to shake; his hands could barely hold it. Slowly, numbly, he approached the driver's side of the car. There was blood down the side of it; a thin, red trickle.

There wasn't much left of his car.

His mouth dry, he turned to look at the watchers. And he was suddenly alone in the forest. They were gone; there was no car.

The wax begonias had been drowned, all right; on close inspection the thick leaves were almost mushy. The old man cactus wasn't going to make it either. The jade plants were tough enough to take Chris for a little while, and Justin was pleased to think he could save them. The solarium, with its plant-covered walls, wasn't the best place for them, but he could move them around.

The Japanese maple by the door was in need of repotting. And the violet . . . he lifted it from the shelf and looked more closely at the planter. Then, slowly, he set it down. He began to look at the dying plants more carefully.

It was cold in the solarium.

"Where are you going?"

"For a walk."

"Don't you think that you've done enough walking, Justin? I'm really starting to worry about you. Look at your eyes, they're—"

"Chris, you aren't my mother. I've got to walk." He saw her start to pull a sweater over her head. "Alone."

"But—"

"I'll be fine." He tied the last knot and stood up.

"Justin—I'd like the company."

He shook his head, feeling pained. "I'll be back, I promise. And I'll be better company then."

When he left the garage, he was pale. He carried a flashlight in one hand and a shovel in the other; the shovel was heavy. He walked westward, with purpose. To the rowans.

He wasn't surprised when they came. They fell into lockstep around him; he was certain they were growing in number at his back. Almost, he felt as if he were leading them to a bizarre religious service. They weren't silent, of course.

The rowans stood out in the moonlight and the bitter, bitter cold. But they were not the trees that he had once disliked; they were guardians, they were living henges. He passed through them with ease, but his followers did not. He turned to see them, wide-eyed, as they began to ring the rowans.

"Spring, eh?" he said, as he lifted the shovel. "I'll do my best." His hands were shaking so much that he dropped the shovel three times before he managed to clear away some of the snow. The dirt was frozen, and it was harder than the ice to get rid of. But he worked; he didn't even sweat.

The night passed into dusk, and finally, when dawn broke, the ground had been shifted enough so that Justin Larkin could see what was buried at the heart of the circle. It was what he expected, no more, no less.

No one heard his scream; it was voiceless.

"Chris?"

She looked up from the paper, but the smile that was beginning shattered when she met his eyes. She set the paper aside. "Yes?"

"How did I get up here?" He came and sat down beside her on the old couch; she was a foot away, but the distance could just as well have been miles.

"You drove."

"Where's my car?"

Her face paled. "Your car?"

"My car."

"It's—it's at the garage. Repairs."

He nodded. Passed a hand over his eyes. "Why do you have my plants?"

"Y–your plants?"

"Chris, I recognize those planters; I should've seen it right away. Why do you have 'em?"

She looked down at her hands; they were clenching and unclenching almost convulsively. "I—" Her eyes teared.

"Chris—I'm dead, aren't I?"

"No, you're not!" She stood suddenly, and the tears began to fall; her eyes were red, her lips shaking. "You aren't dead—don't you see? You're here, you're with me!"

"How long have we been here? How long has it been winter, Chris?"

"And we don't have to leave, don't you see? The circle keeps us together. You aren't dead, Justin."

"I'm not—alive." It was hard to talk. Justin was afraid. "I dug up the circle, Chris. I saw my body."

She blanched. Shook her head, covering her mouth with both her hands.

"This is a forest of dead things," he continued, "of dying things. It's going to be winter forever. Nothing will grow, nothing will change." He caught her hands; they were warm, where his were not. "What happened to Bill—you were starting to date again, remember?"

She shook her head. "It doesn't matter anymore." She turned away from him, and stared blindly into the fire; the tears running down her cheeks were orange.

"I—I took your plants, you know? I took them, even though I knew I'd kill them. I had to try; they were like a little bit of your life. But when they started to die—it was like I couldn't even keep that part of you."

He walked over to her back, and put his arms around her, being as gentle as she would let him while still holding on.

"And then, your body." She began to cry harder. "I identified it, sort of. It was—" She couldn't speak. Minutes passed as she gulped air. "After a few months, I couldn't stand it. I disinterred you, and had you brought here. I wanted you to be near me. I'm sorry; it was selfish. I know you never loved the rowans, not like I've always loved them.

"They were the heart of the forest, and you—you were such a big part of my heart. It—it made sense to bury you there." She tried to pull away, and then changed her mind and burrowed back into his arms. "I prayed so hard. I'd've died for you, Justin. I prayed there, in the circle."

"You always were a sentimentalist and a romantic," he said, crying softly into her hair.

Her voice changed, softening, lightening. He heard the miracle in her tone; she had always been too prosaic to deliver it with words. "And then, I woke up the next morning. You were here. It was winter. And I knew it was going to be winter forever. All the animals left. All the birds. It was sudden. Like they couldn't be where you were.

"And I didn't care. Winter—frozen—I didn't care. I don't care, Justin." She put her hand over her mouth. "I don't want to lose you, I don't want you to leave me."

He held her. He just held her.

After she had fallen asleep, exhausted, he cradled her in his arms. He had choices to make, and he was afraid of all of them. He loved Chris, he loved life—and he understood that he was supposed to have neither.

Well, what of it? He could live as he chose; the rowans had seen to that, for her sake.

For her sake . . .

He gazed out of the window, at the brilliant, icy day. They were waiting for him, with their hungry eyes, their angry eyes, their painful eyes. They had no life, and they belonged to the green.

And Chris—admit it, Justin—Chris had no life, either. Just a shadow of it, a tiny, small slice of unending winter. Because of him. Because he died, but she was better than most at holding on.

Oh, Chris, he said, although it was silent. *You're going to break my heart.*

It snowed that night, for the first time that Justin could remember. The window was shut, but not shuttered; he stared at it as if it were a television. The flakes fell, fast and furious, as the wind whipped them around the barren landscape. The rowans were seeing to his body.

For five days, he refused to think about it at all. Life in the cabin was almost normal, if nighttime visitations by hissing nightmares were discounted—and as long as he stayed indoors, they gave him no trouble. But . . .

The plants were the worst. He went to them daily, spoke to them, watered them, moved them to where the light conditions were right. But they didn't recover; they didn't grow.

At least, he reflected, they hadn't died. But they weren't alive either. He wasn't sure what the difference was between life and death anymore, but he knew there was one—knew there had to be one.

". . . and this is why it has to be repotted. The roots have gotten too large for the—Chris, you aren't listening." He caught her hands as she stared at his face. "Look, if you can love a bunch of smelly trees, you can learn to appreciate a beautiful jade plant, okay?"

She said, "why are you teaching me this?"

"Because I want you to know it. You can't go around just killing every plant you're given."

She tried to laugh, but it was the ghost of a laugh that she offered him. He hugged her. "Now comes the most important part so far. It's about the water—"

The sixth day. The world in winter was bright and cold. Breakfast was good—and he didn't even worry about cholesterol. He had cream with his coffee, used liberal amounts of butter, ate bacon by the half pound.

"Justin—the way you eat, it's not good for you."

He looked up from his plate and grinned. "I'm dead. Food is going to hurt me?"

She couldn't laugh. Her silence, uncomfortable and tight, stretched between them until Justin left his chair. "Where are you going?"

"For a walk."

"Can I—can I come with you?"

"Chris—" He walked around the table and hugged her tightly, thinking that he had never hugged her so much in his life. "Of course. Come with me."

He let her fuss about his boots—too light, and too short—and his snowshoes, and when that didn't satisfy her, he left his coat unzipped. He also neglected to put on a hat, and her gentle haranguing took the edge off her tension and made her seem almost normal.

It was cold out, of course, and Justin could feel it at the bone level. *I'm dead,* he told himself sternly, but apparently it didn't make a difference, and after about ten minutes, he put on his hat, scarf, and mittens, even though it made Chris insufferable.

Behind the naked trees, they were watching him.

"We're being watched, Chris," he said, casually.

She whipped around, and he covered his face.

"You have no idea what the word subtle means, do you?"

But she was scanning the same trees that he saw; her brows were furrowed, her face pale. "Watched by what?"

"Just checking."

The dead voices sounded like the rustle of dry leaves gone mad. Justin listened to them whisper and mutter, and it was always with a longing for spring, the turn of seasons. He looked at Chris' face, seeing the winter written there.

"Do you like the snow?"

"I've always liked the snow." She looked over her shoulder surreptitiously—or at least, she tried to.

"What about spring? Summer? Fall?"

She was quiet.

"There are no birds at the feeder this year, are there?" He slid his arm around her shoulder and she pulled away.

"Justin, please—"

"Come on, Chris." He held out a mitten, and after an awkward pause, she put her hand into it. She was shaking. "Don't do that," he said gently. "Your eyes will freeze."

"Justin, I don't want to go there."

"But you love the rowans," he replied. "And you'll never see them in spring again either."

She bit her lip and nodded. "I don't care."

"You don't have to right now. I do." He pulled her through the snow, and because it was him, she came. She always had, really.

Behind her, they followed, shuffling awkwardly. He turned once to look over his shoulder, but he contented himself with a nervous glimpse. He didn't want to meet their eyes; he knew whose death he saw there.

The rowans were cold and ice-coated, but they were still a circle. Within their confines, the snow was pristine and perfect. If he had come with a shovel, had broken the crust of snow, ice, and dirt, no trace remained of his labor. He was grateful for it.

"Come on, Chris."

"I can't."

"Why?"

She swallowed. "I just can't."

"It's the circle. That's all. And I'll be with you." He hated to make her cry in this cold.

"You won't be with me," she said; it was an accusation.

"I'll be with you for as long as you want." He held out his arms, and after a minute, hesitating on the boundary, she stepped into them. The circle seemed to close; the trees almost huddled over them, as if for warmth. "Come and sit down."

She looked a bit dubious, but as they were dressed for cold, she bit her lip and settled down to the right of the circle's center. She wouldn't sit over the center itself, but he didn't push it. He didn't want to sit there either.

He sat in front of her, and she pulled him back into her arms, the way she had often done when they were both much younger.

"What's the worst thing about me that you remember?"

She was quiet for a long time. "The worst thing? Mom."

"What about Mom?" The question was a bit sharp.

Chris laughed. "You asked. I don't have to answer—I mean, it hasn't bothered me for years."

"No—I want to know."

"Mom was the worst thing. She wanted a boy, I don't know why. She always loved you best." She caught his hands and pulled them up. "But I guess I learned from her, too. I love you, even if you did try to sell my diaries. Closest you ever came to dying—" She stopped speaking, and he pulled her arms into a closed circle around them both.

"What's the best thing?"

"Best? There isn't a single best thing. There are so many, I could go on for days. I tried to remember everything I hated about you. I even hated you a bit, for dying. You know, I'm wrong. Mom isn't the worst thing.

"The worse thing about you is that you died."

"I'm not thrilled about it either."

"You don't even remember it."

"True. But I'm not thrilled about the idea." He swallowed. "But if you want me to make sense of it, I can't."

"I don't want you to make anything of it. I want you to stay here, as if it never happened."

"And if I stay here, you'll stay here, as if the rest of your life never happens."

"Maybe you should let me make that choice," she replied. Her hands became tight, even through two layers of mittens.

He was quiet; her hands gripped his like anchors imbedded into the skin. "You know," he said quietly, "When we were really young, you were like another mother, but closer. You went to school with me. You protected me from Tony Fisker—remember him?" He laughed. "You promised you'd protect me from anything."

"I remember."

"I didn't realize just how serious you were." His voice was light. "But I can't let you make that choice. And I think I understand, now, why no one should have to make it." He pulled his hands away from her; it was hard; her grip was fierce. "I'm your past, Chris."

"And what's wrong with the past? All our lives are made up of our pasts! Our futures come from it—how can you just say you'll walk? Justin, you selfish—"

"I'm selfish?" He said, wheeling. "Me? You've killed an entire forest because you can't face the death of one man, and I'm selfish?"

The rowans creaked in the wind that rose suddenly, lifting a veil of powder-fine snow. She looked up, her voice lost.

"They weren't meant to live in eternal winter," Justin said quietly, as his sister turned, slowly, to look at the perimeter of her living circle. "You always loved life. You said nature was your gardener."

She began to weep. "But th–they're o–only t–trees."

He put his arms around her awkwardly, and held her, because he knew she was lying.

"The worst thing about you," he said softly, as if changing the subject, "was that you were always so damned insecure as we got older. You were afraid that I'd grown away from you, that I didn't need you anymore.

"The best thing about you . . ." He thought about it for a minute. Laughed. "You're right. The best thing isn't easy to pin down. I've got so many memories, Chris—it'd take days to sift through them all."

She was tense.

"My death doesn't change those memories, or the truth of them."

"I don't want just memories."

Justin began to laugh. "That's exactly what you want—can't you see it? That's exactly what I am, now. Memory, Chris."

"No, you're—"

"How long have we been here?"

She didn't answer.

"Have I gotten older? Have I learned anything, made any new mistakes, had my heart broken another dozen times? Have I found a job I finally like, found a way to contribute to the causes I believe in? Have I changed at all?"

"Justin, why are you doing this to me?" Her voice was so small, he wanted to stop.

He didn't. "I don't remember dying," he said, his voice the monotone of someone deep in thought. "I don't even remember living anymore. I remember things that happened years ago, but I don't remember the details of last month." He pulled away from her gently shaking body, and stood. She started to get up but he waved her back, into the snow beneath the rowans.

They were watching it all, but their sibilant chant had ceased. He could hear a collective drawing of breath, like the death rattle of a man with emphysema.

"Tell me how I died."

She was silent for so long, he thought she was going to refuse. He turned to look at her face. The afternoon sun was wending its way toward the horizon; they had been here longer than he thought.

"You were speeding," she said, her voice toneless, almost cold. Her eyes were on snow, on the circle's center; they were dark and wide. "It was raining and the roads were slick. I always told you I hated it when you sped. You weren't drinking, thank God—I think it would have killed Dad if you had been.

"But it was dark, it was late. I guess you must've been more tired than you thought. You knew that stretch of road. I'd've bet you could travel it in your sleep." She laughed feebly. "Anyway, you killed four trees. The fifth one was a large, old maple with a trunk like a steel girder."

"Figures."

"They told me how fast you must've been traveling. I don't remember it—the number only came up once, and it just wasn't real. I nodded a lot. I remember that. Everyone would ask me questions, and I'd nod and smile. It was really important to me that I not embarrass Dad or you by having a stupid breakdown. I wasn't going to be the typical hysterical female, not me."

He knelt a yard away from her, like a religious pilgrim at the feet of a very holy man.

"Funerals are expensive, but funeral directors aren't very tacky. They know how to deal with people made stupid by grief. It's the rest of the world that's hard. People feel like they have

to fill up all the silences with words, that they have to trip over
themselves to make it clear how much of a loss it was—as if we
didn't know it already.

"And they mean well, so you can't tell them to drop dead."

"I'm not sure they'd get the joke," Justin said, smiling.

"Joke? What—oh." She rolled her eyes; tears slipped down
the rims and onto her lashes, where they began to freeze. "And
then your close friends and relatives—they know when to leave
you alone. They give you privacy and space. But . . . but sometimes they don't know when not to leave you alone.

"I hate it. The first week, I thought I'd die. I wanted to. But
I held on, because I wasn't about to add my death to yours, and
because there was work to do. All your papers to go through,
your house, the plants.

"But after that . . . after the funeral, everyone seemed to think
it was just over. And it was, in a way. You were gone. But I kept
thinking about what I could have done differently. I'd fantasize
about turning up, like magic, at just the right moment to save
your rotten life. I'd dream about selling my soul, just to get you
back.

"Do you know that I woke up one morning, and I called you?
I wasn't thinking. I just picked up the phone and dialed. And
then, when I got the stupid message about the number being no
longer in service, I screamed. I just screamed and screamed—I
thought I'd never stop. Because you were gone, and it was suddenly real.

"Eventually, I talked to Dad, and he said we could move your
body from Mount Pleasant to here. He was worried about me, by
then—and he knew it couldn't hurt you any." She smiled with a
shadowed shyness. "The rest you already know."

It was his turn to be quiet.

"Are you afraid, Justin?"

"Of death? I don't feel dead, but I'm not afraid of making you
let go."

She nodded as if she believed him. "Is there an afterlife?"

"How the hell should I know? I can't even remember dying."
He shook his head. "But if I had to guess, I'd say yes. I mean,
I'm here."

"I wanted to believe in God and heaven. But I couldn't, because you were dead."

"People die all the time, Chris."

"Yes, but none of them were you. Will you wait for me on the
other side?"

"I don't know. I don't know if there is another side." He saw that she was crying openly now, but it was important to him—had always been important to him—to tell her the truth. "I can't make sense of death for you by giving you false promises or platitudes. Death doesn't make sense. That's not the way it works."

"Then what am I supposed to do?"

"Make sense of life. Just because I don't have mine anymore doesn't mean I'd like you to lose yours. I can't tell you for certain that I'll wait for you, because I don't know if I can. I can't tell you there's a real afterlife, because I don't know it. I can't tell you anything that'll make any of this any easier. But I always made your life difficult—why should I stop now?" He held out his arms.

She scrabbled to her feet and hugged him.

"I can tell you the two things I know for certain: I want you to go on living."

"That's only one thing."

"And I love you."

"That's t–two."

He raised his head and looked out into the trees. "Is it getting warmer in here, or is it just me?" He let her go very gently and removed his winter wear.

"It's warmer," she said faintly. She pulled off her hat and held it in shaking hands.

"The spring is coming." His voice was soft. He looked over her head to the periphery of the circle. "The spring is coming!"

They knew it. But they did not leave, or move, or even speak. He saw the knowledge in their eyes as they stared, unblinking each one, at the center of the rowan circle.

"Justin—"

"It's really getting warm in here. Maybe there is an afterlife, and I'm going to hell."

"That's not funny!" she said, and she whacked him on the side of the head. But her lips twitched at the corners.

The snow began to melt. Or rather, vanish. It receded from sight, shrinking and dwindling as a warm, brisk breeze blew in through the trees. The scent of the rowans coming to spring life began to fill the air. Justin caught Chris' shaking hands, and together they watched the trees unfurl, leaves springing up along multiple branches, flowers blossoming like a spray of white and gold in time-lapse photography.

As if the center of the circle were a pebble, and the forest itself a lake, green rippled out in concentric circles. Silence reigned for seconds, but it was overtaken by birdcalls, forest songs, the sound of life returning.

It wasn't spring; it was summer's height.

"Jesus, Chris—how long has it been winter?"

She didn't answer. She was facing, not him, but the forest itself, her mouth half-open, her eyes unblinking. Everywhere, the snow receded, called back to the season in which it belonged.

He smiled crookedly and watched her face. Saw it changing slowly as she recognized the birdcalls that pierced the silence. He had never been able to tell one bird from another, and obviously being dead didn't give him any extra information. But the rowans' scent was strong and sweet, as it never had been in life.

"Take care of her," he said to the trees, and they seemed to nod, although that was a trick of the wind.

We will.

He looked up, and saw that the edge of the circle was still guarded, but by no winter creatures. *God,* he thought, *it figures. My sister had to find a stretch of forest with imaginary people and walking legends in it.* He didn't know what or who these summer people were, but they were grand and glorious—a miracle of life. What had once been mummified was now restored; the gray pallor of lifeless skin was gone to a golden glow, and eyes that had been slate and steel were now greener than the forest itself.

They smiled at him, these forest beings; smiles that were full and wise and heavy with the unsaid. "Don't hold it against her," he said. "People—we're like that. Help her, if you can."

"We can't," one replied. It was hard to tell if the voice was male or female, young or old. "She will not let us in."

"Not yet. But she will. The forest was always her biggest weakness."

"Then we will be there, when the circle opens again and we are free to dance within its confines. Thank you." They turned and began to walk, almost to prance, back into the woods.

He wanted to ask them where they were going, but he knew it didn't matter. They weren't of the dead. He was. Their roads didn't coincide further. *And how the hell do I know that?*

"Hey, Chris?" She looked up at him. "The tears'll catch up to you all the time. You always were a mush-brain." He hugged her again, because it was the last time. "I gotta get going."

"Where?"

"I don't know. But I'm getting restless." It was true. The

breeze almost made him itch with the desire to be gone. "I'll write you a postcard."

"Bullshit," she said, but she smiled, even if the smile was faint and sad. "You never wrote a damned thing to me when you were alive."

"I called sometimes."

"When you were near a phone." She hugged him back, fierce. But she couldn't hold him that way for long. "You'd better be waiting for me when this is all over."

"If I can, I'll wait. You'd better take your time coming." He wanted to wait and watch her; to be certain that she would return to the life she'd been leading before his accident.

But that was a matter for the living, and he was truly dead. Very quietly, he kissed her on the forehead. "Gotta go," he said again.

"I know." And her face seemed lighter somehow; the weight was gone. "Can I walk with you?"

"Not a chance." He began to whistle quietly as he left the rowan circle.

Chris watched him go, and because she did, she missed the sudden rush of life in the circle's center, as a sprig popped out of the ground, unbending and leaning toward the sun's light.

It was a young rowan.

SANCTUARY

*There is danger in the Forest
but also peace*

The Monsters of Mill Creek Park

by Susan Shwartz

Susan Shwartz has edited several anthologies and is the author of The Grail of Hearts; *she co-authored with Andre Norton* Empire of the Eagle. *Several times nominated for the Nebula and once for the Hugo for short fiction, she is currently working on a long novel about the Byzantine Empire.*

Today was Marty's turn to sit by Mark on the worn front seat of the battered blue Rambler. He steered, careful not to jar the campers crowded into the car, past the fancy Boardman houses, the low shining waterfall by the Old Mill where crazy Lindsay That's *Mister*-Vickers-to-you actually drank milk he squeezed himself from poison ivy, and down the spiral ("you little monsters stick your hands out the windows one more time and I'll roll them up!"—the windows, not their hands) roads into the great well of Mill Creek Park where the leaves of old trees that Indians had probably walked under turned the sunlight into a green summer glow.

Pressing happily against Mark's side, Marty strained to see over the warm dashboard. Life was good. Her lunchpail was frosted silver in her lap, and she'd finally worked big holes in her sneakers. Best of all, she got to sit beside her favorite counselor. Mark Mantle was tall and cute with a white grin. He could hit a ball like Mickey, he told the best stories of all the counselors, and his mother's gardens let him supply all the campers in his car baby tomatoes. She was too happy to yell or sing. That would be trouble if someone noticed and said something. Then they'd *watch* her again.

She knew they wanted her to play, especially Outside. As Dr. Thomas told Mom and Daddy when they left her room and didn't think she could hear, Marty was a solemn child. *Too smart!* he had said the last house call he made before he retired to raise dogs.

Don't push her. Get her outside. So ever since then, they had tried so hard not to push—while pushing her outside—that she was sure she could never please them.

"Martha, are you *reading*?" they'd call through the door they worried if she closed.

As if reading was bad, like chewing with her mouth open, bubbling her milk, or not-sharing. "Martha, go outside and play." Being watched all the time was hard on the kid.

Still, it got her summers at M&S. M&S was only a day camp, not like that snobby Wood Echo where the kids sang stupid boom-di-ada-boo songs with sappy looks on their faces. But at least it wasn't the Center's day camp, where they even took the boys in the pool through the girls' side of the locker room. Everybody knew that showed how awful the Center was.

M&S Day Camp's colors were blue like Mark's car and green like Mill Creek Park, though Daddy said that Morris, who ran it, was really a pinko. His wife Sophie taught Piano. Sophie was all round and brown, but Daddy said she was a pinko, too; and when Marty had asked what it meant to be pink, she had gotten a Look and been sent to her room. But, because Sophie didn't pressure kids to play recitals like the Tavolarios, Marty got to take lessons from her. Already, she could play "Spinning Song," though Mom and Daddy were starting to get scared that that was pushing her too fast.

Even if Morris and Sophie *were* pink, Marty's parents approved of the M&S Day Camp. So summers meant singing "Give a shout and a yell, and grab your lunch pail because the M&S Camp is on the run!" Even if it didn't quite rhyme. Marty suspected that knowing what rhymed and what didn't might get her into trouble about pushing, so she tried not to care when she sang the song.

You always had to be careful when Mom and Daddy worked so hard to bring you up. That's why she said her name was Marty now, not Martha. Marthas were careful and stayed inside and did homework even if they didn't have any. Marthas even *dusted*. Marty, though, as in Spin&Marty on their new TV, got to do things. Okay, Marty in Spin& was a boy, but who did they want her to act like—that icky Annette?

Marty knew she'd made her parents happy the day Mark told them she was a good camper, not a little bookworm like he thought she might be. And he hadn't tattled when she told all the kids that her silver ring with the one turquoise missing was actually a utility ring from outer space.

So she was glad to sit beside Mark. If she were like Annette, she'd probably want to marry him; but Marty wasn't creepy like that. What's more, he had promised to tell them the story of "The Monster of Flaboongie" at lunch. He said it was an Indian story, but that didn't sound like an Indian name to her like Ohio and Shenango and Mahoning. But if he said "Flaboongie" was an Indian name, it was an Indian name; and she liked the funny sound of it anyway.

Here, in the deep heart of the park, the leaves closed overhead like the water in the swimming pool if you held your breath till your eyes bugged and stood at the bottom of the pool in the deep end and looked up. She hoped they'd go all the way down to the "bottom" of the Park.

Not that she didn't like the new place with the metal merry-go-round you could sit in the middle of, not just on the benches, and where you could roll down the hill after lunch till you were almost sick. And she loved Lake Newport where they sat on rocks left by the glaciers and sketched trees that had so many leaves that the whole camp couldn't count them if they'd tried. She liked the rowboats there, too. She'd peer through her glasses and the brown water for devil-horned catfish.

Or she'd stare at the bubbles in their wake and imagine that each bubble was an entire world that God had made, grew up, and blew apart in the lifetime of the bubble. When she tried to explain that, Mark decided real fast that it was her turn to row. You couldn't talk and row, and Marty was a *good* rower. Rowing wasn't pushing, though you had to push against the oars to do it. But talking about the lives of bubbles—she saw that made Mark worry, and so she never talked about it again.

Flaboongie. She thought she could maybe scare the kids in the other cars with that name.

Mark turned the car. They *were* going to go to Slippery Rock. Marty gave a little bounce of joy. They didn't get to go there too often. Everybody's lunchbox had begun to smell of damp bread and warmed-up tuna and apples by the time Mark turned down the lefthand road. It was so quiet here he didn't even beep the

horn "we're here first!" to brag to the other cars when he parked
the car.

Slippery Rock was the smallest pavilion in the park, and the
darkest. The bathroom's smell made all the kids giggle, and
the water from the pump and taps tasted like eggs. Slippery Rock
had a pool, formed where a sleepy edge of Lake Newport flowed
over an old wall. When the campers came down here, they were
allowed to wade the pool, hunt for snails and teeny fish, and
climb the slippery rocks that gave the place its name. They actually got to climb a waterfall!

Behind them, Morris' Buick crunched over the gravel to a
stop. He had the big campers, who'd probably want to go off and
play baseball. If those were senior campers, Marty was glad she
was a kid. What good was a game when you had a chance to
hear a story and climb a waterfall?

Mark even let them sit and eat on the damp ground. That, too,
was neat. It meant that mud and grass stains were going to soak
through their Bermudas, and they'd have to ride home sitting on
their beach towels and change their clothes outside the house.
The limp sandwiches and milk, smelling of old Thermos bottle,
tasted good. They left their spare carrots and lettuce for the
squirrels, then lounged against the mossy trunks of the trees;
they'd get green stuff all over their blouses and T-shirts, too, and
Mom would really have a fit—and waited for Mark to tell about
the Monster of Flaboongie.

He pointed to the edge of the pool. "You see that moss?"

They nodded yes at Mark and at the moss.

"You see that mud, how red it is?"

Again, the six campers from Mark's car nodded, big-eyed and
solemn.

"Well, that isn't just any moss, I'll have you know. And that
isn't just any mud. Long ago, there was a creature called the
Monster of Flaboongie."

Oooooh went that drip Beth Herman. She *liked* Annette in the
Mouseketeers. She even liked Hayley Mills in *The Parent Trap.*

Marty hugged her grimy knees and stared up at the roof of
leaves overhead. Here in the deepest part of Mill Creek,
"Flaboongie" sounded weird, not stupid.

"How did he get here, you ask?"

The kids all nodded.

"The Indians think he followed the rivers and wandered down
by Lake Newport, down and down and down . . ." Mark dropped
his voice. Marty could *see* a monster, following the water, catch-

ing and eating catfish, maybe eating them raw because everyone knew monsters didn't cook.

"Until he came HERE!"

Everybody jumped and screamed. Marty laughed, but she was mad at Mark, who shouldn't have taken them in with such a baby trick.

"After a while, people who came in here started never coming out. The place got a bad name. Everyone knew a monster lived here."

Now *that* made sense. Slippery Rock was a strange place, with its stinky water (you weren't supposed to say stink, but it was the only word that fit), its pool, its long, stringy moss and roots, and its waterfall with the caves along the shore, heaped up by rocks dumped off the ice from long, long ago.

Maybe there *was* something here. Maybe they'd find fossils. Marty had found fossils in the park by the school, maybe not a dinosaur, but a little shell. Last fall, she had organized her class into heaping up rocks that were pitted like craters. "We're building a meteorite," she'd told her second-grade teacher. When the teacher called Marty's home, her father had laughed and laughed, then opened a bottle from the cabinet Marty never opened. Marty had "pushed" again, and she had been wrong. Now she knew better: meteorites were mostly iron. Limestone, like the rocks she carried, would have melted in the air.

Marty jolted upright as Lisa nudged her. *Listen to Mark,* she hissed. Marty listened.

". . . the Indians got tired of losing their boys and girls in the woods—they had to come into the woods to learn to hunt, you know, and if they went away from their group, the monster got them—so finally the chief prayed to the father of all the Indians—"

"His name is Manitou," Marty blurted. The other kids whispered behind their hands. Marty flushed worse than sunburn. *I didn't mean to push!* she wailed silently. She thought she had read that in *Classics Illustrated.* Hadn't she? She knew she had read *Last of the Mohicans.*

"That's right, Marty," said Mark. "His name is Manitou, and the Indians prayed to him. And do you know what happened?"

Marty knew what happened. Mark had saved her from being laughed at again. Mark was wonderful. Maybe *she* would marry him after all.

"Manitou came down to earth."

"How did you know his name was Manitou?" someone whispered to Marty. She managed to look mysterious and held up her silver and turquoise ring, her utility ring from outer space. Randy's eyes went round.

Morris, who was very old, maybe fifty, with his graying hair and blue shirt, came up and stood behind Mark where he sat on the ground in the center of the circle of kids. Mark started to get up. A hand on his shoulder kept Mark where he was.

"Go on," said Morris.

"Anyhow," Mark said, drawing their attention back to him, "Manitou traced the monster of Flaboongie to this place and to one of those caves over there." He gestured toward the pool and the lazy waterfall, more a tumble of a stream down some rocks than an actual falls. "He made himself real small and went into the Monster's cave, and what do you think he saw?"

"Bones," whispered Randy.

"That's right. All over the floor. Oh, the monster of Flaboongie was a *messy* eater. Manitou saw the bones of boys and girls who got lost in the woods because they wandered off. He saw the bones of old people. And he saw the bones of animals."

"Eeeuw," Beth went again.

"But not many animals," Mark put in rapidly. "The monster of Flaboongie liked the taste of *people* better.

"Anyhow, Manitou said, 'Oh Monster of Flaboongie, you have been eating my people.' And the Monster went *chomp!* on another bone. Manitou said, 'Monster, you must leave this place.' The monster threw his bone away and laughed, showing all these awful green teeth—he never went to the dentist—and said 'I will never leave this place because the hunting is so good. And now you never will either, because—' " Mark leaned out, hands like catchers' mitts opening wide, " '—I'm going to eat you too!' And he reached for Manitou like *this!"*

Everyone laughed and screamed. Beth tumbled onto her side. Morris picked her back up.

"And do you know what Manitou did?"

Better not say, Marty warned herself.

"Manitou let himself grow to his full height. His head broke through the roof of the cave. And he grabbed the Monster of Flaboongie, picked him up, and *threw* him into that part of the lake. He threw him so hard that he sank all the way to China, and the ground closed up behind him."

It would have had to, Marty thought. *Or lava would have*

*come up through the hole, and anyway, Morris wouldn't let them
come here.*

"Even after all these years," Mark was finishing his story,
"you can still see traces of the Monster if you know where to
look. See those roots and that moss and mud? You only think
those are roots and moss and mud. That's really the Monster of
Flaboongie's hair and blood you see—all that's left of him, just
like bones were all that's left of the children—*just like you!*"

He lunged forward, and the boys jumped him, screaming and
laughing. Morris tapped him on the shoulder.

"Coming, Morris. Kids, you clean up, and then we're going to
beat the Senior Campers in baseball."

"Awwwww," whined Randy. "They'll skunk us."

"Not if you've got me on your side, and Morris promises to
strike out to handicap the Seniors," said Mark. "The game'll start
just as soon as Morris and I finish our talk. So don't wander off
anywhere or . . ."

"The Monster of Flaboongie!" Randy, Beth, and Marty
screamed.

Marty wadded up the wax paper and tin foil from her lunch in
disgust and threw it away in the trash bin. It wasn't fair to come
all the way here and then not get to wade in the pool and climb
the rocks, maybe even go into one of those caves by the water's
edge. Who cared about an old Monster of Flaboongie, anyway?

She shut her lunch box—a real workman's box with leather
straps, not one of those tin things the other kids had with stupid
pictures of Lassie on them—and trotted back to the car to put it
away. Morris and Mark were talking low by the Buick and didn't
see her.

"If we keep the kids busy and together, we can finish out the
day without scaring them," Marty heard Morris say. She went
quiet. *Make like a tree and he won't see you.* Her parents called
that "eavesdropping." It was a you-rotten-kid thing to do, but
she'd always heard a lot by just being quiet.

"Do the police definitely think it's a prowler?" Mark asked.
He sounded angry, though he never was. "That's why I told them
a 'don't-stray-from-the-group' story. . . ."

"Your monster from . . . what kind of Indian is 'Flaboongie'?"

"Schmohawk, Professor," said Mark. Both men laughed.

"For this, you had to study psychology?" asked Morris.

Grownups talked so much! What was this 'professor' business? Morris was a teacher. It was always a problem to figure
out what they actually meant. She usually knew all the words

they used, but sometimes she worried about how they used them,
even after she'd looked up the hard ones.

"They found the girl. She lives around here. She was more
scared than hurt, but do you want him touching one of our kids?
Aside from the damage to the child, think of the parents . . ."

"What do you want me to do?" Mark asked.

"Keep 'em busy. Keep 'em out in the open and together. Tomorrow, maybe it'll rain. If it does, we go to the Unitarian
Church and there's no problem. If it doesn't, too bad it's not the
day we go to Packard Park in Warren. We'll have to go to the
tennis courts at Crandall Park. That's safe. For now."

Marty nodded to herself. They were making sense again. Usually, if you waited long enough, grownups did.

So all the Monster of Flaboongie meant was don't-go-with-
strangers. When you were carefully brought up, you already
knew that. You didn't talk to strangers (she'd had to tell that to
a man outside the Court House. He'd turned out to be a Judge-
call-him-Your-Honor and she'd been ashamed, but Daddy said
she'd done the right thing). You didn't take candy from them.
And you never never never went anywhere with them. Not into
cars. Or caves.

She set her lunch box softly down and went back to the clearing. Most of the other campers had already run toward the softball field. Some of the girls hung back, looking as bored as she'd
be in a few minutes. Hmmmm, maybe . . .

"I don't want to play ball," she announced to the other girls.
"They'll stick me in the outfield, and I'll never catch a ball.
Even if I do, they'll laugh and say I throw like a girl."

"That's silly," said Beth. "We *are* girls. But I want to stay
with Mark." She was almost whining. Sometimes she got like
that when she didn't get her way.

"I want to wade and climb the rocks, don't you?" Marty
asked.

"We're supposed to stay close," said the third girl, Lisa, who
didn't say much, ever.

"Well, if we all went, we'd be together, wouldn't we? Like
buddies in swimming?" Marty pointed out. *A natural leader,*
she'd heard a teacher call her. *In-sti-ga-tor,* she had also heard;
which didn't sound as nice. "We all know all about strangers. So
we stick together real close, and if we see anyone strange, we
can scream for help."

"I don't know," Lisa said. "The rocks are slishy. All that green
stuff. Moss. Whatever. Last time, I sat down in the water and had

to wear my bathing suit home. Mom had to throw out my shorts. She was really mad." Lisa's mouth turned up in a smile at the memory. "I caught a lot of tadpoles."

She and Marty looked at Beth. If she said she wanted to go play ball, she'd spoil it for the others. She knew that. She also knew that if she tattled, no one would ever, ever tell her things again. Lisa sighed.

"Okay," she said. "But I get to ask Mark if I can sit by him going home."

She could *ask*. Asking was free. But it was Marty's turn, and Mark knew that.

The three girls headed for the pool. They sat and took off their sneakers on a bank of what Mark had described as hair from the Monster of Flaboongie. It was damp on Marty's backside. *Eeeuw.*

The three girls waded in. Marty held a long stick. Maybe it would help her not to fall.

"You look like you wet yourself," Beth said.

"Did not."

"Did too."

"Oh, come on," said Lisa. She gave Beth a shove, and she sat down in the water. Her eyes widened as if she were going to cry. Then she giggled.

"Let's *all* sit down in the water," she suggested. So they did.

Marty got up and headed toward the pile of rocks. Some were cut and some weren't. Streams of water flowed down them and swirled into smaller ponds like little sinks. The mud between her toes felt, like Lisa said, slishy. Like the bottom of Lake Erie, only you could see through this water. Black tadpoles zipped by. She wished she had a paper cup, but Mom would only make her throw them out, and they would die.

Carefully, she started to climb the rocks. She'd never made it to the top but maybe she could today. Behind her, Lisa and Beth were talking as they splashed along. She knew they wouldn't want to catch up. They'd be too scared.

She wasn't scared. Not of strangers, not of monsters, not of anything as long as she was in this park. The old trees with their leaves overhead like a princess' canopy bed made her feel safe. When she was here, just hiking or learning to shoot a bow at a target, or row a boat, she felt grown-up and strong. She wanted to come to the M&S Day Camp every summer till she got to be a Senior Camper. And then, maybe, if she ever grew up, maybe she could be a counselor with a car and kids.

She waded across a rock where the moss grew springy underfoot toward another one that glinted in the sunlight. Under the mud and the green slime, it was shining white, the biggest luckystone in the world. She'd never be able to dig it up and carry it home, the way you were supposed to when you found a luckystone. And even if she did, what good would it be? There probably weren't enough dimes in the world for the fairies to pay for a luckystone that size.

Good campers had to try.

So Marty dug her stick in at the lucky stone's base and started to push and dig it out of its bed. For a while, pushing and puffing and panting and splashing filled her whole world.

Finally, the rock budged, and Marty rested, leaning on the stick.

Splash . . . splash, the girls were behind her over in that shadowy patch near where the caves were. They were making so much racket they could forget it if they wanted to catch any fish or tadpoles.

She turned to tell them that. And froze. Lisa and Beth weren't standing there. It was a man. Her blood froze worse than her feet in the water. A Stranger.

He had a beard and a dirty face. His clothes were torn, and he had his hands out below his waist. In them . . .

"What's that you've got?" Marty asked. "Is it a rabbit's foot?"

He started toward her, making a goony laughing sound.

She stamped her foot in the water, an angry splash. She *hated* it when grown-ups didn't answer her questions. "What *is* that?" she asked again.

Again, the laughter. She didn't like the way he laughed. She didn't like the way he looked. His eyes were funny, bloodshot and sort of flat.

"You're crazy," she told him. "Crazy!"

Her voice was louder than it should be when a kid talks to grownups, especially if the kid is talking back. She knew Beth and Lisa heard because they screamed, and she heard them falling and running, always screaming, toward the shore.

"Go 'way, you crazy, you," she said. She pulled her stick out of the water and shook it at him.

He jumped forward and tried to pull the stick out of her hand. Now Marty screamed. He was going to grab her and drag her into that cave and then . . . she didn't know what happened when strangers dragged little girls into caves, but she knew it was Bad.

If she tried to run, he'd tackle her and she'd drown. So she had to face him.

"You go away!" she said, keeping the stick between them like she'd seen in *Robin Hood*. Maybe she could knock him over, and *then* she could run.

He grabbed for the stick again.

"No!" she shouted.

Then she screamed again. What looked like a wall of brown fur dashed growling from the rocks between her and the Stranger, grabbed him, and flung him like Manitou flung the Monster of Flaboongie into the pond.

The Stranger belly-flopped. For a moment, Marty thought he was dead. Then he crawled out of the water as fast as he could and ran away.

The monster that had saved her turned to look at her. She let her stick drop with a useless little splash. She looked at her hand with its turquoise ring. It wasn't a *real* ring from outer space. If it was, she'd have magic powers and could fight or get away. Her hand, stupid ring and all, came up toward her mouth, the baby way it did whenever she was going to cry. Her eyes blurred and her nose ran—and the monster picked her up and carried her into the cave.

The monster set Marty down on her feet inside the cave. She got ready to run. You couldn't let monsters see how scared you were. Then she forgot her fear and just stood there. For one thing, she wasn't in a real cave. It was just two or three rocks standing on end and hanging over each other. Light shone in through the spaces between them, plenty of light to see that two *other* monsters lived in the cave, and they were watching her and, as best she could tell, giving her friendly monster smiles.

There was the great big monster who had brought her into the cave—call it the papa monster. There was a middle-size monster, a little rounder than the great big monster—a mama monster? And, even though it was the size of a regular grown-up, half-hiding beside its mother was the baby monster.

Marty had seen bears in the zoo. These were monsters, though, not bears, and Marty wasn't Goldilocks. The biggest monster had thrown the Stranger harder than any bear could. They didn't have claws on their paws, hands, whatever, or she would have felt them when the monster picked her up. And what was strangest about all three monsters was their feet. They were the biggest she had ever seen. If she set her daddy's shoes in a

line, she'd need three or four shoes to be as long as one of the
biggest monster's feet.

Maybe they weren't monsters at all, but space people, Marty
thought. She only knew three words of space-people talk, and
maybe "Klaatu barada nikto" wouldn't mean anything to them if
different kinds of space people had different words for things
like Americans and Russians.

Marty raised one hand *How* the way they did on TV and
opened her mouth to try. . . . But the smallest bigfooted monster
came over and laid its hand over hers and stared at her. Just like
meeting new little kids at a birthday party. Marty looked at the
bigfoot child—the *other* child—and smiled.

Something in the cave changed. Grown-ups were grown-ups;
you could always tell if they were mad or scared or happy with
you. These acted like they had found a kid they'd lost in a parking lot. *Relieved.* Or the way Marty's parents did when she used
a new big word: trying not to smile and hurt her feelings. Unlike
bears, which had little squinchy angry eyes, these monsters' eyes
were gray and calm: they were *smart,* the idea came to her.

Voices touched inside her mind. Marty jumped a little. The little bigfoot holding her hand let out a squeak and backed off toward its mommy. She looked up at the gray eyes and knew the
voices came from inside the bigfoots' heads.

<Child, do not be . . .>

<She has no fear . . . how remarkable! Is she the same type of
creature as the others?>

<*Amusement*—sometimes they wonder.>

<She *likes* us, wants to know us. Can't we . . .>

<*Confusion*>

<*The mama bigfoot looking over at the daddy . . . doubt*>

<You know we must stay hidden. Only I could not let harm
come to a human child any more than to you and . . . *the
thought-word didn't make sense. Maybe it was a name.*>

<I will get our things. We must leave tonight.>

<*Whine* . . . but I wanted to play with her!>

Marty wanted to play with the monster kid. With feet like that,
she'd bet he'd *never* fall down in the water. And maybe he could
catch better fish than any of the campers. The boys could show
him how to hit a ball, but she could show him the swings and
merry-go-round and maybe bring him home for dinner. She
couldn't wait to show these . . . . they were *people* . . . to her parents. Daddy gave her books about bigfoots and spacemen. He
would know how to talk to them. Lawyers could talk to anybody.

<I am sorry, child. We cannot leave the forest.>

<*Sense of love for the forest, wrapping out like green light, shining in the cave, reaching out to touch her like a hug*>

Yes, Marty thought. *Oh, yes.*

She smiled her best smile at the bigfoot family and tried to make her thoughts real clear. *Couldn't you stay? You could live here, and he could go to school with us. And we'd be* friends.

The mother bigfoot shook her long mane and turned away. The young one darted to a rock, sat down, and pushed at it. The biggest bigfoot—and his feet were *huge*—came over and dropped down so his eyes could look into hers.

<*We are pilgrims looking for our own place, our own people. But your forest was so beautiful we stopped here for a while . . . you would say "vacation."*>

<*So now we have to go, or your people will hunt us down.*>

Marty blinked. Pilgrims wore gray and black with big hats. They carried muskets and you drew them in November.

They gave her a great idea. "*I* know!" she cried before she remembered to think instead. "You're hunting for religious freedom. Aren't you?"

She reached into her blouse and pulled out the tiny gold Star of David her mommy gave her two years ago. "My people came here. Couldn't you be our neighbors? This is a *good* place."

<No, dear one. We must find our own.>

The other child was holding out something to her. She held out her hand and felt him put something into it. It was warm from the monster's hand and it felt smooth, except where it had been cut. It was a tiny statue with such a friendly happy look on its hairy face that maybe it was a holy statue like the kids at St. Edwards got to have. If you wore a Jewish star, you couldn't have a statue. But it would be mean not to trade for it. Monster or not, he was a real nice kid, and Marty knew his people worked hard to bring him up right.

She took off the star and held it out. The strange kid's eyes lit up, and he smiled.

And the monster mommy and daddy spoke over the children's heads, just like real grownups.

<If he's found, carrying gold . . .>

<How can we refuse to let her give a gift?>

<*Worry. Sadness.* It does not matter. She will have to forget. And we will keep *voice/name sound* safe with us when we go.>

<We must go now! *Fear/pictures of dogs, police, guns.* Do you hear them shouting outside? Soon, they will come . . .>

The mother went to the mouth of the cave. <Don't hurt her.>

"I don't want to forget!" Marty let her voice rise, though that was bad manners. TV had a word for what the monsters planned to make her have. Am-nes-ia. You were hit on the head, and they found you. You woke up in the hospital and didn't remember.

The papa bigfoot put his hands ... paws ... whatever—they were big, too—on her shoulders. He smelled like a wet dog. She loved dogs, which should have made her feel safe; but *remember that they are animals,* Dr. Thomas said. He raised them, so he knew.

<Do you really think I'd hurt you?>

Marty shook her head.

<Sometimes we have to do things we don't like.> He looked over at his boy like Daddy looked when he kissed her good night.

<The way your parents would to keep you safe. I never broke a promise to *him,* and I won't break my word to you. I promise I won't hurt you.>

<The child's people get closer. Hurry!>

He was asking, not telling, not *making* Marty do anything; and she knew that, big as he was, he was getting scareder the longer he waited.

"Let me say good-bye first."

<Quickly.>

He waved his son over. He wore her star on his wrist because he was too big to wear it round his neck.

"Sorry, I can't keep this," Marty told him and handed him back the statue.

<We'll hide it. One day, we'll come and dig it up.>

She watched him set the statue in a little hollow in the rock. Its big feet didn't quite stick out.

<Now, the star, too ...>

<*wail*>

<Don't *whine.*>

So, the bright star followed the ivory statue. He set a flat rock gently on top of them, then laid a bigger rock on that. She had seen hiding places like this on *Spin and Marty.* They were called caches. Even if the monster daddy said he'd make her forget, Marty'd remember. She always did. She even remembered in the doctor's office when he put the mask over her face and she woke up with her tonsils out.

She turned to meet the eldest bigfoot's eyes. "I'm ready," she said. Then, what felt like the doctor's mask came down over her face.

Marty started to forget.

Sun slanted down on her face. The water below her rippled and flowed, making Marty feel like she really ought to get up and go to the bathroom. Scared voices shouted her name over the water.

She pushed herself up. She must have fallen asleep here at the mouth of the cave. From how the sun shone, she knew it was late afternoon. Funny. She didn't remember climbing this far. She'd have to be careful climbing down, but she'd have to hurry, too. Mark would be looking for her in the parking lot by the car so they could drive home.

"Marty! Marty!" That was Mark's voice. She heard Morris' voice too. It was deeper, furrier-sounding; and it reminded her of . . .

"I'm here! I'm coming!" she shouted as loud as she could over the water.

"Thank God, we've found her!" Grown-ups always said you weren't supposed to say "thank God," and then they always said it. Mark came up the rocks, two, three boulders at a time, followed by Morris. She ran forward to meet them—why did they look so scared?—and hug them, but they dropped back.

"It's okay, sweetheart. We'll get Sophie to come take care of you. You don't have to be afraid."

She wasn't afraid, except they were acting strange. Strange . . . there had been a Stranger. That was right.

"Sophie!" Morris yelled. "Get up here!"

Faster than Marty would have believed a brown berry like Sophie could move, she had clambered up the rocks and was holding Marty. Sophie's arms were cold where the water splashed them, but they felt good.

"Listen, sweetie, we've got you safe. We've been worried for you, going off like that. Beth and Lisa said they saw a stranger. Did you see him, too?"

Marty nodded. Sophie shut her eyes like she was going to cry.

"Can you tell me what happened?"

"He had a rabbit's foot, and he was waving it." Again, Sophie shut her eyes. She pulled Marty's head against her shoulder, but not before she saw Mark and Morris look at each other, then look down. They *growled*, that was the only way to describe it.

Marty frowned. Someone else *had* growled, but it wasn't the Stranger. She was sure of that. If of nothing else . . .

"It's okay, Marty. Now, be brave and tell me, darling," Sophie was having a hard time getting the words out, "did this bad man touch you?"

Marty shook her head against Sophie. "I yelled at him. I had this stick and I shook it, and he went away."

Sophie let Marty pull free, though she kept hands on her shoulders as she looked her up and down. "Morris, you round up the other kids. Don't let them see the sheriff."

"Oh, God," said Morris, and started back down the falls.

"Yes, we've got her safe!" he shouted as he went.

Oh, no. She had Wandered Away. She had been Lost.

"Am I in trouble?" she asked.

Again, Sophie hugged her. Her shoulder shook. "No," she said. "You're a good, brave little girl, and we're going to take you home right now."

And so Marty sat on a towel beside Sophie all the way home, while Lisa got to ride with Mark, which wasn't fair.

For once, Mom and Daddy didn't make her change her messed-up clothes in the back yard by the hose. She had a bath, and Mom sat with her while she was in it, while Daddy and Morris (whose car squealed into the drive in a way that could get him a ticket) made phone calls.

"Doc, I know you're retired and don't make housecalls," Daddy's voice sounded the way it did at three in the morning when someone called because a big truck crashed on the highway. "But no one knows her better and can make sure she gets through this without permanent damage. Please? Thank God. I'll get out the Scotch."

Why did she have to see Dr. Thomas? She wasn't sick. She asked Mommy. Her eyes had the look that Sophie's had when she said she'd seen the Stranger. Then Mommy cried. Marty had only seen her mother cry once, when the radio said something about a man named Salk. (Later, it had been Marty's turn to cry when she saw the gleaming needles, and one pinched her arm.)

"I got through to Paul Cress at home."

"You called the chief of police," that was Morris.

"Sure. He's an old friend. Look, I know it's not your fault, Slavin. In fact, your people probably helped her toughen up just enough . . . anyway, Cress's got his boys turning over every rock in Mill Creek Park to see what's under them. And as soon as Doc Thomas gets here, I'm going . . ."

Mom went to the door of the bathroom. "Oh, no, you're not! Not if I have to hide that damn gun of yours myself."

Dad laughed. "You'd actually pick it up?"

There was a pause. Marty knew her mother was giving Daddy a Look.

"Martha needs her father here with her. And I have to get back to her now. You calm down."

Mother came and got her, and put her into bed even though it was still daytime. Marty thought of telling her that, but she didn't really want to get a Look either.

"I think that's Thomas' car in the drive," her father said. "Her old pediatrician. Retired to breed Dobermans, for crying out loud. Christ, will you look at the monster he's got with him?"

Marty was glad to see Dr. Thomas, even though he wouldn't bring his dog—it was a dog, and not a *real* monster—in the house. (Mom looked relieved.) He pulled her nightgown up, looked over her, tickled her ribs with his stethoscope, then covered her back up.

"You're fine," he told her, then looked up at her parents and nodded.

"Can I go back to camp tomorrow?" Marty asked.

"Honey, you wouldn't rather stay home and read? We could go to the library and get some new books."

Marty shook her head. "I bet it's going to be nice tomorrow. And I want to go back to the Park. I love the Park, all the trees. You feel so safe in the forest."

"Maybe Monday," said Dr. Thomas. "I think once Marty's over her *chill*—" he came down hard on the word like it was important, "—it's a very good idea for her to enjoy her friends and camp again. But now, I think she ought to try to nap until supper's ready."

He pulled the ruffly curtains and took her parents out of her room with him. She watched the sun try to sneak through cracks in the blinds while Dr. Thomas's voice made kind of happy growls about "resilient" (she would look that up tomorrow) and "amnesia" (she knew that one already) and "I can't tell for sure until I do an internal, but . . ."

"Hasn't she been through enough?" Her mother cried out at that. "As long as she's all right now . . ."

"That's your decision. Just don't make it worse by keeping her inside. All she needs is people thinking she's some sort of monster. She's not. She's a beautiful, brave, little girl, and she was very lucky."

She heard the glug-glug-glug of Scotch. "Here, you drink this too," Daddy said. Mommy hated Scotch.

On Monday, the kids at camp looked at Marty funny, but that was the day they went to Zedakers to ride, and they forgot. Except for one thing. They didn't go back to the forest for weeks and weeks. And Mark didn't tell any stories the rest of the summer.

Something did change that summer. By fall, Marty was Martha once again. If anything, she was being brought up even more carefully than before. After all, Pushing her might make her a brain, but it would keep her safe indoors. Marty/Martha the girl was different. She had gone all quiet again. Granted, she wasn't so quiet that she didn't lead her class when she didn't have better things to do. But those things never again included summer camp.

And she grew up into Martha Charney, Ph.D. in psychology. Dimly, she remembered that Mark had studied to be a psychologist so long ago. She wondered if he ever made it all the way through. He enjoyed just living too much, and it had been Dr. Charney's experience that students like that tended to avoid the really demanding programs. She, of course, had sought them out and mastered them. Distinction was what she'd gotten instead of the sunlit world in which Mark swung a bat while all the campers cheered. He was back there in those memories Martha thought of as being walled off from her emotions by a kind of psychic plexiglass (now, that was *bad* terminology). And her emotions were walled off from the rest of her. She had her compensations, of course: but the thing about compensations was that they never quite succeeded.

At least, she had them. She had her sanity. And she had her life. Her parents had been so afraid and taken such pains after that season of summer camp to keep her safe.

Dr. Martha Charney steered the rented car down the twisting narrow road into the green well of Mill Creek Park. Budget cuts in the Rust Belt town had deferred maintenance on the park. The road was cracked, and faded by summers of baking, winters of freezing, until it crumbled into as much a part of the woods as the leaf-mold that half-covered it.

She had been away for so long; it surprised her that she could be grieved by the neglect she saw. After all, she had seen a monster in the Park.

Old growth the Park definitely was: maybe even first-growth forest. It was old; it was peaceful; but it was not quiet. She had turned off the air conditioner and rolled down the window so she could hear the leaves rustle, the song of birds way up in the canopy, the distant rush of water, the occasional crack of a stick as some hiker or deer moved before it thought.

Light slanted through the arching trees just as it had when she was a girl, and if leaves and moss covered the split-oak rails of the tiny bridges over which her car rattled, that only made the park quieter, wilder-seeming. The tension ache that had ridden her shoulders since college had already subsided. She was home. Something stirred behind the barriers she had set up between her and memory. Oh, she had been right as a child to love this forest. Maybe she could recapture even a crumb of the old love, the old freedom from before she started to push herself.

Because she had been right about a lot of things, she had come home to see if she had been right about the main things, too. The serious, sturdy, and curious girl had become a serious, sturdy, and curious woman—and a shadowed one. In recent months, though, she had grown weary of shadows. She had been troubled by dreams, fragments of memories—the "Stranger" who had exposed himself to her and whom she had driven off by a combination of luck and guts that made Martha, fully grown, break into a cold sweat; the cave by the water; even flashes of something large, something furry. A Jungian could have published a book on that.

Fragmentary memories returning—had she really been abused, and were the memories only now coming back to her? They came back when you were strong enough to face them. That would mean she had even a greater fear to face: had the people who loved her most lied to her?

She knew the child Marty's promise for joy had not been fulfilled in the woman she had become. But all her life, at least, she had prided herself on her honesty. What if everything she had grown up to accomplish had been based upon a *lie?*

That was enough to wake her at 4:00 a.m. But the student and the psychologist in her knew she had to find out—and there was still that damnable honesty of hers.

It was not, and had never been, a particularly popular trait. Her old neighbors here? "You turned out good; leave well enough alone, not that you ever could." Or "that silly mess? I'm surprised you still remember. Oh, well, I suppose *you* would."

That kindly fog might be adequate for them, but not for her.

She *didn't* remember, at least not clearly enough. That was the problem. They didn't understand. But then, they never had.

As she drove deeper into the park, the reassurance she had always felt in the ancient wood reached out to her. A rabbit dashed across the road, and she slowed, just in case.

Another turn. Even thirty years later, Slippery Rock was familiar to her: the blackened wood of the old pavilion, the musty fireplace, even the reek of sulfur water from the pump.

Beyond shone the pool, serene at the shore, but sparkling higher up, where water still poured over the tumbled rocks, where, please God, it would pour forever. She parked and locked the car and headed for the rocks. Her eyes traced their shapes, trying to recall the cave in which, thirty years ago, she had hidden from what, even now, she called the Stranger.

Was she really going to climb the waterfall again? She was older now, much older. Her tolerance for the squishy and slimy was way down; and if she didn't get tetanus from something on the rocks, she'd probably get hepatitis from the water. And what if another Stranger had made the cave his lair?

You're lying to yourself, Mart, she told herself. She was gut-scared to go in there, to confront her memories—or the lack of them. But if she didn't face them, how would she ever face her patients? *If you can't do it for yourself, do it for your career.*

With her usual skewed thoroughness, she had prepared for her ordeal. ("You're *nuts,*" she'd been told, but she remembered her day camp training enough to want to be Prepared. So she had her pocket phone and her Capstun, illegal as it was, tucked in a fanny pack. Her Swiss army knife, the one with all the blades. No pistol, though she'd been tempted: bullets ricocheted on rocks. And, just for old time's sake, she'd pick up a big stick. After all, it had worked the last time. *Are you really enjoying this?* she accused herself.

It was a nice, tidy arsenal, but she'd have traded all her armament for her old "utility ring" from outer space.

Martha walked to the pond, still bordered with moss and long pallid tendrils that an unfortunate exposure to college botany helped her to recognize as exposed roots. The mud was reddish brown. There was iron in the soil here, iron throughout the Mahoning and Shenango valleys where the burning open hearths of the great steel mills, after more than a century of wealth, had finally been quenched.

Nevertheless, right now, the "hairy stuff" and the reddish mud were the hair and blood of that bogey Mark had scared them with the summer that she was Marty and free, for the last time in her life: *The Monster of Flaboongie*. She hadn't thought of that for years either.

From the softball field near the pavilion shrill voices rose. Still playing ball, were they? Bless them. She waved. Good: they would remember seeing her. If only she could play with them; but she had never been that good a player.

She waded into the water and toward the first line of rocks. Water swirled over and around them. The rock glowed gold and green as the sun pierced the water and struck the stone beneath Black tadpoles and a few fish fled her ankles.

She planted feet and stick carefully. Up to the next level, then to the slippery rocks of the next. *This is really stupid and dangerous*, the grown-up in her mind told her. *Nonsense*, she told it back. *I'd have to pay to do this in the Rockies. And they'd praise me for surviving Outward Bound.*

Up ahead loomed the cave—or was that really the cave she remembered? The rocks didn't seem to slant over the same way, and the opening they framed was dauntily black. She fumbled in her pouch for her flashlight, which could double as a club.

She tucked the light between her teeth as she started up the last course of rocks. Now she hung on with her hands as the water poured over them at about the strength of a really good shower. Despite herself, Martha laughed.

Water splashed in her face. She jerked her head back. For an instant, as she blinked, a memory returned: *she had* not *climbed this high. She had not been carried.*

Her stomach chilled. So the Stranger *had* caught her after all. What then? Had he carried her to the cave, and then . . .

She didn't have to know. She could turn around and go back right now.

And then she would never know, except that she would know one thing: she had countenanced a lie about herself.

You don't have to think the worst. Not yet. But if you were carried, it explains how the rocks look different from here than from below.

Despite the chill of the water, sweat streaked her sides and face as she pulled herself from the water onto the rock platform leading to the cave. She wouldn't have to bend over to get in. That was right. They hadn't had to, and they were tall.

Had there been more than one Stranger, then?

Something splashed behind her. Martha thrust out with the

stick, jumped, and scuttled forward. Before she knew it, she had taken refuge in the cave, her heart pounding.

Her flashlight glowed on a broken bottle, but only one. Why, it wasn't bad in here after all. No old condoms or needles, nothing but a little mud, some rocks—her knees suddenly went limp, and she sank down on a rock so well-placed you'd think someone set it there on purpose.

She stretched out a little and played the light about the cave. Her own shadow loomed up, huge with huge feet.

She blinked, and memory flashed across her thoughts once more the way light and darkness flash together when film breaks in a movie camera. Huge feet. Big feet.

It wasn't the Stranger who had brought her here at all. It was someone else. Someone with huge feet. Big feet.

Bigfoot. Sasquatch, though she thought they all lived in the Northwest.

Apparently not. This one had thrown the man across the pool and brought her to this . . . this refuge. How could she have forgotten?

Easy, if she were made to forget. <She will have to forget.> Just as clearly as when she was a child, memory produced the voice that had spoken in her thoughts. <Do you think I would hurt you?>

Bigfoot had saved her, at considerable risk to himself—and to his family. There had, she remembered now, been three of them. Like Goldilocks. If she'd been fearful, so had they. Not, of course, of the child she'd been, but of the fate a missing child could bring upon them. So they had fled a wood that they, too, loved. She hoped they'd made their way up North and found others of their own kind.

Martha laughed, surprised at the heart's ease she felt. Despite the darkness, this cave held only peace. And memory.

How can you be sure?

Little Bigfoot. Baby sasquatch. The child she'd been had liked the bigfoot child. Had traded gifts with him, gifts neither was allowed to keep. If she could find those gifts . . .

Think back, Martha. Think back.

A hollow in the ground. A flat rock. A heavy rock. She trained her flashlight on the ground. Ahhhhh. There! She was down upon her knees before she knew it. Her adult strength made heavy work of what a Bigfoot child had accomplished with ease, and she pushed the upper rock away. Yes! There was the flat rock. The bigfoot child had laid it over the treasures two children gave each other, treasures too dangerous to let them keep. In all those years, the rocks had not been disturbed.

Use the stick, idiot. No telling what else might lie beneath that rock.

She poked the rock aside. A worm slid out. "Eeeuw," said Dr. Martha Charney.

And then she bent closer, shining her light on what she saw; an ivory statue, like an ancient chesspiece or something prehistoric—Sasquatch in miniature. And, placed lovingly beside it, the tiny Jewish star her parents thought she'd lost as she fled the Stranger.

<We'll hide it. One of these days, we'll come back and dig it up.>

Tears flowed down her face, making the star twinkle in her grimy hand. She had, she had returned and dug the treasure up, but she could never, ever tell the friend whose dad had saved her from the Stranger.

Unless, of course, she turned into one of those people who stalked the trails for Sasquatch: some kind of nut. There were enough nuts in the world; certainly, in saving her, the Bigfoot dad hadn't meant her to grow up that way. She had been *very* carefully brought up, just like his son. Too much so. The cautious creature she had become was never worth the risk they took. Perhaps, if she had remembered . . .

Oh, she *did* remember now. They'd risked breaking out of hiding to protect her, and all they really wanted was to be left alone. Nice people, she thought. Decent people she'd have been glad to have for neighbors. So she would keep this old cache safe and go away quietly. But she remembered now, and she would do what neighbors did: she'd repay them.

They had saved her. The least she could do was leave them in peace. It was the neighborly thing to do. The star she carried glittered. Before she left the cave, she put it around her neck.

I hope you found the peace you wanted, she thought across the years. *I hope you found it too.*

The Memory of Peace

by Kate Elliott

Kate Elliott is the author of the novels of the Jaran, including Jaran *and* The Law of Becoming. *Upcoming novels include* The Golden Key, *a fantasy co-authored with Melanie Rawn and Jennifer Roberson.* Dragon's Heart, *the first volume of the fantasy trilogy* Crown of Stars, *will be out next year.*

Spring came, and with it, clear skies, clear days, and a clear view of the ruins of Trient falling and rising along the hills in a stark curve. Smoke rose near the central market square from a fresh fire sown by the guns of the Marrazzano mercenaries. Jontano crouched next to the sheltering bulk of a fallen column and watched the smoke drift lazily up and up past the wall of greening forest that ringed the city and farther up still into the endless blue of the heavens.

When it was quiet, as it was now, he could almost imagine himself as that smoke, dissipating, dissolving into the air.

"Hsst, Jono, look what I found!"

He jumped, caught himself, and managed to look unsurprised when Stepha ran, hunched over, through the maze of the fallen temple and flung herself down next to him. She undid the strings of her pack.

"You've never seen things like this!"

But Stepha always bragged. Jontano wasn't impressed by the pickings: an empty glass jar, six painted playing cards, a slender book with crisped edges but no writing on its leather cover, a length of fancy silver ribbon, four long red feathers, and ten colored marbles.

"That won't buy much flour," he retorted. "Where'd you find this?"

"You're just jealous I went by myself. It all came from the Apothecary's Shop, the one midway down Murderer's Row."

"You idiot! Not one thing here is worth risking your life for." Murderer's Row had once been known as Prince Walafrid Boulevard, but no one called it that now, since the entire Boulevard was well within reach of the cannon and, at the farthest end, the muskets of the Marrazzanos.

"Everyone said Old Aldo was a witch. Maybe these have some power."

"Ha! If he was a witch, then why couldn't he spare his own shop and his own life?" But the cards were pretty. Jontano picked one up even though he didn't want Stepha to think he admired her foolhardy courage.

"No one saw him dead. He could still be alive." Her expression turned sly, and she lowered her voice for dramatic effect. "I heard a noise, like rats, when I was in the shop. Maybe he was hiding from me. Everything was all turned over and broken, except for that old painting of the forest that hangs behind the counter. It was the strangest thing, with the hole in the roof and all, but it still hung there, as if it hadn't been disturbed at all. Not even wet."

"Here, this isn't wet either," he said, showing her the face of the card, "and it has a forest painted on it."

"You *are* jealous! Ha!" But she examined the card with him.

The colors were as fresh as if they had just been painted onto the card: the pale green buds of spring leaves, the thin parchment bark of birches, the scaly gray skin of tulip trees and the denser brown bark of fir; a few dots of color, violet and gold and a deep purpling blue, marked clumps of forest flowers along the ground.

"I don't see how anyone could paint things so tiny," said Stepha.

"They use a brush with a single bristle. Don't you know anything?"

Before she could reply, the sky exploded. They both ducked instinctively. Cannon boomed. A nearby house caved in. A wailing rose up into the air, the alarm, and farther away, smoke rose from newly-shattered buildings.

Stepha shoveled her treasures into the bag and scuttled down the hill, dodging this way and that. Jono, still clutching the card, ran after her, not bothering to bend over. Not even the famous Marrazzanos could aim well enough to hit them here, as far away as they were from the lines, but if a ball or shot happened to land close by, then it scarcely mattered whether you were bent in two or running straight up like a man.

He caught up to Stepha just as a great crash sounded from the ruins behind and a column fell, smashing onto the hollow where they had just sheltered. Shards flew. Stepha grunted in pain, and Jontano felt a spray like a hundred bees stinging along his back.

As they darted into the safety of an alley, a double round of shot hit what remained of the roof of the old temple. It caved in with a resounding roar. Dust poured up in the sky in a roiling brown cloud. Then they turned a corner, and another, and ran through the back alleys and barricaded streets, strewn with burnt-out buildings, fallen walls, and an endless parade of little refuges, shelters built from bricks and planks salvaged from once beautiful houses. In some of those tiny refuges people lived, but most simply served as a hiding place to any man, woman, or child caught outside when a bombardment began.

By the time they got back to their house, in the relative safety of the north central quarter of the city, Jontano could feel tickling fingers of blood running down his back. Stepha was limping.

They burst in through the gate and, panting, walked past the newly-planted vegetable garden. Once Mama had grown flowers here, and it had been a lovely place in the spring and summer; she and Papa had entertained guests and laughed and talked and sung to all hours of the night while the children watched from the windows above, faces pressed to the glass. But that had been a long, long time ago. Now most of the windows were covered with boards and the flower garden had been transplanted to vegetables.

Great-Uncle Otto was standing guard over the well. He looked them over with disgust. Stepha yelped when he probed her thigh with his fingers, and Jontano saw a gaping red wound where she had been hit with shrapnel.

"Now your mother will have to sew these clothes up," he said, looking angry as he examined the back of Jontano's shirt. Jontano knew it ought to hurt, but he felt as if Otto's hands probed someone else's body, not his. "There's little enough thread to be had," Otto went on. "Nor do I hold with those who go looting shops. We might as well fall into the hands of the Marrazzanos as become looters ourselves. Look what barbarians this war has made of us and our children!"

Stepha, brave enough up until now, began to snivel. Otto spared her not one sympathetic word and turned his black gaze on Jontano, who squirmed.

"You'll be old enough to go into the militia next year, but I suppose next you'll be saying you'd rather prey on the dead than honor those who have died before you by behaving as a man ought, taking up arms and fighting nobly."

Jontano snorted. "I don't know what's so noble about fighting against cannon and musket with wooden staves and butcher's knives."

Otto slapped him. "I won't say a word against your sainted mother, who has suffered enough, but her mother and her mother's mother were Marrazzanos, and I can see their dirty blood has tainted you."

"What do I care about Trassahar and Marrazzano? I wish I had no blood of either kind! All we do is fight and die. What's the point of that?" Jontano could not help but shout the words. His throat tightened with the familiar lump. "I'd just like to grow up to be a painter like Papa was."

Otto swung his musket around threateningly, but in the next instant he said in a low voice, "Get inside."

Stepha bolted in. Jontano followed her, but just as he crossed the threshold he heard a shot fired, then silence. He turned.

Great-Uncle Otto staggered and dropped the musket, left hand clutching his chest. Jontano ran out to him, shoved him aside to get at the musket, and raised it just in time to stare down the muzzle at a ragged band of men and women, armed with a single musket and several buckets.

"Give us water," said one of the women. She was filthy, skinny, and her hands and arms were a mass of red sores. Beside her, an emanciated man reloaded the musket.

Shaking, Jontano stared them down, but by that time Mama appeared in the door with the pistol and Uncle Martin leaned out of the second-story window, his musket propped on the flowerbox, pushing aside the leafy stems of carrots. He had no legs now, but he had once been a sniper in the militia.

The ragged band retreated. Mama stuck the pistol in her belt and hurried out. With Aunt Martina's help she carried Otto inside, leaving Jontano on guard while Uncle Martin dragged himself down the stairs and together with the two women treated Otto's wound.

It took Otto five days to die, and because of that, everyone was too busy to scold Stepha for looting along Murderer's Row.

"Why shouldn't I?" she whispered to Jontano in the bed they shared with the two surviving youngest cousins, who were asleep. "Why should I care if I get killed, anyway? The Marrazzanos will never leave. And even if they did, I don't have any friends left, and no Trassahar boy will ever want to marry me because I'm just a Marrazzano whore."

They had saved the stub of a candle and they lit it now, while the house was quiet. Great-Uncle Otto's body lay in state in the parlor, until the burial tomorrow. He was the last but one of his branch of the family, having lost wife, sons, and all but one of his grandchildren to the war. He and his surviving daughter-in-law had fled to the city three years ago after their village had been razed, but she had died of a fever last winter, and now only little Judit remained, snoring softly beside Jontano.

Stepha played with the marbles, turning them round so that highlights of bright color caught and winked in the light, yet Jontano could not help but be drawn to the cards once more. They were shaped like playing cards, made of stiff cardboard cut into rectangles as large as his hands, but they were like no deck he had ever seen. A plain hatched pattern of black and white was printed on the backs. The front of each card looked as if it had been painted lovingly by a gifted hand. He spread the deck out to examine them.

A crane stands on one leg in a pool, its form silhouetted in a sunset of red and gold.

A fetid marsh stretches to the horizon, marked by small hummocks and a few twisted old trees.

The restless sea, infinite, surges and swells, without any sign of the safe harbor of land.

A blindfolded woman dressed in a shift runs through a dark forest. Spiders and strange, unsightly creatures peer at her from the branches. As she runs, unseeing, she is stepping on a snake.

Two birch trees bend, their highest branches intertwining so that they form an arch, that leads . . . but here the artist had depicted a haze of golden sunlight in which Jontano could make out only a suggestion, of Trient, perhaps, a golden city where once Trassaharin and Marrazzano lived in peace, together.

And the spring forest, his favorite, the one he never tired of looking at.

As he ran his fingers over the painted surface, he could almost feel the touch of the painter's brush, as if by concentrating hard enough he could become the painter painting the card, as if he could see through the painter's eyes the act of creation, the grinding of the paint, the careful preparation of the brushes and the backing, each brushstroke, each spot of color laid on with exact care.

When he touched the pale green buds of the spring forest, he could feel himself walking there along the path which wound through the wood, darting this way and that through clumps of goldenrod and violets. It sloped down, then crossed a narrow river and ascended a hillside. He walked up. Loam gave under his boots. Wind brushed his face, bringing the scents of the dense forest to him. He heard the rustle of birds above and the little scrabblings of rodents below. A spare outcropping of rock thrust from among the trees. He scrambled up onto it and, turning, saw the land below him, curved like a bowl, filling the graceful little valley with trees and emerald meadows. Suddenly he realized this was Trient—but Trient without the city, without the fighting, at peace, in the quiet of a spring morning.

A crash tore him out of the forest.

He lay in the crowded bed, frozen, feeling Stepha snoring against him—she always had a cold—and listened to the pound of the Marrazzano cannon. They had launched a night attack. Little Judit woke up and began to cry.

Jontano stuffed the cards into his worn but clean pillowcase and gathered the little girl into his arms. After a while she fell asleep, and he did as well, though the cannon boomed intermittently and once an explosion sounded very near them. What did it matter if they were killed in their sleep? At least it would spare them the agony of dying. So he slept, and dreamed of the spring forest.

At dawn as he and Judit walked hand-in-hand to the old central park that was now the main cemetery—all the other graveyards being full—the little girl tugged on him until he leaned down to hear her whisper.

"I dreamed that I was in heaven with Grandpa. It was all the prettiest forest, and a red and yellow bird sat on my fingers. And there were flowers."

Aunt Martina and Cousin Gregor carried the body wrapped in the most threadbare sheet, the only one they could spare for burial. Uncle Martin, ever quick to see the twisted humor in any situation, had waved good-bye to them where he sat on guard in the one unboarded upstairs window and then shouted after: "See, it'll be the last burial in this house—we've got no more sheets to spare!"

They paid the gravediggers three coppers and stood by while

a hole was dug next to the others in their family. Jontano led
Judit to each wooden cross in turn, Stepha following at his heels:
Papa's grave, the oldest one there, Jono's two brothers and one
sister, Baby Lucia, cousins, an aunt, and uncles. More men than
women, because the men all went to the militia, as Cousin
Gregor would go next month when he turned fifteen, as Jontano
himself would go next year.

Stepha stared at the graves, dry-eyed. Her parents weren't
here. Their graves lay on the other side of the lines, and everyone knew that at least one of her brothers fought in the
Marrazzano army, but Mama had taken the girl in because she
and Stepha's mother were first cousins, and no woman with even
a trace of Trassahar blood in her was safe on the Marrazzano
side.

It was another clear day. For once the Marrazzanos weren't
shelling Trient. One of the cousins had died while burying his
own father. They buried Great-Uncle Otto without much ceremony, and Mama decorated the grave with a few shoots from his
beloved potato plants. Here and there on the overgrown grass
that was all that was left of the once-manicured park, other fam-
ilies stood, burying a newly-lost relative. Dogs nosed at fresh
dirt. The gravediggers threw stones at them.

"This park used to be so lovely," said Mama to Aunt Martina
as they walked back. The silence lay heavily on them, it was so
unusual. "Do you remember?"

"All the trees," said Aunt Martina in her hoarse voice. "I remember all the trees."

Not one was left, of course, not even the stumps, all cut down
and dug out for firewood. Jontano remembered the trees vaguely,
too, from picnics, from running down by the lake, from Papa's
canvases and sketches, flowering tulip trees, elm trees, beech,
oaks and birches, ash and aspen, cherry with its spring blossoms
and apple and pear.

"It all used to be trees," he said suddenly, and Mama looked
at him questioningly. "Trient. The city. Before the city was here
it all used to be trees, one great forest. And it was quiet. It was
peaceful then."

Aunt Martina snorted. "Except for the wolves howling at
night. There are always wolves, Jono. Don't forget them."

"I'd like to be a wolf," said Stepha, "and rip out the throats
of my enemies."

Little Judit burst into tears.

"You've scared her, Stepha," snapped Aunt Martina. "I

shouldn't have to remind you, but I'll whip you if I've found you went out prowling around Murderer's Row again."

Now Stepha began to cry as well, so they looked properly like mourners as they came home empty-handed.

The house was quiet when they got back. Uncle Martin sat on his chair, elbows and musket propped in the window, and smoked a pipe.

"Where'd you get that tobacco, you good for nothing?" scolded Aunt Martina. "Did you sell the rest of my silver forks?"

Uncle Martin merely grinned at her and flourished the pipe. He had a network of old friends. Once a week they carted him off to a mysterious place in town where only men from the militia were allowed to congregate. When Uncle Martin came home from these jaunts, he always had a new piece of news from the front, and occasionally a trinket for the children or some luxury item for the women—yarn, lamp oil, a piece of fruit, once a pair of good shoes that, with a bit of paper stuffed in the toes, fit Aunt Martina perfectly.

Aunt Martina called him a few rude names, but she was too weary to really lay into him, as she usually did—she and Martin liking good arguments. They argued about everything, the King, the Parliament, the Marrazzano generals, battles fought four hundred years before, treaties signed and broken. Uncle Martin was a good Royalist: He believed in the Trassaharin King, whom, Martina reminded him, had escaped years ago to another country where he lived in peace and plenty; he believed in the Parliament, and in the cause. Aunt Martina believed that they were all of them, Trassahar and Marrazzano kings, generals, and ministers alike, scavengers feeding off the body of the farmers and the shopkeepers and the artisans, who had once populated Trient and the surrounding countryside without civil war, marrying each to the other with more attention to economic considerations than to blood ties.

So Mama, half Marrazzano, had married into a good solid Trassahar craftsman's family. No one had thought twice about it, because her own family were craftsmen, tile makers, and she had a good dowry, a fine hand for painting pottery, and liked well enough the man who became her husband. So she had in her turn fostered in her cousin's daughter, Stepha.

So Uncle Martin, Royalist that he was, patted Stepha on the head when she brought him up his dinner of potatoes and onions, and told her that she'd had an offer of marriage.

Stepha dropped the plate. She began weeping, but whether

over the shattered plate or the marriage offer Jontano couldn't
tell. No one scolded her. Aunt Martina scooped up the precious
food and Uncle Martin ate it from a tin cup.

"Who would offer for me?" Stepha asked through her sobs.

"My old friend Zjilo Berio."

"He's only got one arm," objected Aunt Martina.

"Which he lost fighting," said Uncle Martin. "His wife died
last winter, and he's got the two little ones now."

"They had the three children," said Mama, having come upstairs to see what the commotion was about.

"They had three, it's true, but he lost the boy to a sniper's bullet one month ago."

"Ah," said Mama. Jontano saw her wipe a speck from her eye.
He wasn't sure if it was a tear or not.

"How old is he?" asked Aunt Martina.

"About thirty."

Aunt Martina considered this. "That's not too bad."

"That's *ancient!*" protested Stepha.

Uncle Martin stared her down, and she wiped her nose and
clasped her hands obediently in front of her blouse. But she
wrung them, twisting her fingers about each other, and Jontano
couldn't tell whether she liked or was terrified of the idea of
marrying a man as old as thirty. Jontano didn't know what he
thought of it. He'd known Stepha so long that he couldn't imagine her being old enough to marry, even though she was almost
two years older than he was.

When Uncle Martin spoke again, he measured his words carefully. "Zjilo is a good man. We fought together. He never raised
a hand to his wife, though she came from an aristocratic family
and spoke down to him once the war came and they couldn't
have the luxuries they had before."

"He's rich still!" Aunt Martina leaped on this point. "I thought
the family lost their warehouse. I thought they had nothing."

"Or you'd have pursued him yourself?" Martin grinned at her.
"The family kept something by, or must have. He's taking the
children out of Trient. He can't bear it any more for their sake
now that he lost the boy. He's afraid of losing the little girls, too.
They've a small estate in Kigori."

"There's no way in or out of Trient," said Mama suddenly.
Jontano felt more than saw the pain on her face, in her body. His
eldest brother had died that way, trying to get out of the city to
fetch the herbs—the apothecary having long since run out of

such supplies—that kept Baby Lucia's heart going. So the two had, in a way, died together.

Martin snorted. "How do you think this tobacco got here? There are ways, if you've enough money, or important enough news, and are willing to run the gauntlet and take the risk. It would be a good life for you, Stepha, but if you agree to it, you must understand that you might not live through the crossing. Zjilo's agreed to take Judit, too, now that she's alone, and raise her as his own."

Stepha glanced over at Jontano, but he only shrugged. He tried to imagine what it would be like without her, but could not.

"Why does he want me?" Stepha asked sullenly. "To use me as a servant and a whore?"

Uncle Martin slapped her. This time, though, she didn't begin to cry. Jontano saw something different in the way she stood, as if she had already made a decision but was refusing to give it away easily. "As a favor to me, my girl, and don't you talk back to me again. He needs a wife. A young girl like you will be strong enough to do the work and bear him more children. You're a pretty girl, too, when you're not making faces and acting wild. If we don't get you out of Trient, you'll either get shot or end up in the marketplace with the rest of the goods that are bought and sold."

Stepha flinched.

"Martin!" scolded Aunt Martina, but Martin looked at her gravely. Whatever Martina saw in Martin's gaze caused her to nod her head once, shortly, and gesture at him to go on. Jontano watched in confused silence.

"When Zjilo began talking of leaving, of getting a new wife, I reminded him that you'll be sixteen next month and that you're a good girl and better off out of Trient. He doesn't care that you've got Marrazzano blood. If you agree and are a dutiful wife to him, you'll have a good life, with servants, land, a good kitchen and decent clothes always for yourself and your children."

Abruptly Mama spoke. "Can he get us out, too, Martin? All of us?" Her voice held a passion Jontano hadn't heard in it for years. Ancient memories resurfaced, clawing out of him, growing, consuming, memories of happiness, of Mama and Papa planning the garden, sketching new patterns for plates and vases for the family business, and in her voice as well he thought he heard a whispering note of hope, that somewhere peace might be found, a place where happiness could, grain by grain, brick by brick, be built again.

As if the Marrazzano guns had opened up again, Martin's next words shattered that fragile thread linking Mama, linking Jontano himself, to her dream.

"Do you have a thousand florins?"

She gasped. It was an enormous sum.

"Relatives to go to? We've got nothing but what we have here, Constance. Zjilo stayed this long because of his wife's family, and because of the risk to the children. But they'll die quickly enough in this hellhole, so why wait? I wish him luck. I wish we hadn't lost everything and everyone, but what's the use? We can't leave."

"We mustn't leave," said Aunt Martina. Her voice, forever scarred by the men who had raped her and then tried and failed to kill her by cutting her throat, sounded hoarser than ever. "That would give Trient to the Marrazzanos. Why else have we suffered? What have our beloved ones died for? I will stand here until the day I die rather than run away and give it to those bastard Marrazzanos."

Stepha stared at Martina. Mama walked to the window and looked out over the city. Her face was pale and the line of her jaw tight with an emotion Jontano could not understand, knowing only that he loved her desperately for her strength—the strength that had allowed her, of all of his family, to survive when the rest had perished. All three of her brothers, her sister, her husband and children, her parents, all gone, leaving her with in-laws and one last child. Uncle Martin got a funny look on his face, and he took Martina's hand in his own and kissed it, as a lord gives respect to a lady.

Martina made a noise in her throat, then pulled her hand free from his. "Huh," she said caustically. "All that fraternizing with former officers is giving you airs above your station, Martin. I hear old Widow Angelit is looking for a new husband."

"Ha! She's buried four already. I'd rather not know my own fate, thank you."

"I'll go," Stepha blurted out.

That simple statement brought its own, new silence to the room. It was so quiet that Jontano heard the distant yell of hawkers in the Wildmo marketplace, where a morning of quiet had brought brave and fatalistic souls alike to set out their wares, to shop, in the ruins of the fine old market stalls.

So it was done.

Zjilo Berio came to the house the next Sunday. He was a quiet man with tired eyes, but he wore a golden pocket-watch and his clothes were neat, pressed, and made of the finest cloth—old clothes, from before the blockade, well cared for and smelling slightly of the cedar chest, where they had perhaps been stored against better days. His daughters were even quieter. They stared at Stepha with great dark eyes. After the brief ceremony, Judit showed them her doll, and with this treasure, while the adults toasted the new bride with precious wine and ate from a table laid with as great a feast as Mama and Aunt Martina could manage, the three girls played together in whispers in the corner of the parlor.

The food was eaten, the wine drunk, and as dusk settled in over Trient, it was time for them to go.

Jontano hugged Stepha, but he could think of nothing to say.

"Take care of my treasures," she said. Then she was gone with her new husband and children.

Jontano gave the marbles to Roman, and the rest of the things from old Aldo's shop he gave to Mama, thinking that she might find some use for them, keeping only the six cards for himself.

At night, the bed seemed enormous with only himself and little Roman, Aunt Martina's youngest child. For the next ten nights he barely slept, wondering, each time he heard cannon blast, each time he heard shots ring out, if Stepha and her new family had won free to Trassahar-held countryside, or if that had been the barrage that had killed them.

"You must accept that we may never hear," said Uncle Martin. "That is the way of things now."

"Why must it be the way?"

Uncle Martin smiled crookedly. "My poor boy. We had a decent life when I was young."

That night Jontano ran his hands over the painted card that showed the forest. Strangely, the trees looked slightly different and it took him a moment to identify what had changed: The leafy buds were no longer tight and pale green. They had begun to unfurl.

If only he could walk the paths that led out of Trient toward the west, and freedom. He recalled once walking with his Papa, years and years ago, when he had been just a little child, up in the woods to the west of the old temple, so that Papa could paint. Jontano traced the painted forest with his fingers, and he felt himself walking there, on quiet paths among the trees. The violets were fading, but now new flowers bloomed in patches of bright sun, flowers his father had names for, names he had known once but now forgotten.

The path wound up into the hills and he followed it, feeling strangely that it was this path that fugitives followed, fleeing the city. He came to an open escarpment and looked out over the valley of Trient. There, across the bowl, lay the rock outcropping where he had stood before, a gray smudge against the distant trees.

Water fell, racing away down the hill. He was alone, except for the animals. There were no bodies, no furtive travelers, no one skulking but a lone fox that darted from cover, then vanished into a thick stand of shrub.

He walked for hours. He saw no one, found no one, heard nothing but animal noises and the flood of wind through the leaves. The silent weight of the sun scattered its light down through budding foliage. It was so peaceful.

"Jono? Jono!"

His mother's voice jolted him out of the forest.

He felt her hands on his arms, shaking him, and he dropped the card and tried to sit up, only she was holding him down and Aunt Martina and Uncle Martin looked on, their faces worn tight with anxiety.

"What is it?" he asked, coming to his senses. "Do you have news of Stepha?"

Mama began to cry. Oh, Lord, they had received terrible news. Pain stabbed in his chest.

"Can you walk?" Aunt Martina demanded.

"Lord, boy, you scared us."

Jontano felt dizzy. What had frightened them? What had happened?"

"Can you stand up?" repeated Aunt Martina.

"Of course." He threw his legs over the side and stood up, and only then did he realize that it was full morning outside. He didn't recall being asleep. Indeed, he felt very tired, as tired as if he had been walking all night.

Mama crushed him against her in a hug. "Jono," she whispered. Then she pushed him away, dried her tears, and straightened her apron and dress. "I don't care what it costs. I am going to send for the doctor."

"Is Stepha back? Was she hurt?"

All three adults examined him so closely that he became nervous. Aunt Martina asked him to raise and lower his arms. Uncle

Martin jerked his chair closer to the bed and peered into Jontano's eyes and ears and mouth, and listened to his chest.

"He's never had such a fit before," said Mama in a low voice. "You didn't hear or respond to me, Jono, and you lying there with your eyes wide open, seeing I don't know what. It's as if you weren't there at all."

"I've seen it take soldiers," said Martin, "after they'd had too much. They just go out of themselves."

"If only we had more food," said Aunt Martina. "The boys get little enough as it is. They're all so thin. He needs more meat. And milk. Ah, if only I'd been able to bring the goats. They'd have done well enough on weeds. Then we could have had milk and cheese every week."

Jontano knew he couldn't tell them what he'd really been seeing. He didn't know what they'd do, except he knew they'd take the beautiful cards away from him. "I feel fine. I was just asleep." He sat down on the bed and searched through the rumpled quilt. Finding the card, he tucked it into the drawer of the sidetable—one that had escaped being broken up and burned for fuel last winter.

"What's that?" asked Mama sharply.

"Only some cards Stepha found when she got the other things at old Aldo's shop."

"What kind of cards?" asked Aunt Martina.

Uncle Martin shook his head. "Old Aldo had a way with things. He wasn't the kind of man you cross, or he'd have his revenge, whether in little things or great. I remember the time about eight years ago now, when the girl in his house got into trouble. I don't know whether it was his daughter or granddaughter—no one did, and it wasn't the sort of thing you'd ask a man like that. She'd come from the country when she was a tiny thing, and he'd raised her. He doted on her, which we all remarked on since he was as ill-tempered as a caged wolf. He was the kind of man who would as soon throw a rock at a boy as give him a piece of candy."

He smiled his twisted grin, and Jontano wondered which of the two had happened to Martin. Jontano's own memories of Aldo were hazier, mostly his parents' prohibitions not to bother the old man who stood in the dim doorway of a shop from which wafted the most interesting and bizarre smells.

"But that girl—Lord, I don't even recall her name now—grew into a taking thing. Even we married men liked to stroll down the boulevard just to get a glimpse of her sweeping the sidewalk or grinding herbs into pastes and such. She had two suitors. One was the son of an officer in the Trient militia, a Trassahar boy, back when there was a city militia that any boy from the city could join . . ."

"One of General Vestino's boys, wasn't it?" asked Mama. "He had six or seven. No one could count them all."

"The youngest of them, yes, I think it was. It scarcely matters now. The other was the son of a Marrazzano merchant, grain and oil, if I remember rightly. That was the proof of how beautiful she was, that sons of good family like that came courting her. But she was a good girl, too, well-spoken, polite. She could read and do figures, and some even said she had the touch of healing in her hands."

"Yes." Mama's voice grew soft with remembrance. "People would bring ailing children to her, and she'd make poultices and drinks for them, and more of them got well than got sicker, as I recall. Girls would go to her for love potions, which I heard she never gave out, but if they would give a tithe to the church or donate some bread for the poor, she'd tell them when they would get married. I remember her."

"What happened to her?" Jono tried to remember a pretty young woman stationed at old Aldo's shop, but he could not, only the old man standing in the doorway, and the musty, inviting scents that came from the shop.

"It came to insults first, between the two suitors, and then to blows. Alas." Martin sighed. "She broke into the fight, trying to stop it, and by one means or another, she got a knife in her side and died. Ah Lord, that was a bitter day. No one knew which boy's knife had taken her. Perhaps they didn't either, but what did it matter by that time? Old Aldo cursed them."

Mama rested a hand on Martin's shoulder, as if to stop him, but he went on.

"He cursed them to be at one another's throats ever after, like dogs worrying at a bone until there was nothing left to be had; and only then would they find peace again."

He lapsed into silence. Mama went to the window and looked out over the city. In the distance, they heard the crack of musket fire.

"Nine months later the war started," said Mama in a soft voice, "as if it was a babe born of the curse. People shunned old Aldo after that, but he stayed in his shop. I suppose he also had nowhere else to go."

"Or nothing to go for," added Uncle Martin. "But the war got him in the end. That's the trouble with curses. They're as likely to rebound on you as to stay fixed on others."

"I haven't heard this story before," said Aunt Martina. "What happened to the two suitors?"

"The Trassahar boy joined the militia and got himself killed in the first month, defending Saint Harmonious Bridge before it was blown to pieces. As for the Marrazzano boy—who knows? He might be up in the hills now, firing down on us. He might be rotting in his grave."

The adults had by now all gone to the window, to look out, Martin bumping his chair over, following the well-worn scratches in the plank floor—this was the window where Martin sat with his musket. The lush greenery of carrots lapped over the windowsill, and Aunt Martina absently thinned a few out as she stared toward the center of the city. Their home stood on just enough of a rise that they could see out over the rooftops below, and the tall boulevard trees that had once obscured the central city from view were now all cut down.

Downstairs, Cousin Gregory sang a counting song to his little brother. From two doors down Jontano heard Widow Angelit singing in her robust voice a tune from an opera popular when he was little—when the opera house in town had still been open. It cheered him, hearing her sing a rousing chorus, even if she was off-key.

Uncle Martin laughed and turned away from the window. "Lord, Martina, you'd want me to marry a woman who can't sing?"

"Better a woman who can't sing than a woman who can't cook, like that woman you courted last year."

"All to no use!"

"Better luck for us!" Martina tilted his chair back and dragged him out of the room. A moment later Jontano heard him bumping his way down the stairs while Martina followed with the chair, hectoring him about his poor choice in sweethearts.

Mama remained. "I don't like you having things from old Aldo's shop."

"Please, Mama. They're so pretty." He opened the drawer and took out the cards, displaying them for her. "Look at the brushwork. Doesn't it remind you of something Papa could do? Please let me keep them."

"Some said the girl wasn't his daughter by the flesh at all, but that he'd created her by sorcery. It's not safe to touch the things of a man who might have worked magic." She sighed, handing the cards back. "But these are just playing cards. I suppose no harm can come from something like that."

"Thank you, Mama." He kissed her on the cheek.

She tousled his hair, then swatted him lightly on the back. "Go do your chores. The rain has made the weeds sprout like flies on a rotten apple."

So the days passed.

But every night, drawn by the lure of green trees and silent paths, he took hold of the card and wandered in the forest. Only now he made sure to keep track of the time; he learned to recognize the path that would take him out of the woods back into his bed, back into the damp spring air of Trient, back to the serenade of intermittent explosions and musket fire, to the wailing of the alarm and the wailing of the newly-grief-stricken, to the constant guard they set over their well and garden.

No trees stood within the city now. It was only by walking in the forest hidden in the card that he could watch the trees unfurl their leaves to their full grandeur, only by squinting out over the bare and broken rooftops that he could see the distant line of forest surrounding the city turn a deeper green. There, concealed by the trees, now and again he saw the puffs of smoke that betrayed Marrazzano cannon emplacements as they fired down onto Trient.

"You're tired all the time," said Mama, looking worried, and Aunt Martina braved the marketplace to look for decent cuts of meat. They traded away the sidetable for a slab of pork, so he had to hide the cards in his pillowcase.

Cousin Gregory turned fifteen and left to join the militia. Aunt Martina wept, a little, but she told him to fight bravely, to protect what remained of his father's heritage. Now there were only five in the house, the three adults, the two boys.

Clouds rolled in and settled over the valley. It rained for days.

On the ninth day of torrential rain, when the streets ran with water and the roof leaked, and even the clothes hanging in the wardrobe exuded a damp odor, the Marrazzanos chose to launch a new and brutal bombardment.

"It's taken them that long to build shelters over the guns," said Uncle Martin, "or they'd never fire in such rain. I don't know how they manage it, even so."

Jontano leaned out the window next to Uncle Martin, watching the flash of fire in the hills, hearing muted explosions and watching smoke rise, dense and packed heavy with moisture, and then fall again, unable to catch fire, or to rise up into a sky drenched with rainfall. "I heard from Bobo's son that the Marrazzanos got a new kind of cannon, a better kind."

Uncle Martin only grunted. He peered out at the distant hills. He was renowned for his keen vision, sniper's sight, and now he frowned and shifted the muzzle of his musket through the carrots so that droplets of water sprayed down on his hands. "I don't like it. They're closer than they were a month ago, new guns or no. Our people have lost ground to them, the bastards."

Was he calling the Marrazzanos the bastards, Jono wondered, or the Trassahar militia that had failed to do its duty? He thought about asking, opened his mouth, even. The next instant he was thrown to the ground.

The foundation of the house rocked beneath his body. Whimpering, he grabbed for a leg of Uncle Martin's chair and realized that the chair had tipped over, spilling the legless man onto the ground.

"Curse it!" swore Uncle Martin, scrabbling like a turtle to roll himself from his back onto his chest. "That's taken the widow's house to pieces. Run downstairs, Jono. Get the others into the root cellar."

Even as he said it, a shattering noise deafened Jontano. The wall beside him cracked, splintering.

"Run down, boy!" shouted Martin. "Those bastards have us under their sights and they don't even know it!"

But Jontano grabbed Martin under the arms and dragged him toward the stairs. Just as they got under the safety of the lintel a ball crashed into the window. Dirt and carrots and glass and shards of wood sprayed the room. Jontano yipped in pain. Uncle Martin merely grunted.

Aunt Martina ran up the stairs. "Down, you fools! Can't you come down any faster?" She shoved Jontano aside and heaved Martin up and with him cursing and her shouting, their argument drowned out by the rain of cannon balls on their house and the neighboring houses, by the sudden onslaught of a driving rain, got him down the stairs. They fled to the root cellar and there, huddled together with only musty old potatoes and the few precious remaining bottles of wine and ale, with a finger's deep pool of water turning the dirt floor into muck, they sheltered while the bombardment went on and on and on. They listened to their house being destroyed, and to the shouts and cries from neighboring houses, and, later, to the silence, except for the endless drone of rain.

At last, when the light began to fade and the bombardment

had, seemingly, moved on toward a new neighborhood, they ventured out. Jontano tried to go out first, but Aunt Martina shoved him back.

"I'll go," she said curtly. "I've had a life, a good one, before this war came. You deserve a chance at a decent life, so we won't go taking chances with you yet, my boy." She lifted Roman from her lap, and he wailed and clung to Uncle Martin, sobbing as his mother pushed open the root cellar door and crawled out into the gloomy, wet afternoon.

After a while, when they heard her footsteps overhead but nothing else, she came back. Her face was drawn and white. Her hair lay in wet strings over her dress. She was soaked to the skin, and it still rained.

They crawled out, all except Martin. The house was destroyed. One wall still stood its full height, but the others were shattered. The roof had caved in. The stairs veered crookedly up to a nonexistent floor above.

They stood in silence for a long time, sheltering under a blessedly dry corner, and watched the rain pour down over what remained of their home. Dimly, Jontano heard Uncle Martin calling to them from the root cellar.

Finally, Mama shook herself. "There's no point in waiting here. If we wait until the rain stops, looters may come. Roman, you go down and wait with Uncle Martin. There's nothing he can do until we've salvaged what's left."

"I'll walk down the street," said Aunt Martina. "Perhaps our neighbors need help."

So Jontano and Mama picked through the wreckage. Of their armament—two muskets and a pistol—one musket was dry and still usable and the others were not too badly damaged. The powder and shot had remained dry because they kept it in metal tins, and those in a cupboard which had come through the bombardment mostly intact. Mama set Jontano in the dry corner and put him on watch while she filled bags and blankets with what remained of their possessions: clothing, a few jars of pickled figs that had gotten wedged into the corner of the cupboard, the kettle and three unbroken plates, two pots, silverware, Roman's toy horse and wagon not too dented from its fall from the upper story, a bucket, a shovel, the last of the bread from the morning, a length of silver ribbon, and the butcher knife. She piled the bags and the single intact headboard next to Jontano.

After a while he realized that the street and alley were empty and likely to remain that way. The bombardment had quieted and moved back south again, and the rain had slackened to a steady drizzle. He ventured out of the ruined house to the well. The little roof had fallen in, and a few of the stones had tumbled out, crushing turnips, but as he tugged the boards out, he saw that the well itself remained intact. And though the garden was half covered with debris, as he picked up boards and tossed bricks aside he found that a fair portion of the vegetables were only crushed but not severed. He leaned the musket against the stones of the wall and began to clean up the garden, his heart racing with excitement each time he uncovered an unhurt plant.

Later, as it grew to dusk, Aunt Martina came back. "Widow Angelit is dead. I helped Bobo Milovech pull his daughter from the ruins, but I doubt she'll live. She lost one of her legs below the knee. We bound it up as well as we could, but she's too frail to sustain the loss of blood. Bobita went to see about a doctor, but what's to do when everyone needs a doctor? At least none of us were hurt."

Mama looked at her strangely for a long moment. "Ai," she said at last. "I'm so tired, Martina." She was weeping, but quietly, and Martina hugged her. They stood that way a long time while Jontano watched over them, watched over the well and the garden. Then, leaving Jontano on watch, the two women crouched beside the root cellar stairs to discuss their predicament with Uncle Martin.

Jontano stood in an eerie silence and listened to Roman sneeze and cough, listened to the hopeless sobbing of a woman farther up the street—Bobita Milovech, perhaps—to a single shot followed by a second, then a third, echoing through the empty streets.

"Water," said a child's voice, weak in the twilight. "Do you have water?"

Jontano started around, raising the musket. A small girl stood at the gate, a waif in tattered clothing. She held a battered tin cup in one hand.

He peered down the musket at her, his hands shaking, waiting for the adults who were with her to show themselves.

But there was no movement in the shadows, no threats, whispers, or coughs. The girl had preternaturally pale hair—Marrazzano hair, people called it—and gorgeous brown eyes and a sweet face only partially obscured by dirt. She couldn't be more than seven or eight years old. She was alone.

Jano glanced back toward the shell of the house, but one of the walls hid the entrance to the root cellar from view. Hastily, he

dragged away the boards that protected the opening of the well
and lowered the bucket, having to winch it hard to get it around,
now that a stray hit had bent the axle. The bucket came up half
full of clear water, and he dipped her cup in and gave it back to
her.

"Now go," he said in a low voice. "I'm not allowed to give
any away. Don't come back."

Mutely, she drank the cup dry. He filled it again. This time she
padded off, barefoot, down the street, cradling the precious cup-
ful of water against her thin chest. Where were her parents?
Lost? Dead? But he heard Mama's voice, calling to him, and as
he turned round, he faced the dead house and knew that even if,
before today, they might have managed to feed just one more,
they had too little left to do so now.

"Martin is going to stay here," said Mama, picking her way
around the house. "We'll set him up in the corner, rig a blanket
to protect him from wind and rain, and he'll guard the well and
the fountain. The rest of us will have to find shelter another
place. Roman is getting sicker, the grippe. It's going down into
his lungs, I fear. We must find someplace dry and warm for him
tomorrow."

"I'll watch tonight," said Jontano. "It's clearing, and I'd rather
be up here than down in the cellar."

He caught her answering smile, a ghost in the twilight, and
then she went away. So he stood watch, but after the terrible
bombardment of the daytime, after the loud, pounding rains, it
was now oddly silent. It made him nervous, because unlike the
silence in the forest, it was an unnatural quiet.

In the morning, Jontano helped Aunt Martina haul Uncle Martin out of the root cellar. While Martin took the parts of several
broken chairs and repaired them into a semblance of one good
chair, Mama and Aunt Martina divided up their possessions. Roman huddled in a blanket, coughing so that Jontano's lungs hurt
to hear him.

"No sense you staying with me, boy," said Martin when
Jontano offered to bide with him. "You'll come over every day
and weed the garden and bring me bread, but until this cursed
weather lets up, we won't have a chance to rebuild here."

Rebuild! Jontano couldn't reply. How could Martin even think
of rebuilding the shattered house? What was the point? If the
Marrazzanos had better guns and better positions, it would just
be destroyed again. And yet, Martin had been born here, as had
he himself.

"Go to Rado Korsic's shop," Martin added. "That's the first thing to do today, once you get Roman to a safe place. You must give him the musket and the pistol to repair."

Aunt Martina and Mama each gave Martin a kiss on the cheek, then slung bags over their shoulders and set off down the street, Roman trudging between them, his thin shoulders shaking under the blanket. Jontano picked up a blanket wrapped around the cooking gear and the bag containing plate wrapped in a cushion of clothing, said good-bye to his uncle, and with a heavy heart picked his way through the ruined house.

A flash of white, the suggestion of green life, the respiration of trees, the dense scent of unbroken loam . . . He bent down and pulled the six painted cards from underneath a fallen plank.

"What is it, Jono?" asked Uncle Martin sharply. "Are you well?"

"I'm fine," said Jono, straightening up and steadying the bag of plate. He set both bag and blanket down, stuck the cards inside his shirt and cinched his belt more tightly so that the cards lay snugly against his skin. "Just thought I saw something." He hoisted up his burdens again and left the house behind, following his mother and aunt down the street.

Mama and Aunt Martina were arguing in low voices. Go here? Go there? No, I won't ask Widow Vanyech, not after what she said about Stepha. They'll know in the marketplace. It isn't safe. Nowhere is safe, not after yesterday.

So they walked down into the bowl of the valley, down toward the central marketplace, down toward Murderer's Row. Heavy clouds scudded in, blanketing the sky, and it began to rain again. Roman coughed and snuffled, and began to cry.

"Here, I'll carry you." Jontano lifted the boy up and was aghast to realize how light he was, how slight a burden even with the other things Jontano was carrying. Roman lay his head on Jontano's shoulder and promptly fell asleep.

Even in the rain the marketplace was thronged with other refugees, fleeing their ruined homes. Still holding Roman, Jontano stood guard over the bags and blankets under cover of an empty stall while Mama and Aunt Martina forayed out into the crowd to see if they could find someone they knew who would offer them shelter.

As if they knew and understood—and why not? Why shouldn't they know?—and chose now to launch a new attack because it might demoralize and kill more and even more of their hated enemies, the Marrazzanos opened fire.

The marketplace erupted into cacophony. People screamed, ran, bled, died. Paralyzed, Jontano huddled with Roman in the empty stall. Was it better to stay here, where Mama and Aunt Martina knew he was, and risk being crushed by bricks, if the stall fell in? Was it better to run outside, where rounds filled with shot might explode, scattering like thrown knives into every person within a stone's throw of their landing? He didn't know what to do. He couldn't think. Roman was too terrified and sick to do more than sob quietly against his chest. They were all alone, and outside the panicked crowd surged this way, that, trying to win free of the open market square but for what safety? There was no safety in Trient, not any longer.

The stall rocked, and a few bricks tumbled down. Roman's sobs cut off, and he lifted his head and stared with a glazed expression at the wall.

"Mama!" he said suddenly.

There! In the crowd, Jontano saw Aunt Martina fighting her way through the mob toward them, but then the press of the crowd shoved her back, to one side, farther and farther away, and she was lost.

"They'll meet us at home," said Jontano with more force than confidence. Another hit nearby sent a second avalanche of bricks tumbling from the stall next door. Jontano eyed the bags, sorting through their contents in his mind: which to take? which to leave? He grabbed the firearms and a blanket stuffed with clothes, kettle, the butcher knife, and the last two jars of pickled figs. With Roman clinging to his chest, he heaved the blanket over his back and strode out.

By now the crowd had begun to disperse, fleeing down side streets. Jontano hesitated. The clouds opened up, and it began to pour down rain. He darted into the nearest boulevard, looking for shelter for Roman. If he could only find a place, he could put the boy there and come back for the other things, come back to find Mama and Aunt Martina. He was halfway down the first block of shattered buildings before he realized he was on Murderer's Row.

Roman, drenched, began to cough heavily. More explosions sounded from the marketplace.

"Mama," whimpered Roman between coughs.

"We'll find a dry place to hide," said Jontano. "Then I'll go back and look for her. Don't worry."

Ahead he saw a doorway. He ducked inside. One wall had fallen in, but the rest of the shop looked reasonably sturdy. It smelled dry, oddly enough, musty, as if perfumed with old herbs. A wooden counter ran along one side of the shop, and he set Roman down in its lee and wrapped him in overlarge clothes and in the two blankets. The boy was shivering with fever, half asleep.

Straightening up, Jontano stared into a forest. If he stepped past the counter, he would step into the woodlands. . . .

Shaking himself, he realized that he was staring at a huge picture, a painting, a painting of a forest. A moment later, he knew he was in old Aldo's shop. Without meaning to, he reached inside his shirt and drew out the painted cards. He held up the card depicting the forest, and in the gray light of the overcast day, he saw that the card and the painting were the same. Except the painting, as tall as he was, was somehow more lifelike. It seemed to pulse with life, as if he could step inside it. It called to him. It would be safe there. If only the trees grew again in Trient, it would be safe. There would be no more fighting.

"Mama," whimpered Roman. Jontano jerked, startled to still be standing in the dim shop. He knelt. The boy was hot, too hot. He needed a doctor. He needed his mother.

Oh, Lord, thought Jontano. What if Mama was killed? I couldn't bear it. I just couldn't bear it.

"Listen, Roman, I must go out and look for Mama and your mother. You must stay here and not move. Do you understand?"

"Yes. Don't leave me."

"Just for a little while. I'll come back."

"Just for a little while," echoed the boy weakly.

Reluctantly, Jontano left Roman and the forest behind. Intermittent shelling still peppered the central city, but the worst of it had moved toward the north. There was more musket fire than anything, as if a skirmish had broken out along the eastern line.

Only a few shapes, more ghosts than people, haunted the marketplace. Jontano hurried, giving them a wide berth, and found the stall where he and Roman had sheltered. It had collapsed, burying their possessions. He scrabbled at the bricks while the musket fire got louder.

"Jono! Oh, Lord, Jono."

He leaped up. It was his Mama.

She crushed him against her. "No time," she said. "No time. They're coming."

"Who is coming?"

"Martina went back to warn Martin. I don't know what they can do. The Marrazzanos have broken past General Vestino's troops. That's what everyone's saying in the streets. I came back, hoping to find you. Ah, Lord, what's to become of us?"

"We must get Roman," said Jontano. "He's down—he's down in old Aldo's shop."

Mama looked at him. A brief spark of something—fear? anticipation? anger?—lit her eyes, and then it fled, leaving her looking tired and resigned. "We'll go get him and try to get back home if we can. We might as well die there, even if it is in ruins, as anywhere else."

She said nothing more as they ran down Murderer's Row, hugging half fallen walls, until she knelt beside Roman, who had by now lapsed into a feverish sleep.

"Poor child," she said. "He deserved a better death than this."

"He doesn't have to die!" cried Jontano. Mama looked up at him, and with a horrid shock, like a claw at his throat, he knew that she had given up, that it had all, the years of fighting to survive, become too much for her to bear.

"I'm so tired," she said. "We'll just rest here a few moments." She lay down beside Roman and between one instant and the next, she was asleep.

She had given up. Jontano shivered. He wanted to cry, for her, for himself, for everything, but he had no tears.

The forest breathed, exhaling its scent around him. His hand clutched the card, the leaves unfurled to their full glory, the spring flowers passing into the blooms of summer—for it was almost summer. Tomorrow would be summer. He remembered that with mild surprise. He smelled, not rain, but the scent of the forest shedding moisture after rain, warmed by the new sun of summer. He heard the rustling of leaves, the scrambling of mice in the undergrowth, not the musketfire, louder now but strangely dull, too, as if from behind the mist, behind an impenetrable hedge.

Once there had been no war in the valley of Trient, though there had always been wolves.

Mama slept, curled around Roman. Perhaps she would sleep forever, never have to wake to the death of all that she had held dear, never have to remember everything she had lost.

Jontano circled the counter and came right up to the painting. It seemed to have grown since he last saw it. It filled the entire wall, as if it was straining, trying to fill the shop. He lifted his arm and pressed the card against it. If only he could find a way through, for himself, for Mama, for Roman and Aunt Martina and Uncle Martin. For the graves, so that the dead could lie in respectful silence, as they deserved.

If only the trees could grow again in Trient, as they once had, filling the parks and the boulevards, filling the once-handsome city with their summer fullness and the stark lines of their winter beauty.

He felt the paper thin bark of a birch tree under his hand, peeling away where his fingers scraped at it. He felt the flowers blooming under his feet, vines twining up his legs. A glade of sweet grass filled old Aldo's shop, and a lilac bush grew, lush and thick, to shelter Mama and Roman.

Oaks burst up in the marketplace, an ancient grove, watchful and airy. Murderer's Row erupted into an orchard of pears and apples and cherry trees, all mingled together, and the musketfire faded as the Vestino Line, the ruins of Saint Harmonious Bridge, the far hills were swamped by ash and beech. Aspen sunk their roots into the low places of the valley, blanketed with ponds and pools of brackish water left over from the rains. In the northern hills, tulips and elms lifted toward the sky, and in the meadows where blocks of houses had once stood, around springs made by wells, great patches of flowering shrubs spread out into a sea of color. Jasmine, bougainvillaea, and twining wisteria wrapped themselves around the shell of the house where Uncle Martin sat watch and Aunt Martina cooked over an open fire, her eyes red from weeping, and filled the ruined walls with their fragrance.

There were no more than a few startled comments, which Jontano heard on the wind as if from another life, so quickly did the forest take root in lands it had once had all to its own self.

The cannon, the barricades, the buildings whole and shattered, the boulevards, all were subsumed. Trees sprang up where people stood, Marrazzano and Trassahar alike, beech and oak, birch and aspen.

Night fell and passed and with the new sun, summer came to Trient, which was no longer a city but a vast woodland, populated by trees and the many small, quiet inhabitants of the forest.

The valley lay at peace in the calm of a summer morning.

Everything Has a Place

by Barbara A. Denz

Barbara Denz lives and writes near Poulsbo, Washington, in a house surrounded by tall cedars. She has had careers in libraries, radio broadcasting, arts administration, and desktop publishing. She shares her life with husband, David, a changeable number of ferrets, and a network of writer friends on GEnie.

Siiri held her breath and listened.

Was that her heart pounding so or the riders who followed her and Julianne, her younger sister? A bush snapped. Then another. It was riders, no doubt about it. For once the years of drought worked in her favor. She quit holding her breath and gasped for air. The two riders were getting much too close. Fear's acrid taste was metallic in her mouth.

Fear is for the rabbits they hunt, not for me, she chided herself, pushing the fear aside. *I've feared them since my firstblood last spring. I won't fear them anymore!*

She straightened from her crouch. Sneak and sprint, sneak and sprint. That's how they had spent their night. The moon was now long down and barren clouds hid the stars. Her eyes were tired from peering back across what she knew were rolling grasslands. Strain though she might, the blackness yielded no silhouettes for her to see. She had to find someplace where she could talk to the Goddess. They needed time.

"It will be light soon, Siir." The words were more gasps than speech as Julianne fought to catch her breath, too. She was small for her age and fragile from too many years of not enough to eat, yet she was tough. Siiri gave her that much. Julianne didn't give up easily. "They'll see us before we find shelter."

Julianne pointed to the northeast. A pale gray at the rim of the sky hid behind the rise of foothills and backlit the jagged tops of trees that were their goal. Behind on the still-dark parched plain was Lord Duncan's Keep and their family in graves, dead of neglect, overwork, and starvation. Ahead was the only place left to go.

"We need to find someplace for me to work," Siiri panted. "I'll only need a minute to buy us some time, but I have to get my breath."

A sneeze and a curse from a masculine voice reminded her of who followed and how much sound carried in the predawn hush. As their path rose to meet the treeline, they were passing through thicker and thicker brush that snapped at a breath. They had to be careful. She grabbed Julianne's hand, pulled her forward, trying to find a trace without making the same amount of noise that had given their pursuers away. Julianne pulled her off to the left behind a bush.

"This will have to do, Siiri. Hurry."

Siiri concentrated on her lungs and thought them quiet. *Help me, Goddess,* she prayed. *Help us.*

There was no answer. After a moment she heard the faint whisper that usually told her that the Goddess was listening and ready to help her now. If she could just think of a way for the Goddess to help.

Siiri thought for a moment of what the old Herbwoman had taught her. "For the Goddess' magic to work, you must think of things she knows," the Herbwoman had said. "The Goddess will show you how to work with it, but you have to focus on something natural and show her what you need done. If it is something she understands and it is within her power, she will help you. But be careful what you ask. What may be clear to you may not always be clear to the Goddess. And don't expect her answer to be what you expected."

I know, Siiri thought with anticipation. She imagined them rested, their bellies full, and the day ahead a relaxed run in the foothills on a goat path sheltered by tall brush.

"Let's go," she whispered, hoping the Goddess would see this image clearly. She began to run.

The stitch in her side began to relax and her breathing evened. Siiri's feet found the well-worn goat trace with no brush or dried grass to give the girls away. Julianne's breathing grew quieter, and her feet patted the ground more surely than before. Quietly now, they ran on.

The next problem was the brothers who followed them. Siiri let her feet move automatically as she thought of a small rock, positioned so it would embed in soft hoof tissue. It would not be enough to harm. The Goddess would not allow that. Behind her, a horse screamed, tack jingling, and the man who rode it thumped and whuffed on hard ground, brush breaking as he fell. She heard curses and then ignored them.

Blessed Be, Goddess. She smiled and her parched lips cracked anew. She promised to pray her thanks later and turned all focus on the rise to the rocky foothills and the growing outline of trees.

They reached the edge of the thick evergreen wood just as they could distinguish colors around them. The sky was turning the heat-soaked dark gold of another rainless day. The needles on the trees looked dull. The girls were tired and panting, but they were as safe as possible until they were in Lord Edward's halls. The air was thick with the day's heat when Siiri found a ring of six of the biggest pine trees she had ever seen. On the far side of the ring, against a rock outcropping, another of the huge trees had fallen over, shattering at the base and creating a splintery tunnel to the rock. The gap was just large enough for the two girls to slip through. Limbs long dead seemed to beckon her.

"Over there, Julie."

"I don't like that, Siiri. If we're caught, there's nowhere to go." Julianne stepped back and looked for some other cover.

"The Goddess will protect us. Trust her, Julie."

Julianne's look was skeptical. The eleven-year-old didn't much trust in the Goddess' help. Why should she? The only family she had left was Siiri. Julianne had only followed because her sister had promised she would be safe and better off in Lord Edward's Keep. She wished she could protect her little sister and not just promise help of a Goddess who had seemed to forsake them in the drought years.

Siiri had to tug on her sister, but in the end it was the sound of brush cracking that encouraged Julianne to press her slender body through the splinters and to hide behind and below the tree. Siiri could barely see the ring. She hoped that no one out there would be able to see them, either, once daylight shone through the trees. For now, the light was mottled and it was much cooler than they were used to. Brush cracked further away and Siiri relaxed a little. Maybe the brothers wouldn't be able to find them.

Siiri reverently pushed cobwebs aside to let her eyes get used to the dappling. Two large burls sat free on the ground and held water for the girls to share. Siiri thanked the Goddess again, settled her back against the tree and drank. Julianne sipped cautiously and settled against the rock, carefully unwrapping the small trifold of cloth that carried the only food they had. She broke off a small piece of hard bread and offered it to Siiri.

"No, you go ahead. The Goddess will take care of me," she said, sounding more confident than she felt as she thought of berries and nuts she would like to eat. "I think I'll explore a little and see if I can see the brothers to be sure they've lost us."

Julianne shrugged and broke off another bite of bread. Siiri slipped out the side of the tree and looked for anything she could eat. It was light enough for her to find berries she had hoped for. But with each step she felt the heat press on her. Cautiously, she surveyed the ring. If she was where she thought she was, there should be seven trees in the ring and this glade should be verdant. It confused her that the Goddess would let Her dance of sacred trees fall into the dead, dull, desiccated area before her. Siiri picked a few nuts off the ground, picked up a downed branch, and smoothed over their dusty tracks in the clearing. She munched absently on more nuts as she squeezed carefully around dried limbs and cracked heartwood to return to her sister.

"Are they close?" Julianne asked.

"I didn't hear or see them, but they can't be far away," Siiri said absently, still concentrating on the tree and the Dance. "We can hope they won't find us, but it would be easy to follow our trail." Siiri looked up at the dull, heavy sky. She took another sip from the burl. It was full again, even though she had emptied it twice already. She wondered if her thirst would ever be slaked.

She was tired and she wanted to sleep the day away.

"Have we reached Lord Edward's land yet?" Julianne whispered once the food was gone and her belly swollen.

"I don't know," Siiri replied honestly. "Goddess lands are supposed to be greener than this. I think so, but we won't know until we meet someone from the household. The brothers shouldn't hunt us here. If Lord Edward catches them, I heard it would be a very unpleasant death. The Goddess led us here, so I think this is sacred ground. . . ." Her whisper trailed off.

Julianne scowled at her sister and waited for her to continue.

Siiri sighed. "I guess this could be the Dance of the Seven Maidens," she said. "The Herbwoman said the trees would be bigger than usual, and I suppose this could be the seventh." Siiri ran her hand lovingly along the fallen tree. It felt cold and dead to the touch. She wasn't used to having nature feel cold. Since her firstblood, nature usually came alive at her touch. Without knowing quite why, she began to cry quietly. "Such is the way of these dry times," she told herself quietly. "Only the fittest survive."

"You're sure he'll take us in? With this drought, he'll not want two more mouths to feed," Julianne said quietly after a moment. Siiri realized that her sister had taken another meaning to her comment.

The tears had already dried on Siiri's cheeks, leaving a salty channel to her chin. "I trust the Herbwoman," she said quietly after another long silence. "She says I'll be safe and that Lord Edward honors those who serve the Goddess and the old ways. She says this drought is because so many now worship the new Onegod. She doesn't think that His followers will believe much longer if He doesn't fill their bellies. When the Goddess' lands are strong again and Her ways are honored, then we will have food for all. The Herbwoman said I could help now and that you could probably help, too, if we can keep us both virgins, but Lord Duncan and his sons have a reputation of leaving no hope for the Goddess' ways to return. She said they mean to rape us all." Siiri was quiet for a moment, letting her anger at the horrors she witnessed subside.

Siiri looked around her again. "The Herbwoman said there are many holy spots on Lord Edward's lands and he is careful to keep them for the Goddess." Siiri stopped to think for a minute. Then she giggled softly.

"What's so funny?" Julianne asked.

"I was just thinking. While we are both here, there is one maiden too many in the Dance." As she said it, a cold breeze blew along her spine. She looked over her shoulder. Nothing was there except her misgivings. When she turned around, Julianne was looking at her very strangely.

"Lord Edward will take us," she said softly, trying to regain her composure. She had felt those cold chills before and didn't like them. They always boded ill. "We can give him rain, Goddess willing."

Julianne smiled. "You witch," she said softly, and tangled slender fingers in Siiri's mousy hair. Matched pairs of ice-green eyes smiled at one another.

"Sleep if you can," Siiri whispered. She settled back, nestling against the dead heartwood, and drowsed.

* * *

Siiri awoke with a start. It took a few seconds before her pounding heart focused on what had jolted her awake. Before she could cry out at the whuffling of horses scant paces from their hollow tree and male voices shouting, a hand cupped over her mouth.

"Shh," Julianne whispered "It's probably mid-morning, but they're setting up camp on the far edge of the glade. There's no way out if they don't leave. They're arguing about losing us. They can't find trail marks."

Siiri nodded and tried to peek out without being seen. Her sister pulled her back. The sound of jingling tack alerted them to the movements of the nervous horses.

"Don't," she whispered next to Siiri's ear. "The glade is too light now. It's Morgan and Robert."

"Just as I thought," Siiri whispered. "All he cares about is that the youngest have some sport. So much is ruined in those inept hands."

She fell silent as the young men stopped arguing with one another. Siiri moved to peek around the edge of the tumble of rotting roots. Into her field of vision stepped two lithe youths in riding leathers. Morgan walked toward the horses. Robert was setting a fire, despite the oppressive heat. She pressed against the back of the tree and held her breath. Morgan returned to his brother with a bulging skin and a sack of food.

"We can spend the rest of the day here. It's pleasant enough. They'll be easier to find in an hour or so when the sun is overhead." Morgan's voice broke, betraying his youth. He had filled barely twelve summers and was inches shorter than Julianne, although she was a year his junior.

"Father will understand," said Robert, his uncertain voice not as convincing as the words. He settled down on his heels, stirred the newly lit wood, and set about fixing their meal.

The sound of sizzling meat had stopped, the fire's heat had subsided, and the brothers had quit speaking in slurred tones before Siiri could figure out how to get at the leftover food without being seen. She had almost thought of a way to envision it for the Goddess to help them when she felt Julianne move. Siiri grabbed at the tattered clothes and Julianne tried to pull them free.

"We need the supplies, Siir. Why they brought all that mead, I will never know, but they can't still be awake. And I'm hungry after smelling that."

"The Goddess has provided so far. Why won't you trust her?"

"If the Goddess is going to provide, then she might as well protect me while I get their food."

"Julie, no. If they wake up, they'll kill you."

"They won't catch me if you're quiet. At least let me try. The Laws protect me while I'm not yet a woman. I'll be back quickly. I promise." And with that, she was gone.

"Sweet Goddess, help my sister," Siiri prayed, but before she could envision a safe path for her sister, a cry told her it was too late.

"There," shouted Morgan.

"Get her," yelled his brother and she heard her sister scream.

A resounding slap and a grunt in her sister's voice told her what she already knew. The brothers were not honorable men. At least while they were slapping Julianne, Siiri had time to plan. Where was the Goddess? Why wasn't she protecting Julianne? Such desecration in Her Dance was unthinkable. Didn't the brothers know that? The chill cascaded down her spine again.

"Where is she," Morgan yelled. "We have to bring back both of you or father will torture us. We'll find her anyway. You might as well tell us." Another slap followed that echoed in Siiri's head.

"I don't know," whispered Julianne, her speech slightly slurred. "She left me hidden and ran deeper into the forest to get Lord Edward's men. They will be waiting for us by now. But I got hungry. . . ." Siiri could hear tears in her voice. The rock face behind her would not let her retreat any farther. Morgan's voice was followed by the crack of a hand on face. Julianne no longer cried. She didn't even whimper.

"Answer me," screamed Morgan.

"Give it a rest," his brother said quietly. "You've slapped her unconscious."

No, Siiri cried. The Goddess must have deserted them for this to happen to Julianne. Unless she has made some pact with her unfortunate words. . . . She shook her head fiercely. *No. The Goddess wouldn't do that!* If the Goddess had indeed let them stand alone, then it would matter little if Siiri lost her virginity.

"The witch sister can't be far," said Robert. "They were together at dawn. I saw them both enter the wood." Silently, Siiri cursed again. They had been sloppy.

"If Father finds out we left our lands to go after them . . ." Morgan's voice trailed off.

"It will be nothing compared to what we'll get if Lord Edward catches us here in the wood. We'd be hanged for poachers, sure, and no questions asked. Unless this is one of Edward's Holy Woods. Then we would really be in trouble." Robert's derisive laugh chilled Siiri. How could they joke so nonchalantly about the sacred places?

"Maybe we should just take the one and say the other died in the running," Morgan pleaded.

"Maybe you should let me do the thinking. Father would want the body. And I think I want the other. Father promised."

"If you get the other, then I want this one. I've never had an Underage."

Siiri choked back the gorge that rose to greet the thick-voiced sound of lust and desire. They had no intention of obeying The Laws and didn't seem to care if they were caught. Maybe the Dance could help her somehow. Maybe she could fall on them from above. *Maybe, maybe, maybe! There's no time for maybe!* she chided herself. *If you're going to move, do it!*

She tried to squeeze out the side entrance she had used before. An arm-thick branch she did not remember blocked her path. As she tried to climb under it, roots twined around her ankles and pulled tight. The more she struggled to get free, the more the tree came alive to stop her. Only her sister's scream stopped her struggles. She knew what had happened, but she couldn't believe that it could be done so quickly. Her sister's racking sobs and screams mixed with Robert's laughter and Morgan's panting grunts.

"You bastard," her sister screamed. "By the maidenblood you have spilt on Her floor, I entreat the Goddess to rot that *thing* you just used on me. May you and yours die and rot in hell!"

"Shut up," yelled Morgan. Flesh echoed harshly against flesh through the glade. "Shut up," he repeated, his voice rising with each resounding whack. And again. And again, until Julianne's sobs quieted.

"Get off her, you idiot," yelled Robert. "You don't want her dead, do you?"

Siiri tried to cry out, but could find no voice. Her sister's death as well as her virginity was exactly what Morgan wanted. She knew it was true as soon as the words came out into the Dance. Frantic, Siiri struggled against the tree. Another branch wrapped around her, twigs and heartwood that should have been dead were tearing at skin and clothing. Siiri tried to break off the dead branches, but they were supple and held her fast. This couldn't be! The tree was dead!

Morgan's howl of rage told her she was too late.

"Stop stabbing her. She's dead, can't you tell? Why did you do that?" Robert demanded, hysteria in his voice. "You fool. You've killed her on Lord Edward's land. They'll kill us, Morgan. They'll kill us both. Aye, we're in trouble now."

"We were dead anyway," Morgan's voice cracked. "You heard the witch. I couldn't let her live after she cursed me."

Sobbing, Siiri clawed at the branches, which now parted easily. She wasn't sure if she felt more anger or anguish as she stumbled from behind the tree and across the glade. She was slipping in her sister's blood before she could stop herself. The slender youngest son still stood poised, dagger held high. From it, her sister's lifeblood dripped, now falling on her as she folded Julianne into her arms. The small pool of congealing darkness was dark on the ground. The dry forest floor drank it up. Siiri felt a rage consume her, its strength growing as the blood soaked in.

"Well, well," Robert said, calmer now that they had Siiri, too. "Look who you scared up, Morgan."

"Aye. Looks like we'll both get what we want this night. Shall I hold her for you?" Morgan chuckled and moved toward Siiri.

"You'll not have me. The Goddess may not have protected Julianne, but I can protect myself."

From within her came a mix of a wail and a warrior's cry in a voice that was not her own. She turned, lunging for a burning branch from the fire behind her and fended off the two. She did not know when the cry became audible to them. Rage poured through her like the fire she wielded as she swung again and again, tiny firefly sparks hissing as they found tinder to ignite. Arcs of flame were drawn on the inside of her eyes.

"Stop her before she burns the forest and us with it," she heard Morgan scream.

Stars burst in front of her eyes and a pain centered just above her ear exploded. She remembered a moment of bright light and then nothing more.

Morgan's icy monotone penetrated her haze. Somewhere inside her, a high, piercing wail jolted her awake. She wasn't sure which chilled her most.

". . . kill this one, too?"

"Not till I've had her as you got yours," countered his brother. "At least this one's of age. And not till we get off Lord Edward's land."

Siiri ventured to open her eyes and regretted it. When two

blinks cleared the bloody haze, she was inches away from the open, dully vacant eyes of her sister. She rolled over, retched violently and then could not roll back. Her hands and feet were bound tightly behind her back.

"She's awake and already commenting on her plight," chuckled Robert.

"You bastards," Siiri's strange voice hissed as she tried to steady racking sobs.

"Now, now," Morgan said ominously. "Those were your sister's last words. Don't let them be yours, too."

Robert let out a low, throaty laugh and leaned over Siiri. She tried to kick him, struggling against the cording that bound her. Feeling it cut into her skin didn't bother her. That pain was better than what she felt inside. She screamed in frustration and regretted it as her head exploded in pain.

"Now there, we'll have none of that," Robert said soothingly, and then grabbed her hair and pulled her head back hard. "I'll have you before day's end, don't you worry. But for now, I want to ready myself for the enjoying."

He flung her back so hard that she saw stars again. The brothers' laughter mingled with a roar in her head as she faded first to white and then to black.

When Siiri next awoke, she was ready for her sister's fate. The wail was still there, and its melody was more insistent than ever. She wished it would leave her alone. She squinted at the sunlight, trying to tell how long she had been unconscious. It must not have been very long—shadows hadn't moved much since all this began. How could her whole life be destroyed and the day not notice?

As the throbbing subsided enough for her to concentrate, she realized that her hands and feet were untied and that her back was against the fallen tree. Her head felt thick. She surveyed body parts without opening her eyes. As her mind itemized an ache, something . . . someone? . . . . prodded at it. As each sore part was touched from within, it felt warm and its pain disappeared. Siiri let the healing continue until she itemized the ache in her heart at the loss of her sister. The healing touched stopped. Angry now, Siiri confronted her Goddess.

Why didn't you save Julie? she demanded. *Why didn't you come when I called? Julie didn't deserve to die, did she?*

The voice inside her was quiet so long that Siiri was afraid she had offended the Goddess, not that it mattered anymore. As she began to wonder if the Goddess had gone, she felt that warm assessment of wounds again, and the healing chill-warmth. She didn't have to envision anything. The Goddess was working on her own now. Siiri tried to regain control, but the Goddess wouldn't let her think. It frightened her.

In Siiri's mind came pictures. First was the Dance of seven trees, strong and huge, and a glade lush with foliage, flowers and wildlife. Then one tree crashed, cracking from roots to top needles. The same cries she had heard from Julianne were echoed by the dying tree. Then six trees shrank as the woods became dry and brittle. She watched herself and Julianne run into the wood and the image of two tall and six small trees stood before her. Colors shifted to odd grays and oranges until one tree fell over and turned into Julianne again. The seventh tree stood tall and strong. As blood drained from Julianne, the six other trees grew to join the seventh.

Oh, no. The chill. I knew it. That was my baby sister you let die. Siiri choked back a sob. *Wasn't it enough for her to lose her virginity? Couldn't you have stopped there? I didn't mean for her to die. What must I do to get her back?*

For a long time there was no response. Then the Goddess just showed the seven tall trees in a Dance again and the forest growing green.

Siiri was devastated. *If I stay, will I get Julie back?* she began then halted. Seven tall trees transformed into seven maidens who joined hands and danced in the glade. Julianne did not reappear, but the Goddess did not say no either. Siiri placed all her hope that the Goddess would be fair.

She must have moved, for someone sat on her stomach.

"She's awake, Robert," Morgan yelled. "Come take her now so we can get out of here. We dare not stay after dusk."

In her mind, she saw the seven maidens in a Dance and two naked male bodies from which blood drained into the ground, which drank thirstily. Her muscles tightened and her jaw twitched. Just as quickly, the Goddess prepared the muscles to spring, smoothed her jaw.

Siiri opened her eyes. Robert sauntered across the clearing, britches already undone and shirt pulled from them. His movements were sloppy with drink and hungry with lust. His eyes were crazed. She was sure he was only seeing her. Morgan got off her to let his brother take his place. With Morgan off her and with inner strength she knew they did not suspect, she was ready to spring at Robert, not knowing exactly what she was expected to do or how the six trees and the Goddess would help her.

But Morgan's face was the one the Goddess showed her, not Robert's. None of it made any sense, but the Goddess insisted. Siiri's hand, unbidden, picked up a small handful of pine needles and flung them toward Morgan's chest. Just as they left her hand, she felt them grow. She watched with fascinated horror as the needles extended into spikes twice the length of her hand, each one firm and sharp. Everything seemed to slow as twenty or more two-edged barbed knives found homes in Morgan's body. The leering smile with which he had been watching her turned into a expression of horror first, then pain, and finally realization that he was going to die.

Siiri did not need the Goddess to urge her to grab for more needles and throw. This was for Julianne. Fingers felt in the dust and grabbed and threw handful after handful. Morgan staggered backwards and was finally impaled against a tree, which leached fluids from the small body through the needles and into the trunk. She scrambled to her feet, a strange lightness in body and head, and turned on Robert. He had not moved, but a growing horror on his face told her that he knew his own fate as well.

Siiri did not disappoint him. Two handfuls of needles flew at him. The war cry that was now her own escaped her lips. The horses pulled loose from their tethers and ran from the smell of blood and fear.

It seemed forever before Siiri could move to be sure both were dead. Part of her was numb at what she had done, but another part of her was the Goddess. They were no longer separate. As she looked at Morgan's body, the needles began to shrink and he fell loose from the tree, a desiccated shell of a human. All that was left were the clothes, skin and bones. On the tree, a new branch was forming and the needles were visibly coming back to freshness. She walked numbly to Robert and saw much the same thing. She touched the needles. They were warm. Under his body, fresh grass was poking up and small flowers tufted ground cover at his feet. Rain droplets touched her face. The glade was growing. A wave of green crossed from edge to edge. Bird sounds began and were finally a noisy chorus. Siiri sat down hard, mouth and eyes wide open in amazement. More animal calls joined the birds and animals out of season and those which should not be awake this time of day. Siiri heard each new part join a chorus to the Goddess.

Siiri crawled across the now-plush forest floor to her sister, cradled Julianne in her arms, and rocked. She could barely see through the tears. "Bring her back, too," she called to the Goddess. "Let her grow. You promised."

There was no response except the sound of the rain. Siiri waved at the desiccated skeletons that now lay empty on the ground and the six tall trees in the grove. All that remained to identify the sons were their blood-soaked clothes, jewelry, and skeletons. "She gave her blood so you would have the strength to help me. Now give her back!"

She held Julianne like that until the body was cold to the touch, pleading the entire time. Tears joined the rain that washed her face. Finally, numb with grief, she gathered branches of the downed tree, now dead and dry again, and piled them around Julianne.

She watched, quietly, as the pyre ignited on its own. Fire sprites that all looked like Julianne danced in the flames, each signaling her to join them. She swiped at her eyes, finally acknowledging that her sister was as much a part of this glade as she must be. She took a deep breath. Above her, the clouds parted, and stars were bright. A brilliant moon shone with her sister's face.

Siiri walked to join the six maidens who stood waiting for her. She took the two hands offered and completed the ring. As they danced, a new tree began to grow.

Trees Perpetual of Sleep

by Nina Kiriki Hoffman

*Nina Kiriki Hoffman lives in Oregon's Willamette Valley
where she spends a month or two each year housebound
from grass pollen. She has written many short stories and
a novel,* The Thread that Binds the Bones. *Other stories
about Matt Black have appeared in the Axolotl novella
"Unmasking" and in F&SF.*

They were way too far into the woods and away from human-
made things for Matt's taste. When choosing for herself, Matt
called the whole world home, but she generally stayed in the
parts of the world where there were cars and roads and buildings
and people, things she could talk to. She wished she had never
met Miss Terry Dane, teenage fashion victim and witch.

Cricket noise and stream murmur edged the forest air with
sound. Sunlight was just fading from the tops of the trees around
the clearing, and the intense blue of midsummer sky was staining
slowly into night. Everything smelled green and wet. The marshy
ground squished under Matt's army boots.

Terry laid red roses in a ring on the fire-scarred altar rock in
the middle of the clearing and opened her backpack. She whispered words while she pulled all kinds of weird things out of her
pack. She set each item carefully on the rock, blessing it and pre-
paring it for use.

Matt wished there were somewhere to sit. If she sat on the
grass, she would get her jeans soaking wet. Durn Terry and her
Midsummer ceremony, anyway.

The whispering tree on the far side of the rock, the only tree in the clearing, had big roots, some of them with knees and knuckles sticking up above the ground. Matt edged around the big gray altar stone and sat on one of the tree's upthrust roots.

Terry opened her big time-nibbled book and set it where she could see it, as though it were a cookbook. She made some passes with her hands and spoke some words. She lit red candles, and then she lit a piece of stick incense which she waved in a pattern, leaving little trails of thin smoke and the scent of a distant country. She stacked wood on the rock in a triangle within the circle of roses, and snapped her fingers. The wood blazed up. It was fairly impressive.

Matt pulled her knees up to her chest and leaned back against the tree's trunk. Its rough bark caught at her crewcut. She didn't know what kind of tree it was, but it sure smelled good, a little like fresh pencils at the start of a school year.

Terry spoke softly, reading from the book and touching the things she had laid on the rock, lifting water, crystal, incense, salt, and a knife. Gripping the knife in her right hand, she stood a moment, her eyes lifted to the darkening sky above, then cut across her left palm and dripped blood into the fire.

"Dedication," said the tree Matt leaned against.

"Mm," Matt murmured. She had learned to keep quiet when Terry was in the middle of something; she had talked during a summoning spell Terry was doing once, and the little wind Terry had been calling up got loose and pestered both of them for three days.

"I used to have that. Almost."

"Shh," said Matt. Golden-orange light was gathering around Terry's head and hands. She held her hands up to the sky and spoke some more words, and the light brightened around her. She closed her hands a moment. She opened them again, and red-gold light flowed from her palms, half to the sky, half to the earth. She pressed her palms together and stood silent, and the light seeped away. Everything got quiet.

Terry drew in a deep breath, let it out slowly. She shifted position, her shoulders relaxing. She blessed all her tools and stored them again, and last of all she passed her hands through the flames, which rose up and then died down.

"Discipline," said the tree.

"Shhhh!" Matt said.

"She's finished."

"Shh?" Terry said, shaking her hands and smiling at Matt. The slash on her left hand had closed clean.

"I wasn't talking to you," said Matt. "I was talking to this tree . . . this tree?"

"Thought you didn't talk to trees," Terry said.

"Not usually," Matt whispered.

"I used to have that kind of dedication and discipline," said the tree again. "Well, maybe not as intense."

"You said you only talked to man things," Terry said. "What does that mean?" She patted her backpack and floated up to sit on the highest part of the rock, above where she had performed her ceremony.

"I can talk to things people have messed with. I know that feeling, so we can relate."

"Hmm," said Terry. She opened the outside compartment of her backpack, fished out two granola bars, and tossed one to Matt. "But now you're talking to this tree."

Matt edged out on the root so she could look at the tree's trunk. Its bark was almost fuzzy, with shallow fissures running up and down. She placed her palm against it and felt a rough surface but not a splintery one. "How can I talk to you?" she said. "I don't know anything about nature."

"I'm not natural," said the tree.

"Oh," said Matt. She wondered whether she should stand up. She decided she'd rather sit on an unnatural tree than try climbing on Terry's rock.

"I used to be a witch," the tree said. "Now I just watch witches come and go here at the Gateway Stone. Powerspill wakes me up sometimes."

"So what is it saying?" Terry asked.

"What happened to you?" Matt asked the tree.

"I got carried away during a spell, and it turned on me."

"Wow," said Matt, wondering if it could happen to Terry, and if she maybe wanted it to.

"Could you let me out of here?"

"What?"

"I've been thinking about it for an age. I've worked out a spell that should release me, but I need help."

"Matt," Terry said. "Talk to me." She was using her pushy voice.

"He used to be a witch until he messed up and got trapped in the tree," Matt said, not realizing until the words came out of her mouth that the tree was male. One of the things she hated most about her relationship with Terry was that Terry could just tell her to do stuff and Matt would have to do it without being able to think it over first. Terry didn't do it very often—if she had, Matt would have found some way out of the tether spell, even if it involved not surviving. "He's worked out a spell to let him go. He wants us to help."

"She coerces you?" the tree asked.

"Tether spell," mumbled Matt.

"Sympathies," said the tree. "How did that happen?"

"Uh," Matt said. She should never have stopped to fix Terry's car. The car had warned Matt that Terry was a witch, but she didn't realize it meant literally until too late.

In spite of the tether spell, Matt had liked living with Terry and her mom, at first. Lately it had begun to grate.

"Oh. Right. Not easy for you to explain when she's listening," said the tree. "Hmm. You can hear me and she cannot, eh?"

"Mm."

"Are you a witch?"

"No."

"You're not? Wait a moment. How can that be?"

"I'm just me, Matt."

"Matt," said Terry. She drummed her fingers on her knee.

"What?"

Terry frowned. "So?"

"Do you want to help him with his spell?" asked Matt.

"How good a witch is she?" the tree muttered to itself. "No, don't answer that. I have watched her work, and she's one of the best I've ever seen."

"Have him tell us the spell." Terry unzipped her backpack and pulled out the ancient book, opened it to a page near the back. She got a pen out of the backpack's outside compartment. "I'll think about it."

"She's a good witch, but is she a good witch?" the tree muttered. "Evidence: she does her solstice ceremony alone. Not a communal witch. Cast out, or alone by choice? Evidence: she tethers another to her. Hmm. Hmm. Did she tell you why she tethered you? Did you do something to her?"

"Yes. No," said Matt.

"Does he want our help or not?" Terry asked. She frowned. Matt knew by now that with Terry, irritability was the first step toward true discomfort for anybody she was around.

The tree said, "By wit and by will, I bound myself. By witchings and workings I bound myself. By wood and by water I bound myself. By one into other I bound myself. Now I am ready to release myself. Now I am ready to face my fear. Now

I am ready to go to war. By wood and by water I loose myself. By witchings and workings I loose myself. By wit and by will I loose myself."

"Matt," said Terry.

"Just a second," Matt said. She put her hands on the tree trunk. It was trembling.

"Water," it whispered. Matt ran to the stream and grabbed water in her cupped hands, brought it back and splashed it on the trunk.

"Wood."

She looked around, saw the unburnt end of one of the sticks Terry had used in her little bonfire on the rock, lifted it, and touched it to the trunk.

"Will," whispered the tree.

Matt put her hands on its trunk and thought about being trapped. Terry didn't seem to know how to make friends except to manufacture them. She had a twin sister who had left on some kind of magic quest and it was driving Terry nuts, though mostly Matt knew about that because the room she stayed in was Terry's twin's room, just a closet away from Terry's room, and at night Matt could hear Terry calling and crying in her sleep. Terry also had an ex-boyfriend, and a witch teacher who wouldn't talk to her anymore. This much Matt had learned from surreptitious talks with things in Terry's room. No wonder she's lonely, Matt thought; but does that mean I have to stay tied to her like this? I might even like her if she gave me a chance.

"I will you to be free, I will you to be free, I will you to be free," Matt said, leaning on her hands on the tree, which felt warm, and still trembled against her. She spoke the words for the tree and for herself.

"Matt!" Terry cried.

The tree shook harder. With a loud crack it split open and spilled out a mushroom-pale boy.

"But we don't know who or what or—" Terry said.

The tree closed its mouth. Its bark welded back together beneath Matt's hands. She patted it and stepped away, looking at the boy, who lay shuddering and twitching on the wet grass. He was naked, his limbs wraith-thin, and his hair long and dark and tangled, a few strands still caught in the bark of the tree. His eyelids fluttered. He coughed.

"—whether he's even a good person," Terry said.

Matt stooped. "Are you cold?" she asked, pulling off her plaid flannel shirt and draping it over him. She still had her black T-shirt on.

"Thirsty," he whispered.

Matt went to the rock. "Gimme the bottle of water."

Terry raised her eyebrows, but opened the pack and fished out the water bottle, then handed it to Matt.

Matt knelt on the grass, oblivious to wet knees, and lifted the boy's head onto her thigh, tilting the bottle so water trickled into his mouth. For an instant Matt was back in an alley, helping her friend Denzel drink from a bottle in a brown paper bag, trying to talk the bullet in his gut into coming out, trying to talk the blood into staying inside him, trying to talk his clothes into binding against the wound, trying even to talk to germs, though she never had before. It was a terrible time when talk got her nowhere.

She cradled the boy's pale head, giving him water a little at a time and waiting while he swallowed, stroking his hair. His eyes were green and he smelled like the tree.

After a little while he reached up and took the bottle from her hand. He struggled and sat up, then drank the rest of the water. "Thanks," he said. "All these years of witch-traffic, and you, a nonwitch, you're the first one who helped me."

Helped him . . . That was how she had gotten into trouble with Terry. When Terry dropped the tether spell on her, Matt had decided that in the future she should leave witches alone. Usually she kept her promises to herself.

"What's your name?" she asked.

"Lewis," he said. He stretched, first one arm toward the sky, then the other. He scratched his nose and grinned at her, showing a dimple in his left cheek.

"Matt," she said, holding out her hand.

"Pleased to meet you." He shook hands with her.

"That over there is Terry," Matt said.

"Hello," said Lewis, smiling toward Terry. She nodded without smiling, her hands resting on her knees.

"How'd you get stuck in that tree?" Matt asked after a short uncomfortable silence. "What were you trying to do?"

"I came up here to get away from the war. All the men and boys were going overseas, except the ones who had some sort of exemption or those who were too old. I thought if I changed myself, I could stay home. But I wasn't as specific about what I wanted to change into as I thought I was."

"What did you want to change into?" Terry asked.

"Well," he said, "not a tree, anyway." He pushed to his feet and leaned his back against the tree, flattening his hands on the bark. "This is still me. It's all the growing I've done." He tilted his head back, looking up the trunk into the branches. Then he closed his eyes.

Frogs chorused from the stream as the longest day of the year was swallowed by the shortest night.

"Is there still a war?" he whispered.

"There's probably a war," Terry said. "There's usually a war. People don't have to go against their wills right now, though. You're a witch, and you couldn't come up with a better plan to evade the draft than this?"

In the gathering darkness Matt couldn't tell for sure, but she had the impression that Lewis was filling out, losing his starved thinness as he lay back against the tree. Above them the branches rustled, though there was no wind. Small scaled twiglets pattered down. Matt caught one. It felt dry; she rubbed her fingers over it and it came apart, leaving behind the ghost of a scent of green.

Terry pulled three candles out of her pack and lit them with a touch of her fingers. She dripped wax and set the candles in it on the rock beside her. The flames burned straight and unflickering.

"I had a better plan," Lewis said at last. His voice had deepened, added overtones. "It just didn't work." He stepped away from the tree. He was definitely bigger. He paused, lifted one foot away from the ground, then the other. "Oh," he murmured, touching the sole of his foot. "This is so strange." He pressed his palm to his chest, then touched the bark of the tree. "I feel so naked. No wonder people wear clothes." He lifted Matt's discarded shirt and slipped it on without buttoning it. The sleeves were far too short. "Not quite right, but better than nothing."

He went to Matt, grasping her elbows from behind and lifting her to her feet. His hands were warm and strong. Her first impulse was to kick back at him and twist free, but she suppressed it. He said to Terry, "I suppose you have some sort of master plan that involves tethering this boy?"

Terry's eyebrows lifted. A moment later she shook her head. "I have no plan," she said. "I realize that sometimes things come into my life when I need them—spirit gifts—and I needed Matt."

"For what?" Lewis and Matt said together.

Terry ducked her head, her gaze on her hands, which lay nested one in the other in her lap. "You know," she said. She looked up into Matt's eyes, her own eyes catching glints from the candle flames. Light turned half her face to butter amber.

"Oh, you're such a teenager!" Matt said.

Terry brushed the hair out of her eyes and offered a brief smile.

Lewis let Matt's elbows go, touched her shoulder. "You understand her?"

"She's a power nerd," Matt said after trying to figure out what she did understand.

"Whaaat?" said Terry.

"What does that mean?" Lewis asked.

"You don't—you run out of—you don't take the time to make the—it's a shortcut." Frustrated, Matt waved her fists up and down. "To get to know people, it takes time. It's not easy. Sometimes they hurt you and you hurt them. But you, you don't have to wait. You have this power. You use it to get what you need, because hoping someone else will help you takes too long and it might not work. You can make a—a relationship happen without even listening to the other person. You never have to risk getting hurt. You just . . . force it . . . and you don't have to be scared there's anything I can do."

"No," said Terry, shaking her head. "That's not right."

"I know you're doing it because you've lost them all," Matt said. "Everybody else has gone, except your mom, and she's scared of you. It's still cheating."

"No, dammit," said Terry, slapping her thighs with open hands. "No. Shut up."

But she didn't use her pushy voice, so Matt said, "You never asked me. How do you know I would have said no?"

"Everybody I've asked lately has said no."

"You didn't ask *me*."

Terry gripped one hand with the other. The tip of her tongue touched her upper lip. "Would you be my friend?"

"Take the tether spell off."

Terry sat for a long moment with her head bowed. She zipped open her pack at last and pulled out a small dark bag, reached inside, took out something about the size of a walnut. She murmured words and held the little thing over one of the candle flames. It burned quickly and left a smell like sizzled hair behind. Matt felt a lessening of tension somewhere in the region of her stomach.

Terry brushed off her hands.

"Okay," Matt said. "Yes."

"You won't go away?"

"I will go away. Doesn't mean I stop being your friend. You

have to treat me with respect, though, or to take care of myself,
I'll stop being your friend."

Terry hesitated, then said, "I'm not sure I know how to do
that. Will you help me?"

"Sure."

"Beautiful," said Lewis. From behind, he locked his arms
around Matt's upper body. "Now that you're free . . ."

"Cut it out," said Matt, tugging at his arms. She couldn't
budge them. He had certainly bulked up since the tree expelled
him.

"I won't hurt you," he said.

"Then let go. Haven't you been paying attention? Forcing
hurts."

He hugged her, then dropped his arms. "I've missed human
contact. I've missed just being able to move around." He reached
for the sky with both hands, then rolled his head back and forth,
lowered his arms, and twisted his upper body. He bent over and
touched his toes. He walked away from the tree, at first striding
fast, then slowing as he came to the edge of the meadow. He
looked back over his shoulder at the tree. "I still can't
believe . . ."

Matt edged over to the rock, and Terry grabbed her hand and
pulled her up, with maybe a little lifting help from air, or whatever it was that kept Terry clean and dry amidst all this dirt and
water.

". . . that I can just walk away. I haven't seen the meadow
from a different direction in decades." His voice faded as he ventured farther.

"Do you feel safe in the forest at night?" Matt muttered to
Terry.

"Most of the time," Terry muttered back. "I respect the spirits
of trees and streams and places, and they know I respect them,
and we regard each other but do no harm. It's only people that
scare me." She stared toward where Lewis had disappeared.

"What about big animals that eat people?"

"There aren't any around here."

"No cougars or bears? How can you know for sure?"

Terry laughed softly in the darkness. The candles were on the
side of Terry away from Matt, and from Matt's viewpoint, only
lit some grass and half of the tree Lewis had come out of. "If we
run into any big scary animals, I have a very quick distract spell
that ought to turn them away."

"Have you ever tried it? What if it doesn't work?"

Terry reached behind her for her backpack, pulled it onto her lap. "If you like, I can whip you up a ward-off-evil spell," she whispered.

"Would that work on people, too?"

"I don't know. It's another thing I haven't tested."

"I'm starting to wonder about Lewis," Matt muttered.

"I've been wondering about him from the beginning."

"Why?" Matt asked. Did Terry have some extra-sensory reason?

"Because I have a suspicious nature."

Out of the darkness, Lewis's voice said, "You know what I'd really like? A nice thick steak. And maybe a beer. Ice-cold. Yeah. There's a restaurant, Morley's Landing, where you can tie up canoes and rowboats and eat right beside the Millrace, a lovely place of a summer's night—do you know it?"

"What town are you talking about?" asked Terry.

"Spores Ferry."

"There's no Millrace in Spores Ferry," she said.

"What?"

"There's no Millrace, and no Morley's Landing."

"How can that be? Oh. Time." His voice sounded sad. "Will you . . . take me to town and let me see if there are any landmarks that survive?"

Terry lifted one of her candles. Matt watched as the dividing line between light and dark moved across Terry's face. "Well, I've done my devotions," she said after a moment. The light just touched Lewis's form. He stood near the edge of the forest, like the dim dream of a god. "I'm ready to go. Matt?"

"I'm more than ready to go." The night was finally cooling, and she had given up her extra shirt. She scratched a mosquito bite on her arm.

"Jump down and I'll give you a candle."

Matt slid down off the rock. Terry said a spell over the candle she held and handed it to Matt. "It will burn steady, but not set anything else alight," she said. "Lewis? Would you like a light?"

"No."

Terry pinched one of the candles out and spelled the other one, then packed up everything except the lit candle, the roses, and the ashes. She shouldered her backpack and drifted down from the rock with the candle in her hand. She kissed the rock, then set out across the meadow.

The wax felt warm and soft inside Matt's hand, and its melting smell reassured her as though it were the essence of safety. She glanced around at the dark meadow and the star-shot sky, then trailed Terry, conscious that this time it was by choice. Matt's boots slapped sound from the marshy ground; Terry walked silently. And Lewis, when he fell in behind Matt, made no sound other than soft breathing. The back of her neck prickled.

The footing was firmer on the path. Matt listened to the path: "You are walking away from me you are walking toward me you are walking on me you are making and destroying me." She liked its song better than the unknown mutters of the forest, louder now that it was night. The way back to the car went faster than the hike out from it had. Twigs and branches didn't grab at her as much, either. Maybe the forest was glad to see her go.

Matt crawled into the back seat of the Terry's white Fiat. She stroked the seat, touched the window and the carpeting, relieved to be in the wide world of home again. "Who's that?" asked the car as Lewis climbed into it. "It tastes like change."

"Don't know," Matt muttered.

"Not sure I want it inside me."

Terry tossed her pack in back and climbed into the car, started it, and drove away.

"It doesn't feel right," Lewis said.

"What?" asked Terry.

"Not only does this car look freakish, and the dashboard looks like something from a rocketship, and the engine doesn't make half the sound it should, but this—this moving away from a place—it feels wrong."

Terry said, "Do you want me to take you back?"

They were twisting and turning down a mountain road in the darkness. Matt was leaning sleepily against the back of the seat, which had shaped itself to cradle her. She closed her eyes and waited for Lewis's answer.

"Part of me wants you to," he said after time had gone by. "Being rooted felt . . . right. All this movement is confusing me. Yet for ages and ages, I longed for nothing but freedom."

"Come down to the valley and look around. If you don't like it, I'll take you back."

"You are very kind."

"Not really," Terry said, glancing toward him. Matt saw dashboard light glinting on Terry's teeth as she smiled.

They completed the drive in silence. "First off," Terry said, as she pulled up in front of the house she shared with her mother, and for now with Matt, "you need a few more clothes. There's some things of my dad's still in the house. Could you use a shower? Though you don't really smell like a guy who's been locked in a tree for years and years."

"A shower would be great," said Lewis. "I'm not really here yet. I mean . . ."

"I know. Changing shape, it takes a while to get used to the new one," Terry said.

"You've done it?"

"Oh, sure. My sister Tasha and I used to have spell fights. I turned her a lot more often than she turned me; she wasn't a very good student. But she was really good with this one spell. She liked turning people into Pekingeses. That is, until she got religion. So I know what it's like. Before you get out of the car, would you wrap something around your waist? Our neighbors are always watching our house. They've seen enough weird things already."

Lewis shifted around and took off the shirt Matt had given him, did something with it. "Best I can do," he said.

"It's pretty dark," Terry said. She snapped her fingers, and the light over the front door went out. "Okay, door's unlocked. Go for it," she said.

Lewis dashed across the lawn and managed not to drop the shirt until he had the front door open. He ducked inside. Matt and Terry followed more sedately, at least until Terry's mother screamed.

Lights switched on across the street and next door.

"Damn!" said Terry. She snapped her fingers. "Phone lines . . . Mom, I can explain. . . ."

In the front hall, Lewis stood with his back to the wall, one hand covering his genitals, the other his mouth, his eyes wide. Terry's mother Rebecca stood backed up against the sofa, both hands over her mouth, her eyes as wide as Lewis'.

"I can explain," Terry said again, but then she burst out laughing.

Terry's mom started breathing again. Her hands came down from her mouth. "Better be a good one," she said.

With effort, Terry smothered her laughter. "Well, we went up to the forest. You know why. And we found this guy, Lewis, up there, and he didn't have any clothes, so I thought maybe some of Dad's castoffs might still be in the basement and I invited him home."

"Not good enough," said Rebecca. "What was he doing up there naked in the woods?"

"He was under a wicked enchantment."

Rebecca's cheeks lost color. "Terry . . . I don't appreciate that kind of humor. I don't like the—I'm not comfortable with you bringing strangers into my house."

"I'll take him out again as soon as he showers and has some clothes, Mom. And it wasn't a joke. And I thought this was my house, too."

"She's talking about me," Matt said.

"Oh, I am not, Matt," said Rebecca, irritation in her tone. "I'm glad you're here, and I hope you stay as long as you want."

"I only want to stay as long as it's okay," Matt said.

"It's okay, dammit."

Matt sighed. "Mrs. Dane, this is my friend, Lewis. Lewis, this is Mrs. Rebecca Dane."

"Pleased to meet you, Mrs. Dane," Lewis said, red staining his cheeks. He didn't hold out a hand.

"I apologize for my lack of manners, Mr. Lewis," said Rebecca.

"I understand. It's enough to turn anyone's hair white, a naked stranger running in your front door. I didn't know there'd be anybody home."

"Well," she said. "Well . . . welcome to my home. Let me show you to the shower. And you may drop your hand. You don't have anything I haven't seen before, and if I hadn't seen it before, I wouldn't know what it was, as my grandmother used to say. Obviously the kids have already gotten an eyeful."

"I'll go hunt up some clothes," Terry said as Lewis followed Rebecca down the left-hand hallway.

"What sort of enchantment was it?" Rebecca asked.

"I was trapped inside a tree for fifty years, more or less," said Lewis as their voices faded.

Matt went to the kitchen while Terry searched the basement. She was starving after all those hours in the wild. Part of Terry's intense discipline involved regulating what she ate and when, and while Matt was tethered to her, Matt had followed Terry's eating habits. It had been nutritious, but not much fun. She opened her arms to the kitchen and said, "Talk to me, food."

A cupboard popped open and a bag of pretzels jumped into her arms. "Oh, thank you!" she said, and sat at the table to eat some.

Lewis stayed in the shower a long, long time. Listening to the sound of water in pipes, the three women sat in the kitchen, talking in murmurs, Rebecca and Matt sharing pretzels, Terry taking tiny sip-bites of unflavored yogurt. At last Terry said, "Matt, what the hell is he doing in there?"

Matt asked the house. "Uh-oh," she said when she heard the answer.

"What is it?" asked Rebecca.

"Putting down roots."

Terry knocked on the bathroom door. "Lewis? Get your toes out of the drain or I'll turn you into a porcupine!"

"Wha-a-a-at?" His voice sounded sleepy and slow.

"Turn off the water and get out of the plumbing."

"What? Oh ... just a minute."

Matt leaned against the wall and listened to what the house had to tell her. The invasion of its systems by this stranger had worried it, and it was glad that he was withdrawing parts of himself that had gone where people parts weren't supposed to go.

"I've got clothes for you," Terry said in a less cross voice. "Anytime you're ready."

The door opened a crack and steam billowed out, carrying scents of soap, shampoo, and—green? "I'm sorry. I don't know what got into me," said Lewis. Terry handed the clothes to him and he shut the door again.

"It's what got out of him that's interesting," Terry muttered to Matt.

The waitress brought a still-steaming steak on a platter and set it in front of Lewis. She set down Terry's lemon herbed chicken and Rebecca's garlic shrimp, and then gave Matt her hamburger. Matt picked up a French fry and bit it. It was nice to finally order just what she wanted, instead of picking the same thing Terry ordered, or something else she thought might stay in her stomach even if she got too far from Terry and felt sick. Lewis' steak smelled good. Matt wondered if she should have ordered that instead.

Lewis picked up his steak knife and fork and cut into his meat. Red welled up behind the knife, and the flesh was still pink inside, rare, the way he'd ordered it. He stared at it a moment. He lifted his fork, with the morsel of steak on it, and studied it. He licked his upper lip. He blinked several times. He paled.

He shook his head. "I can't eat this," he said, setting the fork down. He swallowed. "I can't ... I can't even stay here. Excuse me." Jumping up, he dropped his napkin over the platter and its cargo and dashed from the restaurant.

"Nuts," said Terry.

Matt picked up her hamburger. If they were leaving, she was taking it with her.

"You want to check on him, see if he'll wait while we eat?" Terry asked Matt.

Matt sighed and put her hamburger down.

"Why don't you do it?" Rebecca said suddenly. "Why this lady-of-the-manor delegation thing? It's really getting on my nerves. Matt's not your servant."

"What?" said Terry.

"Just because you can turn people into pinecones, it doesn't give you the right to order them around as though they were less important than you are."

"Mom, what's gotten into you?"

"Nothing's gotten into me. I'm just letting a little of what was always there out. I love you, and I'll always love you; that doesn't mean I approve of everything you're doing. And yes, I darn well expect immunity from your powers."

Terry stared at her mother for a moment, then set her napkin beside her plate, rose, and walked out.

"That wasn't too harsh, was it?" Rebecca asked Matt.

Matt shook her head. She had never had a conversation alone with Rebecca, and she felt shy. "If you're going to live with somebody, I guess you need rules," Matt said. "I usually move on before I get to that stage."

"She's been walking all over you."

"People do, sometimes. Usually I leave when they start, but Terry wouldn't let me."

Rebecca blinked. "Oh. I don't like that at all."

"Got her to let me go today."

"You're still here."

Matt nodded. "You said it was okay. Lewis is kind of my responsibility, since I let him out of the tree."

"*You* let him out?"

"Yeah. I'm not a witch, but I talk to things."

"Ah. Yes. I noticed."

Matt smiled. "He said people had been coming to that stone where Terry did her ceremony for years, but nobody noticed him before. I haven't run into other people who can talk to things like I can. When he was a tree, I could hear him talk, but Terry couldn't."

"Hmmm," said Rebecca. She ate a shrimp. "While watching Terry operate since I found out she was a witch, it occurred to me that it would be very difficult to let go of all the advantages you gain when you have these special abilities. Do you ever *not* talk to things?"

"Lots of times," Matt said. "I usually only ask questions when I feel like something's coming at me. When I need help or I need to know something to survive. I don't know anything about you, really."

Rebecca patted her mouth with her napkin and smiled. "Thanks, Matt."

"You're welcome." Matt ate her hamburger.

"I don't know much about you either."

"We could talk about it," Matt said.

Rebecca grinned.

"For starters, I've done a lot of traveling," said Matt.

Terry returned, subdued.

"He okay?" Matt asked.

"He wants to go back."

The four of them sat out on the back lawn at Terry and Rebecca's house, drinking lemonade and looking at city-hazed stars. Someone on the block was watering the lawn; the air carried the sound of false rain and the scent of wet grass.

"Everything," Lewis said, "everything is different. I can't eat this food, and I'm starving. Music is different. Buildings are different. People dress differently, and they use a lot of words that don't make sense. The prices on that menu scared me! I could have rented a room for two weeks for the amount of money that steak cost, and I couldn't even eat it. How can things be so expensive? There are all kinds of devices in your house that I have no idea what they do, and I don't want to find out. All these years, the witches have been the same; but everything else has changed."

"So you want to run away and hide?" Matt said.

"I don't see how I can survive here. I can't just mooch off Terry and Rebecca, can I? But how could I get a job? I don't understand anything about this new world."

Matt thought about mooching off Terry and Rebecca. She didn't want to do it much longer herself, now that she had a choice. Something in her, the wandergod part of her, longed to move on, wash her present off, and start over someplace new with no complications or expectations. She had been living her life in short bright sections for more years than she bothered to count. The road was continuity enough.

"Aren't you ever curious?" she asked. "Don't you even want to find out?"

His answer was a long time coming. "Maybe. In a way."

"You were a Crafter once," Terry said. "What happened to your desire to shape things?"

"Hmm," he said. "I think . . . as time passed . . . I figured out what to want. Sunlight. Rain. Snow. Dead organic matter. And freedom, and someone to talk to. Maybe I was shaping as much as I could. Or maybe I was just accepting what came. It was almost enough."

"Dead organic matter is mostly what we eat," Terry said thoughtfully. "You're doing okay with the lemonade, aren't you?"

"Hmm," said Lewis, looking into his cup. "It tastes good."

"What kind of tree are you when you're a tree?" Rebecca asked.

"Something local. A cedar, I think. I'm not sure exactly."

"You could put down roots," Rebecca said slowly. "And pick them up again."

"I don't know," said Lewis. "I left my tree behind."

"You started rooting in the house."

"Huh. Yes."

"We could use some more shade in the back yard," she said. "You could just . . . stay here a while and maybe learn some more about now."

"You could stay here for a while and then go somewhere else. Learn new things all the time, and new places. Root, uproot," Matt said. "That's how I live. Try a different place every little while. You could come with me. I could teach you." She touched her mouth after the words were out. Part of her lifeway was to be alone; to always make friends, but never to take them with her on her journey from one piece of life to the next. What had come over her?

"Matt, don't go," said Terry.

"What am I doing here?" Matt said. "I need to go."

"I could teach you to root," Lewis said. He laid his hand over hers on the lawn. His fingers plunged down into the soil, caging hers between them.

"No!" said Matt, tugging, but her hand was locked to the Earth.

"Relax," said Lewis.

"No!"

"I'll let you go in a minute. Relax."

Everything in her was twisted tight and squirming. Every lesson she had learned early in life was about getting away before the Bad Things could find her, and now she was trapped. She pulled in breaths and let them out slowly, trying to relax. At last she asked Lewis' clothing if it could strangle him for her, and it said it could do that if she wanted. She relaxed, and felt—

Her fingers aiming downward, digging into dirt, reaching deeper than their lengths, seeking and finding deep cool comfort; and a language that spoke so slowly a word would take a lifetime but be worth waiting for; and things seeping into her through her fingers, things that tasted like steaming mashed potatoes drowning in butter, and hot apple cider, and chocolate ripple ice cream; and a sense of strength infinite and offering itself to her: all she had to do was stay. Warmth. Comfort. Eternity. A cradle.

The pressure on her hand went away. Her hand pulled back into its own shape, and she was sitting, bereft of contact and comfort, on the lawn again, a world away from the eternal community. Shivering started in her arms and traveled through her.

"Are you okay?" Terry asked, gripping her arm. Matt shook for a little longer. The warmth from Terry's hand felt good.

When the shaking stopped, Matt patted Terry's hand and said, "Don't do that to me without asking, Lewis. Don't."

"You would have said no. And I could never describe it."

"Don't do it like that again."

He hesitated, then said, "I won't."

Matt sipped lemonade. Half had sloshed out of her glass while she was shaking. "I'll try it again tomorrow," she said, "if you'll come to town with me and Terry."

"All right," he said. "For tonight, I'd just like to stay out here."

"Pick a spot away from the house and not under the power lines," Rebecca said.

"I will. Thanks to all of you, for everything."

Matt was brushing her teeth while Terry rubbed astringent over her face. "Pay attention to your dreams tonight," Terry said. "It's a time of pollination. Seeds get set."

"I don't want any dreams," Matt said, but her mouth was full of toothpaste and the words didn't come out.

She dreamed of Home.